Return of the African Diaspora

A Mother for Celeste

OTHER BOOKS BY LINDA PACE SAMUEL

Book II

Return of the African Diaspora
Exodus Village

Return of the African Diaspora

A Mother for Celeste

'N Gratitude Publishing
Aquarian Age Books

Published in the United States by 'N Gratitude Publishing Company
Atlanta Georgia

www.ngratitude.net

ISBN 978-0-615-29417-9

Printed in the United States of America
2015

Cover Design: Sean Collins - www.TenTen71.com

Cover Photo: David Martinez

For my mother –

a loving spirit who taught me

unconditional love by example

♥ ♥ ♥ ♥ ♥ ♥ ♥

Love is the most healing power in the Universe.

Our willingness to Love unconditionally

helps raise our spiritual consciousness.

It helps us recognize our connection to the Omnipotent,

Omniscient, and Omnipresent God-Spirit:

The Divine Healer.

We are all made in the image and likeness of the Creator.

We co-create our experiences with our thoughts

– whether consciously or unconsciously.

Each loving spirit is given free will at birth,

and the ability to create Heaven on Earth.

Yet some, blinded by ego attachments of the flesh,

choose to create Hell on Earth instead; for themselves

and others they seek to control.

When we allow ourselves to surrender to Unconditional Love,

we pave the way for creating our hearts' desires.

We simply allow – giving Love freely and holding nothing back;

rejecting fear that would have us wait

until we're certain Love will return our way.

Love heals all.

It inspires us to create that which works together for the common good.

In doing so, the energy of the entire planet becomes elevated.

God is Love,

and only when we see ourselves as Love

can we recognize the God-Spirit within us.

It is only then that we remember our Divine Purpose

for this incarnation on Earth,

and our intended expression of Love.

Acknowledgements

I have many people to thank for supporting me in writing this book—from friends, to family members, to neighbors, to passing souls who offered me jewels of wisdom during random encounters. I am grateful to all of you for your encouragement and your boundless charity in accepting my "I'm almost finished" progress reports, as though hearing them for the first time.

A special thanks to Karen Bishop for writing "*Remembering Your Soul Purpose*," and other gifts of the written word. Your writings have given me and countless other souls much needed direction during these turbulent times of change on planet Earth. It was truly Divine Timing to have been introduced to your work, as I emerged from my own ascension-inspired health challenge and life-altering detour. Your encouragement and insight has meant more than you might ever imagine.

Thank you to Khari, to my mother and my late father; to Mena, Aunt Mamie, Cassandra, Denise, Woubit, Owen, Linette, Becky, Richmond, Emma, Brad, Craig, Tracy, Jose, Bill, Edwina, Donnetta, Mindy, Debra, Sheri, Jan, David, Tina, Jean-Louis, Shirley, Tanya, and my many other friends and family members who helped me through this writing project. I thank you for your creative, technical, and artistic advice; and for allowing me to bounce my ideas, photos, and other choices I had to make off you. Thank you for your willingness to critique my manuscript and for sharing your opinions. Many thanks to you, Sean, for your exceptional talent as a graphic designer—you were truly a Godsend.

Finally, I would like to express deep appreciation to my friend, Brenda, for helping me with this project from start to finish. Thank you for believing in me and for reading all my painfully written earlier drafts. I will forever be grateful.

This book is dedicated to Dr. Willie J. Fluker

Former Professor of History

Tuskegee University

Special Thanks

Kelly Robinson and Cassandra M. Turnipseed
Atlanta-Fulton Public Library System

~~~~~

The George Washington Carver Collection,
RS 21/7/2, Special Collections Department,
Iowa State University Library.

Taken From Merriam-Webster's Online Dictionary[1]

Main Entry: di·as·po·ra

a) the breaking up and scattering of a people:

<u>MIGRATION</u> <the black *diaspora* to northern cities>

b) people settled far from their ancestral homelands <African

diaspora>

c) the place where these people live

Main Entry: ex·o·dus

Etymology: Latin, from Greek *Exodos,*

a) literally, road out, from *ex-* + *hodos* road

b) a mass departure

---

[1] http://www.merriam-webster.com

Prologue

*T*he explosive sounds of the water pounded Kristin's eardrums mercilessly, magnified to a deafening noise that seemed a hundred times over; like cannon balls being fired in rapid succession. Her weary eyes squinted as the water swirled around the toilet and down the drain; carrying with it the mucus-covered remnants of what she'd failed to digest a short time earlier, despite her best efforts. As the sun receded through her small bathroom window, signaling the end to yet another day, the cold white toilet remained the only witness to her body's rejection of the food. Her longtime friend, Niyla, had been more persistent this time before she left. She had finally coerced Kristin into swallowing a few bites of the crackers she had brought with her and a sip of juice.

Kristin had long since lost count of the number of times she had stumbled down the long hallway to the bathroom. It had taken nearly all her strength to get there each time, only to retch into the toilet like a frail old woman. Her stomach muscles had tightened from their constant spasms. After nearly a full week the eruptions still persisted, as volatile as an active volcano that had sprung to life without warning after years of dormancy. Its explosions were regular and without ceremony; in her weakened state Kristin vaguely remembered that she and Niyla had often referred to the toilet in their dorm room at Tuskegee as the "porcelain god." They had each taken turns bowing to it on more than one occasion, and clinging desperately to its smooth cold surface after having had too much "punch" at an off-campus party.

Kristin's stomach had always been a source of difficulty for her as far back as she could remember. As a student at Lewis Adams Elementary School, named for the former slave who had been responsible for founding what is now Tuskegee University, Kristin had often been sent home sick after witnessing the aftermath of some other child's upset stomach. Days had usually gone by before her own body regained its equilibrium once she became ill. During the first trimester of both her pregnancies she had been unable to keep much food down at all — or at least not long enough to fully digest it.

Each trip she took down the long hallway had become more of a struggle than the one before and required more effort. And each time, the toilet had waited patiently for her inevitable return. So far, she had made it—though usually without much time to spare. Now, she lingered against the commode with her head bent down until she had gathered enough strength to move again. It took a great deal of effort to change her tenuous position, but eventually she managed to brace herself against the vanity that stood a short distance away. Kristin lifted her head and steadied herself so she could look into the mirror above the basin. She squinted even harder as she sought recognition of the reflection staring back at her from the beveled glass frame. Her locks, usually well groomed, were matted and twisted into strange coils flattened against one side of her head. For a reason she didn't fully understand, she felt compelled to look at herself before starting her long journey back to the living room couch. It had become a part of some strange new ritual; she would stare at her reflection for several minutes, struggle onto the digital bathroom scale next to the vanity, and then slowly make her way back down the long hallway.

She had only recently purchased the high-end scale that also calculated her body mass index. She had bought it in an attempt to compensate for her seeming inability to judge her own weight accurately by looking in a mirror. She had often been surprised by how far off the mark her guesses would be from her actual weight. She had been using the scale every day since she first bought it, hoping that in doing so she could keep those few extra pounds at bay that had always seemed to creep back onto her body.

Kristin struggled to bring the scale's display into focus, but then took little interest in the drastic drop that it showed in her weight. She was unaffected by the urgency of the bright yellow numbers that flashed in an alarming rhythm. She ignored its warnings that her total body fat registered as a single digit, and that her weight was just over one hundred pounds. She hadn't taken much notice of her face yet that day, and when she leaned over the vanity for a closer look she was surprised that the reflection in the mirror did not seem to resemble her at all. The profile staring back at her was almost identical to that of one of her aunts, who had been resting in a well-worn rural Mississippi hospital bed the last time Kristin saw her. Her aunt had been in the final days of a three-year battle with cancer that had ravaged her body. Her bulging eyes had stared at Kristin the entire time she was in the room, as though she had some final message for her niece that she opted instead to take to her grave.

Now Kristin saw the same expression looking back at her from her own bathroom mirror. The same taunt skin was drawn back around teeth that appeared exaggerated in their size and stark whiteness. As she gazed deeper into the Hollywood-styled looking glass, she realized she no longer saw anything of her former self in the dark eyes that stared back at her. Before she could react to that staggering thought, a voice suddenly emanated from deep within her soul. She heard it clearly though it made no sound, and she recognized it immediately as her super-conscious mind - her inner Spirit. Without question, she knew it to be the omniscient voice of her eternal God-self. Calmly, the voice inquired whether she would have further use for the body she had been occupying for the past thirty-eight years.

"Are you staying?" The voice asked her.

The abruptness of the question startled Kristin, though the face in the mirror revealed no hint of concern. She looked deeper into the vacant eyes staring back at her and saw that they were devoid of all emotion. The life or death decision she had been asked to make seemed to be of no consequence at all. In that same moment, she recognized that the question had been the same one asked of her loved ones who had gone on before her; those whose bodies she had stood over as they were being lowered into the ground. She also realized the dilemma she had been presented with was hers alone to reckon with. Aside from the Creator, there was no one else who was entitled to any say-so in the matter at all. Nothing or no one would ever take precedence over the pact that her soul had made with God before she came to the planet.

A distant surprise registered as she made her way to the living room and realized a response to the question had not immediately been forthcoming.

As night began to fall, Kristin still couldn't give a definitive response to the unexpected question she had been asked.

The following day saw her thoughts turn toward her experiences in Ghana during the two years she had lived there. She thought about the people she had met as she rode around the countryside and the lasting friendships she had formed as a visiting professor at the University of Kumasi. Her time in Ghana had also heightened her awareness of the cultural divide that existed between Black Americans and West Africans. She had pondered this realization constantly, wondering what might ever be done to change it. It wasn't long after her return to Washington, and her teaching position at Hunter University, before Kristin felt her optimism for any kind of meaningful reconciliation between Africa and its Diaspora in America, begin to fade. For some time thereafter, she had merely gone through the motions during her lectures. She had been unsure whether she would ever instill anything in her students' minds that would challenge them to embrace their connection to Mother Africa, to help find a way to interrupt the cycle that so many Black Americans were still stuck in. A renewed hopefulness that she might actually affect substantive change for the "underbelly," as she referred to that segment of Black America, had only returned shortly before the physical ordeal that she currently found herself in had taken center stage in her life.

This time, her optimism had been prompted by a business venture she would soon start with a friend she had met in Kumasi. They had reached a partnership agreement for a travel and tourism company that would be based in Accra, the capital and largest city in Ghana. It would bring her one step closer to her plans of forming a deeper connection between the two cultures, something that she somehow knew to be imperative. And she felt in her heart that this first step would lead to much more.

Kristin had decided to prepare herself for her new venture and her transition into a Ghanaian businesswoman by fasting, something she had done many times before. She never dreamed that this time the same course of action that had been intended to restore herself mentally, physically, and spiritually would propel her into a state of rapid health decline. And she had *no* idea that it might end with her being asked to decide whether or not she wished to remain on Earth. Something had gone terribly wrong during the first few days of her fast, but she had failed to heed her body's swift and cautionary reaction. Instead, she made the unwise decision to dramatically increase the amount of cayenne pepper she had been adding to a mixture of water, lemon juice, and Grade B maple syrup to drink every day, con-

4

trary to the precise measures called for in the Master Cleanse recipe. The drink stimulated a release of toxins from her body but she had increased the amount of cayenne thinking it would raise her energy level. She had no idea of the dangers involved in consuming such a large quantity of the powerful natural detoxifier within such a short span of time.

The intensely grueling experience she had been going through all week had directly resulted from it, leaving her body in a weakened state of vulnerability from its rapid weight loss of over twenty-five pounds. When she was finally strong enough to attempt to break her fast, Kristin had only managed to keep down small amounts of food. She soon discovered she had no appetite, making it difficult for her to even try to eat. And she found that the morsels she *had* finally succeeded in swallowing were as tasteless as cardboard. It had taken quite an effort and much coercion from Niyla before she finally chewed the crackers that her friend insisted she eat, sufficient enough to swallow. But despite her defunct taste buds and her disinterest in eating, her body still managed to extract enough nourishment to sustain itself as she continued to ponder the question she had never imagined she would be asked.

Even with all the ups and downs of her life, there had never been a time when Kristin entertained any conscious thoughts about ending her own life, not even in her worst moments. She had jokingly made Niyla promise once that she would pester the police until a thorough investigation had been made into her death, if suicide were ever suspected as its cause. "Someone," she had told her friend jokingly, "would most likely be trying to get away with murder."

Kristin had faced far too many difficult situations in her past that had made an unexpected and sudden change for the better. She knew the answer she would give to the ever-pressing question would have nothing to do with feelings of hopelessness that suicide victims often expressed in the notes they left. She also found herself vaguely relieved that Winston would play no role in her decision. It comforted her that her lingering feelings for her ex-husband would not interfere in the business of her soul.

After another day had passed, she became aware of random events from her life that had begun a parade across her consciousness. A plethora of memories from her long-forgotten past began to make brief appearances across the center stage of her mind, and it was she who most often played the leading role. Some were pleasant remembrances, while there were others that dredged up more difficult emotions. She had recollections about conversations she had with people she had only known in passing, and other interchanges with people she hadn't thought about in years. Some visits from her past were mere impressions that flashed across her mind and then slipped back into the recesses as quickly as they had materialized. But each scene brought with it a vivid memory of the exact emotions she had felt at the time.

Despite the futility of her efforts, Kristin had begun making her way from her living room couch to her bed every night before the midnight hour, and then back downstairs to the couch again in the morning. It was her way of marking time against a hazy reality that otherwise had no beginning and no end, as memories of her life continued to flood her mind. She would close her eyes as soon as she was in bed, ever hopeful of the sleep that continued to elude her. After several more days of this routine, her body began to shiver frequently and threaten its intent to go into shock. Still, Kristin remained unmoved by these warnings. Perhaps because she had long since lost her faith in the practice of western medicine, it never crossed her mind to dial 911. She had observed the healthcare "industry's" desire for profits grow over the years, slowly tainting the inspiration that once motivated community physicians whose only goal had been to restore their patients' good health. The frightening side effects from many of the drugs they now prescribed, with handy samples always tucked inside their black satchels, were of far more concern to Kristin than her body's natural reaction to her overdose of cayenne pepper. She had pleaded with Niyla each time her friend stopped by to check in, her own fears threatening to override Kristin's objections and forcing her into an emergency room for treatment. She had begged Niyla for more time to let her body heal naturally, knowing that the very sight of her in such frail condition would immediately prompt a battery of invasive "rescue" drugs and procedures.

Once the cayenne had run its course in physically detoxifying her body, it immediately turned its focus toward an emotional cleanse. A slow trickle of unexplained tears would run down her face and then escalate to uncontrollable sobs with little warning. Kristin was certain that the overworked medical responders in the ER would have quickly diagnosed her symptoms as evidence of her need for psychiatric care.

But eventually the shivers subsided, and after she had watched the endless dramas swirl around her head for several more days she had a sudden and stunningly clear realization. All the stuff that had happened in her life, all that had been replaying over and over in her head had been just that – it was all just stuff. That simple thought had been a significant turning point for Kristin in her seemingly uncontrolled traumatic experience. While it was true that some of the events that paraded before her had helped to shape her into who she had become; none of it had anything to do with who she really *was*—who she *had always been*. Kristin finally understood what it all meant, why her loved ones would never influence her life or death decision. But she also knew they would understand the choice she *did* make at their own appointed hour. She was certain that the children would be devastated at first, should she choose a sudden departure; but she was equally sure that both Trazi and Celeste would heal in time. She suspected Winston would carry his grief with him until he had transitioned from the Earth himself. She found herself unconsciously sending silent assurances to his Spirit that she would come back and help to ease his pain, if need be.

As for her own feelings, she had no doubt that to leave her body behind would be a liberating experience; especially in the fragile condition it had been left in. It never crossed her mind at any time to dread the prospect of departing. The experience had given her a clear realization that her authentic Self was indeed immortal, just as she had learned in Sunday School as a young girl. She accepted it now as an absolute truth and with the same certainty that she anticipated the sun rising each morning. Her physical "death" would be of no real consequence because her immortal Self would *never* die. Only the shell that was her body would change, and in the grand scheme of things that would only matter to those who would miss her daily presence.

After that realization had sat with her for a time, she began to regain her strength, little by little, until she felt well enough one afternoon to walk out to her sunroom. She lay relaxed on a chaise, surrounded by large wide-leaf dark green plants that partially hid her from view. Taking control of her thoughts, she allowed her mind to drift for a few moments as she lay listening to the sounds of birds singing in nearby trees. She began to think about the people she had been impacted by in her lifetime, and Rosa Parks, the gentle warrior of the Civil Rights Movement, naturally came to mind.

Her "shero" had spent the first few years of life in a house nearby Kristin's family home in Tuskegee. It was in a modest neighborhood known as "Brickyard Hill" and Kristin had learned from her father that it was also the place where George Washington Carver had brought students to collect clay they used to make bricks to construct Tuskegee's first classrooms and dormitories. Kristin had often thought of Mrs. Parks' decision to stand her ground on a legally-segregated bus that day in Montgomery Alabama. She had refused to walk to the back of the bus when there were seats available for her to sit in near the front. Could she possibly have known that her action would literally change the course of the world?

Eventually, Kristin's thoughts turned to a consideration of the Divine Plan for her own life. She wondered whether any of the life experiences that had paraded before her during the past days indicated she had fulfilled her purpose. She realized that ultimately would be the major factor in answering the still-unanswered question of whether she would remain on the Earth. She began thinking about the impact she had made on the lives of the people she knew–her family, friends, and especially her students at Hunter. She recalled some of their faces and wondered as she always did whether she had been able to get through to any of them yet; whether her lectures had prompted any one of them to have a passionate interest in changing the plight of the Black American underbelly. Then, she thought about the travel agency that she planned to open with her friend, Solomon, and the impact she might make through their new business.

Her thoughts became more fluid about their plans until she began to gently push any that surfaced in her mind away, choosing instead to rest in the stillness of the moment. She gradually lost all awareness of time as she drifted into a meditative state, feeling her connection to Infinite Intelligence grow stronger. Her relaxed mind drifted in a sea of unlimited potential, amid vast still waters. Then, from the creative darkness that contains all possibilities, a sudden burst of clarity commanded her attention. In an instant, it ended all indecision and she no longer had to speculate whether she had already fulfilled her purpose. No sooner had the flash of revelation popped into her head did Kristin recognize it as the answer she had been seeking. It was finally crystal clear to her what she had come to planet Earth to do.

"It's time to go home." She said it out loud to the Universe after another moment of reflection, confidently speaking the words into being.

Chapter 1

1990 — Six Years Earlier

*K*ristin expertly shifted gears on her Saab 9-3 convertible, as she sped along Rock Creek Parkway toward Hunter University. She glanced down at her watch quickly and accelerated as much as she dared on the curvy road, soaring past every car she encountered in the heavy rush-hour traffic. It seemed that no matter how early she woke up these days, she always wound up on the verge of being late for her eight o'clock classes. And as much as she dogged her students for straggling in late, she wasn't about to end up arriving late herself. So predictably, her morning commute was always the same action-packed adventure. Finally, she approached her exit ramp and the university gates were within view. She glided the green-silver sports car into a reserved parking space; after a quick look in the mirror she crossed the lawn in long strides toward the old academic building.

Her first class was just inside the main entranceway, the only classroom left on a long hallway of rooms the school had converted into faculty offices. As she opened the door, she let out a deep sigh of satisfaction that she had made it on time yet again. And she had well over ten minutes to spare; ample time to meditate briefly and center herself from her hectic drive through the nation's capital. Moving quickly, she dropped her briefcase onto the wooden floor that reeked of sawdust the custodians used to keep it oiled and clean. In one fluid motion, she tucked her purse inside the bottom drawer of a large framed desk and sat down behind it. With her back firmly against the chair, she planted her feet squarely on the floor, placing her hands in her lap with palms upward as she gently closed her eyes. She began a systematic scan of her body, mentally searching for tense muscles after her chaotic race through traffic. Area by area, she directed constricted tissues of her body to relax as she took in slow methodical breaths. She held each one briefly before exhaling to resume her scan. Almost immediately, she began to feel knots in the back of her neck and shoulders loosen, as they responded to her mental commands. Kristin took in deeper more deliberate breaths, remaining conscious of her body's movement and remaining attuned to the mechanics of her breathing. After one last elongated breath, she forcibly exhaled air from her lungs with a sigh, visualizing the remaining stress float away from her body.

Guardedly, she opened her eyes against the blinding sunlight streaming through the room's large windows. She took a moment to acclimate herself to her surroundings; holding the peace and serenity of the moment until she heard muffled sounds of approaching students drift down the hall. Kristin had organized her four classes in such a way that the last two lectures of the quarter were the same, regardless of course title. She had devised a specific format designed to stimulate her students and plant seeds of hope in their fertile minds. Her wish was for the seeds to germinate over time and become a catalyst for substantive change in the Black community. She had made the radical adjustments in her style after taking her first trip to Africa the year before. Kristin had restructured her entire grading policy for all her classes; she changed nearly all procedures she had followed since she first started teaching at Hunter, fresh out of graduate school. Now, her approach was similar to that of one of her undergraduate History professors at Tuskegee.

Of all her professors, both graduate and undergraduate, Dr. Keenan had made the greatest impact on her. She had hardly appreciated him at the time, but now she realized how driven he had been to reach his students through his lectures. His singular focus had been on what he must have considered his true purpose for being on the faculty. Dr. Keenan had used a variety of unconventional tactics to encourage students to register for his classes. Included, was his practice of providing all the answers to his exams, in the form of study questions, before he gave them. Everyone around campus knew that studying was not a requirement for his classes, so the competition was always stiff to get in. Dr. Keenan had been very bold in his defiance of the watchful eyes of an administration that was alarmed by his unorthodox methods. A friend, who had been assigned to a work-study job in the provost office, told Kristin once that the provost had complained constantly about Dr. Keenan. Her friend had actually seen his formal complaints made to the president, in which he described Dr. Keenan's method of teaching as a "blatant disregard for official warnings that he conform to standard school policies." But somehow, Dr. Keenan always managed to prevail. In spite of the attempts to get him fired, he had remained undeterred from his mission for decades—long after Kristin graduated and moved to Washington.

Leading the pack of students who always clamored for his class cards were those who majored in subjects that required all their time for studying. Dr. Keenan's classes were magical gifts to the pre-veterinary medicine, business, architecture, engineering, nursing, and agriculture students, and to others who had science-related majors. His classes helped satisfy their general education requirements without much effort, for an easy boost to their grade point averages. It meant more time could be allocated for those subjects they considered to be their "real" classes. The only catch was Dr. Keenan's insistence that any student who registered, including the jocks, had to come to class and be there on time. Otherwise, he had no qualms about giving *any* chronically absent or late student a failing grade. And he always made a point of reminding them about the school's official policy on attendance, citing it verbatim from an official student handbook.

Tuskegee always had a reputation for its beautifully manicured campus, and that had especially been the case in the early '70s when Kristin took her first class from Dr. Keenan. Had it not been for his strict no-nonsense rules about attendance, she would likely have opted to cut his classes that spring semester too, as she had so many others. Sitting on "the fountain" had been one of her favorite pastimes; it was a prime location for students to hang out and pass away the time since scheduled activities were relatively rare on campus and there was little else to do. The rectangular brick fountain could hold fifty or so students along its four-and-a-half-foot high walls; the same number could sit comfortably on concrete benches built around each side. Or, on sunny days when everyone was outside, other students would sit underneath a small grove of nearby trees. The fountain sat in the middle of "the yard," as the campus was called, and had been a large part of student-life back then. Kristin preferred to hang out with her friends there in the warm sunshine rather than go to class, even if she *did* find Dr. Keenan's lectures intriguing. But that campus spot had been her only opportunity to socialize during her first year at Tuskegee, when she had still lived at home and was expected to *be there* by dinnertime.

The "caf"(eteria); student union – or "rec" as it was called, with its busy sandwich shop that was always jammed with students between classes; as well as several girls' dorms, were all built around the perimeter of the fountain. The structure was surrounded by a lush green lawn with colorful flowers that always bloomed just in time for their annual spring festival, "All Day Music." It was a day that brought student and local musicians together along with at least one other well-known group. They would perform all day and well into the night, for small clusters of students who lay on blankets that would be strewn across the crowded lawn.

A sturdy wooden platform would be erected across the fountain every year as it was transformed for Spring Commencement exercises at Tuskegee, complete with large potted plants lined across the front to adorn the stage. A procession of cautiously grateful students would move quickly toward a short flight of stairs that led to the makeshift stage. They were the survivors of the registrar's last-minute "gotcha;" a dreaded two-color system of disqualification, with lines drawn through names at the last hour. There were red lines drawn for students with financial obligations left unpaid; and blue, for those would-be graduates who still had academic deficiencies. The survivors would march proudly up the steps to await their names being called, all breathing sighs of relief that they had made it past the final hurdle. Unlike their unfortunate peers who had been pulled out of line, their symbolic "walk across the water," in deference to the water that had once flowed in the center of the fountain, had finally been assured. Still they would hurry across it, stopping only to pose for a quick photo op as they collected their well-earned diplomas.

From the vantage point of the fountain Kristin had been able to easily spot her friends; it was where she had been that first time she laid eyes on Winston. He had still been nearly a quarter-mile away, but she had been attracted instantly by the pronounced swagger of his natural walk. The weather had been especially nice that day too, the kind of day when *everyone* had made an appearance on the yard at least once. On days like that, she had been tempted to hang out with friends who would join her group one by one. But when she had her History class, Kristin had always kept track of time so she wouldn't be late for Dr. Keenan's class.

He had spent several years in West Africa before beginning his teaching career. Now, she could appreciate how captivated he must have been by his experiences. He had been so determined to get them to understand the significance of Kwame Nkrumah's courageous leadership. Dr. Keenan had tried hard to help them see how one man's vision had led to the entire African continent freeing itself from colonialism. It wasn't until after her own trip to Africa that she fully understood what had motivated him. After she traveled to the Motherland herself, she knew exactly why Dr. Keenan had been so willing to risk his career, and why he had used any means necessary to entice students to register for his classes.

She understood it because now she was willing to risk it all too. She had adopted a new twist to his teaching methods, completely reorganizing her classes and making her grading policy entirely dependent on a two-part final exam she gave her students at the end of each quarter. The first half was a take-home multiple-choice test. The second part was an essay that she would only accept from students who had attended the previous lecture, and turned in their take-home tests as instructed. Kristin's new class structure placed a much greater weight on these combined test scores than on any other test she gave. It virtually guaranteed that any student who missed either part of the last two lectures only received a 'D' grade, at best.

She gave her students the answers to all of her multiple-choice tests as Dr. Keenan had done, usually on a study sheet that she handed out on the day before the test. But she was careful to stay under the radar of her college dean, because she realized she would need to remain on the faculty to carry out her mission. Toward that end, she made a point of basing all lectures and tests she gave during the rest of the quarter on materials that were specific to the course. Nevertheless, she was still prepared to let the chips fall where they may, if it ever came down to that. She was driven to the same extent that Dr. Keenan had been driven, and she did not hesitate to do anything she could to get more students registered for her classes. *Her* mission was to enlighten them about the ingrained subtle ramifications of the slave trade that still existed, and the consequences it had on all their lives in one form or another. She felt it was the best starting point for many Black Americans in turning their lives around. She presented her students with an alternate approach for considering the African slave trade, which examined, and then stripped away the emotional distractions so the subject could be viewed from an objective standpoint. She began by pointing out the enormity of the practice itself, instead of just glossing over the fact that it had existed for almost four hundred years. She tried to help her students grasp that for centuries the slave trade had robbed Africa of its greatest resource—its people.

Kristin's goal for each quarter was to awaken her students to the realization that many descendants of those who had once been enslaved were *still* reeling from the aftermath. She focused on making them aware that everyone bore its repercussions because of the world's increasing interdependence, and that the unresolved dark energies created by all the suffering, violence, and fears that persisted for centuries had never been reconciled. Kristin believed the destructive heaviness from that dark energy was being passed down from generation to generation in some Black American families, though this went largely undetected by those not directly affected. She believed the consequences of slavery continued to be very real, though a tangible connection became more obscure over time.

When her book club made its impromptu decision to visit Ghana a year earlier, she had no idea how dramatically her life would change from the experience. Someone had suggested the trip after they read *Roots* for a second time, choosing Alex Haley's book after they could find nothing of interest on *Essence Magazine's* best-seller list, or on Oprah's book club list that they hadn't already read. *Roots* was a fictional account that chronicled the life of one of Haley's ancestors who had been captured as a teen in The Gambia, and forced into slavery. The trip had seemed like a natural extension of their book discussion; they chose Ghana because they were all interested in learning more about that country's history and culture.

Shortly before they left for Ghana, Kristin had come to realize that accidents and coincidence usually went much deeper than it appeared on the surface. She had often thought back to the sequence of events that led her to Ghana and the radical changes it brought to her life. For several weeks after they returned, everything had felt foreign to her. She had watched far less television than was normal for her; she shied away from conversations with anyone she could avoid, and canceled any interactions she didn't consider crucial. All she wanted was to spend time replaying untarnished memories from her trip. She would sit alone for hours and look through photos she had taken, holding onto her experiences as long as she could.

Kristin had been stimulated in more ways than she ever expected; the trip also prompted many questions that had been left unanswered. So she plunged into research at the Library of Congress as soon as her jet lag subsided and she became mesmerized by what she uncovered. She examined countless books that documented the African slave trade and the atrocious acts that had been committed during the years it existed; unimaginable conduct that had become a matter of course when slavery was a legal and customary practice in America. She also found accounts of valiant white Americans and the roles they had played in helping to end slavery, and to extend the same civil rights guarantees that were given to other Americans, under the Constitution, to descendants of those once enslaved.

There were many condemnations of slavery made by the Society of Friends, or Quakers, as they are commonly called, as early as the 1600s. Kristin studied the history of the abolitionist movement and found evidence that there had been a great deal of empathy for it among whites, and for underground assistance that was provided to those in the process of escaping slavery. Only wealthy whites could afford to own slaves, although there were wealthy whites who never did. Many felt that the practice was wrong from the beginning, but they did not care to face being ostracized for holding such an unpopular sentiment. Many were forced to hold their views about slavery in secret—especially in the Deep South.

As Kristin continued to pour over volumes of recorded history in the Library of Congress, she soon realized the people who were victimized by slavery were often spoken of as though they existed only as a group. Seldom were they mentioned as individuals, when in fact, they weren't "the slaves" at all. Instead, each person was but one of millions of *individual* human beings who had been enslaved. That observation caused her to take a fresh approach in her thinking and to fully consider its implications. She took a new look at negative statistics that are usually associated with lower-income Black Americans in particular, especially those living in large urban areas. She began to rethink the phenomenon of Black-on-Black crime, the relatively high rate of unemployment, illiteracy, drug abuse, and other social ills that tend to be persistent in the Black community.

Next, she began to chart out the psychological impact of slavery, and how it would have been passed on to individual family members—some more than others—from one generation to the next. For the next several days, she tried to identify a more plausible explanation than her theory; something else that she could point to as a root cause of the stagnant dysfunctions that have continued to plague segments of Black America. She finally concluded that her explanation was much more plausible than a dismissal of such widespread and chronic issues as being random occurrences.

Nothing in the books she read made a connection between the lack of a safe environment to heal scars from generational slavery, and the segment of Black America she referred to as "the underbelly." This group continued to be most affected, Kristin believed, because their ancestors were likely wounded psychologically during slavery, or immediately afterwards. They were never aided in restoring their psychological balance. Now their progeny were increasingly perceived as misfits of society, their circumstances no longer linked to their ancestors' tragic pasts. Intense therapy would have been recommended for the average person to prevail over such trauma, a degree of psychotherapy that wouldn't have been available to *anyone* in 1865. Nevertheless, that bore little significance to the end-result. A valid justification for the omission wouldn't invalidate their need for help. The fact remained that they were unceremoniously "freed" from the most inhumane form of chattel slavery that ever existed in the history of the world, with little support beyond the first thirteen years of freedom.

Kristin had been moved to delve even further in her research; she began to pour over the results of studies that had been conducted about the phenomenon of post-traumatic stress disorders. Many of the studies had been commissioned by veterans' organizations in response to a growing number of soldiers who returned home exhibiting unsettling symptoms of the affliction. Years ago, military strategies began to take into consideration that prolonged duty in stressful combat situations might create the disorder, to varying degrees. Yet, Kristin could not find any comparable research that had been conducted on the long-term effects of the trauma resulting from having been victimized by generational slavery. The violent displacement of a people, who had been forced into bondage in a foreign land with their tribal enemies, and who had been stripped of their families, their religion, their language, history, and culture had apparently not been thought sufficient enough to produce any long-lasting or damaging consequences. There seemed to have been no thought that there might be a toll to pay for all the emotional and physical suffering that had taken place. But, the majority of those who were enslaved had summoned the strength somehow to withstand their experiences, and to make a gradual emotional recovery after they were freed; just as many soldiers returning home from war were able to do. On the other hand, many soldiers took much longer to make a full enough recovery from their trauma before rejoining society. Still others have *never* been able to regain their emotional balance after war, and have remained off-center for the rest of their lives.

Over time, her research started to take on a life of its own. Before she realized it, Kristin had transformed her notes into an outline that became the basis of her second book, *Which Way Out?* As she thought back later, she realized the book had practically written itself. After it was published, she approached her dean about developing a new class around the subject. She had used the same approach after the release of her first book on African American politics. The dean seemed genuinely receptive to the idea but ultimately rejected her proposal, citing budgetary constraints. His hands were tied, he said; he wouldn't be able to add any new classes in the near future. But Kristin's passion for continuing an exploration of that line of research had become uncontainable. She had been driven to take positive action, as her thoughts kept returning to the dysfunctions that each generation of afflicted Black Americans continued to pass on to their children. She decided not to wait for budget approval before beginning a dialog with her students; she didn't feel she could *afford* to wait.

Little by little, she incorporated parts of her research into classes she was already teaching, spending time organizing her notes so her message could be presented succinctly in the limited time she had. Kristin hoped at least one student from each class would hear something that piqued their interest. Once a seed was planted, she was optimistic they would continue exploring their interest one day, just as she had done. She hoped the spark would be strong enough to light a path for those who had been left behind.

Since the ruling planet of her astrological birth chart was Jupiter, known for its expansive energies, it had been quite a challenge for Kristin to condense all the materials from her second book into four broad topics. But she had managed to do it, and from there she created a more detailed framework for each component and used it as an outline for her lectures. She tweaked individual topics again and again until she was satisfied with what she had done. She was more than willing to hand out easy grades to coerce students into registering for her classes. They were her captive audience and played a large role in her plans to reach the masses with her message. So far, most of her students had been receptive; many had been eager to relate their own experiences when they were given the opportunity. The second part of Kristin's lecture often ran over her allotted time because of it, but she always managed at least a brief discussion of each major bullet point representing the total picture she wanted to paint.

She had lobbied the clerks in the registrar's office at Hunter, until they agreed to schedule her classes on Tuesdays and Thursdays whenever possible. That gave her an extra half-hour of continuous class time, which had proven to be a much more efficient way of covering her material. She also started interjecting historical facts about the slave trade throughout the rest of the quarter, if she found an appropriate opening. It had helped her bridge the gaps as she transitioned to her final lectures, which had otherwise seemed to distract some of her students from what she was trying to convey. She did what was necessary to make sure she didn't waste one valuable second of time.

Chapter 2

It's All About the Money

*A*t exactly five minutes past the official start time for her class, Kristin got up and closed the door. It was her signal to any tardy student that they had missed their opportunity for a free 'A' in her World History class. On the way back to her desk, she began to talk to her students about the trip to Ghana she had taken the previous year. She described the warm feeling of welcome she felt at the Kotoka International Airport in Accra when they arrived, and her strong familial sense of belonging from the moment their plane touched down, until she and her friends said their tearful good-byes two weeks later. She told her students that one of the most fascinating things she had experienced in Ghana was the meticulous certainty with which everyone could talk about their family's history, and the major events that had shaped it. She had been amazed how people could rattle off the names of their ancestors going back for generations, and that they did it effortlessly in a way that few African Americans were able to do. She told them she had never gotten used to it the whole time she was there – that everyone she met knew *exactly* who he or she was, and where they had come from.

She followed with a brief history of Asanteman, a loose confederation of unified states in Ghana. They are the Twi speaking members of the Akan ethnic group, she told her students, who make up the majority of Ghana's population. She described the country's physical boundaries,

18

which, as with many other African countries, had been created by European colonialists in the late 1800s, with an end-result of having ethnic groups geographically span several countries. This purposeful disregard of ethnicity, language differences, and social culture also formed the basis for disharmony that has plagued many countries with tumultuous political evolution since gaining their independence; and has included an occasional military coup in recent decades.

Kristin then described her impressions of being inside the two slave castles she had visited on the Gulf of Guinea. She told them how it felt to be closed off in the pitch darkness of the clammy dungeons that had once been used as holding cells. She shared what she had learned about the system of captivity that had existed in Africa for centuries, long before the Europeans arrived. In Ghana and many other countries, it had been customary for captives to be taken as slaves for a specified period as a spoil of battle. The practice had coincided with similar crude behavior that existed in Europe and other areas around the same time. Kristin touched on the "Dark Ages," a time of barbarian invasions across Europe, and the violent notoriety of King Henry the Eighth, who had beheaded his wives for having failed to produce male heirs.

She told her students how an organized system of colonialism had seamlessly replaced the slave trade after human trafficking was outlawed in European countries. And that many Africans who had been fortunate enough to escape capture and enslavement outside of Africa had been subjected to the detrimental effects of colonialism instead, until the middle of the twentieth century.

"That word "*colonialism*," sounds so innocent, doesn't it?" She asked rhetorically. "Yet, according to Webster, "colonialism" is a system of one country's complete domination over another, after forcefully taking control of the dominated country's resources; without providing any benefit to the exploited people of origin, or the 'natives,' as they are often called." She paused a minute to let the definition sink in.

"I imagine that it would have been relatively easy for the roots of colonialism to be firmly established in Africa, after so many of its people had been forcibly removed in large numbers for centuries. The Asante were the last of the die-hard rebels against colonialism in Ghana, and since the British had suffered defeat at their hands in all previous battles, they imported large armies to make certain the West African warriors would finally be defeated. In doing so, the British secured their hold over the entire country and annexed the most populated areas of Ghana to the territories along the coast that they had already forced under their control.

"Now, what does all this have to do with you? I'm sure might be asking yourselves." Several students began fidgeting uncomfortably, as though Kristin had read their minds.

"Well, that is precisely what we're going to be looking at during our last few classes this quarter." She had let them off the hook. "Hopefully, you'll have the answer to that question by the time your papers are due."

She could tell from some of their expressions that they knew exactly where she was going with what she said. She was aware that her classes were generating a growing interest around Hunter's campus. Many students knew how they were structured far in advance of her handing out her class syllabus. She looked around the room and urged them to remain open-minded as they explored new theories about the American slavery experience. She could sense that she had everyone's full attention. There was a sense of intrigue and anticipation as she wondered whether someone from that particular class might be the one to help her take up the cause of the underbelly's transformation.

Kristin then moved into the first topic of her lecture, giving her students a brief sketch of slavery as it had existed in other areas, such as the Mediterranean world of the 1400s. She noted the Italians had operated a lucrative slave trade that mainly victimized Greeks and Eastern Europeans. She touched on historical evidence showing there had been African members of expeditions that had been launched to the newly discovered world across the Atlantic in the 1500s, mentioning Coronado's expedition specifically and several others her students had studied in grade school. She told them that some of the Africans were documented as having been servants, but there were others who had played very important roles in Spanish and Portuguese explorations. She added that she had found no evidence that any of them had been considered subhuman or thought to possess any racial stereotype associated with people of African descent and adopted much later.

Then Kristin moved on to the origin of American slavery, focusing on aspects that were generally not given as much attention as others. She began by touching on the special relationship that existed between African slaves and Native Americans, who the American "colonists" had initially enslaved to supplement the indentured servant labor force that came from the downtrodden of Europe. Native Americans were captured during battles that the colonists waged in order to take control of land they "discovered" when they first arrived in America.

"But as we know," Kristin quickly reminded her students, "the land the Europeans found was only new to *them*. Many Native American nations existed across the land now known as the United States, long before the first group of settlers arrived at Plymouth Rock.

"When we look at things objectively, we can see that the strategy of depending on Native American slave labor had been a risky business model from the start. The indigenous people were highly susceptible to the diseases that Europeans brought to the new world. Some diseases, like chicken pox, were often fatal. And those who managed to escape were also difficult, if not impossible, to recapture. It was the land of their fathers and they knew it well.

"How many of you were aware that the first Africans on record were brought to this country as indentured servants?" She asked, and was pleased to note that at least a third of her students raised their hands.

"Okay, good. The first record of Africans being sold as indentured servants was in Jamestown in 1619, and the first public slave auction was held there about twenty years later. Twenty-three Africans were sold to a small number of Virginia plantation owners during that sale at an average price of twenty-seven dollars each."

After that revelation, a wave of murmurs went around the classroom. A young man toward the back of the room made the observation that the cost of a person had been equivalent to buying dinner at a mid-priced restaurant. Even more of a buzz went around the room as other students commented on his outburst. Kristin waited several seconds until she had regained their full attention.

"I'm afraid you're right," she confirmed. "I can also tell you that I didn't find anything to suggest that any of the Africans who were brought here as indentured servants volunteered to come. But, be that as it may, they were only enslaved for a specific period of time at first, very similar to the traditional system of captivity that still existed in Africa. There were many people of African descent in America who shared the same temporary servitude status as the Europeans, who *did* volunteer to come here. There were also rebellions planned and executed by black and white indentured servants together. It was much later that the slave population was transformed to a mainly African-based system; for many decades during that transition, plantation owners in the colonies employed both European and

African indentured servants as their labor force. And they supplemented it with Native Americans they captured.

Kristin divulged that the Virginia colony had begun to adopt formal laws to protect the rights of slaveholders in the 1640s, but it had been the Massachusetts Bay colony that passed the first law legalizing slavery in 1641. There were slaveholders in all the colonies but the turning point didn't come until a few decades later, when the demand for tobacco products began to grow by leaps and bounds. That flourishing trade created a demand that led to the establishment of great tobacco empires and all the power that came with their wealth. She told her students that as the demand increased, it became clear that the labor model they had been using up until that point would no longer be adequate. With it, they would never be able to take full advantage of the newly discovered profit potential from tobacco.

"Now, I'm giving you this bit of history because it's important for you to understand that the catalyst for changing the slave labor system had nothing to do with the Africans' skin color or with any other physical distinctions they may have had. Those things did play a role however, and we'll talk more about that later.

"Virginia lawmakers bowed to the powerful tobacco farmers' interests and helped them resolve the issue of the increasing cost associated with having to replace their indentured servants. The first major change in the slave trade came in 1662 when a new law passed in Virginia that reversed the English presumption of patrilineal descent, previously used to govern the then-English colony. It allowed children who had been born to female slaves to be considered slaves, instead of having the father determine their social status as had been the custom. In effect, the new law made it possible for slaveholders to produce their own labor force."

There was a rustle in the back of the room again as several students reacted, and Kristin waited for them to end their comments before resuming.

"Many other laws were passed in individual states to regulate slavery: Some of them restricted enslavement and declared it to be imposed on non-Christians only; some provided that all Africans who arrived by ship would be presumed slaves; some provided for the re-enslavement of freed African indentured servants, who didn't leave the state's jurisdiction within a certain length of time after gaining their freedom.

But between 1667 and 1669, the Virginia Assembly passed laws that effectively sealed the fate of enslaved Africans in America for the next two hundred years. The legislature passed the first of its compulsory life servitude statutes in the colonies, which compelled enslaved Africans and the children who were born to female African slaves, to be slaves for life. Around the same time, Virginia passed the "casual killing of slaves" statute, which exempted slaveholders from felony charges that normally would have applied for such an offense.

"Those series of laws officially instituted chattel slavery in America and provided powerful protections for it," Kristin ended. "It began a period of generational slavery, and separated African slavery into its own institution after a few decades. But what I want you to be clear about is that the driving force behind these changes was the plantation owners' quest for increased profits—and nothing more. Other states quickly followed Virginia's lead, as local business leaders assessed the situation and realized the enormous potential they were missing out on. Their motivation in seeking these changes was solely to reduce the costs associated with producing tobacco, and thereby increasing their profits.

"So, that's another excellent reason to quit smoking, don't you think?" Kristin stopped for a minute and looked pointedly in the direction of several students she had observed obeying their tobacco addictions outside the building.

"Unlike Native Americans," she continued after the laughter had subsided, "the Africans who were captured and brought to America were much more resilient. They adapted to their new environment easily and had a natural instinct for survival. They flourished in captivity despite the harsh treatment they received, and despite being forced to work from sun up to sun down every day, with only minimal food and shelter provided.

"And, unlike Native Americans," Kristin added, "the enslaved Africans had no idea of where they were or how they could find their way home."

❈❈❈

She looked up at the clock above the doorway and realized she was out of time. Kristin told her students that she would pick up where she had left off when their class met next that week. She added that they would discuss some of the common experiences shared by Native Americans and Africans who were held in captivity together.

Chapter 3

One in a Million - Chance of a Lifetime

Vivian had always known her striking features gave her an exotic flair that men seemed to appreciate, and her young daughter had inherited the same look. Vivian usually wore her thick, naturally-straight hair piled up in a twist on top of her head—a style she had copied from one of the hair and beauty magazines she was forever reading. On Saturday mornings when she ran her errands, she would usually let it hang in a ponytail that nearly fell to her petite waist. She had a curvy figure from the day she was born, according to her mother, and rarely needed to exercise to keep up appearances. Vivian could eat pretty much anything she wanted to without gaining an ounce. Her smile could light up a room, and she would always attract most of the attention whenever she and her girlfriends went out. The clothes she wore fit her like tailor-made gloves, although she usually bought them off the rack and usually after they had gone on sale. She always had at least one man vying for her attention too, at any given time. She had her pick from any available man that she happened across, and some who weren't quite so available.

But, she had made it clear to all of them that she and her daughter were a package deal—no negotiations. Some of them had kept asking her out anyway, even when she knew they had no interest in a ready-made family.

More often than not, she could tell that right away. Men like that would seldom bother responding when she brought her daughter up in a conversation. Several of them had seemed to expect her to act like she didn't even *have* a child. They would sometimes try to get her to stay over after a date, or seduce her with fancy brochures about trips they could take all over the world—like she could just up and go or something! Sometimes, Vivian overlooked her suspicions if she thought the man had any real potential. But there was something that always happened to force her to choose between the man she was dating and her daughter.

And she had chosen Malaya every time without even hesitating—even if it was someone she would never have dreamed of letting go otherwise.

Vivian had known Sam was a good catch from the moment she first laid eyes on him. She had gone out dancing with her girlfriends one night and spotted him right away. As soon as he came over to strike up a conversation, she knew that Sam was her one-in-a-million chance for the life she had always dreamed about. She could tell he had plenty of money, and he hadn't seemed to mind at all when she told him she already had a young daughter. After that Vivian just *knew* he was the one.

She found out later that Sam had never known his father. Although he never said it, Vivian figured he must have been white because Sam had such a smooth, light-brown complexion and everyone said his mother had been real dark. Vivian had been attracted to the pretty boys all of her life, but Sam was a real *looker*. They got along great together too. And best of all, he couldn't seem to keep his hands off of her.

Still, she decided she would be cautious and she waited until they had been dating for over a month before she took her chance. As soon as she did, she began to wonder whether she had made a huge mistake. She hadn't noticed until then that Sam would always change the subject whenever she brought her daughter's name up. But it was far too late now. She had a sinking feeling in the pit of her stomach that she should have waited a little longer to be sure of how he would react around Malaya. She had never even *considered* the possibility that Sam might not want to have children, but she had already taken matters into her own hands. The opportunity for second thoughts had long passed; Vivian had already gone through the door of no return so there was no going back now.

She had grown more hesitant about it as each day went by, and she also knew that the longer she waited to tell Sam about the baby, the more difficult things would be. So she had made up her mind that she would tell him that night over dinner.

※※※

There was a hodgepodge of smells coming from the restaurant's kitchen that assaulted Vivian's nostrils as soon as they walked through the door. She immediately began reconsidering her plans, especially when she saw they were being seated far away from the lady's room. At first, she had been convinced that her morning sickness this time was as much under control as it had been when she carried her daughter. But lately, she had been overcome by unexpected nausea at all hours of the day and night.

She knew that part of it was just her nerves, and thankfully, her stomach had gradually settled itself by the time she and Sam were seated. As an intense hunger quickly replaced her fleeting queasiness, she decided she would wait until after they had ordered before she sprung her news on Sam. Vivian knew how he was about his image: He always showed a good face in public, no matter what. She had been counting on that in case it turned out that he wasn't as happy about the baby as she hoped. She prayed that all her hesitation would turn out to be unjustified, but after the fiasco with Malaya's father she knew all too well that you could never tell how a man might react to that kind of news. It would have to be Sam's idea for them to get married too, of course, if her plan was to work at all. Or, at least, he would have to *think* it was his idea.

She had been horrified when Sam only sat in stony silence after she finally did work up the nerve to tell him she was pregnant. She knew he didn't like surprises so she had expected him to be thrown off guard. But he had just sat there without saying one word until she became understandably alarmed. Vivian tried to figure out what he might be thinking whenever he looked her way long enough to look into his eyes. Unfortunately, he was an excellent poker player so she didn't detect a hint of his honest reaction.

But, as suddenly as the wall of silence had engulfed them Sam began talking again. He only talked about things that were of an impersonal nature, but anything was better than the silence. Given the circumstances, she had taken it as a good sign at first, but as the meal went on Vivian grew nervous again in anticipation of their drive home. Then, just as her panic

26

began to settle in, Sam had proposed to her out of the blue! She was so relieved that she quickly accepted before he had time to change his mind.

In the days that followed, she had managed to convince herself that he had probably been taking time to carefully consider how they would all fit together as a family, to be certain of it before he made a commitment. After all, she had given him a lot to think about and had forced a big decision on him. They would have a rocky start but Vivian still thought they made a great couple. Sam had always made a point of showing her a good time; he gave her the royal treatment whenever they were out together. He did seem a little distant sometimes, but she had learned to overlook that side because his generosity more than made up for it. He took her to exciting new places and he always encouraged her to order the most expensive thing on the menu. And Sam just loved showing her off to all his friends.

Vivian had been nearly bubbling with excitement by the time he dropped her off after dinner. She told Malaya the good news right away, and her imagination shifted into high gear as she pictured her new life as Mrs. Samuel King. She envisioned herself decorating their house in any way she wanted. Sam could certainly afford it since he was a very successful construction manager. From that point on, she would never have to concern herself about money again. Her husband would want her to have the very best and she would finally be able to buy nice things for her daughter.

Vivian's heart had been broken when she realized the children at Malaya's school dressed so much better than her daughter. She had been worried her little girl might begin to think less of herself, but she hadn't been able to do anything about it then. Once she and Sam were married, she would see to it that both her children dressed as nicely as anyone else did.

After a point, Vivian realized Malaya had been very quiet since she shared her news with her. For the first time, she contemplated how her daughter and new husband might get along together. They hadn't spent all that much time around each other yet, and it suddenly dawned on her that Malaya might not even care very much for her fiancé.

But, on the other hand, her daughter had never seemed fond of any of the men she had dated in the past. Vivian made up her mind right then and there that she would think of ways to bring Sam and Malaya closer together. After all, they were going to be a family now; she wasn't about to let *anything* ruin her chances for real happiness.

Chapter 4

The Call for Freedom

"*G*ood morning everyone." Kristin greeted her World History students for the second time that week. "We have quite a bit to cover today so let's get to it, shall we?" She closed the door firmly behind the last student and moved back to her desk at the front of the classroom.

"...So, last time we talked a little about the relationship that naturally developed between Native Americans and Africans during the years they were enslaved together in this country. I already mentioned that the two groups merged certain aspects of their respective cultures. They developed recipes, exchanged herbal remedies, shared legends, and escaped together from plantations at every opportunity. They also intermarried, with unions most often between African males and Native American females. Why? There were large numbers of Native American males killed in battle, leaving their women and children vulnerable and unprotected. Also, initially there were many more African males captured and brought to America than females."

As she continued her discussion about the links connecting the two cultures, Kristin could see that some of her students were beginning to have "aha" moments. She guessed that they were perhaps reminded of some vague piece of their own family history that included Native Americans.

"So, let's look closer at other factors that contributed to the make up of their unions," she continued. "As I mentioned earlier, the plantation owners' initial preference had been for African males, and that of course was because of the greater potential for them to survive the grueling work that they were to do. Females didn't become as valuable an asset, from a business standpoint, until after the colonies passed laws providing that the children born of slaveholders and female slaves were to be considered slaves, as well.

"A number of states passed restrictive laws to control their slaves as time went on. The State of New York passed laws in 1685, for example, that prohibited slaves from carrying firearms and from holding meetings. South Carolina legislators passed a new Slave Code in 1740, primarily in response to a failed insurrection known as the Stono Rebellion of 1739. Those brave freedom fighters organized their uprising on the banks of the Stono River, just twenty miles outside of Charleston. It was the largest uprising that had been carried out in the American colonies up to that time, starting out as a small group of twenty or so people who had armed themselves. They wrote the word "liberty" across banners they carried and traveled from place to place in the area, convincing other slaves to join in on their revolt. The rebels also killed any whites who stood in their way.

"When the new slave code was instituted, it became illegal for those enslaved in South Carolina to assemble in groups or learn how to read and write. The rebellion took place on a Sunday and a new "Sunday" law *required* whites to carry guns on that day of the week, since most of them had been unarmed during the time of the revolt. The new South Carolina slave code specifically described people held captive as being Africans, Mulattoes, Mestizos, and Native Americans; all of whom had been enslaved in that state at the same time."

Kristin stopped to call on a student in the back of the room who had his hand raised.

"Okay," he started, after being recognized, "I know that Africans who were mixed with whites were called Mulattoes, but what exactly was a *Mestizo?*"

Kristin answered, explaining that the term had been used to describe people of Native American ancestry who had one white parent, most likely the father. She mentioned similar terms that had been used in other countries to classify people born of mixed races.

"So, let's move on to our next point of discussion," she continued after the clarification. "There was an area in northern Florida around that time to which both the British and Spanish colonists laid claim. The Seminoles had also claimed portions of this same volatile area, long before the Europeans ever arrived. There is documentation in the Library of Congress to show that in 1565, African farmers and artisans were part of the Spanish expedition that established St. Augustine as the first European city of record in North America. The Spanish," she said, "provided a safe haven for runaway slaves in that area of Florida for more than a hundred years before the Stono rebellion took place. The Seminoles also aided Africans who escaped and who sometimes lived among them for years, before moving further south. The runaways established themselves as productive members of the undisputed Spanish territory in and around St. Augustine; many were loyal allies of the Spanish against their mutual British enemy.

"King Charles II of Spain even sent an edict to the Florida colony in 1695, officially welcoming fugitive slaves as free and full citizens. The only stipulation was that they convert to Catholicism and help defend the territory. News of the King's proclamation and of the Spanish safe haven quickly made its way from plantation to plantation in states to the north of Florida. The news spread like the sound of African drums and likely inspired the Stono rebels in the Carolinas, and many others, to hope for freedom. That hope gave rise to an increasing number of organized slave rebellions in the years leading up to the Civil War. But we'll talk about that in more detail later."

Most of her students registered surprise as Kristin introduced them to a colorful figure she had uncovered. "According to my research, Captain Francisco Menéndez escaped from a South Carolina plantation when he was only a teen. He was aided in his escape by the Yamassee tribe in the same state, and he immediately headed for the Spanish territory. Later, he played an important role in defending the territory for twenty years after his arrival. He was commissioned as a senior officer at Fort Mose, located two miles north of St. Augustine.

"That post became a major point of defense against the British under Menedez's command, and Fort Mose also became the first formally acknowledged free Black community in America. For years, native inhabitants of The Congo, The Gambia, Nigeria, Guinea, and other West African countries escaped to live there. They were joined by people of African descent who came from South American countries, the Canary Islands, and the Caribbean; all settling in and around Fort Mose."

Kristin got up from her desk and began walking around the classroom. She could see from their expressions that only one or two of her students had been aware of this rich chapter of their collective history. Most of them had no idea that there had been people of African ancestry living freely in the South for centuries, while slavery had still been a legal practice elsewhere in the United States.

"Yes, there were many African Americans who were born free in the Spanish territory of Florida," she confirmed, "and were never enslaved in America. Some of them however, like Menéndez, were recaptured at some point and sold *back* into slavery only to escape it once again.

"Now, we talked a bit earlier about the distinctly different physical attributes of African descendants. It caused them to be very conspicuous since their features sharply contrasted with those of whites, making them hard to miss. The possibility of enslavement was therefore a permanent yoke around the necks of *anyone* of African ancestry in America. It made no difference at all whether they had been born free, had worked to purchase their freedom, or had taken it by escaping.

"And let's not forget that the states had adopted their own *individual* laws too. In many states, all people of African origin were considered property, and weren't allowed to have a voice in defending their freedom. The ones whose African blood dominated their physical appearance had to remain vigilant to avoid capture — no matter what their actual circumstances. This was especially true beginning around 1810, after the practice of human trafficking in Africa was outlawed. It meant that no more slave ships would bring what had once appeared to be an endless supply of captured Africans to the American shores. A 'black' market replaced the auction blocks after the laws were changed, and those practices were even more unscrupulous."

Kristin gave her students an example of one of the more infamous black market operations, involving Dr. George Washington Carver. The soft-spoken agricultural scientist had been born in Diamond Grove Missouri only a few years before slavery was abolished. While still an infant, "night riders," as they were called, abducted him alongside his mother under the cloak of darkness. "Who knows what might have become of him had Moses and Susan Carver – the white couple who owned the young George, his brother, and mother – not sacrificed their prize horse to hire someone to look for them," Kristin stated emphatically. She had become a great fan of Dr. Carver's as a second grader at Lewis Adams Elementary school.

"By all accounts, the Carvers had always treated the people they held as slaves with kindness, considering the circumstances. George's mother was never found and was most likely sold on the black market in a distant state. But the Carvers cared for her two young sons who had been left behind, and the couple nursed the sickly George back to health."

Kristin looked at the clock above the door and realized she would need to move things along if she were to have any chance of finishing what she had planned to cover that day. She switched topics and began talking about the Religious Friends of Society, also known as "the Quakers," and their vocal opposition to slavery. She told her class that their voices had grown even louder as states began to pass chattel slavery laws, creating generational slavery that would last for over two centuries. The abolition-ist movement had slowly begun to gain momentum, she told them, and its members had put increasing pressure on the federal government to end slavery.

"But there was another important factor behind Lincoln's decision to force an end to slavery," she countered, "although it is not frequently dis-cussed. That less-acknowledged aspect was the slaves' increasing determi-nation to free themselves."

Kristin's students were already familiar with Harriet Tubman's Under-ground Railroad, of course. Most also knew about the bloody uprising that had been led by Nat Turner in 1831, who declared his actions to have been at the direction of God. Few of them, however, had heard of Gabriel Prosser, the twenty-four-year-old who had planned the first large-scale slave revolt in America in 1800. Kristin told them that Prosser had orga-nized thousands of slaves and had planned to attack and capture Richmond Virginia. He directed his followers to kill any whites they came across, except for Quakers, Methodists, and Frenchmen, whom Prosser consid-ered as being "friendly to liberty."

"Revolution was definitely in the air during that time," Kristin declared. "Prosser's plans were close on the heels of the 1791 Haitian uprising, quashed after Napoleon sent secret orders to Major General Charles Leclerc, who led a French army of eighty-two thousand soldiers against the rebels. The brutality of Napoleon's orders reflected his fear of the dis-proportionate number of Blacks who had been brought to Haiti to work the plantations there. The Haitian rebellion closely followed the revolutions launched by the citizens of France and the American Colonies, who had both broken away from their respective oppressors in turn.

"Prosser created quite an alarm among slaveholders in southern states and all over America. Up until that point, they had been under the assumption that their enslaved workers were relatively under control. Many whites became extremely nervous after they realized how close Prosser had come to carrying out his plans. As with the plantations in the Caribbean, a massive number of laborers had been brought in to work the tobacco plantations in America. A large slave population had been required to keep up with the growing demand for tobacco products, although it had still been a small number in comparison to the number of slaves brought in to produce sugar, coffee, indigo, and cotton in Haiti."

Only a handful of her students had ever heard of Denmark Vessey either. Kristin told them about the West African-born man who had been considered among the upper echelon of those enslaved in Charleston South Carolina. Vessey, like others of his statue who had been carpenters, artisans, engineers, and the like, had never been required to do hard labor as a slave. His skills as a carpenter were considered to be of more value; he didn't have as many restrictions on his life either. He had eventually purchased his own freedom using lottery winnings that he also used to buy his own carpentry shop. Vessey lived as a successful free man in South Carolina, and became an outspoken critic of slavery once he had his own taste of freedom again. In 1822, he organized a large insurrection of close to nine thousand people. His followers were both slaves and Blacks who had been freed in and around Charleston. But his plans, like those of so many others before him, were foiled when a confidant alerted authorities before his intent could be carried out."

"Aw, man!" A student sitting in the row of seats closest to the window groaned and Kristin acknowledged his frustration.

"Yes, I'm afraid that many of the freedom fighters were betrayed, usually because of fear of retaliation by whites. Everyone was forced to bear the brunt of punishment when there was trouble, whether he or she had been an actual participant or not. And let's not forget that there was little accountability for whatever retribution was decided on.

"It is noteworthy in this instance that the informant also named four *white* men, who played a major role in Vessey's thwarted plans. Again, only wealthy whites benefited from slavery, although not all wealthy whites owned slaves. Many were very much against the practice but were outnumbered, until an increasing number of rebellions finally forced lawmakers to reconsider abolition. Regrettably, some rebels, whose oppression had reached a boiling point before exploding, used physical characteristics that distinguished them from whites against *all* whites. Thus, the consequences of slavery were borne by many innocent white people too; though all but the severely damaged among the revolutionaries would usually spare the lives of children and other innocents.

"The wealthy slaveholders, on the other hand, often played on the emotions of whites who were at the lower end of the economic totem pole. They coerced them into doing their bidding; seeking them out as allies to make sure they had some degree of insulation against the people they kept as slaves, and whom they had begun to fear. There were always lower-class whites who were eager to believe the stereotypes that were adopted about Blacks. Many of them were blinded by their own frustrations and unknowingly became the pawns of wealthy slave owners; a strategy that is still used to a large extent today. In the meantime, many more whites became vocal in their opposition to slavery as they grew more aware of the looming dangers in continuing the practice. Many more became actively involved in ending slavery and they began to stand firm in their convictions.

"Take John Quincy Adams, for example, who was the sixth President of the United States. Adams successfully argued the rights of revolutionaries aboard the slave ship *Amistad* to defend themselves, before the U.S. Supreme Court. He had previously served a term as Secretary of State and later a member of the U.S. House of Representatives, after leaving the presidency. He was also the first President who was the son of a *former* President. Adams defended the thirty-six survivors of the *Amistad* insurrection, who had been arrested when the ship they controlled docked off the coast of New York. He based his appeal on the illegality of the slave trade at the time the rebels had been kidnapped from Africa, in 1839. The Supreme Court ultimately agreed with Adams, ruling that the Africans had merely defended their rights as free human beings in fending off the would-be slaveholders. The group was freed, even after it was shown that they had overpowered and killed nearly all the whites on board the ship."

As she looked out at her students, Kristin could see that most of them had been unaware of all the slave insurgencies that had taken place in the years leading to the Civil War. She told them that the increased number of rebellions had finally brought people together who had a variety of motives for ending slavery, and who were all looking for a way to resolve the "Negro problem." That list included government officials, abolitionists, slaveholders, and even some of the former slaves, who were still living in America as free men and women.

"Paul Cuffee," Kristin said, "who was a Quaker and ship owner of Native American and African descent, instituted the first widely publicized campaign to establish a settlement in Africa for former slaves. His ship carried thirty-eight freed men and women from the U.S. to Sierra Leone in 1817; unfortunately, Cuffee became ill a short time later and died. After his death, the American Colonization Society (ACS) was formed, and through it the Liberian colony was established. The ACS initially had support from abolitionists and free people of African ancestry, with many viewing the organization as a continuation of Cuffee's mission. But as we take a closer look, it becomes evident that the ACS's existence had only served to benefit businessmen in slave states. For example, the organization did not permit free Blacks to become members. Their primary mission was to rid the United States of African Americans who had been freed or who had been born free, and were "agitating" Blacks who were still enslaved just as Vessey had done. Their mission had been to protect the institution of slavery, on which the net worth of so many people by that time had been based.

"On a side note," Kristin added, "there are certain southern politicians who have continued to use this same means of getting the masses to rally behind their causes, perhaps because it has been so effective in the past. Many southern whites used the term "outside agitators" during the Civil Rights movement in particular, making reference to Jewish people who traveled South to join in the struggle."

"The first attempt made by the ACS to establish a colony consisted of a small group of freed Blacks who were transported to Sherbro Island, off the coast of Sierra Leone, in 1821. The colony was all but wiped out after a sudden mass illness swept through. During a second attempt, Lt. Robert Stockton, acting on behalf of the ACS, "persuaded" the king of Cape Mesurado to sell land needed for a new settlement by pointing a loaded pistol at his head. King Peter, the traditional ruler over the land now called Liberia, was forced into a treaty with ACS in 1825, as were other kings in that same area. He ultimately "agreed" to accept a small amount of tobacco, rum, and similar items in exchange for his people's land."

Kristin told her class that it was important to understand that the Liberian Settlement of freed African Americans, which in 1947 became the independent nation of Liberia, had been established through violent means.

The rightful owners were forced from their land and a series of white governors, appointed by the ACS, were established as the ruling authority.

"A tiered class system existed in Liberia for well over one hundred years, with Mulattoes from America falling just below the ACS governor. Next came other African Americans, and finally, at the bottom, were the native-born Africans whose property had been taken; or who had escaped from some slave ship and somehow ended up in Liberia.

"The abuses of the indigenous people became so bad that the League of Nations, the precursor to the United Nations, was called on to investigate charges of slavery and forced labor in 1927. It was all finally brought to a head in 1980 when Samuel L. Doe, a non-American Liberian, led a military coup in which the president was assassinated and the government overthrown. A West African peacekeeping force had to be called in to maintain control over the area, putting an end to Liberia's first republic of terror.

"Wow." Someone in the front of the room blurted out. There was a buzz of conversation among her students for several minutes.

※※※

Kristin looked at the wall clock again and saw that she had gone over her allotted time. When she announced that she was at a stopping point for the day, many of her students seemed genuinely disappointed. But her announcement was quickly punctuated by the sounds of other students who were scheduled to be in the room next, and who had begun to lurk noisily outside the door.

She responded to comments from her students as they filed past her desk, picking up their take-home test and study questions from a neat stack. After the last person had left the room, Kristin gathered her things with a smile of satisfaction on her face. She was comfortable that she would be able to complete everything she intended to present to this class when they met again for the last time. She sensed that many of them had already gained a new perspective and she felt very satisfied.

Then she remembered it was her turn to pick up Trazi from his karate lessons to drop him off at his father's place. Kristin hurried out to her car, remembering how much she had disliked being the last person to be picked up from her piano lessons when she had been a young girl.

Chapter 5

Malaya

Malaya had sat passively watching as her mother paced back and forth across the room. She barely understood what she had been saying at first. Vivian rushed straight into her bedroom after her boyfriend dropped her off from their date. The young girl couldn't remember her mother ever being in such an agitated state. When she finally understood what her animation was about, Malaya had been stunned to silence. She kept hoping she was having a nightmare; the kind where you don't realize you were dreaming until after you've awakened. But this had been no dream. Sam had finally popped the question, she heard her mother say through a cloud of disbelief. He had asked her to marry him while they were waiting for their dessert after dinner.

Malaya had been horrified and had no idea what she should say. Her mother was obviously so happy to be marrying Sam. The young girl managed a weak smile despite the knot she felt instantly growing in her stomach. Later, when her mother playfully warned her not to be such a stick in the mud with her soon-to-be stepfather, Malaya had no concept of what she meant by it. She had been sitting down with Vivian on the loveseat in her dressing room so they could talk, her mother said. It was probably the last thing Malaya had expected her to say. They were having their talk on

Vivian's wedding day after her mother's friends had helped her into her gown and put the final touches on her hair and makeup.

The wedding coordinator had been so organized that Vivian wound up with nearly an hour left before the ceremony was to start. It was such a beautiful day for a wedding, everyone kept saying. Malaya sat quietly through all the hustle and bustle of activity in the bride's room of the wedding chapel. Vivian's friends kept telling her how happy they were that her dreams were finally coming true.

Then abruptly, Vivian had looked at the clock on the mock fireplace mantel to confirm the time, and then she told everyone she wanted to have a private conversation with her daughter before the ceremony started. The women had all smiled knowingly to each other as they left the room to give mother and daughter a few moments of privacy. Malaya had been so proud that her mother wanted to spend time alone with her on her special day. The girl and her grandmother had exchanged smiles too, as the older woman left the room with the others.

Malaya had once overheard the lady who lived next to her grandmother say that her mother should pay more attention to her, "*instead of being in the streets all the time.*" Malaya had been surprised by what she heard. She knew in her heart that her mother loved her, even if they didn't get to spend as much time together as she would've liked.

She had spent the night before at her grandmother's house so her mother could sleep-in on her big day. Vivian's friends had made plans to pick her up around ten thirty that morning and they had all gone to the spa for a massage and facial. Afterwards, everyone had come directly to the wedding chapel so they could all get dressed for the ceremony together.

Malaya's grandmother had taken extra pains with her long straight hair that morning too, piling it on top of her head and pinning it in a bun like her mother sometimes wore her hair. Her grandmother had put special hairpins in her hair with tiny white pearls on their tips. She had tied a white ribbon around Malaya's bun and left the long ends of the ribbons hanging to the shoulders of her white satin dress, also trimmed in pearls.

Vivian had taken her daughter's dress directly from the store to her mother's house after she bought it. Since Malaya and her grandmother were to get dressed there, she had seen her dress for the first time that morning. The young girl had heard her mother tell her girlfriends earlier that she had spent a small fortune on the dress, and only afterwards had she felt uneasy about how much it had cost; or what Sam's reaction might be. Her mother told her friends that she had been on cloud nine getting everything arranged for the wedding and didn't want to spoil things by fighting with her soon-to-be-husband over money. Her plan was to wait until the credit card bill came the following month before she said anything to Sam about the dress.

Vivian had bragged to her girlfriends that she would have her new husband wrapped around her little finger by then. "I've been trying to think of ways to get him used to the idea of having a daughter," she told them confidently, "so he can be just as generous with Malaya as he has been with me. I think her dress will give me the perfect opportunity to do that," she reasoned, more to herself than to them. Vivian said she would tell Sam that since he wanted *her* to look like royalty at their wedding, she had naturally assumed he would want her *daughter* to look like a princess.

After her grandmother unzipped the garment bag that morning Malaya had barely been able to believe her eyes. It was the most beautiful dress she had ever seen in her life, and she couldn't believe it was for her!

Her grandmother had stood back from her after she pulled the dress over her head and had fastened all the tiny pearl buttons. "Baby, you look just like an angel," she had said to her granddaughter, "a beautiful little angel."

Malaya's eyes quickly glistened as she fought to hold back her tears.

※※※

After all the women had finally left the room, Vivian turned around and looked at her daughter slowly from head to toe. It was almost as though she was noticing her for the first time that day. She told Malaya that she looked like a beautiful princess and the child felt her heart swell with pride. Then her mother started talking about Sam abruptly and everything seemed to change after that. Vivian told her that Sam was a good man and that many men wouldn't want to marry a woman who already had a child. She said they were lucky that Sam didn't mind, and they would *both* have to work real hard to make sure he never regretted it.

She stopped talking for a moment as she looked at Malaya guardedly. "It might take him a little time to get used to having such a grown up little girl for a daughter," she continued. "But I promise you, both of us are going to have better lives than we've ever had before. Sam has enough money to take care of us—the way we deserve.

"But you've got to be nice to him," Vivian told her daughter. "Don't be such a stick in the mud around him all the time, okay? The nicer you are to him, the better it's going to be for everybody."

Her mother had made Malaya promise that she would do her very best. After she agreed that she would, Vivian had sent her downstairs to wait with the rest of the wedding party. Malaya remembered being very confused as she slowly walked down the steps, being extra careful so she wouldn't get her feet caught in the hem of her dress.

She didn't like Sam at all, especially the way he looked at her sometimes. She wanted to tell her mother that the night she told her that she planned to marry him, but Malaya didn't know what she should say.

After she had finally made it to the bottom of the stairs, Mr. Tim, who was a friend of her grandmother's, looked up and whistled as Malaya walked toward where they were sitting. Neither he nor her grandmother noticed that her eyes had started to dampen.

"Look at you!" Mr. Tim said in exaggerated admiration.

"You look so pretty, baby. You look like *you* should be the bride!"

He had always teased Malaya whenever he came to her grandmother's house and she was there. He was trying to bring her out of her shell, she had once heard him tell her grandmother.

Malaya was a beautiful child with very striking features, just like her mother. But unlike her mother, she had always shied away from the attention that it brought her. And for some reason, hearing what Mr. Tim said made her feel sick to her stomach.

Chapter 6

... *The Chicken or the Egg?*

*W*ord had apparently spread around Hunter's campus pretty fast after Kristin switched to her unorthodox grading practices. For the last two quarters, all her classes had filled up during the first day of pre-registration. She sat back in her chair and smiled to herself as she went over her student lists for the upcoming quarter. She had just pulled them from her faculty mailbox and already recognized the names of several students she had taught during previous quarters. She liked having repeat students because it challenged her to keep her historical references fresh. There had been many well-documented mentions of slave rebellions in the U.S., and to the restrictive laws that the colonies passed to hold onto the practice; Kristin always had a variety from which to select.

She looked up from her desk from time to time as her American History students trickled into the classroom. They were a somewhat younger group than her World History class and she tried to gauge their level of interest as they wandered in for their final lecture of the quarter. As students filed by her worn desk, they dropped the first part of their final tests into a large wooden tray. A few of them made comments to her about points she had raised during their previous lecture, and she thought they were very astute observations. To her way of thinking, it was clear evi-

41

dence that she had started getting through to them and that gave her a sense of accomplishment.

She was greatly encouraged that some students seemed to have given thought to the material she had shared with them from her research and last book. They seem to have reflected on the contrasts she had pointed out between their own realities and that of the people who had lived through the slave experience. It was what Kristin had hoped for, and she was convinced that after she uncovered fallacies about racism that so many had accepted without question, they would wake up to the truth about who they really were.

She knew that what she visualized as the outcome for the next phase of her lecture would be challenging to achieve. There were few, if any, of her students who had ever experienced overt racism. For them, integration had always been an established reality, with the only possible exception being their churches. But by now, even that last bastion of segregation faced disintegration too—even in the Deep South.

Many of her students had friends and relatives who were of a different or mixed race. Most either didn't know about, or have any concerns about, the small number of isolated white communities still scattered across the country that held on tightly to their racial hatred. A minority now, their residents participated in rituals that passed the evil venom of racism down to their descendants in its purest form, deliberately separating themselves from Blacks and from the views of mainstream America to hold on to it.

Kristin's students had never known the pressures that came with being "a credit" to one's race. They had no idea what the term "white privilege" even meant, and only had an inkling about "Jim Crow" laws that were adopted by states after Reconstruction of the South ended. Most had no understanding of the significance of those informal codes that continued to oppress former slaves and their descendants for nearly a century after slavery ended. She understood that the young people who enrolled in her classes had no frame of reference for forced separation that had been based on color, and had affected nearly every aspect of life in many parts of America. They didn't realize that it had only ended a few decades earlier in some areas of the country. She knew that in the minds of her students and many Americans, all that was something that was a part of the country's long ago past and would be best forgotten.

Most truly believed that racism was now a non-issue and that it no longer affected the majority of Americans in any tangible way. Still, the subject continued to be a sensitive topic and usually not one that was welcomed in racially mixed company. Outside of one's immediate circle, only the most obligatory and politically correct comments were generally made about racism now. And since the subject itself was taboo, everyone's opinions about it remained largely unexposed and therefore unaffected.

Kristin had also come to realize that for many Black Americans, it wasn't quite as simple as forgetting about racism. She suspected that for many, their vivid memories of the Civil Rights Movement of the '50s and '60s were still too painful to bear. It was probably too frightening for those who had witnessed racial violence first hand, to even consider the possibility that it might still exist in America today in any form. Some had chosen to believe that it had been annihilated years ago, because it was too troubling for them to acknowledge otherwise. They couldn't bear to think there was a possibility that their grandchildren might be subjected to the same illogical, sadistic mistreatment that had once been a way of life for them.

The very notion of skin color as a basis for subjecting an entire race of people to a lifetime of slavery seems ludicrous, at best, to the majority of people today. The profitable indoor tanning industry is a testament to that; non-black people of means pay large sums of money to darken their skin. For the most part, skin color has become inconsequential to the latest generation of Americans. To use that or any other physical feature as a justification for slavery would be seen as preposterous to all except a few.

Yet, Kristin believed the trauma of racial terrorism that had been prevalent in America from the end of Reconstruction until a few decades past, still affected many Black Americans. She became convinced of it as she spent days in the Library of Congress doing her research. It was clear to her that a major obstacle for many was still the undetected and lingering genetic memories of their ancestors' trauma. She believed that the dark energies from those experiences created a massive heaviness in their genes that was never reconciled.

Nearly everything Kristin had done since returning from her trip to Africa was done with the thought of easing the unspoken predicament that some Black Americans still found themselves in, until a permanent solution presented itself. Thoughts of this group had been heavy on her mind as she wrote her last book. She risked her tenure at Hunter to send this underbelly of Black America some ray of hope to hold onto, until something more tangible could be found. She was forever thinking of ways to help them transform their lives. She had felt a strange sense of responsibility for this group in particular, after having been in the slave castles of Ghana. And she now felt she had identified what was certain to be the root cause of their social imbalance. Kristin believed that segment of Black America had been silently stuck in the throes of their ancestors' miserable experiences and her mission had become one of finding a means of breaking that cycle and delivering them from it. She looked for ways to inspire a more constructive use of their God-given collective potential, which she believed to have been misdirected after their ancestors lost their psychological equilibrium. Kristin became convinced that they too could live productive lives if they could be made to believe it.

Any effective solution would have to provide support for the men who had yet to learn how to break through emotional barriers, unknowingly erected by ancestors to help survive their *own* trauma. They unwittingly passed these deficiencies on to *their* sons in turn, as they themselves learned to hide their shame at being unable to protect and support their families. Kristin knew a permanent remedy would also have to champion Black mothers who had resigned themselves to doing what they felt they had to do to feed their children. Many no longer found any joy in their lives without the haze of drugs or alcohol in place to mask their despair at making constant sacrifices that never seemed to make a difference. Some women were forced to learn of their *own* children's accomplishments second-hand through relatives; yet they faithfully witnessed each important event in the lives of "Miss Anne's" children, who had placed in their charge.

Kristin was concerned that if something weren't done about it soon, the descendents of *their* offspring would have even less hope. She felt compelled to help the underbelly construct a new legacy to replace the one left by their ancestors' battered souls. She longed to help them create a new flag to replace the invisible banners that waved tirelessly from their substandard communities for the entire world to see. Those furling pennants only emphasized their generational poverty and underachievement; calling attention to their uneducated and unmotivated single-mothers, and to the mental instability in their communities that was most frequently treated with alcohol and illegal drugs. Those very visible banners also brought widespread attention to violent crime that often plagued their neighborhoods and that caused them so frequently to be *victims* of crime.

It wasn't surprising to Kristin when she realized there were some successful Black Americans who had become impatient with the underbelly. She could sense their increasing frustrations that were becoming more and more vocal - that the underbelly had never heeded the practical solution proposed by Booker T. Washington for newly freed slaves to "cast down their buckets where they were" and develop a skill to sustain themselves.

Some Blacks had grown resentful over the decades that the "veil of ignorance" had still been left over the heads of so many.

Now, they were wondering why the underbelly just couldn't get it together. So much had changed since the time that their ancestors were brought to America. These Black Americans were tired of hearing the excuses. Others had made it; why couldn't these people make it too?

Their exasperation was easy enough for Kristin to appreciate, but recently she had begun to question the passion that seemed to be behind some of the comments they made. She couldn't help but wonder whether there was an unspoken fear that some in white America might try to use the underbelly's failings as proof that all Blacks were inferior. Though such a scenario was unlikely to prevail for many reasons, Kristin had to wonder whether some Black Americans actually feared the possibility. If something like that were to happen, it might mean that those who had risen from the ashes and had been living the American dream for the past decades along with everyone else, just might find themselves right back in the hellish nightmares of their ancestors' past.

Kristin also held the belief that many who were still struggling had begun to see their continued failures as confirmation that they somehow *were* inferior. They had begun to believe they were merely suffering their fate in life. Though few said it aloud, she believed it was that very shameful despair that made them resign themselves to passively accept failure. And in that belief, living a life of crime was of little consequence.

So far, all she had was a message of hope for the underbelly and she relied heavily on her students to help her deliver it. She knew that they all had friends and relatives who hadn't been as motivated to secure their futures as they had. Those friends and loved ones had never tried to find any reliable means of supporting themselves, and were well on their way toward joining the ranks of the underbelly. Kristin dared to believe her message would be delivered by her students in their interactions with them during breaks from school, bringing unmotivated friends and relatives some ray of hope. She knew that it wasn't a solution by any means, but it would have to do until she could think of something better. She could only pray that her message would reach those who needed to hear it most, and that it would stimulate some shift in their way of thinking.

She was positive that the first step was to expose the truth about slavery and racism. It was the key that would finally release the hold that had kept the underbelly in bondage, long after the practice of slavery ended.

"Please come in and shut the door," Kristin called out to the last student to arrive. "You made it just in time," she chided, as the grateful sophomore scurried to his seat. She didn't necessarily relish the idea of having to take such a hard stance but she had stood her ground on more than one occasion. Kristin had turned away several students in the past who disregarded her rules on punctuality and arrived after her door had already been closed. She wasn't much older than most of her students and she had a youthful appearance that made her seem closer to their ages than her own. She knew that if she didn't stand firm, it might affect the survival of her class structure and that she couldn't afford.

"Good morning everyone," she greeted them all from behind her desk.

"Before we pick up from where we left off, I want to take a minute to emphasize an important point. As we finish the quarter, I want to be sure that you're getting what these discussions mean for you, as individuals." There was a brief pause before she continued. "As children of the African Diaspora in America, I want you to be assured of who you truly are. The African blood that runs in your veins and your ancestors' heritage of having survived the American slave experience makes you, without a doubt, among the most resilient of humans ever to walk the face of the Earth.

"I firmly believe that we are descended from a spiritually powerful people. It was their spirituality that empowered them to withstand extreme emotional, physical, sexual, and psychological abuses for centuries. As their descendants, we have not only managed to climb up from the hell of their past in large numbers, but countless among us have also excelled.

"And, yes," she added with a smile, "we all know people who haven't started the climb yet, but that doesn't mean they don't have the potential."

The room erupted in laughter after Kristin's candid observation. She took in their faces as they quieted down. She saw an acknowledgement of what she had said on several of them, while on others she was met with doubt and confusion.

"So why then, are there those among us who appear to be stuck, you might ask? Why is it that one hundred and fifty plus years later, there are so many who still haven't even considered a climb out of hell?

"We've all heard the statistics on the rising number of single-parent Black families. We know that many of us don't have the family resources to call on for help when we need emergency cash. We know about the setbacks to family plans that arise after an unexpected illness or pregnancy, a job loss or some other emergency. Yet, there are many who have experienced these same things and have still managed to pull themselves up. They accept the temporary help that's available, as the welfare system was intended, and after a brief period of recovery they make a fresh start.

"So why then is it so difficult for some Blacks? What contributes to one person's repeated failures, even when they start out with similar resources and aptitudes as others?

"Think about it," Kristin urged. "There is quite a bit of savvy required for operating an illegal drug business, for example. The successful kingpin would have to have a solid aptitude for accounting, and he or she would need other skills that are required for running a legal business, as well. So why drugs?

"What is it that holds so many down in a counterproductive cycle of poverty, drug abuse, disease, sexual assault, and physical violence?

"It may be true that other racial and ethnic groups experience these same dysfunctions," she acknowledged hastily, "but Black Americans are unique to any other group in this country. The majority of our African ancestors did not immigrate to America voluntarily; most were kidnapped and brought here in chains. After the Civil War ended and the Constitution was amended to end slavery, the Union troops provided former slaves with only *thirteen* years of protection; then they were left to their own devices while still at the scene of their enslavement.

"So the real focus of our final lecture is the "underbelly" of Black America–those still bearing the consequences of slavery; the demographic that is *still* struggling for survival. But before we get further into that, I want to take a few seconds to remind you of how your final grades will be calculated."

Kristin looked out into the sea of faces before her and was pleased to see that some were genuinely put off by her unexpected diversion. But after the first few quarters, she had come to realize her best bet was to take care of this final bit of housekeeping first, since she had found herself constantly running over her time.

"As I mentioned at the beginning of the quarter," she continued, "the take-home exam that you turned in today will count as forty-five percent of your total grade. Since the questions were taken directly from the study sheet I passed out earlier, I don't expect that anyone should have had a problem with it."

Someone in the back of the room made a muffled comment that Kristin couldn't quite make out and the rest of the class erupted in quiet laughter.

She presumed their amusement had been at the expense of a rather large football player who sat in the last row of seats and was grinning sheepishly. There was no reason that anyone should have made less than a perfect score on the test. Kristin could only surmise that the jokester's remark had questioned the athlete's ability to copy answers onto his test sheet. She had to force herself not to smile as she waited for the laughter to subside.

"Another twenty-five percent of your grade will come from the essay that you are to turn in by next Friday. And don't forget, they must be in my office no later than 5 p.m."

And with that said, Kristin got up and wrote the essay topic on the chalkboard behind her desk in large block letters:

'American Slavery—What will it take for the descendants of those traumatized by their enslavement to make a permanent change in their circumstances?'

She turned around to challenge her students with the question and size up their reactions. Most seemed in no way surprised by what she had written on the board. Not one word of her essay question had changed since she implemented her new class structure several quarters earlier. She had been encouraged by the growing number of students who referred their friends to her classes now. The number had increased steadily with each quarter; she knew that they also expected that she would grade their essays generously, since the topic itself was entirely subjective.

Her main goal in having them write the paper had been to have a way of verifying that they weren't just daydreaming the entire time she spoke. They were required to reference some portion of her last lectures in a logical way, and then each paper would be graded an automatic 'A.' It was that simple. But Kristin had been pleasantly surprised lately as many of her students had begun to take the question more to heart. She had freed them from the distractions of Kate Turabian's *Manual for Writers of Research Papers* and their grades, and had given them creative license to write whatever they wanted. Now she was being presented with some interesting concepts from her students and looked forward to reading their papers.

"So, let's continue with a look at some of the consequences of freedom for the former slaves," she continued. "As you may recall, the Emancipation Proclamation was really a set of executive orders that were issued by Abraham Lincoln prior to the Civil War. In his first order, signed in 1862, the president named ten southern states that had seceded and would be exclusively penalized if they failed to comply with a January 1, 1863 deadline to rejoin the Union. The punishment to be imposed was to have all people being held as slaves in those specific states alone, declared free."

"Just *those* states?" Someone in the back of the room yelled out the question. "What about everybody else?"

"I'm afraid that was it," Kristin responded. Only one of her students had been aware that the Emancipation Proclamation had not applied to all slaves, before taking her class.

"It affected slaves differently because their release was totally dependent on the state that they were being held in." She continued by saying that many of the Northern states had already passed individual statutes to abolish slavery after the colonies won their independence from England, winning the Revolutionary War.

"The second executive order was signed on the January 1st deadline date that Lincoln set. It officially declared that only those who had been enslaved in those states specified were to be immediately freed.

"It may be surprising to some of you that New Year's Eve that year was the beginning of the "Watch" services that are still held in many Black churches each year. The slaves in those ten states gathered, under the guise of celebrating the new year, to wait for word on whether they would be freed after midnight."

"Wow! We always go to those services but I never knew that!" The student in the back again.

"That's because a good number of churches never mention it," was Kristin's best guess. "It started out as a means of protection, of course, against retaliation for them daring to want to be free. It probably continued for the same reason for a long time afterwards, as they quietly celebrated their freedom under the noses of those who spewed hatred and resentment because they finally had it. At some point, all association with New Year's Eve and slavery was lost in many churches." She paused to give her students time to form their own opinions and thoughts.

"At any rate," she continued, "Lincoln's order had no effect on Union slave states; like Tennessee, parts of Virginia, or the new spin-off state of West Virginia." She looked at all the surprised faces in her classroom. "The City of New Orleans and its parishes," she went on, "were also exempt from Lincoln's executive orders. Those states and local governments retained their rights to practice legalized slavery until it was abolished.

"It was because the states named in the first executive order rejected Lincoln's ultimatum that the Civil War was fought to enforce it. Thaddeus Stevens, who was part of the House Republican Leadership at the time, pushed for an all out war against the southern states, arguing that the loss of free labor would deal a deadly blow to the Confederate economy. There were countless family fortunes wrapped up in the shameful enterprise of slavery, and many suffered severe losses because they had used the people they enslaved as collateral for their mortgages and commercial loans."

"So how did everybody else get freed?" The question came from the same student who had been yelling them out all day. He seemed to speak for the others, asking questions that they all seemed to want answered.

"Fortunately, the abolitionists had forced Lincoln to also push for a formal Constitutional amendment instead of just ending slavery in a few states. After that joint resolution passed Congress and was ratified by the required number of states, slavery was then officially abolished across the entire country. The political bartering that had gone on for decades over the issue finally ended with the ratification of the Constitutional amendment.

"Lincoln, however, was killed only a week after the Civil War was won. He had been dead for eight months by the time the required three-fourths of states voted to make the amendment the law of the land."

"What?" Several students expressed surprise at the same time.

"Yup, that's right," Kristin assured them. "I was surprised myself when I found that out. And Lincoln's successor was from the South, so he immediately set about trying to undo the damage that his predecessor had done. The Republican majority in Congress at the time, and their abolitionist supporters, managed to hold onto power for a few years longer. But Lincoln's replacement gained notoriety for failing to execute the new anti-slavery amendment. As a matter of fact, Andrew Johnson was the first president to be successfully impeached by Congress because of it, and he came within one vote of actually being removed from office."

There was another murmured conversation around the room as several students expressed their surprise. Kristin waited for them to quiet down before continuing. She told them that the southern states rejoined the union one by one, and the Democratic party soon regained enough power to force the withdrawal of federal troops that were providing order and protection for the former slaves in the South.

"And that was the point in which everything changed drastically for many," Kristin emphasized to her students. "The troops provided protection only for a short while after freedom was declared," she reminded them. "Federal assistance was made available on an individual basis through the Freedmen's Bureau and through General Sherman's Special Field Order No. 15 that I'll get more into later.

"During Reconstruction, the federal government established schools for former slaves," Kristin continued, "who had been kept from learning to read and write in most states after the Stono Rebellion took place in South Carolina. And those same schools became the foundation for today's American public school system. Large numbers of Blacks were elected to local and federal political offices during the thirteen years of Reconstruction. It's very likely that the African Diaspora in America would have continued to thrive had barriers not been erected to block their progress.

"Except for a brief thirteen year period, the newly emancipated slaves were left entirely defenseless," she summarized. "They suddenly found themselves at the mercy of the same economically depressed people who had been most impacted by their free labor, since slaves had been used for work that poor whites might have otherwise been paid to do.

"It soon became apparent that because they were no longer considered someone else's property, the security against random violence the former enslaved once had was also gone. Before slavery ended, they had only been at the mercy of their so-called owners or the plantation overseers, for the most part. After that unknowing safeguard was removed, many found themselves in constant physical danger. They were subjected to physical violence from virtually any white person who had such an inclination.

"Many of the defeated southerners freely used the former slaves as their scapegoats. They held them responsible for the loss of their loved ones during the Civil War, and for the enormous loss of wealth and property that had been built around the notion of owning other people. It was all "gone with the wind" and in the blink of an eye. Researchers at the Library of Congress estimate confederate soldier casualties to be around 260,000—more than a quarter of a million people. Resentments ran high against those who had once been enslaved; they were associated with all the visible loss and devastation and they were blamed as its cause."

"That's a lot of people!" One of Kristin's students made the observation.

"It is, isn't it? The total number of whites killed during the war is estimated as being between 618,000 and 700,000 people. That number is higher than for any other war that the country has fought–and all over our ancestors." A brief conversation ensued around the classroom in reaction to the statistics she had quoted on the number of people killed. "And don't forget, that number doesn't even include Black soldiers who fought for their freedom.

"It took another hundred years before Civil Rights amendments for Blacks were adopted as part of the Constitution," she continued after they had all quieted down again. "Ratified by a majority of states, the new statutes affirmed the legal rights of all slave descendants to vote and have equal protection under the law. Before the late '60s, many slave descendants had been left vulnerable in certain areas of the country; like sitting ducks at a carnival booth. They were randomly victimized, sometimes based on little more than a whim. There were many who survived some of the worst imaginable acts of terrorism for a full century after slavery ended, and there were many others who didn't survive. Until the Civil Rights amendments were ratified, there had been few legal remedies available against the violence committed against people of African descent.

"And as a quick side note, the former 'Dixiecrats' in the southern states who regained power after Lincoln's death almost uniformly abandoned the Democratic Party, in the late '60s. After Democrats sponsored the passage of Civil Rights legislation, the Dixiecrats joined the Republican Party in droves and they still make up a sizeable portion of their 'base' support."

※※※

The basis for Kristin's final lectures included an assumption that her students already had a basic knowledge of the Civil Rights movement. The faces of some of its most courageous leaders—like Congressman John Lewis, Ambassador Andrew Young, Reverends C.T. Vivian, and Joseph Lowery—were still occasionally seen during national news reports. In the interest of time, she had been forced to forego a more in-depth discussion of that very important era of African American history. Instead, she moved directly to the part of her lecture where she would have preferred to start had she any reasonable expectation that her students knew about their true history. She knew that an accurate account of their ancestors' collective past was crucial in moving them beyond the limitations that so many had set for themselves, and offering them a different viewpoint of slavery would be a vital part of that process.

Kristin reminded her class that a recovery plan had not been devised for those who had been traumatized by their ordeal during and after slavery. She challenged her students to consider what it must have been like not to know from one moment to the next what horrors might befall them. She asked them to form a mental image in their minds of the period just after Reconstruction ended; when all that had been familiar had abruptly changed, and those newly freed had found themselves on their own in an "anything goes" and violently unpredictable environment.

"One thing we haven't discussed yet is the annihilation of the family structure that resulted from American slavery; the family being a very important entity and considered to play a major role in most cultures. In contrast, those who were brought in to work the diamond mines in South America were encouraged to marry," Kristin said. "They were allowed to stay together, unlike those enslaved in the United States. In America, slaves were always subject to having family members sold away and their legal status was the equivalent of being personal property. They weren't permitted to enter into marriage contracts but undeterred, hopeful couples compensated by creating their own ceremonies and jumping over a handmade broom to mark the occasion of their commitment. They made the best they could of their reality and they could never be certain they wouldn't be forced to say good-bye at a moment's notice, without any prospect of being reunited.

"Now the importance of the family unit in society is widely accepted," she added, "so keep in mind that the Black family, as we know it, was largely undefined during slavery. The sense of family that *did* exist, however, had a profound impact for as long as those relationships were allowed to last."

Kristin got up from her desk and erased the essay topic she had written on the board earlier. In its place, she wrote "post-traumatic stress syndrome" in large block letters. As she turned to face her students, she began describing a graduate psychology course she had once taken. She relayed that based on what she had learned in that class, some form of massive dysfunction most certainly should have been expected, considering the circumstances. She noted the well-documented trauma that Nazi concentration camp survivors sustained during World War II. Long after their rescue, there were many who were still disturbed by what they had witnessed and experienced.

✳✳✳

Kristin checked her watch quickly and was pleased that there would be time left for a brief exchange with her students. She listened as they shared their thoughts, with most confiding that they couldn't imagine how they would have survived slavery. After several students had spoken, Kristin pointed out how widely their opinions varied, suggesting that their differences were likely based on who they were as individuals. She pointed out that each of them had been colored by a different set of life experiences.

53

When asked, several students shared their thoughts on whether the people who had been taken from Africa toward the end of the slave trade would likely have adapted more easily to their freedom. Kristin compared that group to those who had been born ten or fifteen generations into slavery; whose parents, grandparents, and great-grandparents had all been slaves and who had known nothing different in their lifetime. To that group, she compared the group whose ancestors had been freed a few years after being brought to America; who, along with their descendants, had remained free since that time. "How do you think freedom would sit with each of these different groups?" She asked rhetorically. "And what about those whose spirits had been broken during slavery, the Middle Passage to America, or even before they were forced from the slave castles in Africa onto waiting ships? What do you think it would take to stop the energy of their broken spirits from being passed on to each successive generation?"

She asked her students to consider what might motivate a freed slave to refuse to leave his or her so-called owners. Many had lived out their days as sharecroppers, afraid to venture away from the plantations they had been born on and land they had always lived on. "Do you think this was merely a classic expression of Stockholm syndrome?" She referred to a more recently identified phenomenon of hostages who developed positive feelings toward their captors after a certain length of time.

"Is it possible that they were just shell-shocked?" She asked finally. She used a term that had been coined to describe veterans of the "Great Wars," as World War I and II were known in other countries; soldiers who had been traumatized during battle.

Kristin walked back to the blackboard and erased what she had written. She took with her the notebook she had used to copy down definitions from a collegiate dictionary she found in her office. She wrote the definitions in large letters on the board:

Patriotism—love for one's country, zealous support and defense of its interests.

Nationalism—the doctrine that one's national culture and interests are superior to any other.

Ethnocentrism—a belief in the intrinsic superiority of the nation, culture, or group to which one belongs.

She stood back from the board and read what she had written out loud before turning around to look at her students.

"Like many other words in the English language," she stipulated, "the definitions of these words have evolved over time. I selected these particular ones because I believe they still accurately reflect current meanings."

She moved to the opposite end of the blackboard and wrote down another single word, with an expectant hyphen next to it.

Racism –

"So what exactly is racism?" She asked, observing her students as she waited for a response. Several of them raised their hands hesitantly, and Kristin went around the room randomly giving an opportunity to each one who wanted to share their ideas. She listened attentively and then turned back to the board. She wrote down the definition for racism she had copied from the same dictionary she had copied the others.

Racism - 1) a belief or doctrine that inherent differences among the various human races determine cultural or individual achievement—usually involving the idea that one's own race is superior and has the right to rule others; 2) hatred or intolerance of another race or races.

After she had finished writing, Kristin turned toward her students pointedly. She asked how the definition of 'racism' differed from the other words she had defined, and what they all had in common. Some of her students began to shift uncomfortably, hoping perhaps that someone else would respond. She could sense that they were beginning to feel trapped and put on the spot. After a few more seconds, she asked them whether they thought the definition of racism was pretty much the same as the others. She allowed the question to linger in the air for a few seconds, not really expecting an answer. Kristin knew that her silence would force them to focus. She guessed that some of her students had become frantic, trying to think of something reasonable to say in case she called on them.

"I believe that the element missing from the definition of racism is its origin," she said finally. She sensed an immediate sense of relief around the room after she let them off the hook. "Except for ethnocentrism, the origin of the other definitions is more or less insinuated, don't you think? The definition of racism seems to imply ethnocentrism, but wouldn't there be some degree of ethnocentrism expected within a culture?"

She shared with her students that until the late '60s, the Black American community had been the only culture she was aware of that had not laid claim any degree of ethnocentrism. "Before things began to change in the '60s," she informed them, "if one Black person referred to another as being 'Black' it had usually led to a violent fight that might easily have ended in death.

"Thankfully, there were two major catalysts that led to an end to this internal hatred so many were taught to have," she said, "which was a good thing for us all. The first push came with the arrival of the Honorable Elijah Muhammad onto the national spotlight. He materialized rather suddenly from rural Georgia with a radical message for Black America. He urged discipline within the Black community, and Muslims and non-Muslims alike were influenced by his teachings—either directly or indirectly.

"The other major impetus was surprisingly "the godfather" himself— Mr. James Brown. It was *his* catchy song that had most Black Americans suddenly saying it loud: 'I'm Black, and I'm proud.'" Kristin was aware that her students were all familiar with the song.

She walked closer to the side of the chalkboard, now filled with definitions she had written. "So, let's take a look at what we have again," she connected her points. "If we change the word "superiority" to 'pride,' the definition of ethnocentrism reads: a belief in the intrinsic *pride* in the nation, culture, or group to which one belongs.

"Would there be any objection to ethnocentrism if it were defined that way? Wouldn't that be a normal attribute—one that our ancestors in Africa and nearly every other culture has exhibited to some degree? What could be wrong with having a healthy dose of pride in who we are, or in some of the things that our cultural history represents?

"And what do you suppose caused African Americans not to feel any sense of ethnocentrism for such a long time? Why didn't we always feel pride and self-respect in who we are? And why are there so many who still don't feel a healthy sense of self-worth?"

Chapter 7

Tell Me This is a Dream

*W*ithin a few months of her mother's marriage, Sam had already done the unthinkable. Although Malaya was only seven at the time, she knew it wasn't right for him to do the things that he did– no matter what he said. But as the months went by, she had started wondering whether she might be making too much of it. Maybe she was just being a stick in the mud in spite of the promise she had made to her mother on their wedding day. Sam *had* been nice to her, except sometimes when he came into her room at night. She didn't think that was nice at all and she kept hoping that he would stop. But Sam had even been nice to her friend Celeste too, whenever her brother would walk her friend over to their house to play.

Sam had bought Malaya all the pretty things that her mother had said he would buy her. She only wished that her mother would see how Sam looked at her sometimes, when he thought nobody else was watching him. It was the same look he had on his face the first night she woke up to find him standing over her. Malaya would watch her mother closely whenever they were all sitting in the same room together, hoping she would see it. Her mother had seemed so happy just after their wedding, but now she didn't smile as much as she used to.

Sam's presence this first night startled Malaya and she had been frozen with fear. She hadn't dared to scream out because she was even more afraid of waking up the baby, who was sleeping in his crib right next to her bed. Her grandmother used to say that Lil' Sam cried loud enough to wake up the dead, and she was right. He usually started out whimpering and then he would just keep crying until he had gained more steam. Then he would yell so loud that the soft spot on top of his head would move up and down. Her mother always got mad at her when she woke the baby up — especially in the middle of the night. Once Lil' Sam was awake, he would demand her complete attention; she wouldn't be able to do much of anything else for hours after that, until he finally went back to sleep. So Malaya always tried to be as quiet as she could in her room at night. She wouldn't even get up to pee if she could help it. She was too afraid of making noises that would wake Lil' Sam up.

Before he was born, the doctor had made her mother stay in bed for months. Her grandmother always said Lil' Sam was just making up for all that time. Malaya had sometimes wondered whether her mother might have noticed Sam watching her then, if she hadn't been in her bed so much. Malaya wished she knew for sure whether any of the things Sam said to her were true. But in the back of her mind, she knew the answer. She just didn't know what to do about it.

She wanted to tell her grandmother the day she dropped by to give Malaya her birthday present. Then she remembered what Sam had said to her a few days before. She had been laying across the princess bed he insisted on buying her, coloring in the gigantic coloring book she got for Christmas. As soon as Sam came into the room, Malaya moved next to the wall and huddled as close to it as she could get. She tried not to cry when he touched her; she prayed, as she always had, that he would leave her room soon. She hadn't been able to stop a lone tear from rolling down the side of her cheek, but she turned her head quickly so Sam wouldn't see her crying. Before he left, he had told Malaya that if anyone else knew about their "special friendship," as he would always call it, *she* would be the one that everyone would be mad at and not him. His raspy voice whispered it and Malaya quickly turned away again. She squeezed her eyes shut as though Sam would disappear if she couldn't see him.

Her mother was the one who said she should start kissing her stepfather goodnight. Vivian had followed Malaya upstairs to her room as soon as she and Sam got back from their honeymoon, and she had picked her daughter up from her mother's house. Vivian had started in on Malaya as soon as her bedroom door had closed behind them. Her mother was still been bubbling with happiness as she described how nice their trip had been. Then, she had become more serious abruptly, as she told Malaya that they were a family now. Her mother said she should start treating Sam as though he were her *real* father, but Malaya could barely remember her father at all. She had only been a little girl when he moved away and she hadn't seen anyone from his side of her family since he left them. She had always kissed her mother before she went to bed every night. When her mother said that she wanted Malaya to start kissing Sam goodnight too, that had been the last thing *she* wanted to do.

But she had only been seven years old so she did what her mother told her to do. Every night she would approach Sam nervously after she had kissed her mother on the cheek. He would usually pretend not to notice as she inched her way toward him. Malaya would hold her breath every night so she wouldn't have to smell the stinking liquor he always smelled of. She would give Sam a quick, half-hearted peck and then hurry to her room. She did it as fast as she could but he somehow always managed to brush against her skin in that short time. And every night she would feel his touch long after she had left the room.

Just about everybody else seemed to like Sam, though. Her mother's friends would still tell her what a good catch he had been. Sam always insisted on paying whenever they all went out to eat together. Before the baby came, her mother had bought all the clothes she had ever dreamed of having too, even after her belly got bigger. Vivian loved showing her friends all the things that her husband bought for her and both her children. Her friends would often tell Malaya how lucky she was that Sam had accepted her like she was his own daughter.

But she had heard her grandmother tell Mr. Tim once that she didn't trust Sam; she had said it in a low whispered voice. Malaya wanted more than anything to know why her grandmother said what she did, but she had been too afraid to ask. She knew her grandmother talked low so *she* wouldn't hear what she said, but for days afterwards Malaya had thought about it. Maybe her grandmother *would* believe her. But the young girl loved her grandmother more than anything; in the end, she had just been too scared to take the chance. She had been afraid of losing her grandmother forever but she had lost her all the same.

She had only been in bed sick for a few days before she died. Now, Malaya wished with all her might that she had told her grandmother about Sam. But now it was too late. She was already gone and Malaya had missed her chance to get away from her stepfather.

Chapter 8

The Color of Money

"*T*oday we're going to finish our final lecture series for the quarter with a discussion on race and racism in America."
Kristin disliked having to stop where she had with her African Studies class when they last met. It was now her only class scheduled in the afternoons, for she had long since discovered that she was much more focused during the mornings. It had been a struggle for her to keep on track and she made a mental note to start lobbying her friends in the registrar's office early. Her goal was to have all her classes run back-to-back on Tuesday and Thursday mornings for the upcoming quarter.

"We're going to start by taking a closer look at the aftermath of slavery," she continued. "We'll look at the radical changes in the circumstances of former slaves, and how many found themselves with even fewer resources than they had before their freedom was won. Their change in status literally came overnight; for many Blacks, their lives took a dramatic turn for the worse once they were freed. But there were some who were more fortunate than others, like Blacks who lived in Tuskegee Alabama, for example. At one time, the small town was a safe haven for African Americans unlike any other place in the country. As I mentioned before, there were also many families whose ancestors had been freed from indentured servitude centuries earlier, and former slaves who had bought their freedom or who had run away decades before the Civil War began.

"Now we can see that after having had decades and sometimes centuries of freedom ahead of the majority, some of these Blacks found it easy to disassociate themselves from the newly freed. They had lived successfully in white America and some had even been slaveholders themselves. And they were reluctant, at best, to upset the status quo."

There was a stir in the room, as Kristin's students reacted to what she said about former slaves having been slaveholders themselves.

"It's not that far-fetched when you think about," she spoke to regain control of the room. "Remember, in Africa, tribal captivity had been a long established practice; for those Africans who were brought here as indentured servants during the first hundred years or so in particular, the practice of slavery in America must have seemed very similar to their ancestral customs.

Later, there were others like Denmark Vessey, who had been allowed to buy their freedom. Some slaves were also freed as the wills of their former "owners" were probated; gifts from the grave to loyal servants or blood relatives— perhaps in a final attempt to evade hell."

Several of her students snickered at Kristin's blunt comment. "Okay, okay," she said amid their laughter. "The point I want to make is that today we have one distinct group of African Americans, whose ancestry is one of having been temporarily in servitude. And there is another group that is the by-product of generational slavery. Most people tend to think of African Americans as one homogenous group, and we do all share the history of the slave castles and the Middle Passage. But there are also distinct branches in our history, as well. So, let's get back to our discussion.

"As we said earlier, there were tens of thousands of captives who were freed as General Sherman marched his Union army through the South. Many of them followed him all the way to Savannah, where he issued a field order to resolve the question of resources needed for their new start. Special Field Order No. 15 was issued not as a means of promoting welfare; but rather, it authorized an award of forty acres to each so-called "respectable" Black family that applied. The acreage was also available to whites in the South who had been sympathetic and helpful to the Union army. The property he awarded extended along the east coast, from Charleston to the St. Johns River in Florida, and it was all property that had been seized as a spoil of war.

Black families were required to join with at least two other Black families to establish homesteads in order to qualify. The general's orders also provided a mule to each family for use in working their new land.

"Hey, that sounds like Spike Lee's company," someone yelled out.

"Yes, that's where he got the name from," Kristin agreed.

"Now the order obviously didn't make up for everything they had gone through, but it did give thousands of the newly freed slaves a great opportunity for recovery. Unfortunately, however, Andrew Johnson was sworn in as the country's new president only a week after General Lee's reluctant surrender at Appomattox Virginia. Johnson rescinded General Sherman's field order only a few months after Lincoln was assassinated. That meant the property that had been given to the former slaves was confiscated and returned to its original owners."

"Wow. Lincoln's assassination sure was convenient!" Someone Kristin couldn't identify muttered the comment.

"Yeah, well that's an entirely different story," she agreed, smiling. She turned in the direction that the observation had come from.

"At first, Johnson didn't have enough control to keep Republicans in Congress from sending federal troops to the South to maintain order. As I've mentioned, the soldiers were only there for thirteen years—not a long time at all when you consider the centuries that slavery had existed. But for a while, former slaves had the security they needed to start rebuilding their lives; until the Democratic Party slowly regained power, as the former Confederate states rejoined the Union. When their party was powerful once again, the Democrats forced the troop withdrawal and any progress that had been made toward recovery immediately began to reverse itself. The newly freed slaves were left unprotected from local hostilities that mounted against them, often cloaked in the darkness of night.

"As I've mentioned, many of the former slaves left the South in search of safety and better opportunities, as violence continued to escalate with the troops' withdrawal. The British had taken complete possession of Florida in a 1763 compromise with Spain. Blacks who had lived in and around St. Augustine and Fort Mose had already relocated to Cuba or other Spanish territories, so that area had no longer been an option for runaway slaves by the time the Civil War began. Many of the new 'African Americans' migrated north and to central and western parts of what is now the United States. They also went in large numbers to what is now known as Mexico, as we will talk about later.

"But the majority stayed in the South. It was where their parents and grandparents had been born and lived. Many dug in and made the best of the opportunities that presented themselves. They had kept the knowledge that had been passed down by their ancestors on how to live off the land. They could survive on very little because their parents and grandparents had taught them how. Or, they created their own opportunities, as men like Booker Washington advised them to do. But many of the former slaves did neither, and it is with *their* descendants that I am most concerned about.

"My theory is that there were many who were far too traumatized to do anything. Some had perhaps given up decades before the Civil War ever began. Their experience of physical bondage or the terror that became part of their normal existence after Reconstruction–and sometimes both– rendered them immobile. They passed this apathy on to their offspring; some even opted to continue working on the same plantations they had been born on for generations to come – perhaps too afraid to leave. And where would they go anyway? They had probably heard many horror stories about others who had ventured beyond the relative safety of the plantation. Their status officially changed to sharecropper but the distinction came with little change in their circumstances. As meager as their cabins were, some sharecroppers clung to them as a guaranteed place to live without having a need for money exchange. And today, we can see that same mindset in their descendants, who don't see a need for anything different for their families than the virtually free government housing they live in.

"By the way, there were those who were raised as sharecroppers and who *did* leave the farm they were raised on, but only when the timing was right. Many accomplished all they set out to do in bettering their lives and much more—take Congressman John Lewis, for example.

"At any rate, inaction gripped the lives of many. It is my contention that those who found themselves apathetic to their freedom and unable to spring back as others did, surely passed that apathy on to at least some of their children. And that same dispassion," she said knowingly, "has *continued* to be passed down and *will* continue until something comes along to change it.

After a pause, Kristin continued. "Not unlike any other creature on Earth, the African slaves adapted for survival as best they could, throughout all the twists and turns of their enslavement. It had probably not taken long for those living in the slave yards to notice that those their captors preferred in some way had an advantage over others. A favored woman may have been given nicer sleeping quarters separated from everyone else, for example, to make it easier for midnight visits to go undetected. Some slaveholders had been openly partial to those who most closely resembled themselves physically, many times their unacknowledged relatives. It could be observed by all that they were often assigned to work in "the big house," doing jobs that were physically less demanding than work in the fields. The house-slaves' children were often relegated as companions to the slaveowner's children. They were given their hand-me-down clothes to wear and their outgrown toys, which, of course, created another layer of separation in the slave yard.

"This wedge between those Blacks who were privileged and those who worked hardest in the fields only deepened after they were freed. The stakes grew even higher as their physical safety was brought more into question. Eventually, the majority of Blacks began to mimic whites in some way in order to be accepted. They played up any physical features that would help them appear to be as white as possible.

"Some so closely resembled whites that they relocated to different areas of the country after slavery ended, and camouflaged themselves to blend in with white America. Although they were still considered to be of the "colored race," according to an 1896 Supreme Court ruling in the case of Plessy v. Ferguson, many assumed a "white" identity. They married whites and had families with them; many were accepted into white society and took their secret identities to the grave.

"The violent rebellions from the past were forever etched in the minds of southern whites, especially. Some felt justified in making preemptive attacks against Blacks that they suspected of becoming a physical risk, and these were most often Blacks who had darker complexions.

"In contrast, Blacks who did the best job of mimicking whites often found themselves elevated in status in their communities. The closer their whiteness, the easier it was for them to move into positions that distanced them from the dreaded "former slave" status, still the lowest position on the American social totem pole at the time. Blacks who had physical features more in line with their African ancestors, like Booker T. Washington for example, often became obsessed with adopting "white mannerisms." They were quick to point out their white parentage too, if they knew it. They adopted the "proper" etiquette and sought other social credentials that would separate them from the Black majority. And when they did, it seemed to send an unspoken signal to whites that these African descendants would pose no physical threat to them. When you think about it, trying to blend in was the logical thing for them to do," Kristin concluded.

"So, Blacks discovered many low-cost ways to bleach their skin, and all kinds of ways to straighten hair; not for style, but for survival. Black Americans imitated whites in the way they talked and behaved, and did nearly anything they could to be accepted. And who could blame them?

"Who could really blame a mother for being obsessed with steering her children toward friendships and marriages with their lighter complexioned peers? Why wouldn't a woman want her grandchildren to have the best advantages available, if she were given the choice?"

Kristin got up and began walking around the room. Teaching a class on Friday afternoon had also meant having to work harder to keep her students' attention. She ran her fingers through the locs on one side of her head and then used two of them to quickly tie the entire group together at the back, keeping them from falling onto her face.

"As we move further into our understanding of racism and its origin, we find ourselves in a better position to unravel its impact on American culture." And with that prelude, she forged ahead with her primary purpose, determined to stick as closely to her prepared notes as possible.

"Racism alone has been the motivating factor in many cruel and violent interruptions of life," she stated, "both black and white lives. Property has been destroyed, career potential has been thwarted, and intellectual abilities have been stifled. The innocence of love has hard-heartedly been kept from expressing itself on countless occasions. Yet, in many ways racism has also been somewhat of a mystery to some who have been victimized by it; notwithstanding random violence or uninspired epithets that may have been carelessly hurled at them. My gut instinct tells me that the mystery surrounding racism is responsible for many a prolonged and destructive consequence, though the connection may now be somewhat obscure. And I believe that all of this needs to be faced, and the truth needs to be brought to light; not unlike some confused spirit that is finally exorcised from a haunted house it has occupied for centuries.

"I believe that it is very important to unravel all ambiguity about the origin of racism too and its purpose, so that it can finally be laid to rest once and for all. But how do we do that?" She asked the rhetorical question.

"Let's look further into its origin." Kristin answered herself. "I believe that when we get down to the simplest truth, we can see that racism was concocted to justify generational slavery—nothing more and nothing less."

She stopped for a minute to let her words sink in.

"Of course, the application of racism has evolved over time and now includes attacks against other ethnic groups, as well. Many African Americans have even joined in the fray, and have adopted biases against other groups; most notably our friends south of the border. It's no coincidence that their biases became more pronounced after Mexicans began to nudge Blacks out of unskilled jobs in this country.

"But the irony is that Black Americans share a common ancestry with Mexicans. Many are also the direct descendants of African slaves, mixed with the blood of Spaniards and indigenous people of that area. Their lineage is similar to that of Black Americans, whose African blood was mixed with Europeans and Native Americans. In Mexico, everyone was much more thoroughly mixed, that's all. There were approximately 200,000 African slaves sold in to "New Spain," as Mexico was once called. They were brought in to harvest timber and to work in the mines there. By 1570, they outnumbered the Spaniards by a margin of nearly three to one.

"Who knew?" The comment came from a young woman in the back of the room. Kristin continued after allowing the student's question to hang in the air for a second.

"So do you think it would matter to this new group of Black racists if they understood this? Or, if they knew that the Mexican government offered safe haven to Blacks who fled south of the Rio Grande after the Civil War? Hundreds of former slaves migrated during the 1890s to escape the violent aftermath of Reconstruction.

"But, back to our discussion," she redirected herself. "The logical place to start is with the African slave trade. There were huge fortunes made from trafficking; in my opinion, racism as an ideology was adopted to justify laws enacted to keep Africans enslaved for their entire lives. Shipowners and slaveholders quickly adopted racist viewpoints because it legitimized their inflictions as being against "subhumans," as opposed to injury to actual human beings.

"Earlier, I mentioned that the turning point in American slavery had been the cost effectiveness of using African labor exclusively on the tobacco plantations. As we look at it from a business standpoint, we can see similarities between practices of the tobacco magnates during that era and the practices of some corporate entities in America today. Some businesses openly have policies that favor increased profits over human lives. Take, for example, businesses that outsource to certain countries so they can use child labor to make their products. They do this even when there is plenty of evidence to show that children are being forced to work in sweatshops in horrible conditions, all so they can manufacture toys that we, in turn, buy for our children to play with as Christmas gifts.

"Often, the unscrupulous people who own and operate these businesses view themselves as merely taking advantage of the best prices they can find for labor, just as the tobacco plantation owners did. They seldom acknowledge any moral wrongdoing in the way they operate and the average consumer tends to push any unpleasant thoughts about how the toys are being made from their heads. They may feel vaguely uncomfortable perhaps, but in light of the reduced cost in purchasing the toys, they don't let that stop them from buying them. And this is why the child-labor business model has remained so successful.

"Another example is the change in staffing policies by technology firms that once offered generous middle-class incomes to American families. Now, the same companies *outsource* most of their labor to other countries to reduce production costs. Little remorse is shown for the trail of unemployment left in the wake of these decisions, affecting Americans of *all* races. But the color of money has never been black or white—it's always been green.

"After racism was adopted as a matter of course in America, any thoughts about morality and decency regarding the slave trade were therefore moot. A view could be taken that those who profited from the institution of slavery merely chose the most cost effective business models available. By removing any mention of the word "human" from the slave trade equation, the term "human suffering" was therefore no longer even defined.

"When laws were passed to make it illegal to import African slaves into America a new demand was instantly created. Breeding farms became a new source of income, as the children born to enslaved females could boost a slaveholder's bottom line significantly. Plantation owners and overseers used enslaved women for sex and reproduction indiscriminately. Not only did the women not have reproductive rights, but they could also be offered to male 'studs' from neighboring farms at random. And even today, some descendants of these "stud slaves" still seem to think that's all they are required to do." Several students snickered at the remark.

Most of the material Kristin used for her lectures was with the hope that it would give her students a more complete picture, and thus a different perspective about what actually took place during slavery. She felt it was necessary for them to understand their true history as African Americans before they could fully appreciate any concerns about the underbelly, or consider helping her spread her message of hope to them.

Having paused a few seconds to give them time to digest the last segment, she then steered her discussion to the class system that had existed in Europe during the time that slavery had been a legal practice. She noted the works of writers like Charles Dickens, who had so aptly described the immense disparity in wealth among the various classes in Europe. His stories were skillful portrayals of their contrasting lifestyles, and accurately chronicled the paltry existence of the lower class in particular.

They had been treated callously, she told her students, doomed from birth to remain beneath a very low ceiling of life possibilities. The lower class had been forever at the behest of the upper class in Europe, driving many to become desolate enough in their situations that they actually embraced the opportunity for temporarily enslavement in America to escape it. At the same time, officials in Europe seized the opportunity to empty a large portion of its prison population. They all boarded the ships that regularly crossed the Atlantic, after dropping off tobacco and other products for trade. The ships had returned to the colonies loaded down with indentured servants for many years, and the prospect of starting life in America as a slave for the first seven years gave them much more hope for the future than they ever had in Europe. They were free to seek their fortunes after their contracted term of labor was over, no longer hampered by social status from birth or their criminal pasts.

"Boy, things must have been bad for them to volunteer to be slaves!" A voice yelled out from the back of the room.

"It was back then. There were lots of Tiny Tims," Kristin responded. "The upper crusts of Europe came to the colonies too, settling largely along the northeastern coast during the seventeenth and eighteenth centuries.

"But we find that chattel slavery created flourishing new opportunities for those who came from Europe as indentured servants. An abundance of menial jobs were created to support the slave trade; jobs that only men who had once been considered the scum of the earth in Europe would dream of taking. The former lower class found themselves in high demand for jobs that required direct contact with African captives—essentially the dirty work of the slave trade. They worked on the transatlantic ships that sailed to Africa to load captives from the slave castles. They also worked at the auction houses and became overseers on big plantations.

"Now mind you, when chattel slavery was first legalized, the same men who later were hired to help manage it had often only recently completed their own years of servitude. The new opportunities came with a bonus for some, because of the large populations in African countries at the time. Slavers operated their enterprises on a numbers basis, for the most part because of it. They had even gone so far as to label maps of what is now Ghana "Negroland" because there had been so many people at their disposal for capture. Because of the large demand for labor to work the plantations and mines in the Americas and the Caribbean, their business models quickly evolved to cramming their ships with as many captives as they would hold without sinking.

"There were schools of sharks that would trail ships for miles along the Middle Passage, patiently waiting for the next dying or dead captives to be thrown overboard. Shipowner profits were projected based on the percentage likely to survive the trip; since the Africans were physically resilient, requirements for their care were minimal. Those employed by the slavers were given unrestrained authority over them. And as bad as the former lower class had been treated in Europe, the Africans brought to America were far worse off because they were "under" them. Those who worked the slave trade were handed the perfect opportunity to exact vengeance for the way they had been treated, because the only mandatory requirement was that the slaves be kept alive and in good enough condition to be sold. Aside from that, the Europeans were given carte blanche to mete out even harsher treatment than they had been subjected to in Europe. And if a female slave arrived at the auction blocks pregnant it only increased her sales value.

"All-in-all it was the perfect storm," Kristin ended, "for the sea of brutality that American slavery was to become." She started around the room again because she had approached the critical end of her lecture. The sun had been pouring through the open windows for the last half hour and heating the air in the classroom. At first it had been a mild beam that gradually took on more intensity. Kristin knew that she was in danger of having her students' minds wander off and calculated that her abrupt movement might keep them focused a bit longer. The clock above the doorway surprised her; it was much closer to the end of her time than she had thought, although she had no intention of stopping before she was finished.

"As I mentioned earlier," she picked back up, speaking slightly faster, "the Africans' unique features were a natural point of division between the two races. Their differences made it easy to set them apart from whites, in most cases, and the stark contrast was embraced by some whites as evidence of their superiority. And, I suspect that it may have provided an explanation for the wives and children of the plantation owners too. Blacks, who were house servants, had been a familiar part of the household and many times were almost considered as family," she said. "Since racial biases suggested that they weren't really human to begin with, it may have been used to silence questions about how slaves were treated.

Once people accepted racial slurs as factual, it likely helped placate their nagging conscience about holding people against their will and treating them as inhumanly as they had been treated in North America. Slaveholders received support from religious leaders through their sermons too, thus further relieving some of their guilt. Southern clergy were very vocal in defense of slavery at one time, seeking isolated Bible verses like "servants, obey your masters," and quoting them on Sundays.

"The sermons were well received by poor whites too, who were all too willing to believe that slavery was something Jesus would have approved of. This group's thin standing in society was kept stronger with racism firmly in place. It kept them from slipping to the bottom rung of the ladder again, as their ancestors had been in Europe.

"It's doubtful that any rational person actually believes the racial slurs," she added, doubtfully. "And it's really hard to imagine that the people who kept slaves believed it. Not only did they run their households, but the captives were often wet nurses and nannies to their children and were charged with the care of elderly family members. Surely they would have questioned the prudence of assigning such tasks to subhumans.

"Another more significant angle in this whole thing was that the economy of the entire country became dependent on the slave trade over the centuries that it existed, either directly or indirectly, and it happened rather quickly. The institution of slavery took on a life of its own and became ingrained as part of American life.

"But I'm sure many who were traumatized by their experiences also found it easier to accept racist dogma as being fact. Then, they could just stop resisting altogether and numb their expectations. Some sought solace through their spiritual nature as they went about their daily lives, expressing their sorrows through songs. Others, however, never stopped fighting for survival and used the same songs to communicate plans for escape.

"For some, it was easier to resign themselves to a better life in the hereafter, and they passed this same spirit of hopelessness to their descendants, from one generation to the next. Unfortunately, many continue to accept the same fatalistic view of their lives—even today. They fundamentally believe their situations to be so hopeless that even minor setbacks can easily fuel a sense of doom and defeat.

"When we look at records of temporary public assistance, we see that the average applicant requests help for a period of less than two years. The underbelly's longevity on welfare rolls is due in part, I believe, to their genetically shell-shocked minds. It's part of a larger and much more crippling sense of failure that can be attributed to the fabrications about racism that have been deeply entrenched in their minds. Many black and white Americans still hang on to this deception about racism, whether it's on a subconscious level or done consciously.

"There were Blacks back in the '60s who never bought into the lyrics of James Brown's hit song, for instance. They sang it like everyone else because it was popular but they never felt the lyrics—not deep within their souls. They have never felt proud to be Black, because their blackness continues to be a source of misery for them, if only in their minds."

Kristin had finally come to the end of her lecture. She told her students once again that her sole motivation for writing her last book, and for introducing her specialized lectures, had been to expose the deception about racism and find help for the underbelly.

"Exposing the truth to you is a first start but it's not nearly enough," she admitted. "Many began this journey in the '60s, as we learned to take pride in the same physical characteristics that had once been used to make the argument that we were inferior. But a thick residue of darkness from all the ugliness of racism continues to engulf far too many," she concluded. "It has stifled growth and prevented many from living up to their full potential." She had walked back to the front of the classroom and she wrote down their essay topic down once again.

"My question to you is, what can be done about it?" She turned to face her students squarely. "How can we 'un-ring' this bell once and for all?"

She pointed over her shoulder in the direction of the question on the board. Then, she reminded them that their papers were due in her office by 5 p.m. "One week from today," she added, with a slight smile. "No exceptions, so don't even try it."

Kristin gathered her notes and collected her purse after the last student had left the room. She took her time strolling toward the parking lot, anticipating her drive home. She had decided to let the top down so she could take advantage of the warm late-spring afternoon. She started it on its way down after she had pulled out the latch near the rear view mirror. She waited for the beeping sound to confirm it had finished retracting itself and was folded securely inside the trunk. Kristin was looking forward to

71

feeling the breeze against her face on her drive back through Rock Creek Park toward home.

She reached for the small stack of mail she had dropped onto the passenger seat to stick it inside the glove box before backing out of her space. She had pulled the mail from her faculty mailbox when she picked up her class lists and she noticed for the first time that there was an envelope postmarked from Ghana. Kristin held her breath expectantly when she looked at it more closely and saw that the letter was from KNUST— Kwame Nkrumah University of Science and Technology. Her heart raced as she tore open the envelope, careful to preserve the stamps for her son's collection.

She scanned the letter's content quickly and then sat staring at the formal invitation. She read the letter again, more slowly the second time and still scarcely believing what it said. She was being offered a position to teach African American History at KNUST on a two-year contract. The letter included the name and number of someone in Kumasi who would assist her in coordinating her travel arrangements, if she accepted the position, and information on housing that the university provided.

Kristin was ecstatic about the invitation and barely able to contain herself. She had longed to return to Ghana since she and her book club friends boarded the Swiss airplane for their return flight. On an impulse, she had spoken with the head of the history department at KNUST as they toured the school. She expressed her interest in teaching there and they had briefly discussed her experience. Kristin had been given the required application, which she filled out and mailed back before she left Ghana for home. It had been so long ago that she had all but given up hope that anything would ever come of it. Now, just like that, she was going to be living in Africa for two whole years!

She would miss Celeste and Trazi without a doubt. Her ex-husband's daughter had always been as close to Kristin as her own son, and she had always thought of Celeste as being her child. She and Winston had made such a big mess of things, although they both seldom acknowledged it. They had only been married four years before divorcing and she could no longer even remember why their marriage ended. God had clearly put the two of them together, of that she was certain. Even their divorce hadn't made a difference in the way they felt about each other, and neither had Winston's remarriage just a year after their divorce became final.

Chapter 9

Just a Walk in the Park

*T*he strong smell of paint assaulted Malaya's nostrils, but she refused to let it distract her. She remained alert for sounds coming from the living room after she had cautiously peeked around the freshly painted kitchen door. She stood perfectly still, holding her breath before moving forward again quickly; reassured by the faint rumblings of her stepfather's rhythmic breathing that confirmed he was still asleep. He had started painting early that morning and fell asleep on the couch as soon as he had put everything back and cleaned up. Malaya reached the far end of the hallway and inched her way down it at a snail's pace, as quietly as her wiry eight-year-old frame allowed. As she got closer to the French doors leading to the living room, she became mildly aware of steady ticking sounds coming from the grandfather clock.

The clock had been a wedding present to Malaya's mother and Sam. Her grandmother had gotten it from a woman who had been the surviving member of a rich Virginia tobacco family. She had given it to her grandmother as payment for work she had done. The woman had somehow found herself with little cash in the final years of her life; she confided to Malaya's grandmother that she had no idea how she could get along without a housekeeper, but could no longer afford to pay one. Malaya had been happy to see the clock delivered. She remembered it being at her grandmother's from the time she was a baby. It had been one of her most prized possessions and Malaya could remember holding onto the cabinet to pull herself up as she learned to walk. The clock's rich tones always soothed her. The familiar chimes made her feel close to her grandmother, especially on the days that she found herself alone with Sam.

She leaned against the well-maintained mahogany case for a moment of comfort as she waited anxiously. The clock stood like royalty in the hallway. The brass slivers on its hood-columns sparkled from light shining in from the window, as a stream of sunlight fell against its narrow glass panes built into the polished trunk. Malaya peered around to look at the clock's face and held her breath as she braced herself for action. Its large hands inched forward until it finally reached its mark. The chimes began to reverberate loudly, and the rich sounds of its timeless melody filled the air to herald the arrival of a quarter past the hour.

Malaya scurried past the living room doors and down the hallway. She rushed through the front door and had crossed the porch before the door banged shut behind her. She kept running so fast that she was afraid she might run onto the busy street bordering their yard, but she managed to stop herself before she reached the curb. Nearly out of breath, she rested for a second before crossing the narrow street into the park.

She and Celeste were to meet up and walk back to Celeste's house to spend the rest of the afternoon. Malaya was always happy when she and her friend got to see each other outside of school. They had spent the weekend together once; they went to the zoo with Celeste's Aunt Kristin. They had fun that weekend, but after she got home she heard her mother and Sam arguing about it. Sam had told her mother that eight was too young an age for her to sleep overnight with strangers. After that, Malaya could only spend an occasional Saturday afternoon with her friend, and her mother would pick her up from Celeste's house on her way home from shopping. Malaya hoped that she would get to stay at Celeste's house again some day when she was older, but for now she was happy to have that afternoon. She hurried into the park to look for her friend. It was all she had to look forward to since her grandmother passed away.

An older woman who lived in the building across the street looked down at Malaya protectively from her balcony, watching until the girl met up with her friend. After seeing them safely into the park, the woman looked back toward the front door of the house the girl had run out of, shaking her head in disgust. She waddled back inside her apartment and let the gentle afternoon breeze blow her balcony door shut behind her with a loud bang.

Chapter 10

Kumasi — 1991

*K*ristin stood outside the whitewashed fence and looked in on the unassuming graves it encased. Two modest headstones between the narrow walls of the makeshift cemetery marked the final resting places of the former slaves. Several years earlier, they had been posthumously conferred honorary Ghanaian citizenship and repatriated.

An international committee had undertaken the ambitious task of arranging for their bodies to be brought back to Ghana for internment. An enormous degree of coordination had been required, but the committee's persistence had prevailed. They had refused to be shaken by the various obstacles that presented themselves and threatened to stall the project.

Their steadfastness had finally been rewarded when the remains of Samuel Carson, from New York, and Crystal, from Kingston, Jamaica, were finally exhumed from their respective graves and brought by ship to Ghana. The two had been unknown to each other in life but were now eternally bonded by the happenstance of the committee's selection process.

The ship that carried their coffins had sailed the Middle Passage in the opposite direction that ships had once traveled during the slave trade, in a triangular trade route between Africa, the Caribbean, and the United States. The vessel had arrived at the Cape Coast slave fort two weeks later amid much ceremony, and the two had then been carried back through the

Door of No Return into Ghana. The same wooden doors had been the last point of physical contact with the African continent for countless captives. The forty or so castles erected along the Gulf of Guinea were now the only direct links between West Africa and those who had been forcibly taken.

Kristin thought about the ray of hope that must have filled the ceremony, hope that an inherent bond might finally be recognized by the Diaspora and the Motherland. The ceremony had been but a symbolic gesture of the answered prayers of millions who had eluded capture during the slave trade. They had prayed for the return of their loved ones who *were* captured, and who had been carried across the unknown waters of the Atlantic Ocean. Kristin believed their prayers had been for her own ancestors.

She couldn't be certain what had brought her back to the Ancestral River Park as she traveled north from the airport in Accra to Kumasi. She had been moved to tears the first time she and her friends had visited the memorial erected in the Central Region, and she felt equally touched this time.

She moved back from the fencing, allured by colorful wildflowers that grew along the outer edges of the path leading away from the graves. Butterflies darted all around her, alive with vivid colors that seemed especially created for the landscape. Kristin had decided to come to Ghana a few weeks before she was due to arrive at the university to start her teaching position. She wanted to explore more of the area around the coast before heading to Kumasi. Attracted by their fragrance, she stooped to pick a small bouquet of wildflowers that grew around a cluster of nearby trees. She decided to take them with her and she arranged them as she walked down the winding path that led to a short footbridge. Other tourists headed for Donkor Nsuo, also known as the Slave River, joined her on the path.

Millions had been forced down the same path they walked on. It had been the last stop before the captives began a final trek that ended at one of the trading forts built along the gulf. Kristin had seen the iron neck chains that had been used to link the captives together when her book club visited the Cape Coast fort on her first visit. The weight of the chains would have easily compelled the entire line of weary captives to fall into the river, once those at the front were forced in. Shackled together, they would have struggled against the rushing waters that Kristin now stood facing. One end of the heavy chain that connected their neck irons would have been securely fastened around the baobab tree that still stood on the riverbank. The strength of the gigantic tree would have made it possible for most to withstand the strong currents, as the rushing waters stripped away grime and bodily fluids that had accumulated during their long march south.

On her first trip there, Kristin had gently touched one side of the ancient tree trunk only to have small pieces of its bark break off in her hand. She had carefully wrapped the bark in a tissue and managed to smuggle it, along with a small film canister filled with river water, through customs at Virginia's Dulles Airport when her group returned home. She had found the perfect shadow box to display her unexpectedly acquired mementos, and placed it on the mantle of her living room fireplace in Washington.

As she stared into the rushing waters, tears began to form in Kristin's eyes. She imagined how weak many of the kidnap victims must have been, after such a grueling journey south that had covered hundreds of miles for some. Likely, they had been given only minimal food and water during their march; the fierce heat of the African sun would have brutally taxed their bodies. Looking into the rapidly swirling waters of the river, it seemed a miracle to her that any of them would have had the strength to withstand its currents and avoid drowning. She visualized the difficulty that those who could still muster their *own* strength must have had in keeping afloat. They would have struggled hard to avoid being pulled under by the dead weight of others, those too weak to survive the water. Nevertheless, millions had survived and they had been forced to continue marching south to the slave castles along the gulf.

Kristin had always felt an instinctive connection to the people of Ghana that only deepened after she visited the country. She hadn't had the DNA tests yet so she still didn't know for sure where her ancestors had been captured, but she had become convinced of it. All four of her grandparents had been born in Alabama and she had taken that as a clear sign, after learning that many who had been enslaved on Alabama plantations toward the end of the slave trade were taken from Ghana.

The first time she visited the country she had also noticed that the shape of many of the men's heads she saw there bore a strong resemblance to the typical shape of male heads in her family. She had once been told that might be used as a clue to narrow down an ancestor's country of origin. That was before DNA technology made testing more precise, of course. And although she felt in her heart that she already knew the results, Kristin promised herself again that she would take the test to confirm her theory as soon as she returned to the States.

As she walked back up the hill toward the car she had hired, she began thinking about all the children who had been wrenched away from their mothers' arms. With the enactment of chattel slave laws, many a mother and child had been separated when the mother was taken from her village since smaller children stood little chance of surviving the Middle Passage. They had often been left behind after their parents' villages were ransacked, fending for themselves until someone came along to find them.

Kristin could only imagine how heart wrenching it must have been for everyone, but especially for the women separated from their children. Not only would they have been afraid about their own plight, but they would have been tortured by the uncertainty of what became of children they had nurtured and who had suddenly been separated from all they had known.

Then from out of the nowhere, Kristin found herself enmeshed in her own familiar gut wrenching pain. She immediately recognized it although its sting still caught her off guard every time it resurfaced. She stopped short on one side of the trail as a fresh wave of old torment gripped her.

"My God!" She cried out silently. "What would make me think of this now?" The agony that had overtaken her felt as powerful then as it had nearly eight years earlier. "Why here," she wondered, "when I'm thousands of miles away from anyone I could go to for comfort?"

She had always managed to convince herself that she had finally come to terms with that very difficult period of her life. She would confront her feelings and then release them, eventually lulling herself into believing she had put it all to rest for good. Each time the memories came back to haunt her, she felt staggered in the knowledge that her agony was as intense as ever. She was weighed down by her grief, its burden pulling ever stronger at her heart. Kristin felt so overcome by her emotions that she wanted to crumple to the ground; but left with little choice, she continued up the path toward the car.

She settled into the back seat of the shiny black Mercedes shakily, wiping away stray tears. She was grateful now for the stiff formality of her driver; glad that the neatly dressed young man had resisted all her efforts to engage in conversation of more than a few words. She had been working on him since he collected her and her belongings from the airport in Accra two weeks earlier.

Kristin stared out of the car window vacantly, hardly noticing the beauty of the distant mountainous countryside. She allowed herself a rare moment to think about Winston, wondering whether she would ever bring herself to tell him what she had been carrying with her for so long. If she could summon the courage to tell him, maybe she would be able to put it all to rest for good.

※※※

All throughout puberty, Kristin had been able to feel every change her body went through during its transition to womanhood. She had remained in tune with her body from that time on, especially sensitive to her reproductive system. She usually felt herself ovulating each month so the abdominal cramps that soon followed were predictably timed; she was rarely caught off guard when her cycle started.

Because she felt so connected, she had been positive that she was pregnant the instant Trazi was conceived; although she hadn't been able to convince Winston until her doctor confirmed it a month later. But the second time around, she had been taken completely by surprise. When she thought about it later though, she realized a baby was exactly what she should have expected after the night she and Winston spent together.

She had never been motivated to keep track of the actual dates of her menstrual cycle. Winston was still the only man she had ever been with and their sexual relationship ended months before their divorce. The night that they were together again, neither of them had dared a thought beyond the desires they had suppressed for nearly two years. Nothing had been allowed to interrupt the surreal familiarity of the moment, as the spell went unbroken and they were together again as though they had never been apart.

But as soon as the night was over, their reality had immediately resumed focus. Kristin silently held on to her memories even as she forced herself back into her daily routine. She hadn't been sure how long she could keep it up, but she intended to avoid any emotional fallout from their night of abandon for as long as she could. Eventually, she had been able to block all thoughts about what they had done from her mind, which is why the obvious consequences had taken so long to register. She had been in denial and missed all the clear evidence of her miraculous conception, choosing to believe she had some unknown medical problem instead.

It wasn't until after the word "pregnant" floated out of Niyla's mouth so casually that Kristin ever considered the obvious. A baby had been causing all the changes that had been going on in her body for weeks. She and Winston were going to have another baby!

There had always been an easy flow between the two of them, even when the couple was fighting. They had been magnetically drawn to each since the day they met, and things had been no different in 1983—two years after their divorce. Although their physical relationship had ended with their marriage, they had never stopped gravitating toward each other. It happened automatically whenever they were around each other.

Before they officially started dating, Kristin had made a point of asking for Winston's birth data so she could discreetly have a synastry chart created. When properly delineated, their combined chart predicted their relationship potential, and Niyla, who had mentored her in her study of astrology, confirmed what Kristin already suspected. According to her friend, Kristin and Winston had quite a few planetary connections that were considered favorable indicators of a lasting relationship. All the main ingredients were clearly there in black and white: they had a mutual attraction and desire for each other; they communicated well, at least about most things; there was a potential for a deep friendship and respect; and other indicators of relationship longevity were there too.

The biggest challenge to their happiness, Niyla had cautioned her, was their Moon and Mars oppositions. Thankfully, it wasn't always a problem and it had been a non-issue the majority of the time they were together. But when one of them had been in a bad mood, it would sometimes end with the other feeling slighted and eventually provoking a fight. Since the opposing planets in their combined chart were ruled by the signs of Scorpio and Taurus, a bullheaded power struggle would sometimes develop and lead to legendary arguments.

At first, making up after their fights had almost made the few days of their sulking worthwhile, with all the passion that was generated. Since Kristin's natal North Node was at an exact conjunction with Winston's natal Venus, even when their arguments took on more intensity she knew that he loved her—whether Winston wanted to or not.

But his family was Jamaican, although he and his sister, Grace, had been both born in Washington, D.C. Kristin never considered the possibility that cultural differences might materialize between them to cause trouble in their marriage. The thought had never crossed her mind until after Winston had finished graduate school and they moved to Washington. Things had changed quickly and dramatically after that.

Mother Bailey, as she had insisted Kristin call her, was a traditional middle-class Jamaican woman. She was "colored" although Winston's father had been born into the "planter" class. Winston had explained the baffling Jamaican color caste system to her several times before Kristin finally got it. It was based on lineage, rather than on wealth and had evolved during the longest period of British rule outside the U.K., from 1655 until the Jamaican island finally gained its full independence in 1962. At the top level of the caste, just underneath the aristocrats, were the "coloreds," and they were considered part of the upper crust because of their pedigree. Free education hadn't been provided to former slaves in Jamaica as had been the case in the United States. Consequently, the coloreds, who had always been treated royally by their aristocratic relatives/owners, were the only African descendants to be educated in Jamaica initially.

The "planter" class fell just beneath the "coloreds." After she learned that, it dawned on Kristin that Mother Bailey's marriage to Winston's father must have caused quite a stir in her family. The planter class originated when tens of thousands of Indians were brought in from the East as indentured servants and they introduced curried foods and marijuana to the Jamaican culture, among other things. In lieu of a promised return trip home, many had been given land after their period of service ended. Many of the Indians mixed with the people of African ancestry on the island and eventually the planter class was created.

Both the coloreds and planters were considered to be above the working class, who had started their life of freedom with nothing. The "workers" were brought to the island in large numbers to man the plantations and make sugar for the rest of the world. Their class still makes up the largest percentage of the Jamaican population.

Winston had been good enough to tell her after they moved to Washington that his mother had been deeply insulted by her only son's choice of marrying a "Yankee." It had been the first time she heard the term used by Jamaicans in referring to Black Americans. He had warned her not to take anything that his mother said or did personally, before the two women ever met. And telling her that in advance had helped divert some major catastrophes later, because as it turned out Mother Bailey was even *more* annoyed that Kristin had "allowed" Winston to take her to a Justice of the Peace to get married. She had been surprised to learn that her new mother-in-law apparently felt robbed of her right to see her only son married in a "proper" ceremony.

Trazi had softened his grandmother's heart somewhat, and the older woman lightened up quite a bit after he was born—partly because Kristin had always made it clear that Trazi was *her* son. Her mother-in-law started in on her again after they moved to Washington, but everyone had finally adjusted and Kristin managed to find a way to reconcile her issues with Mother Bailey.

The rift that had appeared in her marriage was another story. Kristin had no inkling of how to reconcile her independent nature with the expectations she was just learning her husband had of her. And unfortunately, she never understood how important it was for her to keep trying. Their relationship in Tuskegee had been so laid back that even with an infant and Winston in graduate school, they had still found time for each other. Part of it had to do with the energy of Tuskegee itself that on most days was '*easy like Sunday morning.*' You could drive from any one point to another in the town in less than fifteen minutes, no matter where you started from. There had literally been nothing to do there other than study too, so it had forced all the students to focus on human relationships in general. In addition to providing nourishment for their marriage, she and Winston had both made solid friendships in Tuskegee that were to last a lifetime.

At one time, it had been a Black parent's dream come true—a safe environment for their children to be in as they came of age; where only the most determined truants didn't buckle down and study after their first year or so. Since Kristin had been born there, she was used to the inactivity but for Winston, it had been like stepping back into time, he said. He liked it there though, because the pace reminded him of being in the hills of Jamaica, on his grandfather's farm.

The two of them had spent hours walking through the woods of Tuskegee before Trazi was born. One morning, Winston woke up determined to find what Tuskegee natives referred to as "Broken Bridge". It was a bridge that once crossed a small creek on a road that wasn't far from downtown. Kristin had been telling him stories of how a plane that had been used during training exercises for the Tuskegee Airmen, crashed on the bridge during World War II and destroyed it. Rather than repairing the bridge, the traffic had been rerouted around it, and water from the creek diverted itself around the fallen concrete after the plane wreckage was removed. The creek bank had a naturally sandy texture and people gradually started frequenting the area to have picnics. Kristin had only seen the bridge once herself when she had been much younger. All through elementary school, she had made the assumption that there had been battles fought in Tuskegee during the war and the plane had been shot down by Germans.

She and Winston had finally found the crash site after they had walked a mile or so into the woods. They spent the afternoon having a picnic on the "sandy beach," as everyone called it, since the sand looked closer to beach sand than anyplace else in the town. They sat near the stream of water that ran beneath the collapsed bridge and barely talked, content to enjoy each other's company in the peaceful woods on the beautiful spring day.

It hadn't been until after graduation that either of them had an inkling that the other had any serious ambitions. They had been married over Christmas break of their sophomore year and Trazi had been born just over a year later. They discovered later that they had both expected to have careers all along, but their entire life in Tuskegee had revolved around studying, taking care of their son, and each other.

She had always known that Tuskegee was a one-of-a-kind place, so Kristin expected some changes in their marriage after they moved away. But she hadn't begun to understand the Jamaican culture fully until after they were divorced, and now she wondered just how much their cultural differences contributed to the breakdown of their marriage. She had never imagined that Winston expected their relationship to remain as it had been in Tuskegee. His career with NASA had started with a summer internship and continued on some level until after he had completed his nuclear engineering degree. His future was solid by the time they arrived in D.C., and he had been earning more than enough to support them when he first started working in Greenbelt.

Kristin had no idea that Winston assumed she would be satisfied with being a homemaker and a mother. Not that there was anything wrong with that, she just had other plans for herself. Who knows, she might have been persuaded to wait until Trazi was in first grade before starting graduate school even, if her husband had chosen an approach other than making his usual Neanderthal demands.

He never admitted to objecting to her working either. There had been a lot of flexibility in her schedule and to her way of thinking, teaching at the college level had been the perfect compromise. But once she landed her job at Hunter, her husband's passive-aggressive behavior toward anything associated with her new career told her that he didn't want her to have one. A rift had begun to form between them that both of them felt, yet neither of them acknowledged. Before she knew what had happened, the rift had widened and they were divorced.

Aside from having a crush or two in high school, Winston had been Kristin's first and only love. But she had never fully appreciated the special relationship they had during the short time they were married. They had both taken the other's love for granted until it was too late.

They each came to understand without saying anything that they had to be guarded whenever they were around each other, especially after Winston remarried. Otherwise, it might have been far too easy to fall back into their old pattern of intimacy that came so naturally. Kristin had taken it upon herself to monitor the times they were alone together, just to be on the safe side. But that only accounted for the physical expression of their love for each other; the substance of it had never changed.

It had been a difficult struggle at times but Kristin thought she had adapted fairly well, all things considered. Angela got pregnant within a few months of her marriage to Winston; despite the obvious awkwardness, they had both felt it was important for them to remain friends—for Trazi's sake if for no other reason.

They had both been determined to make things work. Neither of them ever stopped to consider how impossible what they were hoping for really was, until the night that it stopped being possible.

Chapter 11

These Arms of Mine

*W*ith Trazi staying at his father's house all week, Kristin had no reason to think that Winston might drop in on her. Her day had been completely out of harmony from start to finish. She had to force herself to run a few critical errands after her last class ended, instead of coming straight home to put her head under a pillow. She poured herself a glass of red wine as soon as she had finally made it inside the house, and had just been about to step into a hot tub of water with her glass in hand when she heard his knock at the door.

Winston had decided to take a chance that she might be home, he told her. He needed to talk about a note that Trazi had been sent home with from kindergarten the day before. Their son had apparently punched one of his young classmates, and his behavior had prompted a parent-teacher conference with both parents required to attend. Since his teacher knew they were divorced, Winston wanted to clue her in on what was going on so they could be on the same page during their meeting.

On the same day that he told her about the baby that he and Angela were expecting, Kristin and Winston decided to join forces to keep their five-year-old son from feeling left out. Both of them had been monitoring his behavior for signs of trouble that he might be having in adjusting to the new baby. "Like father, like son," Kristin said laughing, after Winston had read the teacher's note out loud. Not that she would ever let *Trazi* see her responding to his aggressions so lightly.

"Yeah, that's real funny." Winston said dryly, with laughter in his voice. He could definitely see a lot of himself in his son. After Trazi first learned to walk, he had followed his father around whenever he was at home, the same way that his mother had done the entire time she was pregnant.

Kristin poured a glass of wine for Winston too and their conversation soon drifted away from their son. She told him all about her 'day from hell,' as she called it. She had a meeting with the acting dean that she had requested to discuss the school's requirements for her tenure. Instead, the man had taken up most of the hour by admonishing her for being "too friendly" with her students. Kristin had only been twenty-three when she landed the job at Hunter, but she had always taken it seriously. The acting dean had made all kinds of assumptions about her, she told Winston, just because of her age. By the time her day was done, she had been feeling quite unappreciated. But predictably, as soon as she started telling Winston about it, all her frustrations were instantly gone. The dean's misconceptions about her no longer seemed important, in just a short span of time.

Winston was the only person she had ever known who could make anything seem better and she knew the feeling was mutual. It had only taken her one glance at him to know that *his* day had not gone much better than hers. She recognized the symptoms and as soon as he walked through the door, and she guessed correctly that there was something he needed to get off his chest too. She could tell how much he needed to relax by the way he plopped down on the sofa they had picked out together in Tyson's Corner. After he had unloaded his frustrations on her, they had both been in a much better place.

That was the way it had always been with them and Kristin had no idea how their relationship had grown so complicated. She had tried her best to accept that they were no longer together. The trouble with that was that they *were* together all the time, even after he first started dating Angela. A part of Kristin had hoped that Winston would have come to his senses before actually marrying Angela, but she had stopped just short of telling him that. And once he went ahead with the wedding, Kristin decided that she would move on too. There had been several men on faculty at Hunter who were attentive to her in the way men behave with the women they hope to attract. But none of them held her interest for very long; she had a way of comparing everyone she met to Winston, and quite naturally, none of them measured up.

To her, the notion of having sex without some degree of intimacy had never had much of an appeal. So she had quickly dismissed her girlfriends' idea that she go out and meet someone to help her 'get over' her ex-husband. Instead, she had buried herself in her career, trying to make the best of things until someone came along who could make her forget about him.

She had deep regrets now about not putting up a fight for their marriage, even after she realized she still had feelings for him. She had been far too stubborn back then; her pride would not let her forget that *he* was the one who had walked out on their marriage. Foolishly, she had ignored what was in her heart and held on to being right instead.

Those thoughts had kept circling her head that night, until she finally forced them to stop. She turned her focus back to the real reason Winston had stopped by her place instead. They put their heads together and came up with a strategy for checking their son's behavior before it got more out of control. Trazi was the spitting image of his father, right down to his little temper. But just like his father, they both knew he wasn't a mean-spirited child. They had agreed that he was most likely testing the waters to see just how much he could get away with.

Kristin had often tried to remember just what happened next, how things had evolved so quickly and gotten so out of control. Normally, she would have been more attuned to the subtle shifts of energy in their conversation and mood. But somehow, everything about that night had been different. She never noticed anything out of the ordinary until it had been far too late to care. She could never be sure whether it had been the awful day they'd both had, or if it was the magnetism of the full moon shining in through her living room window. She only knew that all of a sudden she had been acutely aware that the delicate balance they had created, as a way of managing the mess they had made of their lives, no longer made any sense to her. As she thought back, it could have been a combination of things against a backdrop of relaxed conversation in the home they had once shared as a couple. Something very different had happened that night without warning, and it had left her with an intense and unexpected aware-ness of her love for Winston. The magnitude of what she felt had instantly destroyed any illusion of him being anything to her other than the love of her life, though she still had no intention of letting him know what she felt. To do so would have violated their unspoken rule that had permitted their delicate post-marriage relationship to stay afloat.

But she hadn't been able to force away the sadness that overcame her as she faced her true feelings. She couldn't stop thinking about how much they had lost when they lost each other, and she wondered whether Winston felt it too. She wondered whether that had been the real reason he had been drawn to her house that night.

No doubt, the glass of wine they shared had played a role in it too, lowering their guards that they had put in place after Winston married Angela. But they had shared wine alone on a number of occasions before. It had never been an issue in the past, so she couldn't fully blame it on the wine they drank that night either. She remembered thinking about the psychic connection that they had always had been between them and she had worried that Winston would know that there was something else on her mind. She tried desperately to think of other things to throw him off guard. When they had first been married, their connection was so strong that Kristin could literally wake him up with her thoughts at night while they were in bed.

Still, she had been caught completely off guard when he turned to her abruptly and asked her what was wrong. By then she was too weak to withstand the sincerity in his voice. The look of concern as he offered his shoulder had pushed her over her emotional threshold. Winston had looked intently into her dark eyes as he waited patiently for her to confide in him. It had all been too much for Kristin. Her mind felt as though it had short-circuited; no longer functioning, and leaving her without a plausible explanation for the sadness she knew he had recognized in her eyes.

She felt trapped, as though she had no other options and before she could stop herself she had burst into a flood of tears. Winston quickly moved next to her on the couch before she had time to recover. They had usually tried to avoid touching of any kind, but without forewarning he had put his muscular arms around her and held her to his chest, gently rocking her from side to side. She had fought against herself and tried to regain control, but her body had ached for his arms to be around her for far too long. It had been a losing battle from that point on, as the tears streaming down her face had made him hold onto her even tighter.

It had all started out so innocently with him only trying to comfort her. But unexpectedly, his embrace stirred something that had moved them both beyond the power either had to control. The comfort they felt in each other unleashed passionate feelings that had been burning below the surface; feelings they had pretended not to notice.

At first, Kristin thought she had been imagining it, that her suppressed longings for him had only made her think that his innocent hug was more than just that. But her doubts were transformed when he began kissing her face and then finally her lips, in a passionate kiss that neither of them even attempted to resist. They began caressing each other and their caresses grew almost ravenous. Their feelings were too natural for them to think of stopping. It felt to them like it was intended to feel—like they belonged together. Finally, he swept her up in his arms and carried her into the bedroom. He sat her down carefully on the mahogany sleigh bed in the middle of the room. It had been their marital bed and she saw how pleasantly surprised he was to find that she still slept in it.

They hadn't allowed themselves to think of anything other than that moment as they kissed, more gently now and lovingly. They stroked each other passionately; stopping only long enough to look into the other's eyes with tentative smiles that soon widened into mischievous grins, as they silently began to undress each other. Their lovemaking that night had been sweeter and more tender than it had ever been. They moved in perfect harmony, demonstrating with their touches how much they treasured each other. Winston visited all her familiar places, scarcely able to believe they were together again. She had welcomed him fully and with all her being.

Finally, they lay back on the bed in blissful exhaustion after a simultaneous explosion of love. Still smiling, they rested together while intertwined in a mass of flesh that knew no beginning or end. Winston had been first to fall asleep, with a look of peace on his face that Kristin hadn't seen in a long time. She smiled to herself, remembering how he had teased her when they were married, accusing her of "knocking him clean out" when they made love. After a moment or two, she turned out the lights and fell asleep curled next to him, reliving their passion in her dreams. From time to time, she had opened her eyes to make sure she hadn't just imagined it. She tried to memorize it all not knowing whether they would ever be together that way again.

She had awakened as soon as she felt Winston roll away from her to get out of bed, but she kept her eyes closed and pretended to be asleep. She heard him trip over her rocker at the edge of the bed in the now-unfamiliar darkness of the room, searching for his clothes. He had been up once before, but now she knew he would be going home. He dressed hurriedly and as quietly as he could; hoping, she knew, that she would not wake up before he left. Then, she felt him standing over her and wondered what he was thinking, but she realized she already knew. She had wanted to reassure him that somehow everything would be okay, but she kept herself from saying anything because she knew how awkward it would have been. If she had opened her eyes, it would have forced a conversation between them that neither had been prepared to have.

She remembered wondering how much their night together would affect their relationship, and then she realized it had been their son's behavior that was the catalyst that brought them together. She thought about all the women who so shamelessly used their children as a way of staying in their fathers' lives. She understood it now; the desperation that drove some women to that point, and it had made her appreciate her son on an entirely different level.

Kristin had come to think of Winston as being her closest friend and she had been proud their friendship had survived their divorce. But now, the truth they had been hiding from themselves for almost two years had started its journey toward the light. Her pride had kept her from admitting that she still loved Winston until it was too late. Then, she had suppressed her feelings for him out of respect for his marriage to Angela. But as her mother had always told her when she was younger, *'no matter how well the truth is hidden, it always finds its way to the light.'* The truth was that she still loved Winston as much as she had when they first met, and she couldn't imagine a time that she wouldn't love him.

To make matters worse, Kristin had been first to notice things about Angela that struck her as being odd. She had dismissed them at first, convinced that she had only been looking for something to be wrong out of her own jealousy. She had first met Angela when they were all in school at Tuskegee; Winston had introduced her as his "home girl" one morning as they were dropping Trazi off at his babysitter's. Angela had lived in the same off-campus neighborhood as their sitter, so they had also given her a ride to the campus. After that, Kristin had only seen her in passing for the most part, but she had always seemed a nice enough person.

Her recent concerns about Winston's new wife had been confirmed by him only a few weeks before he came to Kristin's house that fateful night. He had confided in her how distant Angela had become since being pregnant; needing to get a woman's perspective. He had been about to say more, but fortunately he remembered in time that Kristin had behaved the complete opposite of that when she carried Trazi. It had saved them both an awkward moment because she had become extremely sexual after their son was conceived; much more vocal and assertive about her needs.

She had traveled to be in Houston with Winston for his NASA internship only a month after her morning sickness subsided. Since he had to put in such long hours to finish his project by the end of the summer, Kristin had tried her best not to pounce on him as soon as he walked through the door every day. She knew how mentally exhausted he would be by the time he reached their apartment and in need of a shower to help wind down. He would head straight for the bathroom most evenings as soon as he got home, after giving her a quick peck on the cheek.

Kristin had found it difficult to give him the space she knew he wanted. Sometimes, she would sit back and watch him, just as a wild animal watches its prey. She would look for signs that he had completed his mental transition from work to home, odd behavior considering they had each acknowledged their need for personal space when they first started dating. They had respected each other's boundaries after they started living together too, although all of that had changed with Trazi on the way. It was the main reason that they had both been so convinced that Kristin was carrying the baby girl they had dreamed of having.

But she hadn't been able to get enough of Winston during the entire time she was pregnant, and not just sexually either. She would follow him around their apartment all the time, sometimes waiting for him outside the shower door. She had offered body massages and even pedicures until her belly grew too large to do it. Sometimes she would give him a facial — anything that would give her an excuse to touch him. And as soon as she felt the sensation of his skin next to hers, it would be even harder for her to restrain herself. But most of the time, she had waited patiently until after he had eaten the dinners she cooked for him every day. She had put a lot of love into the food she made since had been was her only scheduled activity in Houston. She would make full meals every day, including breads and desserts and nearly every recipe in the cookbook she had bought at the Atlanta airport as they waited for their flight to Houston.

"You're not fooling me," Winston would tease her. "I know you're just trying to make sure I have enough strength."

Kristin's appetite for sex had only grown as her pregnancy progressed; the closer she got to her due date, the more reluctant Winston had been to participate. But she knew him well enough to know that he would always give in to her advances, and that he would think by saying "no" to her he might hurt her feelings. So his reluctance had never bothered her in the least, because she knew he still found her desirable—big belly and all. His only concern had been in keeping their baby from being born "with a big dent in the top of its head," he would say, as he made attempts to beg off.

At his insistence, Kristin had asked her doctor about it every time she went for an appointment, and he had kept assuring them both that it was okay for them to have sex as long as she didn't feel discomfort. Still, Winston had been anxious about it until Trazi was finally born, and he could see for himself that he hadn't caused any damage to their child.

Kristin realized they had both been reliving the same memories the day he sought her advice about Angela, because Winston had quickly dropped the subject of his new wife's reluctance. He had turned away from Kristin quickly to avoid eye contact with her, but he hadn't been quite quick enough. She had seen the sparkle in his eyes briefly before he caught himself, and seeing it had given her optimism about their future for the first time in a long time. She had allowed herself to admit that she had hope that they would find their way back together again some day, only Kristin had never guessed it would happen so soon.

Chapter 12

Good Night My Love

*A*fter she heard the front door close behind him, Kristin got out of bed herself a few minutes later. She knew Winston had already started beating himself up about breaking his wedding vows, and that she would soon have to face her own betrayal. Kristin knew her only chance of falling asleep again would be to allow herself a few minutes to mull things over with a strong cup of chamomile tea.

She had come to think of Angela as a sister, although lately Angela had pulled back from her friendship with Kristin too. Kristin had always tended to be honest with herself, as she was uncomfortable with deception of any kind. She wondered now how her betrayal would affect her relationship with Angela, but she had also questioned whether his second wife still wanted her marriage, long before Winston's knock came at her door.

Surely, Angela must have realized he was an energetic man with normal expectations of intimacy. When she and Winston had still been together, he had seemed to crave Kristin's affections; he even said their sexual relationship had given him an edge at work. He would often tell her that it gave him just the boost he needed to drive him forward toward his goals. As his wife, Angela must have known that she would be expected to be receptive to his needs. Otherwise, she would just be asking for trouble.

Knowing him as well as she did, Kristin was certain guilt had consumed

Winston by the time he left her house, especially since Angela was now pregnant. Kristin guessed that he was also feeling trapped too, because he probably hadn't realized until that night that he was still very much in love with her. But although she knew that he would never hurt her intentionally, she also knew that he wasn't the kind of man to leave his pregnant wife—especially one who needed him as much as Angela did.

And Kristin also loved him far too much not to care that he was having such pangs of remorse, even as she realized she would be the one most hurt in the situation. She had certainly been a willing enough participant, with no reason to blame her ex-husband for anything that had happened; so all that was left was the satisfaction she felt from their honest expression of love. When she closed her eyes, she could still feel his arms around her and it gave her a sense of contentment that matched the look on Winston's face as he fell asleep next to her in their old bed. After a minute or two, she got up to clear away her tea fixings and when she got back into bed, she fell asleep with the scent of Winston's cologne still lingering around her.

It was several days before she saw him again at their meeting with Trazi's teacher; the energy between them had been awkward to say the least. By that time, they had both decided it would be best never to talk about what had happened–there really was no point. It had been a long time before they could even be in the same room together without feeling anxiety. And both of them understood it would be longer still before they could trust themselves to be alone again. Kristin had watched Winston's guilt at their betrayal grow, as did hers, especially seeing the toll the baby was taking on Angela. But Kristin had held on to her memories just the same for as long as she could. She would replay them at night when she was alone, until her growing guilt finally overshadowed any pleasure.

With time and much effort, she had managed to push the entire episode to the back of her mind. She decided that was where it should stay until the day she realized she was pregnant. She had been quickly dismissing the obvious signs of the new life growing inside her, willing to believe almost anything else to be the cause of the mysterious ailments that had taken hold of her body. She rationalized she could have developed a bladder infection, convinced it might be the cause of her sudden need to urinate so frequently. It might also explain the queasiness she sometimes felt in the morning. Over time, she managed to block the entire incident with Winston from her mind and had never considered that she might be pregnant.

It wasn't until after Niyla suggested she might be expecting that the possibility even entered her mind. Niyla had joined the faculty at Hunter after completing her PhD program at Harvard, only a year after Kristin had earned her doctorate. The two women had been huddled together over tea in the faculty lounge while Kristin went through a list of herbal remedies she might take for her body's suspected imbalance. Her friend had made a casual comment that Kristin had a different look about her–almost a glow. She had been stunned when Niyla went even further and suggested that she might be pregnant. Kristin had just been on the verge of dismissing the notion as ludicrous when memories of the night she and Winston spent together forced its way back through the wall of denial she had erected around it. She had been protecting herself from her guilt, as Angela continued to struggle with her pregnancy. Now Kristin had to face the truth, only then remembering that neither she nor Winston had given any thought to birth control. They had been far too intent on being together.

Once she got home she said it out loud for the first time. Through some miracle she was really pregnant! It was easy enough for her to say, but she also knew her life would become considerably more complicated as a result. She decided on two things immediately: there was no circumstance under which she would consider *not* having the baby they had been blessed with, and she also decided there was no way that she would tell Winston. He had already been going through enough havoc in dealing with Angela's pregnancy and she had refused to put even more pressure on him.

But aside from settling those two things in her mind, Kristin had no earthly idea what she would do during the first few days of her new reality. She had mixed feelings about keeping the news from Winston, of course, but Angela's hormones had become even more unbalanced as her pregnancy progressed. Her emotional state had become a major source of concern to them all. The pregnancy itself had seemed normal during her first trimester, but after her fifth month everyone could tell that Angela was teetering well beyond the normal range for hormonal imbalance.

Everyone had already been on edge for weeks by the time Kristin found out about her own pregnancy. They had all been praying that Angela would be strong enough to recover after the baby was born. Kristin could tell that Winston was worried sick, afraid that Angela wouldn't snap out of it on her own. He confided in Kristin that he had talked to Angela's doctor at length, and his only advice had been to wait and see how Angela's body would adjust after giving birth.

And Angela had apparently moved far beyond merely pushing Winston away, the closer she came to her due date. According to him, Angela had started acting as though he was an enemy instead of her husband, clearly blaming him for her ill health and the pregnancy. The only person she would still talk to for any length was Kristin, which had put both she and Winston in a very strange position.

Kristin knew that the last thing he needed was to find out that she was also carrying his baby. Things had been hard on her but she couldn't bring herself to force him to respond to that on top of everything else. More than once, she had considered how much different things would've been if they had all been Muslims. As first wife, Winston would have asked her approval before he even took Angela as his second wife. But the way things had been going between them shortly before their divorce, she might have easily agreed for him to marry the Angela they had both known in Tuskegee.

Kristin had a number of Muslim friends, so she had witnessed firsthand the harmony that could exist in having multiple wives in one family. If they had all been Muslims, she never would have been in the position of having to hide her pregnancy either, it would have been cause for celebration instead of things being in such a hideous mess. She could have been openly happy about her pregnancy; Winston would have been given nods of approval by the men at the Masjid, as they all arrived for Jumu´ah on Friday afternoons as a family.

"How on earth did I let this happen?" She wondered repeatedly over the next several days. "How did I let myself get caught in this position?"

But when she was being completely honest after her initial shock, Kristin had to admit she was *thrilled* about the baby. It was a miracle from God; for the second time she was carrying a baby for the man she had always loved.

Eventually she came up with a plan that she thought might get her out of the sticky situation she was in. Admittedly, it was somewhat convoluted, but she decided she would invent a new man in her life. There would be a brief affair and then she would announce *her* pregnancy, shortly after Angela's baby was born; everyone would naturally assume that her mystery lover was the baby's father. Kristin knew that Winston would be upset, to put it mildly, but she hoped it would stop him from wanting to know anything more about her new lover. She had counted on that even, and later she would tell them all that her mystery lover had decided to move to a different part of the country – Seattle, maybe. And that would be the end of that, at least until the baby grew older. Then, she knew there would be hell to pay – from Winston *and* from Mother Bailey.

The only other option, as she saw it, was to move back to Tuskegee temporarily; which meant leaving fairly soon, before anyone other than Niyla found out she was pregnant. She and Winston had always agreed that Trazi would start living with him full time once he turned six and started school. The plan was to have their son spend only weekends at her house after that, but Trazi could always come and live with her in Tuskegee instead. It would be good for him and everyone else, since Angela was having such a hard time. It would lighten her burden in having to care for two children.

Kristin had been even more careful about her diet once she saw the results of her home pregnancy test. It had only been a few months but she had already been talking to the baby as she went about her day. She would listen to soothing jazz every night as she got ready for bed so she would be relaxed as she fell asleep. The first time around, it had been months before she needed to wear maternity clothes and she hoped it wouldn't be any different with the new baby. She decided she would find a house near campus in Tuskegee and maybe start teaching in the fall. She found herself fantasizing about taking her son and the baby for walks around the sprawling campus. The more she thought about it, moving to Tuskegee seemed her best option; especially if the baby turned out to be another boy, because he would probably be the spitting image of Winston too.

She had almost broken down and called Winston once in a moment of weakness, after she first began to feel flutters of the baby's movement. And she had just loved going for her doctor's appointments because everyone there knew she was pregnant. They didn't know anything about the drama surrounding the baby, so she could relax and get the 'pregnant lady' treatment that she craved. She looked forward to talking to her doctor about the baby's development and he had let her listen to the heartbeat the last time, which sounded very strong.

Then, almost overnight their little love child had begun to get bigger until her stomach took the shape of a round ball poking beneath her clothes. She avoided physical contact with Winston as much as possible after that, knowing he would notice right away. With only a few weeks left before the spring quarter ended, she hoped to be able to conceal the baby longer. She had learned in her yoga and tai chi classes about the need to allow the body's natural flow of energy; her normal style of dress tended toward loose fitting and flowing garments so she thought she stood a good chance.

She had soon changed her mind about being so far away from Winston when she delivered the baby, deciding to put her original idea into motion instead. She had been looking for the right opportunity to mention her new love interest; someone she would say she had been dating for a few months.

For her next scheduled doctor's appointment she was to have her first ultrasound. She was thrilled at the prospect of seeing the baby for the first time, and hoped that the image would reveal she was carrying the daughter that she and Winston had fantasized about having when they were in Tuskegee. But as fate would have it, all her joy had come to an abrupt end only days before the appointment. She had been heartbroken that none of her fantasies were meant to be; she later learned that she had begun feeling the sharp pains in her abdomen at nearly the exact time that Angela had gone into labor.

Winston called to tell her they were on their way to the hospital; when she answered the phone, she had been just at the point of fearing something was going wrong with *her* baby. She had tried to sound excited for him as best she could, but all she could think of was the pain she felt – knowing it wasn't a good sign. She finally promised to come to the hospital just to get Winston off the phone, and then she had called Dr. Foster immediately. He asked her to meet him at the hospital as soon as she could get there and since Niyla was on a trip to Jamaica, Kristin had driven herself to Columbia Hospital for Women. She arrived just minutes after a nurse had wheeled Angela to the maternity and delivery floor, with Winston following behind like a caricature of an expectant father.

The look on Dr. Foster's face told Kristin that what she feared was true; she was in serious danger of losing her baby. She had been Dr. Foster's patient since she and Winston first moved to D.C., four years earlier. The doctor knew how happy she was about the baby she was carrying, though she had never mentioned the father to him. He had hurried from his home to meet her and was already waiting at the hospital when she arrived. Dr. Foster signaled the admissions clerk that her paperwork would have to wait and quickly ushered Kristin into an examination room. As soon as he had begun his cursory exam, she could see that his suspicions were confirmed. He administered a series of intravenous drugs, yet and still, hoping for a miracle that would stop her miscarriage. After that, Dr. Foster quietly told her that all they could do was pray.

So Kristin had prayed for hours, all curled up on the narrow hospital bed. She was in shocked anxiety the entire time; everything seemed surreal, as though it were happening to someone else. The small room was crowded with nurses, technicians, and her doctor, who had all hovered over her as they continued to monitor the baby's vital signs. And in spite of all the people in the room, Kristin had never felt more alone in her life. She braced herself as she waited to find out whether her prayers would be answered, but a short while later, she sensed that the baby was preparing to leave her. Her darling little one had only been giving her time to accept the inevitable, what she could not change. The baby was giving her time to accept that she would have to say good-bye.

As she waited, Kristin wracked her brain and began second-guessing herself about whether she had been careful enough. Was there something *she* had done to cause it to happen? She wondered whether the moderate exercises she had been doing were too much, too soon. Had she eaten enough of the right foods? She had been a vegetarian for years, but once she could keep food down she had started eating tons of tofu to make sure she had enough protein. She had even begun eating small portions of fish again, and vegetables that were high in nutrients that the baby needed.

Then she began to wonder whether she had been *too* happy about the baby. Was that possible? Was she being punished? Had she been too happy that she was carrying Winston's baby? Was it because of what they had done to Angela? Was that the reason she was in such pain now? She had never consciously intended to tell Winston that he was the father; but in her heart, she knew the truth would have come out eventually. She had not allowed herself to think that far ahead, because all she had been able to manage was one day at a time.

As she felt her baby's life slipping away, Kristin wondered whether the truth would've been too much; maybe that was the reason the baby chose not to stay. Kristin knew that she would have to find a way to accept it, to believe that what was happening was in Divine Order. But she had come to love the baby she carried so very much.

Her anguish when she realized she might never get to hold her baby nearly destroyed Kristin. She began to talk to her silently; instinctively knowing she was carrying the baby girl that she and Winston always wanted to have. She told the baby about the night they had first dreamed of her; Kristin told her how much she would miss her if she decided not to stay.

Almost immediately, the activity in the room increased and only verified what Kristin already knew. She pleaded wordlessly with her daughter, asking her to return to her some day; even as the sounds coming from the machines confirmed that her baby's brief sojourn had ended.

And it was exactly ten minutes later that Celeste Akilah Bailey made an arrival for her own expedition on planet Earth.

Chapter 13

The Garden City
(1990)

After what seemed to be an eternity, Kristin realized the Mercedes was riding in had finally approached the outskirts of Kumasi. Only then did she refocus her attention on the reason she was in Ghana, turning her thoughts to more practical matters of getting settled before her classes started. Her driver had stopped only long enough to refuel on the trip north and once to eat, though Kristin had little appetite after having relived the misery of her miscarriage. She looked from side to side as they rode through the streets near the Kumasi Market; after a few minutes more, the driver brought the long Mercedes to a halt. She was glad to be finally out of the car and she took her first long look at the place she would call home for the next two years.

The faculty compound, as it was known around the university, consisted of two large one-story buildings that were kept as living quarters for a small number of unmarried faculty and researchers. Each building was located at opposite ends of a large fenced courtyard with a small patio sitting between the two. There was a very pleasant looking garden to the left of the women's quarters with two wooden benches that had been erected among the coconut trees and sweet smelling foliage. The landscape was beautiful, and Kristin was drawn to the area immediately. It was clear to her why Kumasi was known as the Garden City of Africa, and she could immediately envision herself sitting on the patio in the early morning hours after meditating.

But at that moment she felt drained, as much from the emotional torrent of her memories as from the long drive. Without warning, she began to feel a sense of melancholy come over her again, as the reality of the distance between her and everyone else she knew and loved finally hit her.

She managed a smile as she readied herself to be introduced to the household staff, who waited patiently to greet her. A slender young woman with flawless ebony skin stepped forward with her hand extended. Amina was a new teacher at the university, she told Kristin. She had been assigned as her assistant for the two years she would be in Ghana. Amina also lived in the faculty compound and after introducing herself, she introduced Kristin to the rest of the staff. They all greeted her in the slightly formal way that she was already becoming accustomed to.

A middle-aged woman was introduced as the manager of the women's residence and their cook. "She's been the boss for most of the time the compound has been here," Amina explained. The woman reminded Kristin of one of her aunts and she could tell right away that she ran a tight ship. A much younger woman of around twenty years was presented as the building's housekeeper. And finally, Amina introduced Kristin to Amad, a young man who also appeared to be in his mid-twenties.

"Amad is an excellent driver," Amina told her, "and he will be available to take you wherever you want to go."

As she greeted Amad, Kristin noted that he had the same calm demeanor as the driver that she and her friends had the first time she visited Ghana. Kristin only hoped that he would be equally skilled because she fully intended to take advantage of having the young man made available to her, so she could explore the countryside surrounding Kumasi.

Amina took the small travel bag that Kristin still carried and led the way inside the women's dormitory. She showed her the large kitchen and dining area first and then steered her into the comfortable common room that also served as their library. A large bookshelf held a number of books in a variety of genres and it took up much of the room. There was also a desktop computer, several tables, and two large sectional sofas that were decorated with brightly colored pillows. Adjacent to the room was a much smaller room that contained a small television set; judging by its pristine appearance, Kristin concluded that the room was seldom used.

101

She was introduced to other members of the faculty who arrived home as Amina concluded the tour. Kristin was pleased to find that her bedroom was located next to one of the two bathrooms that were situated on opposite ends of the building. Her room was small, but handsomely decorated and it was also immaculate. Kristin saw that her luggage had been placed on the floor next to a small comfortable bed that was close to the room's only window. A carved desk stood on one side of the bed, with a large lamp sitting on top of it. Next to the lamp was a bowl of fresh tropical fruit and Kristin noted with delight that there was more than ample space for her yoga exercises. The room also got plenty of morning sunlight according to Amina, whose room was only two doors down the hall. The small window in the room provided an excellent view of the garden below, and there was a chair sitting next to the window where she could sit and read, if she preferred not to go outside.

"Thank you so much, Amina."

She told her new assistant that she was grateful to be living in such warm and pleasant surroundings. "I think I'm going to be very comfortable here," she said.

Kristin's comments seemed to satisfy Amina, who began moving toward the door. "I know you must be tired from your trip," she called over her shoulder, "so I will leave you now.

"Dinner will be served in two hours." Amina turned around after she had reached the door. "But please let me know if there is anything you need before then." And then she turned again to leave, closing the door softly behind her.

Kristin looked around her new room again after Amina had left, thankful that her spirits had finally begun to lift. "I'm glad I came," she realized, as her optimism began to replace some of her earlier apprehension.

"Maybe this is exactly what I needed to do to put the past behind me, and get my life in order again."

She wondered whether she might meet someone in Kumasi who would help her forget about Winston. All the while, she didn't hold out much hope that she would. To distract herself from her thoughts, she unpacked all her clothes and grabbed one of the clean white towels that had been left at the foot of her bed. Then she headed for the bathroom to take a long hot shower before it was time for dinner.

Chapter 14

Angela

The green and beige pattern of the tile cast an almost hypnotic spell over Angela, as she followed the swirls it made with her eyes. She sat staring at the backsplash as though she were in a trance, remembering that she had debated with herself for weeks whether she should even buy the tile at all. She wasn't certain whether the mosaic pattern might be too much for such a small space. But in the end, she decided on using it to create a larger pattern in the center of the tile; the colors were an exact match with the kitchen and breakfast nook wall trim. She only wished the tile design *could* hypnotize her. That way she might have had some protection against the hurtful words that had been spewing from her husband's mouth all morning. The things he had said to her felt like tiny daggers being thrown inside her ears, and she had struggled to keep herself from wincing with pain. She had been aware, of course, that things were far from *perfect* in their marriage, but she had been stunned to silence when Winston brought up the subject of divorce.

Everything had started out so wonderfully that morning, or so she thought. The air held promise of an early spring, very early for Washington although it was already April. Angela had been looking forward to a leisurely breakfast with her husband just a short time earlier. She had reveled at the thought of basking in the stream of sunshine that poured through a bay window into their breakfast nook. It was to be just the two of them for a change, and she had even thought they might celebrate a fresh start for their marriage to coincide with the arrival of spring. It was only later that it dawned on her that Winston had orchestrated the whole thing. His mother had just *happened* to stop by their house the night before, and had unexpectedly taken Celeste and Trazi to spend the weekend with her. Winston had been so gracious all morning and had even volunteered to make breakfast for them. He had made all the things that he knew she liked – blueberry muffins for heaven's sake!

As he continued his tirade, Angela realized her immediate concern had been how Trazi might react to their divorce for some odd reason, instead of how his sister might be affected. Angela had adored Winston's son from the day she first saw him again in Washington. The four-year-old cutie had smiled so shyly from behind his father's legs as they were introduced. His honey-brown skin, thick curly hair and smile were exactly like Winston's. How could she have kept from falling in love with his son too?

But thank goodness Kristin had taught Trazi to be self-sufficient, even at such a young age. He had never required much of Angela's attention at all and Winston had always taken care of anything that he *did* need. Her husband had been used to doing that long before they ever started dating.

Celeste, however, had been a different story altogether. After she came along *everything* had changed. Her daughter needed much more of her attention than Angela had to give—and she seemed to need it all the time. After Celeste was born, everyone had just assumed Trazi would be spending more time at their house too, so he could bond with his new little sister. Everyone except Angela, that is. *She* had thought he would spend *less* time with them – not that she didn't love seeing the little fellow. But it had been hard enough for her to adjust to taking care of an infant, and all of a sudden she had been expected to take care of *two* small children.

Before Celeste was old enough to talk Angela would leave her alone in her nursery for hours, pretending she didn't exist for as long as she could pull it off. She would put toys in her daughter's crib and avoid her room as much as possible, as she went about her day. She would fantasize that her pregnancy had just been a disturbing dream that she had finally awakened from. Unfortunately though, she could only do that on those rare occasions when Trazi wasn't around, and he seemed to be around all the time.

Angela had no idea why she had never developed motherly instincts that apparently came so naturally to other women; mothers she usually saw when she took Celeste for doctor's appointments, for example. They were always trading stories and making cooing noises about some adorable thing their babies had done and they needed to share. It wasn't that she didn't *want* to be a good mother; it was just that none of it had come easy for her. And if the truth were known, some of it had never come at all.

Sitting at the breakfast table with her soon-to-be ex-husband, Angela was curious whether her lack of response to motherhood had been the beginning of the end of their marriage. But deep down, her suspicion was that it was something else altogether.

She remained motionless in her beautifully decorated kitchen, thinking back over her marriage to Winston and their life together. It wasn't long before she recognized the clear warning signs that had been there all along. But somehow, she had managed to miss them all.

"How is that even possible?" She asked herself absently. "How could I have completely missed what is so clear to me now?"

Angela finally turned to face Winston, who had been calmly eating the breakfast he had so expertly prepared as he rattled on between bites. He had started in on her as soon as they sat down to eat as though he had rehearsed it. His voice had been droning on and on nonstop for over thirty minutes. He had been saying things to her that she had never dreamed she would hear him say. Somewhere in her distant mind, she recalled how Winston had brought her breakfast in bed every weekend when they were first married. She gazed at her husband's ruggedly handsome profile and tried her best to remember when he had stopped. The only thing she knew for sure was that it had been long before Celeste was born.

Sweet sounds of tiny bells wafted in through the open bay window, from the black resin fountain Angela had bought on one of her frequent trips to the Baltimore Inner Harbor. The small brass bells drifted lazily over the fountain's cascading waters just beneath the window, gently colliding with each other and the fixed bells attached to its sides. She would often listen to their delicate music as she sat sipping her morning coffee. That morning, the chimes seemed only to mock her; they played a cruel accompaniment to her husband's relentless attack on their marriage.

She turned away to avoid eye contact when Winston looked up unexpectedly from his almost empty plate. She shifted her focus to a tiny crack she thought she saw along the side of a porcelain vase sitting in the center of the table. Winston's mother had given them the delicate sea-green antique as a wedding present, and Angela had been captivated by it from the moment she pulled it from its handsomely wrapped box. The sloped eighteen-carat handles decried the vase's rich Italian history. Mother Bailey had already been more than generous in helping to pay for their extravagant wedding, and she couldn't imagine what her mother-in-law had paid for the vase.

Angela had moved it on three occasions in an attempt to keep Trazi, now thirteen, and still in his clumsy stage, from knocking the vase over and breaking it. Now she wondered abstractly whether Winston would let her keep it after they divorced. She found herself speculating on how long it would last around Trazi, without her there to keep a watchful eye over it.

Eventually, she realized that she needed to force her attention on what Winston was actually saying. When she did tune in and listen, it became apparent to her that he had been giving the demise of their marriage a great deal of thought, and for some length of time. He appeared to have conducted his own assessment of their marriage, unbeknownst to her, and had decided that it was beyond repair.

"With no thought of including me in the process, as usual," she thought to herself, feeling anger begin to rise.

She refused to give him the satisfaction of knowing how surprised she had been at first; and later, how infuriated she was after hearing what he had to say. Instead, she merely looked at Winston and asked whether he wanted more coffee. She got up to make a fresh pot before he could reply. She could see that he was taking extra pains to be polite, friendly even, as he continued his quiet onslaught. He seemed visibly relieved that she hadn't thrown a tantrum as he and his mother obviously expected.

Winston laid out all his carefully calculated plans for their separation and divorce. He made several attempts to get her to join in the conversation about how everything should be arranged. He told her he had figured out how they could both still spend time with the children. She started tuning him out again as he began "sharing his thoughts" on how they could integrate the children's extracurricular activities into a master calendar, so they could both coordinate them together and share responsibility.

Angela busied her mind with other things as Winston went from there to talking about a fair way of dividing the assets they had accumulated during their marriage. She started reminiscing again, this time about how long it had taken to find the right tablecloth for the breakfast table they were sitting at. She had gone from store to store until she happened upon the perfect match for their decor. Through persistence in searching, she had also found the cheerful light green curtains that hung on rods around the bay window in the breakfast nook, providing a perfect accent for the room. She had discovered the curtains at Lord & Taylor's, shortly after she decided she would take on the redecorating project.

Winston reached across the table to take another muffin from the bun warmer. In doing so, he brushed against Angela's hand lightly as she reached for a muffin at the same time. His hand recoiled, almost too quickly, to avoid a collision. For several minutes afterwards, an awkward silence replaced his endless chatter.

After he was certain that Angela's slender hands were securely on her side of the table, Winston pulled another muffin from the warmer quickly and began spreading blueberry jam across the top. Angela had always loved the combination of blueberry jam on top of blueberry muffins; now she wondered whether she would ever eat it again.

Her husband seemed almost apologetic as he told her that he no longer felt any joy or happiness when they were together. He said he hadn't felt any for a very long time, but he also wanted her to know how hard he had tried to make their marriage work. He told her he was no longer willing to sacrifice his happiness for the sake of keeping their family together.

Aside from asking about the coffee, Angela had still not uttered a single word the entire time Winston had been talking. She hadn't even asked him to pass the turkey bacon that was on his side of the table. She had been steeling herself the whole time against blurting something out that would expose her anger, and now felt she was finally ready to respond.

Then it was Winston who seemed to avoid looking at her, but before he lowered his head she caught a glimpse of his face. In it, she saw that guilt had replaced the relief he had initially felt after seeing she wouldn't put up a fight. He raised his head again before Angela had a chance to speak and he looked directly into her face, vowing to always love her in a special way. He said it in a quiet dramatic voice, so typical of Winston. He even told her that he appreciated her because she had given Celeste to him.

Winston hesitated for a moment, as though trying to decide whether he should say something more. Then, he told her that he no longer felt they were right for each other, and that he wanted to be free to rediscover joy in his life. He told Angela that he needed both a friend and a marriage partner – someone he could share his goals and his heart and soul with.

She looked deep into his eyes as she searched her own heart and found that she couldn't blame him for what he said. What person wouldn't want all those things in a marriage? But she couldn't help wondering whether he had been thinking about Kristin when he said it.

Chapter 15

Love is a Hurting Thing

*I*t wasn't long at all before Kristin had settled into a routine in Kumasi. The classes she taught were scheduled for Tuesdays, Wednesdays, and Thursdays so she often took off on long adventurous weekends into the surrounding countryside. She met the Vice Chancellor of KNUST only once, but she had an immediate sense of his commitment to excellence for Ghana's top ranked university. She had also come close to meeting the school's Chancellor once too, on a rare occasion when he had attended a faculty reception engulfed in ceremony. By statute, the position of Chancellor has always been held by the Asantehene, the given title of the Ashanti King.

The air of maturity of her KNUST students had impressed Kristin right away, especially since most of them looked much younger than their years. She didn't meet one student who seemed to take his or her opportunity for an education lightly, or who didn't seem grateful for the sacrifices their families been made for them to go to school. Her students who took her African-American History classes had the kind of enthusiasm for learning that required little, if any, prodding on her part. It was quite a different experience from what she had been accustomed to back home.

But she had to admit she had been surprised and touched when her students at Hunter voiced protests when she announced her plans to leave for Ghana. At first, she had chalked it up to their reluctance to lose out on an easy 'A.' Then, they caught her completely off guard by organizing a farewell reception in her honor at the student union building. One of her young female students, speaking for the group, made a very touching farewell toast. She told Kristin that they wanted her to know just how much they valued what she had been trying to do in her classes, in case she decided not to come back. It had made Kristin instantly think about Dr. Keenan, and she wondered why she and her classmates at Tuskegee had never thought to show appreciation to him. It also made her vow that she would step up her classes at Hunter a notch, once she returned from Ghana.

Although she hadn't been able to use the same grading system at KNUST as she used at Hunter, she soon realized it wouldn't be necessary. Her students in Ghana wanted to learn as much about their American cousins as they possibly could, and they would never have dreamed of cutting her classes. Most of them had yet to travel outside of their country and had only been in close contact with Black Americans who came to Ghana infrequently as tourists, and who had sometimes been rude and arrogant.

The format she had chosen for her classes in Kumasi was a twenty-minute lecture, followed by open dialog with in-depth discussions about the economics that had driven the African slave trade. Kristin found her students at KNUST to be as fascinated as her students at Hunter had been to learn how determined those enslaved in America had been to free themselves. She introduced the same theories about racism and its origin as she had at Hunter, contrasting the experiences of enslaved Africans in America with those in Ghana who had been oppressed during colonialism.

The British had ruled what was once known as the Gold Coast Colony for close to a hundred years, beginning only decades after the slave trade was outlawed in Europe. Since millions of Africans had been kidnapped and enslaved in countries all over the world, Britain and other European countries found little resistance to colonialism forming roots, as they invaded one country after another.

Kristin led discussions about how the Queen's English had been forced on Ghana the same as it had been forced on all other British "colonies" around the world. The Europeans greatly influenced Ghana's culture during the time they occupied the country, hindering religious and traditional practices as they gained more control over economic policies.

As with many of her Hunter students, her students at KNUST had only associated slavery with victimization, in one form or another, before they took her class. She introduced them to research that had been conducted by Dr. David Hawkins, a noted psychiatrist and author of the book ***Power*** *vs. Force*[2]. Hawkins, Kristin informed them, had used his knowledge of kinesiology to correlate physical movements and emotions to various levels of human consciousness. According to his Map of Consciousness, created with scaled calibrations, the energy of victimization, resistance, and insurrection all rank low. At the very bottom of his scale, however, was the emotion of 'shame,' which Hawkins calibrated at a consciousness level of 20. In contrast, he recorded 'courage' at a level of 200; while 'reason' registered higher at 400, according to his scale. The energy of 'enlightenment,' on the other hand, which was at the highest level of Dr. Hawkins' Map of Consciousness, calibrated at a point between 700 –1000.

She pointed out to the young people she taught on both sides of the ocean that an attitude of *victimization* ranked much lower than either resistance or insurrection. And while the latter two expressions were not considered *evolved* by any means, they were at least headed in the right direction.

Kristin had come to know several members of the KNUST faculty quite well, largely through her association with her housemates at the faculty compound. Shortly after the school year started, however, she had encountered a male faculty member called Solomon Asare, who had become one of her closest friends. They met when they sat next to each other at a departmental meeting by chance, and since Solomon was also a professor of history they had found an immediate connection. He was only a few years younger than Kristin and she learned that he had once been a student at KNUST himself. He had moved to London after graduating to study Modern History at King's College, and then returned to Ghana to teach at KNUST only five years before Kristin arrived. Since their classes were also on a similar schedule, they frequently found themselves engaged in deep political conversations during tea breaks.

She already had a number of West African friends she had met at Tuskegee and Hunter before her first trip to Ghana. Had that not been the case, she might have been startled at first by some of the fierce expressions that would cover Solomon's face as he argued his points during their debates. Usually, his delivery would be accentuated by a sudden shift in tone that would transform his voice into a dramatic booming sound. One of her friends at Tuskegee, who was from Nigeria, had been her first experience in seeing such an abrupt display of raw emotion. His otherwise mild

---

[2] Dr. David Hawkins, *Power vs. Force: The Hidden Determinants of Human Behaviour* (Carlsbad, California: Hay House Inc.), 68–69.

demeanor would suddenly shift into a passionate outburst during their political debates; when in reality, he would have only been mildly agitated by something she had said.

There was a similar trait often expressed by people of certain European cultures too, like the French and Italians. But Kristin had often wondered how much that same flair for passionate outbursts had played in the prohibition against enslaved Africans speaking their own language in America, or looking directly into the eyes of their European handlers. She suspected the trait had been passed down from ancient times, as ancestors learned to aggressively defend themselves at a moment's notice against dangerous animals that had once roamed across the land.

At any rate, Kristin's friendship with Solomon was well established within a short period and she was soon spending Sunday afternoons with his family at their home. She had quickly bonded with his wife, Liyana, as easily as she had with Solomon. Their three children were also delightful and joyful innocents, who had helped her tremendously in easing her pangs of loneliness for Trazi and Celeste. Over time, the Asares had become like a second family to Kristin; she had been especially grateful to have them in her life when everything happened later with Winston.

Kristin's original intent had been to travel home to Washington for Christmas both years of her teaching assignment. Instead, she had changed her plans twice in reaction to some drama involving her ex-husband. First, there had been the unexpected news that he and Angela were getting a divorce. Kristin had only been in Ghana six months when she got that bit of news. She hadn't seen it coming at all, but, in retrospect, it shouldn't have been a surprise to anyone. There had obviously been no love lost between the two, but it had still been the last thing Kristin expected to hear.

She had found herself becoming more and more nervous as time approached for her to board her flight home after hearing the news. She kept anticipating what being in close quarters with Winston would be like, after he and Angela were no longer together. In the end, her anxiety had gotten the best of her and she cancelled her plans at the last minute. By her calculations, their divorce would have still been pending a final status at the time she was due to arrive in Washington. It had all been too much for her to handle emotionally, since her own wedding anniversary with Winston would have been the day after Christmas. She decided it would have been far too awkward so she opted to remain in Kumasi instead.

Kristin had celebrated that holiday season with Solomon and his family, grateful to have more time to prepare herself for what she had hoped would soon be a reunion with her ex-husband. Liyana and Solomon had been nearly as excited as she was after hearing Winston would soon be divorced. They had been convinced from the beginning that she was still in love with him, despite her efforts to convince them otherwise. And Kristin hadn't even been aware of how often she would bring Winston's name up during conversations until they called it to her attention.

She had been encouraged by news of Winston's divorce too, but she also knew that it didn't necessarily change things between them. Although he had down-played the summers he had spent in Jamaica with his grandfather, Kristin knew well that the older man had achieved his intention in the way that Winston was raised. He had taught his grandson that a large part of being a man was to take special note of the image he projected to those around him, in addition to taking care of his family. Kristin and Winston had been so young when they were married; they both were only twenty-five when their divorce became final. By the time Kristin realized how important the things his grandfather had taught him was to Winston, and how uncomfortable he must have been with the image they portrayed as a couple, it had been far too late.

When they were married, they had each been so bent on having things their own way. Kristin had no idea at the time that her determination had come across as being adversarial to her husband. Apparently, he had felt constantly challenged by her; something she had only discovered during the shouting match that turned out to be the last one of their marriage. No matter how hard she tried, she couldn't even remember what had started the fight. The only thing she could remember was that she had been resolute in standing her ground for once. She had decided that she would not put up with Winston's pigheadedness anymore—no matter what.

"You either love me or you don't." She had announced simply, still preoccupied with having the last word even when she knew in her heart it would be an empty victory. "If you loved me once, then you still do."

She had been sitting on the edge of their bed at the time watching him pack his bags, as though it was all happening to someone else. Winston didn't even bother to dispute what she said, because both of them knew that he did still love her as much as he had when they first met.

Their fight that fateful afternoon hadn't been the first time their stubbornness had led them into such a huge disagreement, one that neither of them was willing to admit to being wrong about. Kristin had merely adapted to their fighting as a normal pattern of their relationship. She had no idea how bad things were between them until the day that her husband of four years announced that he had found an apartment close by, and was moving out. And even as she got over that initial shock, she could tell that he didn't really want to leave. But she had *had* it with him that day, and had stubbornly refused to budge. For some reason, it seemed more important to her that she not reward his bullish behavior by giving in to him.

Instead, she had sat calmly and watched as the only man she had ever loved packed his bags to leave her, without uttering one word of protest. Neither of them had fought for their marriage that day and within a few months they no longer had one. They had stood by passively and allowed their legal union to unravel, knowing all the time that the deep love that was between them remained unchanged.

That love could no longer be denied because of what happened the last time they were alone together, but that didn't necessarily mean anything would be different. Kristin knew that to Winston it was a matter of honor; losing control with her before Celeste was born still haunted him, because it conflicted sharply with how his grandfather had taught him to behave.

So it hadn't been all that surprising to her almost a year later, when their son called to tell her that his father was planning to remarry.

❋❋❋

"Hi Mom." She had known immediately by her the sound of Trazi's tone that something was amiss.

"Hi Sweetheart. What's wrong?" In spite of everything, Winston had always been an excellent father so she had never doubted that she could depend on him to handle all the parental responsibilities, while she was out of the country. But with the distance that separated them, she still didn't care to dally around without knowing what troubled her fourteen-year-old son.

"Nothing, Mom. Well..."

Kristin waited after his voice trailed off. As with her, she knew it sometimes took Trazi a few minutes to say what he had on his mind.

"It's Dad."

She didn't wait much longer after that. "What about your father? Did something happen to him?"

"Not exactly... He's getting married, Mom."

She had been at a loss for words on hearing what her son had called to tell her, but Kristin knew that if she didn't say something soon, Trazi might assume there had been a problem with the phone connection. It would have been even more awkward if she waited until he began calling her name to try and figure out whether their call had been disconnected.

"Who is he marrying?" She heard herself ask.

It was all she could think of to say, but it occurred to her later that it was probably the most natural question to ask. She felt nearly paralyzed with pain as she listened to her son hesitantly tell her about the woman his father had been dating and now planned to marry. Trazi struggled with his words to spare her feelings and she could tell right away that her son didn't care much for his father's latest bride-to-be. It made Kristin wonder whether he would have accepted Angela as readily, if he had been old enough to understand his parents' relationship dynamics. She had heard the glimmer of hope in his voice on the day he called her to tell her about Winston's divorce from Celeste's mother. Kristin had decided years earlier that she would never try to hide the fact that she still loved his father from her son. They had never discussed it openly, but she knew that Trazi wanted them to be a family again as much as she did, and that he was just as disappointed by his father's latest plans.

This time Winston was going to marry a woman that Kristin had never even met, and she was terribly hurt by it.

"What kind of man does something so cowardly?" Solomon demanded to know after he learned the news. He and Liyana had been encouraging her to reconcile with Winston after his divorce from Angela. Now, they were incensed with her ex-husband after seeing how badly she felt about the news of his upcoming marriage.

And after a few months, they had begun to tell her repeatedly that she should be glad to be rid of Winston because he was obviously a fool. They were very helpful to Kristin in healing her wounds, and Solomon began giving her frequent pep talks about being open to having a new man in her life; one who would treat her as she deserved.

"I have just the man for you." He made the announcement one afternoon, as soon as she joined him at a table in the faculty break room. Reluctantly, she had agreed to meet one of his childhood friends, whose family was also influential in the Ashanti region. He was a very handsome man and quite wealthy—but definitely not a man to be toyed with. Kristin soon realized she wasn't ready yet to share her heart with anyone else, so she had politely declined the man's invitations after their only date.

She had been more hurt that Winston didn't have the courtesy to call and tell her about his plans himself. In her heart, she knew it was because his new marriage wouldn't change anything between them. She kept thinking about what she had said to him on the day that he walked out on their marriage. She hadn't realized how true it was at the time, or that the same thing applied to her. They *did* love each other before, and they both still loved each other now.

Nothing short of an emergency would have made her fly back to the States that second Christmas. She had decided to spare herself the agony of being introduced to Winston's latest wife for as long as she could. She knew Trazi would understand her reluctance in coming home, and as for Celeste – she told herself that Winston's daughter already had a mother *and* a stepmother. And Kristin understood now more than ever that she was neither. She decided to spend Christmas in Ghana again and this time she spent the holidays on the Gulf of Guinea, despite Solomon's urgings that she stay in Kumasi and celebrate with him and his family again.

She and Amad, her driver, headed south on Christmas Eve. They stopped to share a holiday meal mid-day at the LaBodi Beach Hotel in Accra, and later that afternoon they made the forty-five mile drive west to Winneba. Kristin had decided on visiting the fishing town in the Central Region because Liyana, who had been born in Winneba, had been telling her all about the colorful Christmas festivals that were held in the town each year.

She and Amad spent an entire week at a small beach hotel near the Winneba University of Education. Kristin had gone for morning and afternoon walks along the shore and Amad would drive her out into the countryside during the times in-between. On the day before they were to return to Kumasi, they happened to drive past the house of an older woman who sat expectantly on a bench beneath a tree in her front yard. She seemed as though she had been waiting for them; the woman got up from where she sat as their car approached her house, and waved to beckon Amad to stop. He quickly pulled the car off to the side of the road at Kristin's urgings and parked near a small grove of trees in the yard.

Initially, Kristin interpreted the older woman's stares to be curiosity, once they were out of the car and had introduced themselves. She had seen similar expressions on people in some of the more isolated areas of Ghana during her travels with Amad on the weekends. She had come across many people who had spent little time in the company of African Americans, and their natural inquisitiveness toward an approaching stranger would often become guarded after she began speaking. Once they realized she was an American, many had seemed unsure of what to make of her.

The woman had continued to stare at Kristin that day with an intensity that soon made her fidget in the wooden chair that a tall young man brought out of the small house, beckoning for Kristin and Amad to sit down with a wide smile. After he went back into the house, the woman finally introduced herself as Nana Adwoa. She moved closer to Kristin abruptly after she had said her own name and stared into Kristin's dark blue eyes.

"So, our Moses has come at last," the older woman said confidently.

Kristin was startled, not only because of the woman's authoritative tone but also because of what she said. She had called her "Moses" of all things and it had thrown her off guard completely. At the same time, she found was she said to be most intriguing and also found that she was eager to hear what the woman would have to say next.

But Nana Adwoa had said nothing else on the subject; she only smiled at Kristin knowingly every few minutes or so. The young man soon came back out of the house with a tray of porcelain cups filled with rose hip tea, and Kristin sensed the tea service was normally reserved for special occasions. She waited politely as they sipped their tea, giving the older woman an opportunity to explain—to reveal why she had called her by a name other than the one Kristin had used in introducing herself. She was reluctant to speak out of turn since the woman was an elder, and she didn't want to risk appearing disrespectful. But after Kristin saw that no further explanation was forthcoming, she could no longer contain her curiosity.

"What did you mean before," she asked the woman shyly, "when you called me Moses?"

Nana appeared to be surprised by the question, leading Kristin to wonder whether she had indeed been discourteous. But then the older woman had just smiled at her again.

"It will all be revealed in time," was all she would say. Then she changed the subject and asked Kristin whether she cared to see her garden. They spent the remaining time walking in Nana's vegetable patch in a lush wooded area behind her house. She pointed out several varieties of herbs in the garden and explained their medicinal purposes. As she walked Kristin back to her car, Nana extended an invitation for her to visit again.

"Come back anytime you need to gather your thoughts," she said mysteriously.

Kristin had no idea of what the woman meant by the invitation, but she smiled her acceptance. And for some unknown reason, she sensed it was only the beginning of her relationship with the baffling older woman.

Chapter 16

Am I My Brother's Keeper?

*W*inston had sensed that there was something not quite right with Malaya the first weekend she stayed over with Celeste at their loft. That had been nearly three years earlier when the girls were only eight. Now, Malaya could no longer sleep over with his daughter, but she only seemed slightly more at ease than on her first visit. He had felt so strongly that something was wrong that first weekend that it kept haunting him long after his daughter's friend had been dropped back off at her house that Sunday evening.

He had developed his habit of walking fast when he was student at Tuskegee, and only had ten minutes to walk from the School of Engineering at one end of the sprawling campus to Huntington Hall, on the other side of "the yard." After he got there, he still had to climb four flights of stairs to his math class on the top floor. Most of his professors had been flexible about the ten-minute grace period students were officially given between classes, but unfortunately, some weren't quite as forgiving.

Dr. Chandra, or "the Big Injun," as many of his engineering classmates had called their math professor behind his back, had always gone strictly by the book. He would start his lectures promptly on the hour, checking his watch periodically until it was time to close his classroom door at exactly ten minutes past. Winston had little choice but to walk fast if he had any chance of making it to class on time. Usually, he had reaffirmed Euclid's familiar axiom: *"the shortest distance between two points is a straight line,"* as he hurried along toward the old academic building that had been built at the turn of the 20th Century. He was aware that he had still held on to his old habit of speed walking, but it was a trait that he also shared with Charlotte. It hadn't escaped Winston's attention how Malaya responded differently to his wife than the girl responded to him whenever *he* walked into a room abruptly. His daughter's friend had all but jumped out of her skin the first time he had walked through Celeste's open bedroom door without warning. They all had a big laugh about it afterwards, but Winston remembered thinking that Malaya's giggle had sounded a bit forced.

For a while after that, he considered whether the loft itself might have been the problem. Thanks to Charlotte, their home looked more like a museum than even Winston's tastes appreciated – and he loved art. She had transformed their living space into an artistically pleasing environment, but it wasn't exactly kid-friendly. Her decorating style completely ignored the fact that young people lived in the loft and were in and out with friends all the time. She had placed expensive and breakable pieces on pedestals all over the place. At first, they had all found it tricky in navigating around some of the pieces. They had seemed to jump out in front of them as they went about their daily routines, moving from room to room.

Later still, Winston wondered whether Malaya might have been nervous about having to eat meals in the type of formal setting that Charlotte always insisted on. She had been setting their dinner table with "a whole bunch of plates and forks and spoons," as Trazi so eloquently put it, since the day she had cooked her first meal for them. Winston secretly agreed with his fifteen-year-old son that it was a bit over the top, but Charlotte had responded to Trazi's comments before he had time to offer his opinion. She had told his children that they would have to learn how to eat in a formal setting eventually, and they might as well learn to do it at home.

Winston had certainly been forced into his share of formal dinners during his career with NASA, so he couldn't argue with his new wife on that. He had to laugh when he thought back to his first black-tie dinner when he was interning in Houston, and the near fiasco that had been. But for the Grace of God, he could very well have ended his career before it ever got off the ground. The whole thing started when he realized the dinner was scheduled for the same day that he had arranged a date with a certain long-legged young woman from Texas Southern. He had met her at a mixer that NASA gave at the beginning of the summer, so their interns could get to know each other. It had taken Winston weeks to work up the courage to ask the young lady out.

He had felt a bit of guilt even thinking about approaching her. He and Kristin had just started hanging out before the spring semester ended but they weren't officially dating yet, so he had figured, "what's the harm?" At the same time, he had no plans to share that particular part of his Houston experience with Kristin once he returned to Tuskegee. And as it turned out, their relationship had taken off quickly and had become so serious that they had been married before the end of Christmas break.

Winston's dinner invitation had been extended at the last minute, after his mentor unexpectedly ended up with an extra ticket. It had been a highly sought after event held in honor of a former astronaut, who had become an influential lobbyist for NASA and was very important to the program. Out of all the interns that summer, Winston had been one of only three to have the opportunity to attend. Before he had left Tuskegee for the summer, his engineering advisor had warned him in no uncertain terms that he was not to decline *any* social invitations extended to him, unless it conflicted with some life or death situation.

So, being a typical male college student he had come up with the bright idea that he could do both. He decided he would keep his date with the young woman and after explaining the situation to her, he suggested that they get together earlier than planned. He had been thrown way off guard when she showed up at his apartment with pot, of all things. But not wanting to seem lame, he had impulsively taken a few hits off the joint she had pulled from her purse as soon as she got there. He immediately regretted doing it; he had tried pot a few times before and quickly concluded that it wasn't the thing for him. He found that his thoughts would become too unfocused when he was high, and that wasn't a good combination for his math or engineering classes.

But he figured that since he wasn't taking any classes that summer and all the interns had been given that Friday afternoon off – what the heck? He and the young woman had ended up spending several hours together, smoking pot and relaxing intimately as they listened to Pharaoh Sanders and the Last Poets on the stereo system he had bought after getting to Houston. Only college students in the '60s and '70s had the opportunity to experience life with the kind of abandon that Winston and his summer friend enjoyed that afternoon.

For a very narrow period of time after rigid sexual standards in America had been relaxed, his generation had it all. It was a time before life-threatening sexually transmitted diseases had become widespread, when there had been openness and honesty in communication and interactions among the country's young adults. The arriving energy of the new Age of Aquarius had also begun to break down racial, gender-specific, physical, religious, and political barriers that were firmly held in place until that time.

Winston's brief encounter with the young woman had been without any deception or promises. They had simply enjoyed a few hours of pleasure to pass the time. But his head had still been buzzing from the pot as he rubbed a generous amount of body oil on his hands and across his hair before heading out the door. The pungent scent of the oil completely covered any lingering aroma of the distinctive-smelling marijuana, but when he arrived at the hotel Winston was still as high as a kite. He began having paranoid thoughts as he waited in line for his table assignment, praying he would be seated at an inconspicuous table near the rear of the ballroom.

His anxieties had grown exponentially when he realized the host was leading him to a large table in the front, close to the podium. Winston had been seated directly across from his NASA mentor. He recognized several VIP guests who were seated at the same table from television broadcasts and from their orientation films at the beginning of the summer. And a new well of apprehension had risen in the pit of his stomach when he glanced down at the table and saw all the silverware and dishes that were on it. They were arranged in small clusters and at different angles all around the table. To make matters worse, the table itself was a bit overcrowded and it was next to impossible for him to know where his table setting ended and his seat-mates' settings began.

But thanks to all of his mother's prodding as he was growing up, the tableware wasn't completely unfamiliar to him. He realized he might be able to wing it if he could only calm himself down. After he began engaging in what he hoped to be casual conversation with the people seated near him, he finally relaxed a little and only prayed that he wasn't rambling. Everyone at the table seemed to have a million things to say to him after his mentor introduced him as an engineering student from Tuskegee.

By the time their meal was served, he had what his friends always referred to as the "mass munchies." Thanks to the pot, it had become extremely difficult for him to concentrate on the conversation going on around the table too. It had taken every ounce of his willpower to wait until after everyone else had picked up his or her silverware before he began eating himself. His strategy had been to observe which pieces were being used to eat which dishes, and then follow suit himself.

Miraculously, he had almost pulled off the entire evening without a hitch. His one error had been a major one and could well have been a fatal blow to his career. Near the end of the evening, he had mistakenly taken a dish of sculptured butter that had been left on the table, for after-dinner mints.

He had already popped one of the rosebud-shaped pieces of butter into his mouth before he realized his blunder. But fortunately, the lingering effects of the marijuana hadn't kept his brain from functioning at that critical moment, and he quickly recovered. After the butter finally registered with his taste buds, Winston had faked a quick cough and discreetly captured it in his napkin as he covered his mouth, without attracting too much attention.

That experience had been the main reason he actually appreciated Charlotte's willingness to teach his kids how to handle themselves at a formal dinner. He only hoped pot wouldn't be involved as a factor with either of his children. Unfortunately though, Charlotte had also taken his acquiescence on the dinner setting thing as a go-ahead for her to have free reign in changing anything in the loft that she saw fit to change. Apparently, she also thought it meant that she didn't need to consult him first *or* consider his children. The more he thought about it, he wouldn't have been surprised if Malaya had been consumed by anxiety that she might accidentally knock something expensive over and break it. Or she might have been stressed about appearing foolish as she tried to eat their elaborate meal.

But it was still hard for him to dismiss the nagging feeling that it was something else altogether. His daughter's friend finally began to relax a bit more after they had finished dinner that night that she stayed over, but it still seemed to Winston that she was only jumpy when she was around him. He found that hard to understand because Malaya had known him for years – as long as she had known his daughter. When he came into Celeste's room to kiss her goodnight that first night, as he always did, Malaya had seemed petrified that he might kiss her goodnight, too.

There was something about the whole thing that bothered him in a way that he couldn't quite put his finger on. He remembered Kristin saying Malaya's mother had remarried shortly before the two girls met. For a while, he wondered whether her behavior had anything to do with her stepfather. He stood outside his daughter's bedroom door for a few minutes, thinking the worst. But in the end, he had decided it was probably only his imagination.

Chapter 17

Stepping Out on Faith

"*T*he truth of the matter is that when our ancestors were forced across the Atlantic in chains, they could hardly have imagined the fate waiting for them on the other side. They likely would have been crammed inside the hull of a ship for weeks, one that had been used to carry countless other kidnapped Africans all over the world. Many witnessed suicides, failed insurrections, and the abuse of their fellow captives during their journey. Those captives being held would have seen both men and women thrown overboard to waiting sharks that encircled the ship that carried them, still with no idea of where they were being taken.

"For most, their final destination in America would have been a plantation slave yard. They would have arrived not knowing the language of their captors, though they must have immediately recognized their compatriots in the strange new place and even their tribal enemies. They would have known them by their physical features, though it must have presented an odd sight in their unfamiliar dress. And the newcomers themselves must have seemed quite strange to the majority in the slave yard, especially those whose parents, grandparents, and even great-grandparents had been born there. Because they had just arrived from the Motherland, the novice would have been alarmed to see that children were no longer being raised in the ways of their elders. The people they saw would likely have still practiced many of the ancient traditions, like making soaps and items they needed for their daily use. But strangely, they would no longer have understood their own language.

"The convention of taking one's rivals as captives had been practiced in Africa and other countries for centuries, long before the Europeans began selling African slaves to the American colonists. These barbaric traditions have been well documented throughout the ages, such as in the Old Testament of the Hebrew Bible, as it was translated for the third time from Greek translated texts into English. The translation was undertaken and supervised by the Church of England between 1604 and 1611, though it was attributed to King James. The practice of enslavement is also referenced in the direct English translation of scriptures from the Aramaic language; likely the language spoken by Jesus, and still widely spoken today in the same region where his ministry took place.

"Yet the African slave trade, as a practice, was unparalleled in its lack of humanity. In America, the cruelty shown to those who were victimized..."

Kristin raised her head from the paper she had been reading and stretched. She lowered it again until her chin touched the top of her chest; she began inching her head slowly to the left, until it had reached its beginning mark. She then rolled her head in the opposite direction until she had made another complete circle. She repeated the exercise once more before forcing her attention back to the paper before her. So far, it was as brilliant as all the others that Kioni had written for her classes, but she found herself so distracted that it was difficult to focus long enough to finish it. His was the last of the American History papers she had to read, and it would also be the last paper she would ever read at Hunter University.

She had saved Kioni's paper for last, as she usually did whenever he was in one of her classes. As soon as she was finished with it, the only thing left for her to do was to turn in her grades. In exactly two weeks graduation would be over and her teaching career would be officially ended.

It only took five minutes before she became distracted again. She had found herself absently looking around the room that had been her office for the past fifteen years, thinking about all that had transpired over the last year in particular. It had taken nearly six months for her to fully recover from her near-fatal health challenge, a fluke that had resulted from a routine fast. She had been on the same fast many times in the past with no issues whatsoever. But this time, she had taken it upon herself to vary the simple recipe for the Master Cleanse she had embarked on, hoping it would start her off spiritually-grounded for her new life in Ghana. The fast had quickly morphed into a calamitous crisis in a way that she would never have imagined. The excessive amount of cayenne she had consumed within a short time frame had caused her body to undergo an accelerated cleanse with a drastic and rapid weight reduction. Within seven days, she had lost more than twenty-five pounds. And with that weight loss had been a loss of all the nutrients in her body that were so critical to its functioning. She had also lost valuable muscle tissue that her organs depended on for just about everything, including her ability to think.

But in retrospect, the spiritual experience had far overshadowed her body's physical crisis, though she still lacked words to adequately describe it. She thought back to how alarmed her friend Niyla had been on seeing her diminished size that first day that she came by to check on her; so much so that Niyla had been unable to process Kristin's attempt to give voice to her experience. She had described it as a re-birthing and that was exactly the way it felt after the experience was over. She had shed a good portion of weight during the episode and damaged several vital organs, but the near-tragic incident had left Kristin with a sense of newness and peaceful contentment. It had left her with an assurance that she was now in-step with her life's purpose, and with a renewed confidence about the underbelly of Black America; that they too could be reborn – in Africa.

Kristin still didn't have a clear roadmap of how she would accomplish it, but now she felt certain that she would. She had decided to step out on faith and let the Universe direct her path. And as her direction came more fully into focus, she felt her body begin to stabilize and mend itself; though it had still taken months before her healing was complete.

It had been her determination to get back to her classes that had motivated Kristin to consult with Dr. Malcolm and begin acupuncture therapy. Going to see him had initially been a compromise with Niyla, who had still pressed her about going to see a western physician once they saw that her crisis had passed. Dr. Malcolm was a tall former chemist who reminded Kristin of a big smiling teddy bear that first day he opened his office door to greet her. He had a gentle non-invasive energy about him that had put her at ease immediately. And as she left her appointment, he had given her the first of many bear hugs to come. She knew instantly that she had made the right decision in coming to see him. He was spiritually conscious and well-versed in eastern holistic medicine. She knew he understood why she had chosen to fast in the first place, so she didn't have to spend unnecessary energy in defending her rationale to him. He also understood that the thought of Niyla taking her to the emergency room, after Kristin began to show signs of impending shock, had terrified her more than anything else.

But as soon as she began describing the excessive amount of cayenne pepper she had added to the mixture of water, fresh lemon juice, and grade B organic maple syrup, Dr. Malcolm had immediately raised his eyebrows. He confirmed what several of her friends from yoga class had already told her: cayenne pepper was an *extremely* powerful cleansing agent. Although it could be safely used to loosen particles of waste from the walls of her colon, he had stressed that caution should always be taken.

But instead, Kristin had indiscriminately shaken very large amounts of cayenne into the lemonade mixture she drank exclusively everyday, far exceeding the amount prescribed in the Master Cleanse recipe. She told Dr. Malcolm that she had done it in the hopes of boosting the energy that was also derived from the spice. But he had countered that the overdose of cayenne was likely the catalyst for everything she had experienced after her seventh day of fasting – including her haywire emotions that came later. The excessive amount of pepper had apparently gone to work all over her body simultaneously. Although Kristin would never regret having had the hideous accumulation of putrefied food expelled from her body during her ordeal, the intensity of the cleanse had almost been too severe for her to sustain.

During his initial consultation, Dr. Malcolm asked her questions that she never expected, including her sexual preference. He explained that the practice of Chinese medicine was much more detailed than was western medicine. The body system was considered as a whole in determining the proper course of treatment; one that would balance her yin and yang energies and restore her good health. He examined her tongue, eyes, lips, and nails carefully; he used tiny sticks of burning incense to test her fingers and toes for heat sensitivity. With this relatively brief assessment, he had been given all the information he needed to determine which needles to place on which specific areas of her body during her treatments.

Her reflexes had been far too slow on that first visit, so she hadn't been quick enough to decline his demonstration of how painless the needles would be. Before she could muster a reaction, Dr. Malcolm had already tapped the first long thin needle into her ankle and she never felt it at all. Had she not been looking directly at it, she would never have known the needle was there.

Over the weeks that followed, the needles energized the proper functioning of her organs that had been damaged during her rapid weight loss, resulting in protein deficiency. As soon as she began her weekly treatments, she felt a boost toward her recovery right away, though it had still been a long road to travel. Every system of her body had been affected by the loss of protein; so much had been purged after her fast took a wrong turn that she had virtually been left with a blank slate. As a result, she became even more conscious of consuming the most nutritious foods available, as she slowly began to regain her appetite. Within only a few months of acupuncture therapy, she had recovered a good portion of her physical strength. And by the beginning of the winter quarter, Kristin felt that her brain was functioning at a high enough level again for her to resume teaching.

It had only been a few weeks after returning to Hunter that her friend and business partner had phoned her with news of finding a travel agency for sale. And even more surprising, it was the same agency she and her friends had used on their first trip to Ghana. The owner was an older gentleman who had owned the business for the past forty years. He had decided to sell it, Solomon told her, so he could move north to live closer to his family. Kristin couldn't have been any happier with the news. She had prayed for clear direction as she continued her recovery; she decided to surrender her very determined will and wait for the universe to point her in the right direction. Her friend's phone call had been the bread crumb she had been waiting for; she could already envision how Heavenly Travel would fit into her long-range plans to bring transformation to the underbelly.

She quickly confirmed her interest in buying the agency and Solomon immediately went about negotiating a purchase price. Everything else had just fallen into place. It was during these negotiations that Kristin first learned that Solomon's father was a paramount chief in the Ashanti Region, the highest rank in the Akan chieftaincy. It had been later still that she realized how powerful her new business partner's family was in Ghana, and that Solomon's father was among the King's closest confidants. The signs the Creator gave her couldn't have been more clear, as far as she was concerned. She could hardly sleep once they began negotiating for the travel agency; partially due to her anticipation, and partly because she was *positive* that their new business venture would lead her toward her destiny.

They finally settled on an excellent purchase price that included the previous owner's client list, a small office building with furnishings, and all the equipment they would need. And all of it, according to Solomon was of excellent quality. They had also drawn up a formal partnership agreement

126

at the same time. Kristin was to retain greater control over the agency's operations; in exchange, Solomon would receive the greater share of net profits. They had faxed paperwork back and forth for weeks until everything had finally been ironed out. Once she arrived in Ghana, her signature would be all that was required for them to make their partnership official and finalize the purchase of Heavenly Travel.

But Kristin still had mounds of things that needed her attention before she would be ready to leave the U.S., and only three weeks left to do them. She had written out a list of tasks that were associated with her house. There were friends that she had to see before she left and she also had social obligations with people she had worked with at Hunter for fifteen years. Over the past few weeks, her time during evenings and weekends had been taken in fulfilling these invitations. And in the meantime, her to-do list had become so long that it seemed impossible for her to finish everything she had to do in time.

She would have to make time for Celeste too before she left, so that they could do something special together. The poor thing had taken the news of her leaving much harder than Kristin had ever imagined. She had always thought of Celeste as being her daughter, but she never knew the child felt the same closeness until she told her she was leaving again for Ghana. Kristin wanted to reassure her that she could always come for a visit whenever Trazi came over, but she knew she would have to talk to Winston about it first. Celeste was, after all, *his* daughter so Kristin couldn't very well make plans for his thirteen-year-old without consulting him—especially for a trip out of the country. Her only consolation in leaving Celeste was that Angela seemed to be finally pulling herself together. Hopefully, with her gone, the mother-daughter relationship that everyone wanted them to have could be finally be formed, so a bond could be established between them at long last.

Although Kristin and Winston had been divorced for nearly fifteen years now, and he had married two other women since they broke up, there had amazingly been nothing that had ever changed in either of their hearts. They rarely saw each other after Kristin returned to the States from her two-year teaching assignment in Kumasi. But she had finally reconciled her disappointment in his failure to tell her about his plans to re-marry.

She had been relieved of that burden unexpectedly one morning before she boarded her plane back to the States. She sat on a hilltop outside the women's quarters of the faculty compound in Kumasi, taking in the panoramic view of mountains in the distance after her meditation. A clear knowingness had penetrated her idle reverie, though she had been reflecting on the beauty of the scenery with no other thoughts in mind. In the cool stillness of the morning, Kristin had immediately known in her heart that Winston only married Charlotte to try to purge himself of the guilt he had carried for over ten years about Angela. He had to marry Charlotte while she was still out of the country, Kristin suddenly realized, because he wouldn't have been able to do it otherwise. That had been the real reason he hadn't come to her, as he had with Angela, to tell her of his plans to remarry. He wouldn't have been able to pull it off, as he had with Angela, and had been deliberately rude in hopes of creating distance between them.

The second that thought came to her mind, Kristin recognized the truth in it that explained everything. Winston had probably been scared to death about what would happen between the two of them when she came back from Ghana—just as she had been on hearing the news about his divorce from Angela. His main concern, she knew, was Celeste. Kristin knew Winston was probably worried sick about how his daughter might react if she found out how the two of them really felt about each other. Above all else, he wanted to always make sure his daughter never thought badly of him.

Kristin had watched her ex-husband wrestle with his guilt over Angela for years. He held himself responsible for everything that had happened with her—all the problems she had during her pregnancy, and especially her lack of an attachment to their daughter. Kristin knew that every time Winston looked at *her*, he was reminded of the night that he had completely lost control of himself. Knowing him, he had likely decided that if he hadn't been so distracted by her, he might have somehow taken better care of Angela. His grandfather taught him that a man should always remain in control of his feelings; seeing Kristin only reminded him of that failure.

She had asked herself on more than one occasion whether Angela might have picked up on their true feelings for each other. The two had never tried to hide that they were still close from the time that Winston and Angela started dating. His second wife had always been aware that he frequently spent time with Kristin at her house. No one could have been prepared for the lack of bonding between Angela and her baby daughter. But Kristin was afraid to even consider that she and Winston might have played a role in it. Angela's doctors had hoped her extreme hormonal imbalance would correct itself after she delivered, but unfortunately she had gone into a post-partum depression that soon morphed into a variety of emotional challenges; finally ending with alcoholism.

As soon as Kristin got back to the States from Kumasi, the early morning message she had received from the Universe about Winston and Charlotte was confirmed. Since she hadn't seen her son or Celeste in over two years, Kristin had gone directly to Winston's loft from the airport as soon as her plane landed. A distinct charge of electricity passed between them in the close quarters of the foyer as soon as he opened the front door. They both felt it immediately and quickly averted their eyes. Her ex-husband's behavior had given him away even more, as soon as they found themselves in the same room together. Kristin sensed a powerful struggle going on between his desire to rush over and hold her tightly in his arms, as Trazi and Celeste did, or move as far away from her as he could. Neither option was appropriate for the circumstances, and she had felt his anxiety as he struggled to appear unaffected the whole time she was there.

And it had taken only one look at Charlotte to convince Kristin that her marriage to Winston wouldn't last long. Kristin guessed that they had little in common and it wouldn't be long before her ex-husband began thinking of his new bride as just another pretty face who happened to live with him.

But what then? Would Winston just marry someone else after he finally had enough of Charlotte?

Kristin had never seen much benefit in trying to fool herself, much less anyone else. As much as she wished it weren't true, she was very much aware that she was still in love with Winston. She had kept her distance from him as much as possible in the three years she was back in the States. She tried to do it discreetly, without calling attention to the silent dance they always did whenever they were around each other.

Her health challenge had been a blessing because it gave her an opportunity to learn what she valued most. She would always love Winston, but she was committed to the urgings of her Spirit. Not even her feelings for him would keep her from doing what she now felt she had been born to do.

Since Trazi had joined the Navy and was no longer living in Washington, a permanent move to Ghana wouldn't make much of a difference where he was concerned. As for Celeste, she was still searching for an answer. Kristin kept wondering whether the role she had been destined to play in the young girl's life had now been fulfilled, since she was already a thirteen-year-old.

She had begun to wonder whether it might be time to force her emotional bond with Winston's daughter to loosen.

Chapter 18

That Midnight Plane to Ghana

*K*ristin had to force her eyes back to the evenly spaced lines of Kioni's paper yet again. She recalled being pleasantly surprised at the beginning of the quarter to see his name on her registration list. It had been the fourth time for the electrical engineering major, who was quite an original thinker and seemed to have an unquenchable thirst for knowledge. Kioni had been the kind of student who had inspired her to teach history in the first place. He was masterful at fitting all the independent pieces of the world history puzzle together. His understanding of the intricacies involved in international politics had also continued to impress her. Whenever he enrolled in one of her classes, he had always helped push her class discussions up a notch.

Kioni had challenged Kristin to stay on top of her game; he was one of the few students who understood that the course syllabus didn't represent all there was to learn about a subject. It had been obvious to her that he had given a great deal of thought to each of the final essays he turned in each quarter. He was quite creative and his writing style had immediately caught her attention. His World Civilization paper during the previous quarter, for instance, had been a thought-provoking discourse on the nature of aggression. He had based his theory primarily on population size and geographic landscaping, as he explored what he called the "natural tendency toward aggression" among the majority population of some specific countries.

He wrote that a country's propensity toward violence could be correlated to the density of its population, and to the availability or lack of natural resources where the majority lived. He noted that there had been certain areas of Europe with a history of consistently combative behavior. He contrasted these with other regions of the world, whose majority population exhibited a comparatively milder demeanor. Kioni concluded that the difference in behavior between the two was the life-sustaining living environment of the second group. It sharply contrasted with areas where the first group lived - an environment of rocky and barren land.

He had even cited exceptions to his own theory, noting people living in highly populated areas of Asia and India. Kioni theorized that it was their customs that had effectively stemmed much of the violent and aggressive behavior that might have otherwise plagued their culture. Many of their rituals included the use of opiates, he asserted, that resulted in a relative docility of the people caused by the effects of the drugs. A natural climate of peace and spirituality, he stated, was most often attributed to these overpopulated areas as a result. Since each successive generation was being taught to adopt the same practices, no aggressive behavior was being passed through their genes to their descendants.

In his paper, Kioni asserted that in contrast, those people who had been forced to compete for survival had only become more and more assertive over time. They developed an innate aggression, with associated fears resulting from it that effectively circumvented any moral questioning of their plans to go out and "conquer" the world.

To support his theory that aggression had been a learned behavior, he offered a conclusion drawn by an internationally acclaimed geneticist, after examining the mitochondrial DNA recovered from the remains of "African Eve." The scientist had determined that modern man originated in Africa hundreds of thousands of years ago, in a naturally supportive environment that easily sustained life. The discovery of African Eve predated all prior evidence of early man, and Kioni's paper cited findings that had been made by noted anthropologists to support his theory, as well.

There had been many well-respected scientists who surmised that a prehuman species of man had migrated across the Sahara and into Europe, thousands of years before *modern* man's discovery of a migration path from Africa. The earlier migrants to Europe had struggled, Kioni noted, in a much harsher environment that didn't easily support their survival. This group evolved into Neanderthal man over a period of time. Their aggressive nature had been likely formed, he concluded, over thousands of years as they adapted to their new environment of scarcity. On the other hand, their counterparts left behind in northeast Africa, had proceeded in their evolution as a species in an environment more akin to the Garden of Eden.

Cro-Magnon man, however, the first modern Homo sapiens to migrate from Africa into Europe, eventually interbred with the Neanderthals who had still inhabited parts of Europe when they arrived. The Neanderthals' innate aggressive behavior persisted for generations, even after their basic survival became less tenuous. Political alliances eventually formed across Europe through strategic marriages between the two groups; and the aggression in the Neanderthals' bloodline, Kioni asserted, continued to be passed on to their descendants through genetic memory. He argued that their inherited traits of combativeness desensitized them to any moral concerns about the unprovoked crusades of violence they organized and perpetrated all over the world.

❋❋❋

Kristin realized she had lost her focus again. She had wasted more valuable time daydreaming, in spite of her determination to give Kioni's paper her full attention. Annoyed with herself, she got up to stand next to a small window—one of two located in the spacious room. Hers was one of the largest offices in the old academic building with a nice view overlooking the side lawn, and the soccer fields across the street beyond it. She had shared the space with a pleasant, middle-aged professor who was new to the History Department that year. That quarter had been the first time she had ever been asked to share a space at Hunter, but their schedules had never coincided and they had rarely been in the office at the same time.

She stood on her tiptoes and stretched toward the ceiling, reaching her arms up as high as they would go. She decided she would indulge herself a few moments longer and noticed for the first time that there were early daffodils mixed in among the thick brown grass below. The flowers saluted the afternoon sunshine that fell across their bright yellow blooms to energize them for the coming spring.

Without realizing it, Kristin's thoughts began to drift again—this time to the first trip she had taken to Ghana six years earlier. She had a hard time believing how much had happened since then. She had hardly known when they organized the trip that she would end up teaching college in Ghana for two years, or that she would some day go back there for good.

She had stayed up until well after midnight before that first flight to Ghana, determined to cram as many school supplies and children's clothing in her luggage as she could fit. Their travel agency told them in advance how much they would be appreciated in Ghana. Kristin had traveled with seven other women, all friends or former coworkers who had been members of a small book club that she and Niyla organized. A much stronger bond had formed between the women during their fourteen days in Ghana, as they explored the country and their possible roots there together.

Another friend from Hunter had recommended their travel agency, whose name they had all thought was funny when they first heard it. An informal appointment had been arranged to give the agency a feel for their primary interest in visiting the country, as a starting point in planning their itinerary. After all their questions had been answered, a schedule was drafted for their approval based on the consensus of the group. Before all was said and done, they had been very impressed by the efficiency of "Heavenly Travel" and by everyone they came in contact with at the agency. There had been many personal touches and after they had signed their service agreement, Kristin and her friends had little else to concern themselves with other than what to pack for the trip.

The agency had really turned out to be a piece of Heaven because practically everything needed to get them ready to travel had been taken care of for them. Their agent had filled out their passport and visa applications, and even coordinated their appointments to get their required and elected travel immunizations. Everyone had been sent a list of travel-friendly snacks to bring along too, that they could have on hand for a convenient bite in the early morning hours before their bodies adjusted to the six-hour time difference in Ghana. They were told about bug sprays they could buy that would be effective, but didn't contain deet or other harmful chemicals. They were sent a list of gadgets from the travel agency to consider bringing, along with an explanation for their use and suggestions on several sporting-goods stores where the items could likely be found. There were other specific things they were urged to consider buying too, since they planned to travel in rural areas of the country.

Heavenly Travel had arranged their transportation to the airport, and also sent a van to meet their return flight two weeks later. They sent enough vans to comfortably transport everyone, along with their purchases, home.

Kristin could still remember how powerful her emotions had been on that first trip, as though it were yesterday. She had paid honor to her ancestors, although she had never known their names. She witnessed a commanding family structure in Ghana that had been at least similar to the one that her ancestors had been forced to leave behind. She and her friends had learned all about the country's matrilineal line of descent. They discovered African women who had been warriors and it had strengthened their pride as African-American women.

They had boarded a Swiss aircraft in Zurich for the final leg of the trip. Kristin craned her neck to take in the snow-covered Alps they flew over, before the plane glided across the Mediterranean Sea into Africa. They had their first glimpse of the Motherland as they flew over the expansive Sahara Desert. The pilot kept the plane at a much lower altitude once they had reached the desert, to mitigate the intense heat of the sun and temperatures that could reach well over one hundred and thirty degrees. The sun's rays added a reddish tinge to the mountains of sand that seemed to stretch into eternity to Kristin. She leaned against the small plane window that was warm to the touch, to take in the sweeping view. From time to time, she spotted an oasis that interrupted the rippling flow of dunes, linked by a solitary winding road that went on for miles and miles. She had stared down in awe at the world's largest desert and then the reality began to sink in: she had finally made it to Africa!

Kristin had always expected that her first journey to the Motherland would be memorable. She had just never imagined that the impetus for making the pilgrimage would have partly been an effort to put distance between herself and Winston. She had finally decided to stop beating herself up for not being able to move forward with her life. Still, she had hoped that her time away from D.C. and Winston would give her a better perspective on making a new start. After all, at the time of her trip they had been divorced for close to ten years. By then, she realized, she didn't want to grow old by herself. She had become keenly aware of how much time she had already lost in her failure to shut off feelings for her ex-husband.

But by the time she boarded the van that took them to Dulles Airport, Kristin's focus had shifted entirely. She had become fully engaged in their trip, though she still had no idea of the depths that her spiraling emotions would reach in the two weeks they were gone.

Her whole body felt stiff from the long flight as their plane finally touched down at Kotoka International Airport in Accra. She had carefully made her way down a narrow set of steps outside the plane; by the time she reached the ground, her legs had been shaking from her excitement. She turned around in a full circle on the runway and lifted her head gratefully to the unspoiled sky above. With tears in her eyes, she had given thanks to the Creator that her dreams of going to Africa one day had been realized. Then, she spontaneously knelt down to run her hand across the tarmac before hurrying toward the terminal to catch up with the others.

Everyone had been deeply moved by signs being held up all over the bustling airport that read, "Welcome Home." Kristin was met with smiles that were warm and somehow familiar, like she was meeting distant relatives for the first time at a family reunion. It had been a feeling of instant intimacy with people who, in reality, were total strangers. But one glimpse at the no-nonsense immigration desk ahead of them had also made everyone grateful that they had thought to hire a top-rate travel agency, rather than going it alone.

Maat, the smiling-faced manager of the local tour company who had arranged their itinerary, was on hand to greet them personally just inside the terminal. He had already prearranged their entry into the country; as soon as they had claimed their luggage, they were whisked through immigration and customs in no time at all. He then led them out of the airport and to a luxury bus that had been parked a short distance from the terminal. They waited as their luggage was loaded onto the bus, for two small groups who would join them, all passengers on the same Swiss flight that arrived daily, and who would travel with them around the country. They were served chilled bottles of water and small cups of mango and pineapple juice, to gratefully refresh themselves as they waited.

Everyone bubbled with excitement as they checked into the 4-star La Palm Beach Hotel that rivaled the popular LaBodi Beach Hotel next door. Both establishments, located directly on the Gulf of Guinea, had excellent reputations for the service and comfort they provided for their guests. Their hotel offered an assortment of first-class restaurants with culinary delights to suit a range of tastes, including pizza and Chinese fare. A gift shop, just off the lobby area, carried a host of beautiful and surprisingly inexpensive local art and jewelry. The exchange rate at the time had been 12,000 cedis to one U.S. dollar. Their dollars gave them an unbelievable advantage while shopping, and they knew that everything they saw would have been priced much higher back in the States.

There were several Olympic-sized swimming pools on the hotel property, all connecting to a large swim-up bar in the center. Four guest rooms were built into each of the cabana-styled buildings that they were assigned to stay in, all scattered among the beautifully sculptured landscape. An alluring fountain formed the centerpiece of each of the circular buildings, creating a tranquil sitting area for guests. The buildings' thatched roofs had been woven from banana leaves and provided more than ample protection from the West African sun.

Kristin and her traveling companions soon came across gigantic versions of the same houseplants that many of them grew in their homes. They explored the expansive hotel property and discovered that the oversized vegetation also provided shelter for large iguanas that darted underneath their mammoth leaves, in an effort to avoid the guests.

It wasn't until after they had left the hotel on their first tour of the city the next day that Kristin's euphoria began to diminish. They had all wanted to be shown what someone from their group referred to as "the real Ghana," and not just the tourist attractions and popular markets. Maat, who had been educated in the United States, was more than happy to comply with their wishes. He knew well the contrast that his country presented to its western visitors and he was encouraged that they wanted to see it all.

They had driven past hundreds and hundreds of lean-tos that were pitched along the sides of the road as shelter. But seeing how many people lived in the shacks had begun to wear on Kristin after a time. The streets that day had been lined with throngs of ebony-colored people who were going about their daily lives. At first, she couldn't keep herself from seeing everything through her own western-tinted eyes. She had been distracted by the glaring lack of material wealth, all too evident as they rode through areas of the city where the majority of people lived and worked.

It had grown increasingly difficult for her to remain upbeat, as they went from area to area; there were so many people who seemed in need. After a few hours, they stopped at a local restaurant for a midday meal that had been specially prepared for them. By the time they were ready to be seated, Kristin had become overcome with sadness. Her mind remained stuck on something Maat had told them earlier; that very few of the people they saw had what she and her friends considered to be the necessities in life: plumbing, electricity, and refrigeration. Kristin had been so disturbed by all they had seen that she deliberately sat apart from the group so she wouldn't dampen everyone else's mood. She had struggled to hold back her tears as her mind replayed scene after scene from their tour that day.

In the end, she lost her battle and began to cry softly as everyone else was served what looked and smelled like a wonderful meal. There was grilled fish; fufu, a West African staple that could be made from a variety of vegetables, and had a consistency of mashed potatoes; kelewele, fried plantains that were sprinkled with a combination of spices; kokonte, or cassava chips; and palm nut soup.

From time to time her friends had looked in her direction with empathy shown on their faces. No one had attempted to console her, though, and no one asked why she was crying. They already knew the answer. They had all been affected by what they had seen on their tour of the city that morning.

But over the next couple of days she and her group had finally begun to adjust to their environment. From that point on, all Kristin had been able to see was the deeply spiritual nature of the people of Ghana. She had sensed their kindness and their good-heartedness in her interactions with them, as they rode around visiting place to place. She began to see them and not just their circumstances; and as she looked closer into their faces she began to recognize them. One woman in a small market they had stopped in could very well have been one of her aunts, there was such a strong resemblance to Kristin's mother. Another woman that they had seen walking along the road once, who had balanced a stack of firewood on her head, was a dead ringer for one of her cousins. The owner of a shop they visited in Kumasi looked just like the father of one of her friends back in Tuskegee. It was then that Kristin's heart began to tell her that the Ghanaian people were *her* people. And after that, she had found herself absorbing as much of their familiar, yet unfamiliar, culture as possible.

Before leaving for other parts of the country, their group had visited a lavish tribute erected in honor of Kwame Nkrumah, the country's liberator from British rule and its first president. There were beautifully designed brass sculptures and fountains all over the grounds, with pools of water that flowed from large brass vessels that were connected by sparkling streams of water. As they browsed through the monument's library and archives Kristin's thoughts turned to Dr. Keenan, who had first made her aware that Nkrumah had been well-respected among world leaders. There were many photographs of him taken in cordial settings with his contemporary European, Chinese, and Soviet heads of state, displayed throughout the halls of both buildings.

Nkrumah had beseeched his compatriots to secure their country's economic future through industrial development, after he had led the successful rebellion against colonialism. Maat echoed sentiments Dr. Keenan had voiced in class, expressing the younger man's own frustrations. The two men agreed that Ghana might well have traveled the road to recovery from colonialism on a much higher note, had Nkrumah's vision been fully realized.

After leaving the monument, Maat led the group to the outskirts of a gated more affluent community. He told them that he didn't want them to leave Ghana with the impression that it was populated entirely by "have-nots," in terms of material wealth. Strangely, knowing that there were many people living comfortably did little to ease Kristin's mind. Rather, it left her in a state of confusion about the enormous disparity of wealth. In comparison, it seemed greater than the economic inequalities in American cities like Dallas, Texas, with South Dallas communities in sharp contrast to its South Fork-type residences.

Only after she had returned home did Kristin fully appreciate the thoughtfulness that had gone into creating her group's travel itinerary. They had left Ghana on a more pleasant note and with a much broader perspective of the country than when they arrived. Maat had earned his degree at Lincoln University in Pennsylvania, which coincidentally was Nkrumah's Alma Mater. The younger man was well-versed on Ghana's history and he had given them interesting insights into the country's economic, social, and political challenges. Kristin could feel his frustration as he talked about foreign corporations that still profited from his country's natural wealth. Their centuries-long business associations made it possible for the economic stronghold that was created during colonialism to continue, in many cases, still with little benefit to the people.

Maat's eyes had been troubled as he described the cycle in which the country's bountiful produce was shipped away every day. It was processed, he said, stripped of nutrients and then shipped back in aluminum cans for his countrymen to consume. After hearing that, Kristin had an even greater respect for the vendors she would see as they traveled around the countryside. They would set up their tables of fruits and vegetables for sale every day, taking great pride in their artistic symmetrical displays. They did it knowing that much of the produce would likely wilt or be spoiled by the heat of the sun, if it wasn't sold and consumed by the day's end.

One phenomenon that Kristin had found fascinating while they were there was the way in which Ghanaian schoolchildren interacted with each other. Her travel group had come across several clusters of children as they drove through small villages and towns. They were neatly clad in their school uniforms and played together with an innocence that she hadn't witnessed since her childhood in Tuskegee. There was an air of chastity about them that made them seem more "childlike" in their physical appearances too. There was no false sense of maturity projected as with many American children. All the young girls wore short-cropped hairstyles; at first glance, their skirts and tiny earrings were the only distinctions separating them visually from their male counterparts.

They giggled and hugged each other as they played and seemed to take genuine pleasure in being together, as children had once done in the United States. Kristin had been amazed at seeing them run in unison with the grace and synchronicity of a flock of birds. She witnessed groups of children who would abruptly change directions as they ran together, in the same way that a line of birds would zigzag across the sky. She had been inspired to see that children who were not physically capable of running themselves, were being pushed alongside their peers in wheelchairs. They had been as much a part of the fun as the other children, giving new meaning to the concept of "mainstreaming" that was once championed in American public schools for children with physical and mental disabilities.

The driver for their tour company had taken great care in maneuvering their luxury bus around Ghana, and his skills had certainly been put to the test on their drive to Kumasi. He had been ever vigilant as he drove along, on the lookout for potholes on the poorly maintained rural roads. In some areas, the holes were so large that young children would spring into action as their bus approached to flap their arms wildly and warn of the impending danger. Kristin had been touched by their goodwill, but when she made a comment to their driver about it later he had explained that the same children would sometimes create the very same potholes, as a means of generating money. He told her that motorists would often reward them with a handful of coins for their gallant action in warning them, and Kristin had been both surprised and amused.

Early on they had all noticed that many of the businesses they saw had similar names to that of their travel agency. They had driven past "God is Love Laundry," "Praise the Lord Barbershop," and many other business names that attested to the Ghanaian people's practice of religion as a way of life.

Kristin had been captivated by the ease with which the women they saw could balance water, bundles of firewood, and other household items on their heads as they walked. It reminded her of Black women she had seen in areas of rural Alabama as a child, carrying buckets of water on their heads from a nearby spring. She also noted that the women on both sides of the ocean would wrap scarves around their heads in much the same manner.

Occasionally, as they drove from one city to the next, they would pass a parcel of land in the beginning stages of house construction. Sometimes there would only be cinder blocks that formed the start of a foundation, but with few other signs of activity. When asked, Maat told them that home mortgages were virtually unheard of in Ghana and in most of West Africa. Families would build as much of a house as they had the money to pay for, he said. The house would remain unfinished until the family had secured additional money needed for the next phase of construction.

Looking out the bus window had almost been like watching a film to Kristin, with the many different scenes they drove past. She had seen old men napping under the shade of trees and some who bathed in iron tubs outside of their houses, to temporarily escape the heat. Occasionally, she had been astonished by what she saw, like groups of people who stood in trenches of stagnant water, often with livestock milling about beside them. Their expressions suggested that they were oblivious to any concerns about health issues in what they were doing, and neither had they seemed in any particular hurry to pass through the sluggish water.

But one of their worst experiences had been after they stopped for gas at a place that was about an hour's drive from Kumasi. They had all agreed immediately that the building where they had been directed to relieve themselves was appalling, to say the least. Kristin had been one of the few who had brought along several skirts to wear, as Heavenly Travel had recommended for trips into the countryside. She had become quite adept at peeing while standing up too. She would discreetly move to a nearby wooded area to use one of the devices that had been recommended and that she had purchased from the sporting goods store—something she had never dreamed of doing. Her friends, who had skipped the agency's rec-ommendations, weren't quite as fortunate. Since none of them had been brave enough to venture too far into the thick woods, the only alternative for those couldn't abide the horrific smells coming from the outside-toilet stalls, was to arrive in Kumasi with very full bladders.

They had gone on a tour of the King's palace and learned the history of Nana Yaa Asantewaa, once Queen Mother of the Asante Confederacy. She had personally led a rebellion against British colonialists who had exiled the King, and she challenged the men of the Asante governing council to arm themselves in defense of the Confederacy. The Queen Mother had chastised the men for having allowed their king to be taken without so much as a fight. And had the British not brought in 14,000 additional hired troops, it was quite possible that Nana Yaa Asantewaa might have been successful. But the Europeans had quashed the Asante nation's last attempt to retain their freedom; the Queen Mother was eventually captured and exiled to the Seychelles Islands, in the Indian Ocean.

Kumasi's international market had been their first experience in a large market since they arrived in Ghana. A few of her travel companions had grown annoyed with Maat for ignoring their pleas to be taken to a large market early on. He had been patient in explaining that they needed more practice at bargaining first; after their experience with the charmingly assertive vendors in Kumasi Market, they all fully appreciated the approach that Maat had opted to take. Everyone had been grateful when he finally came to rescue them from the vendors, and they had all boarded the bus again in relieved laughter. They were surprised to find that they had only been shopping for thirty minutes; after comparing purchases as the bus pulled off, several women confided in embarrassment that they had bought items they had no previous intention of buying.

Some of the women felt guilty that they had even attempted to bargain with the vendors, since the asking price of everything had been so reasonable. Maat had kept assuring them, however, that bargaining was an integral part of their culture and was expected. And sure enough, whenever Kristin tried to give a vendor more cedis than had been asked for, she was always offered more merchandise to account for the extra money given.

Heavenly Travel had informed them before they traveled that the agency would arrange to have anything they bought on their trip, wrapped and shipped back to the States. As a result, nearly everyone spent far more money than they initially planned. Those who bought something that wouldn't fit in their checked luggage, had it shipped separately by an international carrier on the day before their scheduled flight home. By the time they boarded their plane, they had air bill receipts and tracking numbers in hand. All that was required was a signature to receive it, after they had cleared customs and their purchases were delivered to their homes.

Kristin remembered how much she had admired the business acumen of the agency's management back then. That one added convenience had motivated everyone she traveled with to purchase furniture and other larger items, and it provided a much broader support for the local economy at the same time. Now she would be able expand on the previous owner's ideas for Heavenly Travel. Before long, she would see her *own* plans for the agency take shape.

She had always felt strongly that everyone should travel to Africa at least once in his or her lifetime. She especially felt that Black Americans should make the pilgrimage, in much the same way as Muslims are encouraged to visit Mecca when they are financially able to do so. She had planned, once she was behind the helm of Heavenly Travel, to encourage and help make possible for as many Black Americans to make the journey as she could.

Without a doubt, her most arresting memory came after her group had driven south to Elmina and Cape Coast, in the Central Region. With the exception of her meltdown on their first day of touring Accra, everyone had been alive with excitement for the entire trip before heading south. Many of her travel companions had already made plans to have genetic testing done as soon as they were home, so they could find out for certain whether Ghana was the country of origin of one of their ancestors.

But as they approached the heavy wooden doors of the slave castle, the energy level on the entire bus changed. Everyone had grown quiet all at once as they came closer to the entrance of the fortress. None of them knew for certain what they would find behind the massive walls of the old trading fort. They all assumed it would be heinous but they had still been unprepared for the actual experience. Kristin had never considered how much she might be impacted by the slave castles, or what a life altering experience it would become. Like the others, she had only known that she felt compelled to go inside them, and to see whatever there was to be seen.

And it had been an afternoon that she would never forget. They were greeted just inside the entrance by a very polite and soft-spoken young man, who had been assigned as their tour guide. He had taken great care in showing them around the colossal structure, telling them the history of a people who might well have been their own ancestors. The young man was a griot, trained by his ancestors in the traditional role of history keeper. His, was a caste that was responsible for maintaining an oral record of tribal history in the form of music, poetry, or storytelling.

Kristin and her group encircled him and they listened closely as he recited the oral history of that area of Ghana that had been passed down from generation to generation. In a quiet voice, he told them the story of how the slave trade began there. He filled in many of the gaps that Kristin had in understanding how any of it could have ever taken place. The young man began with the story of the first Portuguese merchants to arrive in Ghana; as he spoke, Kristin was made aware of just how much had been left out of the textbooks she had studied on African slavery.

The story he told explained all that had been inconceivable to her before. She had never been able to imagine how such a comparatively small group of people who had generally not been as physically strong as the indigenous people, could have established such a strong foothold. It had become even more puzzling as their bus came closer to the fort and she had seen that it was constructed of heavy stone material.

She had listened closely while their guide described the practice of tribal captivity that existed before the Europeans arrived. After a village was raided by a neighboring one, perhaps as the result of some unsettled dispute or encroachment, the spoils of battle had usually included captives. They had been forced to their captors' villages and into involuntary servitude for a specified period. It had been common for one family member to be offered to another as a servant, or to satisfy a debt.

Many doors of understanding had suddenly been opened for Kristin that day in the Elmina castle. She had learned for the first time that under the traditional system captives had been treated reasonably well, considering the circumstances. After their prescribed period of servitude ended, many of them had chosen to remain in the new village rather than return home. They had been accepted fully into their adopted villages—they were allowed to marry its members and produce offspring.

Their guide had explained to them that not unlike Christopher Columbus, the first Portuguese ship to arrive stumbled onto a water route to Ghana as the ship's captain searched for a new way to get to India, in pursuit of silk and spices. Instead, they had accidently found a more direct source for the alluring gold that was so popular in Europe. He explained that the Portuguese had their first glimpse of the exquisite nuggets in faraway Moroccan markets, in the early 1400's. The gold had been carried north through Ghana and other countries across the Sahara by merchants who were searching for new business opportunities. By accident, the Portuguese merchants had found a much more profitable means of making their fortunes from the gold.

Their countrymen had already begun kidnapping people from Mauritania, a country in the northwestern area of Africa, as early as 1441; forcing many into slavery all across Europe. Ten years later, Pope Nicholas V had issued a papal bull, or charter, that granted the Portuguese King an exclusive right to force non-Catholics into slavery.

Their tour guide also spoke of great clashes that had taken place between the different kingdoms of what is now Ghana, after the Portuguese first arrived on their shores. Some had strongly disagreed with the notion of giving the "toubob," as the Europeans were called, a cordial reception. Many of the kings along the coastline apparently had an instinctive distrust of the Europeans from the start. But there were other tribal leaders who had been entranced by the novel items that the merchants brought with them for trade. Either way, the consequences of their pivotal decision to allow the Portuguese to set up a base of operations, could scarcely have been predicted at the time.

The Elmina trading fort they visited had been built in 1482; during the years that followed, other European countries had joined the Portuguese in setting up trade in that area. Ships from Europe were regularly loaded with ivory, lumber, exotic spices, and precious minerals—most notably gold, for a return trip to Europe. The merchants were allowed to conduct their business unhampered and unharmed in Ghana, although they were vastly outnumbered by the people who were native to the land.

Kristin learned that the Akan had been among the first Ghanaians to trade with the Europeans. The firearms that were bought from Europe provided the Akan with a decided advantage over their local enemies in battle. Not surprisingly, other tribes began to trade with the Europeans over time as well, to gain access to the same powerful weapons.

The guide told their group that the men who had been hired by the trading companies had often brought their families with them to Ghana at first. They soon discovered, however, that the untamed environment of sub-Saharan Africa was not particularly suitable to Europeans. Many of them lost fights against malaria and other tropical diseases, and before long, they began to leave their families behind. Some of the traders took Ghanaian women as their mates instead; many formed lasting attachments to their new African families, who also carried their European surnames. Their group had been surprised to learn that for nearly a century, a mutually beneficial relationship had existed between the Ghanaians and the European merchants.

Even before the first trading fort was built, the Portuguese had begun to take part in the Ghanaian's endemic system of warfare. They purchased and sold African captives to other tribes, in conjunction with their main business of trading for gold and other natural resources. At the time, the Akan nation had been fighting for expansion of its territory; it loosely aligned itself with the Portuguese and other Europeans, to buy captives to work in their gold mines. The bond servants they bought were also used to clear sections of the rainforest for farming.

Finally, their young guide told them it had been the demand for sugarcane that radically changed the dubious relationship between the Europeans and Africans they did business with. The trading forts along the "Gold

Coast" had taken on their more sinister nature as they began meeting the increased demand for workers for the West Indian plantations.

According to accounts passed down for generations, a Portuguese clergyman was credited as being the catalyst for changing the course of history, with an offhanded remark he made. The minister, whose church had been built within the walls of the Elmina fort, was said to have commented on the Africans' strength and resilience. He casually speculated that they would be well suited for the Caribbean sugarcane plantations, especially since the tropical climates were so similar. That observation was said to have sparked a hot topic of conversation among the traders; ultimately, resulting in the inception of the African slave trade.

Hearing her ancestor's history from a West African perspective had been a major revelation for Kristin. She had always assumed local tribesmen had assisted the Europeans in carrying out the slave trade, but she had never understood what might have motivated them. Only that day did she realize that generations of Africans had come to accept the European presence in their homeland. They had traded peacefully with them for decades before the relationship took a fateful turn.

It had become clear as she stood in the middle of the courtyard of Elmina castle that the Africans who played a role in the capture and enslavement of her ancestors, and millions of others, had no way of knowing what would become of them. How could they have known? They had no frame of reference for the kind of inhumanity that was later perpetrated. It would have been impossible for them to even imagine the degree of physical, emotional, and psychological abuse that the captives would ultimately be subjected to.

As soon as the traders realized how much more profitable it was for them to traffic exclusively in humans, rather than in gold, they modified sections of the trading castles to allow them to make the product switch. Kristin and her group were also shown an area of the fort where female captives had been chained periodically. The ships' officers and others important to the trade, had stood on the balcony and selected from among the captured women according to their fancy. An eerie sensation had traveled all across her as they walked up the same stairwell that the chosen female had been forced to walk for the sexual assault awaiting her.

They also went inside one of the dungeons that the captives had been crowded into, as they waited for another ship to return and take them away. Kristin could only imagine the combination of fear, anguish, and defiance they must have felt. Their guide had cautioned them before they entered the cell, because the floors were still moist and slippery. He closed the heavy wooden door behind them so they could get a sense of how it felt for those who had been captured. Kristin had been horrified when she realized they were standing on the DNA of hundreds of thousands of captives who had passed through the castle during the centuries the slave trade operated. The thought had been so disturbing that she had given away the sneakers she purchased for her trip before boarding their plane for home. She couldn't bear the thought of carrying any parts of those who had already been victimized, back to America on the soles of her shoes.

Their guide that day had given them an uncensored account of the many atrocities that had been committed in the castle. They listened in horror as he described the day-to-day activities. His voice was gentle and compassionate, but he had spared no details. As he talked, Kristin noticed a door across the courtyard that had a skull and cross bones painted over the entranceway. She had almost been afraid to hear the guide's explanation of its purpose, and she had braced herself before asking the question. She had been compelled, yet reluctant to hear something worse than they had already seen and heard.

The young guide had paused only a moment before responding. "Many of the captives were determined to escape," he started slowly, "although the majority had been forced into manageable submission in short order. There were extreme measures put in place for those who were considered uncontrollable, and therefore too dangerous to be sold.

"Their fear of reprisal was great so the slavers isolated those particular captives from others, slowly starving them to death. And they waited to be certain that all were dead before venturing inside to remove their bodies.

"But please understand that this wasn't a course of action that was taken easily," the guide had hastened to add. There was concern on his face as he watched the reactions of the horrified group that stood before him.

"Captives were only taken to that cell as a last resort. They were considered to be valuable commodities," he had reminded his astounded audience, "and they were worth nothing to the traders if they were dead."

Once again, Kristin felt weighed down as she confronted the enormity of all they had learned in the trading fort. It became unbearable to think of the cruelty that had taken place within the castle walls. For the second time on their trip, she had been overwhelmed by sadness and despair. She felt as though she would burst apart from her anguish, at the inconceivable inhumanity that had persisted for so long. Tears began to trickle down the sides of her face, bringing her some degree of relief. It wasn't long before the trickle gave way to uncontrollable sobs, as she struggled to wrap her mind around all she had learned. It was hard for her to fathom how anyone could treat another human being as the captives had been treated. The Europeans had handled them with far less care than they managed the gold, lumber, and other items that had been traded in the forts before them.

It was obvious that their guide had grown accustomed to visitors becoming overwrought during his presentation, and he paused politely as several others joined Kristin in her tears. He showed sensitivity and respect for their emotional revulsions at what had occurred in the fort, understanding their difficulty in hearing details they were hypnotically compelled to hear.

It was the moment that Kristin realized the slave castles were the physical connection that unquestionably tied the involuntary Diaspora to native Africa. The young man had been speaking of his relatives and ancestors as he spoke of those who had been held in the castle, but it was possible that he had also been speaking of Kristin's ancestors, as well.

Being in the slave castle had made her finally understand the demons that apparently tormented the English song writer and former slave-ship captain, John Newton. Long after he had declared his repentance for his ways, and had sought atonement and turned to God for salvation, he had continued to play a dastardly role in the enterprise of human slavery. Listening to their guide that afternoon had given Kristin a better insight into the regrets that had surely come later in his life, and had motivated him to write the still-popular spiritual, *Amazing Grace*. Kristin had often tried to imagine the kind of misdeeds that had caused such misery in the songwriter's soul, as she sang it on Sundays as a child at Emmanuel Baptist Church. "Wretch indeed!" It was all she could think of after seeing a small portion of what motivated Newton to write the hymnal.

They had been forced to stoop down in order to enter the final corridor that the captives had been prodded through. The passageway led to the *Door of No Return* and to the waters of the Gulf of Guinea beyond it. The walls of the walkway had been narrowed from their original design, so that only two people could fit crossways in the confined space. Kristin could hear faint sounds coming from the walls still, of the captives crying out. As she moved along the hallway with the others, trembling from the weight of her own emotions, she could sense the sheer terror that must have struck at the hearts of captives' souls. She imagined their outright panic as their eyes adjusted to the bright sunlight beyond the door. It was there that they would have had their first sight of the waiting ships, and would have immediately felt new unanticipated fears about where they were being taken.

Some of the captives had likely been held for upwards of a year in the trading fort, perhaps longer, depending on the ships' schedules and the weather. For many, it had probably taken that long to come to grips with the horrors lying within the castle itself. It must have been clear by then that their captors didn't subscribe to any the traditional protocols of captivity that their ancestors had always followed. Then, they were abruptly confronted with a new reality – they had only been living through a preamble for whatever hell awaited them on the other side of the water.

As she looked out at the waters of the gulf, Kristin had thought back to books she had studied on slavery in America. She realized there had always been a perceptible undertone and quiet inference that the Africans' treatment had somehow been justified. Even still, there remained a subtle suggestion that their lives and those of their children and families were of no consequence. But as she walked down the narrow corridor of Elmina castle toward the ocean, her mind had been left with no doubt that they were indeed people. And in her heart, she knew they were her people!

※※※

Abruptly, Kristin realized she had been daydreaming again.

"What on earth is my problem?" She wondered in aggravation. "Why can't I settle down and finish this?" She looked down at the paper and then up at the large clock hanging above her doorway for the thousandth time.

"Good grief," she mumbled aloud. She realized she had been standing at the window for nearly forty minutes, and that she had been trying to read Kioni's paper for over an hour and a half. She was agitated with herself for having wasted so much time when she had so much left to do. Kristin looked at the paper again and hesitated for only a second. Then, she scribbled "A+ Excellent Paper" across the cover page.

"I can't imagine that this one would be any different than the others," she mumbled to herself She felt only slightly guilty, and she promised herself she would take Kioni's paper with her to Ghana so she could read it later.

She scribbled her star student's final grade onto her grade sheet, and packed up the remaining papers on her desk. In a few minutes more, she was out the door and headed for the registrar's office to turn in her grades for the very last time.

Chapter 19

Celeste

*C*eleste stopped in her tracks for a second, listening closely for soft rustling noises she heard coming from a nearby bush. When she was satisfied that a small animal had probably been responsible, she kept moving through the small grove of trees. It was hard for even *her* to believe that she was back on the footpath that ran behind the mall again so soon after the last time she was there. And once again, she was racing to get home before her father was due back from work.

Her brother had warned her countless times not to walk home that way. He had told her over and over that it was far too dangerous when she was walking by herself. Although neither of them mentioned it, they both knew their father wouldn't have been happy to find out that *either* of his children frequently used that route to get home. But it saved Celeste almost ten minutes off her trip from the mall; being that she was a slippery thirteen-year-old, she was finding the short cut too hard to pass up. She did try to make an effort to take the street route home unless she was in a big hurry to get there. Unfortunately, that seemed to be the case for her quite a lot these days. She had already seen a stray animal on the trail once or twice, but she and Trazi had even come across homeless people several times as they walked home together.

Her brother explained that they would squat in the boarded-up houses on the deserted street at the end of the trail. They were only there trying to find shelter, Trazi told her, and they would usually move on after a few days. Even at that, it had been homeless people who had been seen on the street and blamed for a fire that had destroyed two houses a few years back. But Trazi said they were harmless, for the most part, and had probably started the fire just to keep warm. Some of them had mental problems though, he warned her. And most likely, they weren't taking their medicines because they had no clean water to wash the pills down after they woke up every morning from wherever they had slept. Even if they got their prescriptions filled, which many didn't, Trazi said the pills were too bitter tasting and hard to swallow without water. It would leave a bad tang in their mouths all day, and who would want that?

He had especially warned her about the drug addicts. He told her they would hold up in the abandoned houses too, from time to time, and usually stayed until someone ran them away. Her brother had told her time and time again how dangerous *they* were, and he had taught her to recognize the "crack-head march," as he called it. Celeste knew he had been trying to scare her and it worked a little. He kept saying that the drug addicts were always looking for money to feed their habits when they weren't getting high. He had told her again and again what an easy mark she would make for them, and that had made her start looking out for the unusually quick body movements her brother told her crack-heads always made. Trazi had even showed her one of them once. He had pointed out the vacant look the man had in his eyes and told her it was another way she could tell if a person had been smoking crack.

"But if you're close enough to see their eyes," he had cautioned her, in a very serious tone, "you are way *too* close. So, the first thing you need to do is to get as far away from them as fast as you can."

Trazi had nagged her about it almost everyday before he left for the navy, when she had stayed with him and Aunt Kristin for two weeks. Celeste had finally promised him she would never take the shortcut home, but her assurances had been very short-lived. The first time she had walked home by herself on the trail had only been a couple of days after her brother left for the naval base in Michigan.

Every few minutes, Celeste would look back over her shoulder while she kept moving at the same pace. She zigzagged between low-lying bushes that crossed the short trail and finally climbed up a slight incline onto a narrow abandoned street. She walked even faster down the neglected sidewalk, avoiding the dandelions that grew freely in the pavement cracks. Many of the enterprising weeds had banded together in clumps, encouraged by their growing numbers and defiantly staking out their claims.

It had been thirty years since the fires and looting had ended in D.C., but most houses along the once thriving street, so close to the nation's capital, were still boarded up. Winston had taken both his children to see the area when they first moved into the neighborhood five years earlier. He described what the community had been like before fires were set that destroyed almost everything in the late '60s. He said the store owners on the next block over had fought to save their businesses, after order had finally been restored in the streets. They had formed an association to coordinate all the work that needed to be done, and they found private funding to rebuild their stores in record time. Unfortunately, around the same time, shopping malls had just begun to spring up in the suburbs. Winston called the mall idea a brilliant business move. He said it was "a novel approach to an old and very unexciting chore."

It wasn't long before the people who lived in that neighborhood had started catching buses out to Maryland or Virginia, to do the same shopping they had once done right around the corner. The local store owners hadn't been able to compete with the discounted prices that the people could get at the mall. One by one, most of the shop owners had given up. They abandoned their family legacies that had started out as dreams in the minds of their ancestors.

Winston told his children that most of the white store owners had probably been in as much disbelief as everyone else, when they learned the news of Dr. King's assassination. They had probably commiserated with their longtime customers in their grief and frustrations about it, at first. He said that some may have been just as saddened by the treacherous deed. But then the fires and looting started. When the damage to their property was assessed a few weeks later, it must have been hard for them to feel much of anything other than resentment, bitterness, and perhaps fear.

No matter how hard some of them most likely tried, they just couldn't see a connection between Dr. King's murder in Tennessee and their property being burned to the ground in Washington. Their very livelihoods had been destroyed. It must have been hard for them to understand why they were being blamed for a split second of hatred and cruelty that had been committed hundreds of miles away, by someone they didn't even know. Winston guessed that they had probably been dumbfounded by the seeming ease in which the neighborhood that had supported their families for decades had turned against them, as if on one accord. The fires and looting had destroyed nearly everything their ancestors struggled to build, and most of them had immediately left the neighborhood for good. Her father told Celeste that the white store owners would probably never forget that one week in 1968, when the raging fires had lit up the "Chocolate City" skies of Washington, D.C.

"The ones who had managed to hold onto their shops no longer felt at ease around customers they had once assumed they knew so well," her father said. "When the buildings were burning, there were many people in the streets; some were otherwise law abiding citizens who had decided on the spur of the moment to take advantage of the situation they walked into, and who had taken part in destroying the store owners' property. All of a sudden, people had been able to step inside a store front and pick up a television set or something else they had likely seen in the window, and wished they could afford.

It had been months before the majority of people who lived in the neighborhood ventured out again beyond mandatory trips to the bus stop, for work or for school. By then, the shop owners had become wary of the faces they had seen on the television set every night as the fires burned—and they had all been Black faces. Many store owners had become overly cautious of any Black face they saw after that. They eased their fears by barricading themselves behind thick walls of glass, and securing a fixed distance between themselves and the people they had once greeted warmly. In so doing, they also insulted their best customers, who had never caused them one bit of harm.

❋❋❋

Celeste almost rushed right past the Japanese plum tree that her brother had pointed out to her as a landmark. The tree stood at the edge of a large yard that was now run down, but according to their father, had once been beautifully landscaped. After she made a sharp turn down the narrow street bordering it, Celeste hurried toward the alley that was behind the boarded-up house in the middle of the yard.

She missed her brother so much and had found herself thinking about him a lot in the past few days. It was still hard for her to accept that he had just up and joined the navy. First, he had moved out of the loft and then he had left her completely behind in Washington. It had been the first time they had ever lived so far apart. Trazi had been the one person who had always been there for her, since their dad had always worked such long hours.

For the millionth time, Celeste wondered whether she might have been able to stop her brother from leaving home that night, if only she had heard all the commotion sooner. Her brother and father had been close at one time, at least until Charlotte came into their lives. They used to play basketball together and they would go fishing in Maryland at least three times a year. But a wedge had slowly developed between the two, right after their father remarried. It began after they were introduced to Charlotte as their father's new girlfriend. Her brother had told Celeste right away that there was something about Charlotte that made him want to keep his distance. After Trazi moved from the loft, Celeste kept remembering what he had said from the beginning – that their stepmother was bad news.

Celeste, on the other hand, had always been a daddy's girl. She had at least tried to be nice to Charlotte because she knew that was what their father wanted. In truth, Celeste had never really liked her either, but she had never imagined the woman would end up causing such a separation between the two men that Celeste loved so much—especially when she knew how much they really loved each other.

She and her aunt Kristin had been the only two people who had ever been able to get her brother or father to calm down once they got started. But by the time Celeste heard them that night, it had been too late for her to do much of anything. They were yelling so loud that their voices eventually drifted up to the second level of the loft and woke her up. After her mind cleared enough to recognize their voices through her closed door, she had thrown on a robe and run down the stairs to her father's office, where all the shouting had been coming from. By the time she got there, her father and brother were so angry with each other that neither of them even noticed she had come into the room.

Celeste had forced her way in between them to make sure they didn't come to blows, as she pleaded with them to stop all the shouting. When they kept right on, she had begged them to at least tell her why they were fighting. Neither of them answered her, but they had finally stop their arguing. They were both worked up from all the adrenaline that had been going on for who knows how long. Their chests were rising and falling as they tried hard to calm down.

Celeste had been afraid to move from where she stood because the two men still glared at each other for several minutes more. The sudden contrast of silence in the room had seemed almost deafening. Celeste wanted to say something to clear the air, but she hesitated because she had no idea what had started the fight. She could sense the hostile energy that still simmered beneath the surface. She had been afraid to risk saying something that might unknowingly fan the flames back to the blaze of anger it had been when she came into the room.

She decided to wait for them to calm down more before she did anything. As she looked from one to the other she realized how much alike they were, and wondered whether either of them knew it. It usually took a long time before her father or brother got as angry as they had been that night, but once they reached a boiling point it was hard to keep them under control. Both would usually reject all attempts at reason. It was a good thing that neither lost his temper very often, because there was usually hell to pay whenever one of them did.

They had all stood frozen in silence for a long time before they walked back up the stairs to their respective bedrooms. Trazi led the way, without so much as a glance in their dad's direction, and Celeste trailed behind the two men. It wasn't until after she was half way up the stairs that she became aware of Charlotte's conspicuous absence. When she thought about it later, Celeste couldn't imagine how her stepmother could have slept through all the pandemonium that had been going on. And though she couldn't be absolutely certain, she could have sworn she heard Trazi's muffled voice mentioning Charlotte's name as she neared their father's office. Either way, it was very peculiar that her stepmother hadn't come downstairs with everyone else. And it made Celeste realize Trazi had been right about her all along.

After she was back in her room Celeste had tossed and turned in her bed, afraid of falling asleep again and missing another warning sign that trouble might be brewing between her brother and dad. She had thought about calling Aunt Kristin for help, but it was late and she really had nothing much she could have told her. Celeste racked her brain for hours trying to unravel the mystery of what the two men had been fighting about. She was very worried about the damage done to their already strained relationship. The look in her father's eyes told her that things would be different between them after that blowout. Her father had been really angry with Trazi this time, instead of his normal frustration from trying to communicate with his son.

She had still been wide-awake when she heard the sound of their court-yard gate opening later that night. When it clanged shut again, the clock on her dresser told her it was just after 3 a.m. Celeste hurried over to her bed-room window overlooking the street and pulled the shades open in time to get a last glimpse of her much-beloved brother before he disappeared. Trazi had stopped only once, just long enough to shift his overstuffed gym bag to the other shoulder. Then he hurried down the sidewalk quickly in a long gait and vanished from sight.

Celeste had been so distracted in thinking about her brother that she had momentarily forgotten that she was on a mission to get home. She picked up her pace and quickly sidestepped a large pile of trash that was piled in the middle of the narrow walkway. She couldn't help but wonder what her brother would say if he saw the way she had been acting lately. She had no idea what had made her stay out with Malaya so long at the mall, or for that matter, why she had gone to meet her friend in the first place. Her father had been very clear that morning about what he expected from her. Celeste knew very well that she wasn't supposed to leave home, though for some reason her father preferred not to use the word "grounded."

She started walking even faster when she finally neared the back of the old post office building. Once again, she focused all her attention on get-ting to the loft before her dad got home. She walked close to the north side of the ancient brick building; when she was near the front of it, she inched forward slowly. There was mossy-green algae on the surface of the wall and the damp sensation on her hands felt disgusting. Celeste bit down on her lip to distract herself from the ickiness of the clammy wall, keeping her slender fingertips pressed firmly against the building to brace herself. Her fear of losing her balance and stumbling out onto the sidewalk over-shadowed every other emotion she felt. She clenched her teeth together to silence her disgust, as she moved ever closer to the front of the building.

"Thank goodness, he's not out there." She pretended to be relieved after peeping around the corner and not seeing the boy she had a crush on stand-ing on the steps. She tried to sound convincing too, even though she was the only person who was close enough to hear her. And even as she said the words, she knew that she really wasn't happy at all. She was disap-pointed that Bennie, the skinny kid with tiny twists all over his head, was nowhere to be seen. He was nearly always there among the three or four guys who usually sprawled out over the steps of the Methodist church across from their loft.

Celeste stuck her head out even further so she could get a better look up and down the few blocks that separated the old post office from their loft. She smoothed down the silk fabric of her cream-colored blouse, and ran both her hands down her long legs to straighten out the matching skirt. She had to account for the possibility that Bennie might have gone inside the small corner market for a second to get something to drink. After she had satisfied herself that he wasn't in the store either, she turned her attention back to getting down the sidewalk and home quickly.

She had taken extra pains with her outfit that morning—just in case she ran into Bennie. Malaya had said that it was a good color for her, and the blouse was just loose enough to hide her newly developing bosom. The skirt that went with it was short, but it was still well below her derrière. Her bony legs had begun to fill out all of a sudden, and Celeste had started attracting all kinds of unwanted attention from men that she didn't even know. It was hard for her to believe how much her legs had changed, almost overnight. Everyone who knew her parents had told her that they looked just like her mother's legs.

On the one hand, she was very excited that she would soon become a woman, just as most teenage girls were. Sometimes, she could barely sit still just thinking about it. But on the other hand, she was more than just a little intimidated by all the attention that her body had already started getting, and she was still developing.

Celeste avoided direct eye contact with the scattering of boys who were lounging on the steps, since Bennie wasn't among them. She smiled to herself as she hurried past the old church, thinking how proud Trazi would be. Then she focused again and prayed that she would make it inside in enough time to change her clothes, so her father wouldn't bust her again. She could just imagine how upset he would be if he found out she had left home only thirty minutes after he did that morning. And he would really freak if he knew that she had walked home through the alley.

But knowing all that wouldn't have stopped her from flirting with Bennie if he had been on the steps. She had no idea why she was finding it so easy to disregard the specific warnings that her father had given her about associating with him.

"What on Earth is happening to me?"

She was still contemplating that riddle as she closed the front gate and heard the massive lock slide into place behind her. She breathed a heavy sigh of relief when she glanced at the open garage, and saw that her father's parking spot was still empty.

"Well, I guess that's one more thing I get to add to my list." Her tone was much more flippant than she felt. Celeste had started to become concerned because she didn't seem able to stop herself lately. Breaking the rules had become a regular pastime for her in spite of the warnings that always piped up from the voice inside her head, trying to point her in a different direction. It had never failed to make an appearance so she wasn't surprised that it started in on her right after she had finally made it inside the gate.

No matter how hard she tried, she had never been able to silence the voice–at least not permanently. She was getting pretty good at ignoring it for periods of time, though. It was like some kind of a built-in monitor, always keeping a watchful eye over everything she said and did. It always got much louder if she did stuff that she knew was wrong. It was almost as though the voice was trying to nudge her into doing the right thing.

Once, when she had been around seven-years-old, she had accidentally broken a small snow globe that belonged to her aunt Kristin. The voice had tormented her for months about the incident; not because she broke it, but because she had never told her aunt that she had. The globe had been one of many souvenirs that Kristin had collected during the summer after her first year in college. The snow-covered mountain inside the globe would transform into a blizzard whenever the round glass ball was shaken.

Kristin had told Celeste and Trazi that she had hitchhiked across the country to California with her friend Niyla and two other roommates, during their summer break. It had been her first extended trip out of Tuskegee and she had bought cheap trinkets at every place they stopped. She kept the mementos in a chest in her living room and would pull them out sometimes when Celeste and Trazi slept over. Celeste loved watching her aunt go through all her treasures, but Kristin was quick to remind them that it was no longer safe to do what she and her friends had done. She told them that back then hitchhiking had been reasonably safe, and a popular mode of transportation for college students during breaks from school.

She had a story to tell them about each trinket she had bought, and Kristin loved to tell the stories. One night, Celeste spotted a beautiful turquoise necklace that she had somehow missed seeing all the other times she had looked through the chest. Kristin told her she had picked the necklace up at a reservation in New Mexico. Although it was late, she had let Celeste try it on briefly, because everyone could see that she was charmed by the piece. Still not satisfied with her brief time from the night before, Celeste had hurried downstairs the next morning to try on the necklace again, before anyone else was up. In her haste to pull it out, she had lost her grip and somehow the snow globe fell from the coffee table where she had sat it.

Even before it reached the floor, Celeste knew the globe would be damaged. And sure enough, a small trickle of water ran down its sides when she scooped it up from the shiny hardwood floor. Without hesitation or any thought about the consequences, she had made a quick decision not to mention anything to Kristin about breaking her souvenir. Instead, she hastily put the globe back inside the chest with the broken side up, hoping that would keep the rest of the water from seeping out.

Not only had she known what she did to be wrong, but she had been positive that her aunt would know right away that she had been the one who had broken the globe. Celeste waited nervously to be discovered the rest of the weekend. She had been a wreck by the time Kristin dropped she and her brother back at their father's house that Sunday evening. The days that followed the incident had turned into weeks and then months, as the voice inside Celeste's head continued to badger her. It seemed intent on convincing her to tell Kristin the truth about what happened. But she had never been able to summon the courage, especially after time had passed.

Kristin had never once mentioned a word about the globe and the whole episode had hung between them for months, like a dark cloud. Eventually, Celeste pushed it from her consciousness, although it had never left her mind completely. As she watched things get more out of control, her guilt began to tag along for the ride more and more often, just as it had after she broke the souvenir. Sometimes it felt as though she had a one hundred pound weight hanging around her small neck.

She already knew from hearing her friends' complaints about their parents that she had it pretty good. Somehow that didn't seem to matter much anymore, especially when she and Malaya were hanging out together. She had begun keeping a mental note of all the things she had done that was yet to be discovered by her father, and she briefly considered the likelihood of him finding out about some of the other rules she had broken. All the time, the voice inside her head kept reminding her that she wouldn't even have a list to keep up with, if she would only listen to it.

Chapter 20

Charlotte

*T*he family area just inside the front door was dimly lit as Celeste walked inside the loft. She had been so focused on getting upstairs to change her clothes that she nearly missed seeing her stepmother, who was sitting quietly on the sofa. The music Charlotte usually listened to that Celeste and Trazi had always referred to as "elevator music" wasn't even on.

"Hey Charlotte."

The teen mumbled the greeting without breaking her speed as she walked past the doorway. She was praying that Charlotte wouldn't be in one of her bonding moods again as she ventured a quick look at the clock above the fireplace, before making a right turn to dash up the stairs toward her bedroom. By her calculations, she still had another ten minutes or so before her father would be home.

"Hi Lessa." Charlotte called out to her stepdaughter in a tone that sounded more like a plea."

"Oh great!" Celeste groaned to herself. She had briefly considered pretending that she hadn't seen Charlotte and now regretted her decision to say anything. *And who told her to call me by that stupid name anyhow?*

Celeste clinched her teeth as she turned to face her father's wife.

"Hi," she greeted her again, reluctantly.

"So, where are you off to in such a hurry?" The woman persisted, although she could sense that her stepdaughter didn't want to be bothered. No surprises there, but she had still hoped she might persuade Celeste to stop and chat for a minute or two. Winston had been so consumed with launching his engineering company lately that he had spent very little time with her, even when he *was* at home.

Charlotte hadn't seen any of that coming. Her husband already had a solid career at Goddard Space Flight Center when they first met, with plenty of room to grow at NASA's Greenbelt center. She had no idea that he would want to bail out just because he didn't find any flexibility in nuclear engineering. She didn't find that out until after he had already resigned. Apparently, mechanical engineering had always been his real passion— that and a desire to start his own business.

Their marriage had taken on another dimension once Winston became his own boss. Charlotte was still trying to figure out her best approach for taking control of the situation. He had been so distracted by all the deadlines he constantly had to meet at NASA that she had free rein over their social life at first. But all that had changed after he started his own firm. Of course, she had to thank God that the money hadn't stopped flowing, but it didn't take long before she realized there was only so much shopping that one person could do—no matter how much they liked to spend money.

Charlotte had known all along that her stepchildren didn't care much for her. Who could blame them? She had barely been able to conceal her resentment after learning Winston even *had* children, and that she would have to share him with them. He was probably the only one who hadn't noticed, but Trazi and Celeste caught on to her right away. And no matter how much she tried to fake it afterwards she hadn't been able to convince them to un-think their first impression of her.

Her attraction to their father had been almost immediate, even *before* she did her homework and found out how much money he was worth. They had hit it off right away too although Winston had been quick to tell her that he wanted to take things slowly at first. He had actually told her that he thought they should date for a while and get to know each other first to see if they even *liked* each other. Winston had taken her out for nearly a month before he even kissed her goodnight!

Instead, he would touch her ever so gently with his index finger—just above her navel in the middle of her tummy, after he had walked her to her front door. She had been imagining what it would be like to kiss him for so long that when he finally did, she became weak in the knees just as their lips touched from all her anticipation. She could tell right away that they would have remarkable chemistry together, but it had been several more weeks before they finally made love.

And it was a few months after that before Winston even *mentioned* having children. Charlotte knew he wasn't seeing anyone else, so she had accepted all his excuses for having to get back home at the end of their dates without question. She had been living in Alexandria Virginia at the time, which was quite a distance from Greenbelt Maryland. She had made the assumption that he preferred sleeping at home because of his early work schedule.

"Damn him!" That had been her initial reaction after learning he had two children. She had been taken completely by surprise when he sprang that tidbit of news on her, but by that time it was too late. She had felt herself sinking deeper into those gorgeous eyes of his every time she looked at them. She thought it would be safe with him so she hadn't held her feelings back at all.

Charlotte had never considered herself as the motherly type; she was far from it, if the truth were to be known. Even as a little girl, she felt isolated from her friends who preferred to play with their doll babies. She had absolutely no inclination toward domestication either, but she had always been very practical. She understood that children were usually expected in a marriage, although deep down she had hoped to find one of the few successful men who weren't gay, and just didn't have a desire to produce offspring.

She had earned a law degree from Georgetown but it wasn't as if she had ever intended to practice law. She studied as hard as everyone else did in school, and also went through the trouble of passing the bar in all the metro jurisdictions after she graduated. Charlotte had only done that as a fail-safe, though. She planned to use her law degree to support herself in the lifestyle she always intended to have until she found herself a Winston to take over that role. That had also been her sole motivation for learning how to cook too and how to organize a household. She knew it was the kind of thing that the type of man she wanted for herself would expect. The entire time she spent taking her cooking lessons, Charlotte had daydreamed about entertaining her future husband's business associates, just as she had hosted Winston's colleagues at NASA before he gave up his job. Children had never played a role in her daydreams, but she had already made up her mind she would marry Winston long before he ever thought about it.

After the initial shock of discovering she would have to be a stepmother too, she had been forced to rethink *everything*. Winston seemed fairly content with the two children he already had; he had one of each, which was a big plus. More than likely, it meant he wouldn't be putting too much pressure on her to have a child of their own. And that would be a foolproof way of avoiding all those awful stretch marks she had seen on her girlfriends' bellies that had once been smooth and firm, before their pregnancies.

But when Winston finally *did* take her home to meet his kids, she could see right away that they meant a lot more to him than she had hoped. Charlotte decided right then and there that she would have to have at least *one* child of her own. She had surprised herself by actually contemplating motherhood for the first time in her life; only because she knew that if she didn't, she would be just setting herself up for trouble. Plus, she would probably never get Winston's full attention otherwise.

Once she had been ambushed in finding out he had concealed something as important as having two children who actually *lived* with him no less, Charlotte knew she would need some kind of insurance for herself. Having a baby would guarantee that she wouldn't be abandoned later on with no means of support, in case things didn't turn out the way she hoped and their marriage ended badly. Those regularly scheduled child support checks would supplement her alimony nicely, and give her the time she needed to bounce back from not having access to Winston's money as his wife. Charlotte had already decided exactly how much time she would wait before she got pregnant, long before Winston actually proposed. But now she was forced to postpone all her plans because he had up and quit his job.

Reluctantly, Celeste backed up until she was standing in the door frame and facing her stepmother. They had been forced to stay inside together that winter since the blizzard of 1996 had brought in so much snow that the government and practically the whole city had been shut down for a week. It had taken several days before Winston finished digging them out, and having to be in such close quarters with Charlotte had nearly driven Celeste insane. But she had forced herself to be as pleasant as she could to survive the experience. Now, her stepmother seemed convinced that the interactions they had been required to have as the streets and sidewalks were being cleared, somehow meant that things had changed between them.

"I'm sorry," she lied easily. "I was just trying to get upstairs to put on the dress I made in home economics. I want to surprise Daddy when he gets home."

Celeste didn't even care whether Charlotte believed the tale she had concocted on the spot or not. Technically, Celeste had only told a partial lie because she really *had* sewn a dress in home economics. She just didn't think she had done a particularly good job and she certainly hadn't planned on *showing* it to anyone. Now, thanks to the big tale that had just rolled out of her mouth with so little effort, she would have to show the dress to her father. She had no idea what had come over her in the last few months.

"Okay." Charlotte agreed, as though Celeste required her permission. "Go ahead and change then. We're having salmon for dinner. Your dad called a while earlier so he should be home soon."

"And I'd like to see your dress too," she called after her stepdaughter, who had already turned and was halfway up the stairs.

Celeste doubted that her father would have bought her story, and she wasn't really sure that Charlotte bought it either. For some reason her stepmother had been acting much nicer to her lately; almost like she wanted something, but Celeste just wasn't sure what. Malaya kept saying that someone might have switched Charlotte's birth control pills with "nice" pills instead. The two girls had discovered the pills while riffling through Charlotte's dresser once and they both had giggled for hours at the thought of someone actually doing something like that.

Celeste had no idea what Charlotte's *real* motives were, but she decided she would take full advantage of it. Once she had finally made it to her bedroom, she reluctantly pulled out the almost-forgotten dress from the back of her closet. She ran a hot iron across it to get rid of some of the wrinkles. Her mother had given her a sewing machine for Christmas and she had used it to make the dress. Celeste had casually mentioned that she wanted to learn to sew one day when she visited her mother's apartment. The teen really did hope to learn to sew like her mother one day, and she had begun to feel happy that her mother had moved to a new place that was closer to their loft. Celeste thought her mother had been doing so much better lately; she had started to believe that the two of them might finally get to know each other.

Her home economics teacher had graded her sewing project and handed it back several days earlier. Celeste had been shocked that she had been given a grade of "B" on her dress—especially since she had put so little effort into making it. She had initially wanted to make her dress look different from her classmates' dresses, so she had thought of various ways to change the pattern. But their teacher had insisted that Celeste stick to the same design as everyone else, and she had become bored with the whole thing after that.

Now, she examined the dress carefully before slipping it over her head. She stood in front of the mirror on her closet door to critique it objectively for the first time, and after looking at it for a while she decided that it really wasn't half-bad. Her biggest oversight had been in not following her mother's advice on pressing each seam open as she sewed the different fabric pieces together. If she had, it might have been hard for anyone to tell that she had made the dress at first glance.

And to her surprise, Celeste realized she really *was* anxious to have her father see it.

Chapter 21

Guess Who's Coming to Dinner

"I'm coming!" Malaya yelled down from the top of the stairs to her mother. Then she rushed back into her room to frantically look for something else to put on. She had already tried on nearly everything in her closet, before finally settling on the short navy skirt she had on. The matching top had a cute lacy collar that she liked too, but now she was worried that her skirt was too short. She preferred wearing clothes that made her look more like a little girl, especially when she was around her stepfather. But it had been a long time since Malaya had felt like a child.

'I don't know why I always have to go anyhow,' she thought nervously. *'It's not like it makes a difference to Uncle Paul that I'm there; at least not after the body count is over.'* Her reference was made to her uncle's habit of going through a mental list of all their relatives before they sat down for dinner, until he had accounted for everyone living in the metro area. Not counting his family and the four in her family, Malaya had three aunts and another uncle who lived in Virginia. They were all expected at the table for every family dinner, along with their spouses and all their children.

Her uncle would sit back in his chair and demand to know the whereabouts of anyone who hadn't seen fit to grace him with their presence. If there was no one there who could give a reasonable excuse for their

165

absence, Uncle Paul would then verbally rake the missing party over the coals while everyone else at the table laughed at his antics. It was for that reason alone that Sam insisted they go to every family dinner, and he always tried to get there before everyone else. They all had to be "appropriately" dressed too so everyone could see that Sam still had money and was doing good.

Malaya had dreaded the first Sunday in every month until recently. Not only was she forced to be around Sam for hours, but when she went to her grandmother's house now it was just a painful reminder that Malaya would never see her again. Everyone always seemed to be gawking at them too, lately. Malaya wondered whether her mother had noticed it but she was too afraid to ask.

Her uncle had inherited the family house after her grandmother died. As the oldest surviving male child in the family, her grandfather had left the house to Uncle Paul in his will. Since Paul had already retired from his job at O'Hare Airport by the time his mother died, he moved his family from Chicago to D.C. right after her funeral. Malaya's uncle was seven years older than his next-oldest sibling, so he had quickly asserted himself as the new head of the family.

And it didn't take long before he had started bullying everybody into doing exactly what he wanted. He had a loud booming voice and everybody said he was just like Malaya's grandfather. She had never known the older man because he had died when she was just a baby. But Malaya did know that Uncle Paul was the exact opposite of her grandmother. His energy overshadowed all the warmth she used to feel when she and her mother had lived in the house. In spite of all their criticisms about his ways, they all knew Uncle Paul really loved his family. He took his role as family patriarch very seriously, and at every opportunity he reminded them that it was what their father wanted.

Once he had finished lambasting any unfortunate individual who was unaccounted for, Malaya's male relatives would pretty much take over the dinner conversation. They all sat as close to Uncle Paul as they could manage and carried on rowdy conversations that no one else at the table cared about. And once they got started, they hardly even noticed that the women and children were still in the room. After they first started having their monthly family dinners, Malaya had listened to the men's conversations closely as she waited for an opportunity to join in. But more often than not, one of the older women at the table would anticipate her move. They would shoot her a look to quash whatever she had planned to say before she had time to say it, although she had caught them all off guard once. She had slipped in a question of her own right in the middle of the men's debate about some local political scandal. Rather than answering her carefully worded question, Uncle Paul had just turned to stare at her for a couple of seconds before commenting that "children should be seen and not heard."

Sam immediately shot Malaya an angry look and both she and her mother had been anxious as they anticipated their ride home. That had taught her to keep her mouth shut and eventually she stopped listening to the men altogether. After that, Malaya had been bored the entire time they were there for dinner–that is, until recently.

Normally, her little brother and their younger cousins always made a dash for the backyard right after dinner, if it wasn't raining; as soon as they had been dismissed from the table. They would busy themselves playing on the heavy oak playground equipment Uncle Paul had built for them. He had set up the swings on the exact spot where her grandmother's vegetable garden had once been.

The older women would assemble in the kitchen, finally able to let down their guards and talk freely; while Malaya and her female cousins were tasked with bringing all the dishes in from the dining room table. They had to wipe it down quickly so the men could settle in; but after they were done, the older women made it clear to the young girls that they weren't welcome to hang around the kitchen "trying to eavesdrop on grown folk's conversation." The women would all work together as a team to finish cleaning the kitchen as they talked, while the men quickly converted the dining room into a makeshift speakeasy with an open bar. After that, they would be too busy laughing and drinking to notice what anybody else did.

Although Uncle Paul's twin daughters were fourteen and just a year older than Malaya, they weren't particularly friendly to anyone except each other. They would usually drift upstairs to their room after they were all done clearing the table; the room that had once been Malaya's bedroom before her mother married Sam. It had been repainted now in a color that Malaya would never have chosen for herself, so it was definitely the twins' room now and she never felt comfortable in it for very long. Plus, her twin cousins would usually started having telepathic conversations with each other sooner or later, giggling out loud suddenly when neither of them had spoken a word. It made Malaya uncomfortable not knowing what they were talking about, so she would usually drift back downstairs within a half hour.

But the last time they were there for dinner, her cousin Nathan, who was a senior in high school and three years older than his sisters, had spent lots of time talking with her. She never thought they would have so much in common but they discovered that they had a mutual interest in art. Malaya hoped she would have a chance to talk with him again this time; but with her luck, she would likely end up sitting alone again on the bench near her grandmother's rose bushes.

The roses were all that were left after Uncle Paul's rapid transformation of the yard that Malaya had played in almost every day before her mother married Sam. It was still shocking to her every time they came to the house to see how different things looked. Her grandfather had built the bench so her grandmother could sit near the roses he had planted for her. Her grandmother said he planted them soon after they were married, when they first bought their house. Malaya and her grandmother would sit on the bench together for hours after her grandmother had finished her work in the vegetable garden, just looking at the roses.

Malaya had always loved the way the flowers smelled; sometimes she would close her eyes and it would feel like her grandmother was sitting next to her again. The bench was the only thing at the house that helped her hang on to her memories of the good times she had there when she was younger. She could relax when she was alone in the rose garden too, not feeling as nervous as she usually felt around her relatives. It was almost as though they were watching her constantly now. If she didn't say much, her cousins and aunts would start questioning her like amateur detectives. They would keep their probing going until Malaya finally said something to satisfy them. She was always terrified that someone would ask her the wrong question and she would say the wrong thing because of all their badgering. It made her feel jumpy all the time, because no matter how low her voice was or how far away she sat from him, Sam always managed to hear every word she said.

Any reprieve she felt sitting in the rose garden was always short lived. Sooner or later, there would be sobering thoughts about their long drive home that would replace her fond memories of her grandmother. And usually, she would hold her breath for the first five minutes after they were all were in the car, waiting for Sam to start in on them about something.

Malaya made a quick decision that what she already had on would have to do, and she hurried down the stairs where her mother and younger brother stood waiting. Lil' Sam was the only one who seemed genuinely excited about their monthly family ritual. It gave him a chance to play with cousins that he would otherwise seldom get to see. He dashed out the front door ahead of his mother and sister to join his father, who had already gone ahead to warm up the car.

Malaya followed her mother out of the house slowly. It had become so unnerving to have everyone's eyes fixed on them so much. Sometimes, she would look up from her plate to find one of them staring at her openly. Even Uncle Paul had seemed to develop a sudden interest in her. At times, he would have the most peculiar look on his face, as though he had never seen her before.

And to not know what her uncle was thinking terrified her.

Chapter 22

Keep on Keepin' On

*I*t had been less than a week and Celeste found herself right back on the same trail behind the mall, rushing to get home. She headed down the narrow street that ran next to the plum tree landmark and in no time she was scurrying down the alley leading to the old post office. She was frantic this time because her father hadn't exactly been in a good mood that morning to begin with. She knew she had cut it *way* too close; it would truly be a miracle if he didn't catch her this time.

She was encouraged after spotting a haphazard stack of cartons up ahead. The mountain of cardboard was piled next to an already overfilled dumpster that she recognized from the sign painted across the front. It belonged to the dollar store; she had just started to relax a little, knowing she was getting close to the old post office, when without any warning, a dark gray cat shot out from behind the paper boxes as she neared them. The animal practically scared Celeste out of her skin, but it virtually flew past her and gave no indication that it had been aware that she was even there. Its sole mission was on getting across the fence and to the other side of the alley. Within seconds, all evidence that the cat had ever been there was gone.

The errant teen kept moving again after making stopping briefly for a shaky recovery. She had no choice, because if her timing was off just a little she would run smack into her father on his way home from the train station, a few blocks down from the post office. Celeste had already racked her brain for some explanation she might give him in case her luck finally ran out. He seemed able to read her mind half the time these days, and there was nothing she could think of that he would be likely to buy.

Then, surprisingly, her mother popped into her head from out of nowhere— just like the cat. It had been weeks since Celeste had talked to her mother and she had been debating whether she should call. With her, Celeste had never been quite sure what to do. Aunt Kristin had spent more time with her mother lately than anyone, but now her aunt was back in Africa again–and this time for good. Celeste had no one she could ask for advice about her mother anymore; she could almost feel her father tense up any time she even mentioned her mother's name.

Celeste had only been six the first time her father had sat her down for one of their now-frequent father-daughter talks. As soon as he said he wanted to talk about her mother, Celeste had known he would say something bad. He had such a grim look on his face, one she had never seen before. Her father told her that her mother would be going to live in a hospital for a few months because she wasn't well. Celeste remembered that it was the first time she had heard him say that her mother was fragile, because she had wondered what that meant. Her father promised her that her mother would feel much better when she came back home.

At first, Celeste understood very little of what he was saying; she had heard her mother say that the vase sitting on their breakfast table was fragile. She couldn't understand what her mother and the vase had in common. But she had told her father that she understood. She also shook her head in agreement whenever it seemed like the right thing to do.

He had looked so worried that day. He seemed to need for her to understand what he was saying, and he was obviously relieved when Celeste pretended that she did. She knew she wasn't exactly being truthful but she had only done it to make her father feel better. He sat with her for a long time that day, talking about some of the things they had all seen Angela doing around the house. No one had ever said anything about it before and after he kept talking, Celeste finally *did* understand. She had always known her mother was different but she had no idea what it really meant.

Angela's latest thing at the time had been to lock herself in the bedroom that she still shared with Winston. She would go into the room just as everyone else sat down for dinner. She made it clear that she wanted to be left alone, and it had only taken a few times of her getting snappy answers back through the closed door before Celeste learned not to bother her mother. They all left her alone whenever Angela closed herself off like that. Celeste and Trazi had come to accept it as part of their daily routine.

Eventually, they got used to their father pulling out the sofa bed in his office when it was time to go to sleep. They started looking for him there at night too, if they needed anything. And when Angela began to drink a lot more they gradually got used to that. Everyone acted like it was normal, but it should have been obvious to anyone who spent time at their house that what went on there was far from normal.

But Angela *had* seemed better when she came home from rehab the first time, just as Winston had promised. Unfortunately, she had gone back into the hospital twice before Celeste celebrated her tenth birthday.

A short while later, Celeste could hear the soulful sounds of Gladys Knight and the Pips filling the humid air of the alley. The sounds got louder as she moved closer to the back door of the cleaners, because the music floated out of an open window in the apartment above it:

> *"I've really got to use... (I've got to use,) my imagina-tion... (im-agination...), to think of good rea-sons... (think of good rea-sons!) to keep on, keepin'on... (keep on, keepin'on!). Got to make the best of... (best of, best of...), a bad situ-a-tion... (a bad situ-ation!) Ever since that day I woke up and found that you were gone..."*

Celeste pulled herself out of her daydream to hurry past the cleaners. It was a rare occurrence when she walked by and didn't hear old school music, as her father called it, blaring from the apartment. The man who lived there never seemed to get tired of hearing it, and she could sometimes see him dancing through the curtains as she walked past.

Even though she was barely thirteen, Celeste could still feel the words that Gladys sang call out to her soul. She felt a mysterious strength whenever she heard that song; like it was some faraway promise of courage that would be made available to *her* when she needed it most. It made Celeste feel that she could handle anything! But then again, she wasn't exactly what you could call teeming with experience. In reality, she had no frame of reference at all for the kind of rock-you-to-the-core pain Gladys was singing about.

Technically, she had only been a teenager for a few months. It hadn't been that long since she stopped praying to be spared womanhood altogether. She had begged God for that miracle after she learned the actual mechanics involved in making her girl-to-woman transition. But listening to old school music coming from the man's apartment, or the music in her father's collection, somehow made her curious about womanhood again. The songs her father had listened to in college would sometimes magically conjure up the promise of good times for her too, when she was older.

Her father had once told her that music could carry a person back to a time when they might have been someone else altogether. They had been sitting in his office listening to a few cuts from his collection. Winston told his daughter that just by hearing certain songs a person could relive their past just like that, and it could cause all sorts of stuff to be stirred up.

She had watched him for a few seconds after he said it to try and figure out what he actually meant. Celeste had only intended to stop by his make-shift office long enough to get some money before she left to meet Malaya at the mall. Instead, she had ended up staying there for more than half an hour. When she first came to the door her father had been leaning back in his overstuffed chair, deep into the sounds of his music. Before she had a chance to speak, his eyes had glazed over as the Friends of Distinction started singing "You Got Me Going in Circles."

She remembered wondering whether her father had been thinking about their house on Delaney Avenue. It had always been filled with music when her mom came home from the rehab hospital that first time. She had really seemed like a new person too, one that Celeste had never met before. Celeste had been so hopeful, and for a short time things had seemed better between her parents. The young girl had constantly been on the look out for that spark she could sometimes see in their eyes. Somehow, the music they played in college seemed to play a role in it. Her father said it was the music that had documented their coming of age; the energy of that unstable period of history had been etched inside the music and imprinted in the minds of his whole generation. No matter what their current situation, hearing it quickly transported them "back in the day."

Celeste had witnessed the effects of the music on her parents many times during the first months her mother was home from the hospital. It had taken them to a place where things had obviously been much better between them. They would invite friends over on Friday nights when her father was between deadlines at NASA. Then, he only worked eight-hour days and was free to socialize since he wasn't up against the gun all the time, as he liked to call it. Her parents would have a ball playing bid whist half the night with their friends. They would all make bids like they were playing for money; Celeste loved listening to her father sell good-natured "wolf tickets" to anyone he played against. And his loyalties would come and go as quickly as he changed partners.

Both her parents would transform themselves into the life of the party right before her eyes. Celeste loved seeing them look so happy, especially her father. He seemed to have an endless supply of stale jokes and that's when she discovered he apparently loved to dance too. Any time a song by Brass Construction started to play, he would jump up like some kind of maniac. He would dance around the middle of the floor, temporarily forgetting about whatever he had been doing before the music started. Her father had moves Celeste would never have dreamed he'd have. He had no problem dancing by himself either, if no one else joined in with him.

They would play old school music and dance like that until well after midnight. When certain songs played, they would all sing off key together and make up words to replace the ones they had forgotten. There would often be some pretty rowdy arguments that broke out too, if they couldn't all agree on the forgotten lyrics; with laughter filling the room. Celeste had barely recognized the two happy-go-lucky party animals who entertained their friends on those special nights. And if she remembered to be quiet when it started getting late, and didn't move around too much, they would sometimes forget all about her bedtime. She would fall asleep in her father's big armchair in the living room, often dreaming about her parents. Celeste would wake up in her bed the next morning with no recollection of her father having put her there.

One night, she lay in bed listening to the music that drifted down the hall after one of her parents' parties. She had already heard the front door close behind their last guest and sounds of the minimal cleaning they usually did before going to bed. She kept waiting for the familiar sounds of her parents' footsteps walking past her bedroom door, and grew curious when the music didn't stop. She tiptoed down the hallway and peeped in through the half-opened living room door, and what she saw had made her speechless. Her parents were standing in the middle of the floor, swaying back and forth to the music in rhythm. They didn't seem to be aware of anything else except themselves. It was a side of her parents that she had never seen before and Celeste had watched them, mesmerized, for several minutes. Before she could process that scene, something even more magical happened.

Her parents had stopped dancing suddenly at the same time. They stared at each other for a few seconds and then kissed as though they were the only two people alive. Celeste had only been seven at the time, and the unexpected turn of events startled her so badly that she raced back down the hallway to her room. She dived under her bed covers but she had stayed awake for hours after that, giggling to herself and replaying the image of what she had seen. Before that night, she had never once considered that her parents might love each other, but once she had seen them together like that she became convinced that they did.

The next morning she noticed a change in her mother right away. She wasn't slamming pots and pans around in the kitchen as she normally did. She had practically floated around, humming a tune that Celeste thought she had heard before but couldn't place, with the strangest smile on her face. It was the same look that she had been surprised to see when her parents were dancing the night before. Her father was already in the kitchen too, which was very rare for him. He tried to make Celeste believe that the blueberry muffins he was making for breakfast were for her, but everyone knew they were her mother's favorite.

She had been overjoyed with the change she saw in her parents, although Trazi had been skeptical about it from the beginning. Still, Celeste had held on to her hopes, no matter what her brother said. But sadly, it soon became clear that he had been right all along. That special look she saw flicker between her parents began to fade in time, and gradually it disappeared altogether. Celeste began to wonder whether she had just imagined it and as the weeks went by, she watched helplessly as her parents grew further apart.

It wasn't very long before she was being awakened once again by the abrupt sounds of her mother throwing pots and pans around in the kitchen. Celeste would sit at the table and watch her make breakfast for her father grudgingly again, as though it was the last thing on earth she wanted to do. Soon after that, she would find her father sitting alone with a familiar drained expression on his face. She had seen that look more times than she could remember; for a few short months, Celeste had thought she might never see it again.

But she was a fighter, so she consoled herself with the knowledge that it was at least possible for her parents to be happy together. She had seen it with her own eyes so she spent months trying to figure out a way to make it all happen again. The memory of seeing them kiss was still fresh in her mind, and she had been determined to help them make the magic reappear. She tried one plan after the next but nothing she did seemed to work; over time she became almost desperate. She kept thinking that her aunt Kristin might have helped her if she hadn't already left for Ghana. Celeste had never realized how important her aunt was to her until Kristin told her she would be away for two years teaching out of the country. She remembered, though, that her aunt had always been reluctant to say much about either of her parents so she couldn't be sure that Kristin would have given her any advice at all.

It had been her aunt Grace who had finally helped set Celeste straight and end her dilemma. Her father's older sister visited them during the same summer that Kristin left, and her timing couldn't have been better. Aunt Grace had noticed right away how miserable she was and quickly figured out the cause. Grace made a point of inviting Celeste to lunch before she returned home to Michigan so they could talk privately about anything the young girl needed to talk about. They had taken a taxi to one of Celeste's favorite restaurants, down on the waterfront.

She and Aunt Grace had always had a pleasant time together, although they didn't see each other frequently. Her aunt's obvious compassion had spurred Celeste to open up more than she probably would have otherwise. Before she knew it, everything Celeste had kept bottled up for months about her parents came pouring out. Her aunt hadn't even seem surprised when she told her what had been troubling her. She only sat listening attentively as Celeste told her about some of her parents' more troubling episodes. She told her aunt all about the hopes she had that they would be happy together, and how everything had quickly gone downhill.

Celeste had been unaware that it had taken everything Grace could muster to stay calm as she waited for her niece to finish. It had absolutely killed her to see the sadness in the young girl's eyes. Grace had to glance away several times, feigning interest in a row of small ships that were docked at a nearby pier. She did anything to avoid looking at the forlorn expression on Celeste's face, as she continued talking about the hopelessness of her parents' marriage.

It had broken Grace's heart to know that her niece was taking on the entire weight of her parents' relationship—and at such a young age. Celeste had obviously needed someone to talk to and Grace guessed correctly that her brother probably hadn't even noticed his daughter was hurting. Most likely, he had been far too busy thinking about himself!

After Celeste exhausted all she needed to say, Grace had taken her niece's slender face between her strong hands, smiling lovingly. She told her as gently and as firmly as she could that she would never have the power to control what was, or was not, going on in her parents' marriage.

"You can't fix this, sweetie," Grace told the troubled young child.

Celeste's face dropped quickly as her aunt's words assaulted her ears. She looked like she wanted to cry, but Grace wouldn't let a pitiful look stop her from saying what the girl needed to hear. It was heartbreaking for her to see her only niece so upset, but she knew that sugar coating it would only make it harder in the long run. She couldn't offer Celeste hope about her parents' marriage in good conscious, because she didn't see any hope.

Grace had always considered Angela to be a strange bird from the first time she laid eyes on her. She tried to tell her brother what he obviously couldn't see for himself, but quite naturally he wouldn't listen. Angela was a pretty enough woman and she had just the right pedigree to get their mother's approval, but she had never impressed Grace as having common sense. And things had only gotten worse after Celeste was born; had it not been for Kristin, her poor niece would've been left without any motherly love at all. And why such an intelligent woman as Kristin would let Winston use her to raise his child like that was beyond Grace's comprehension!

Celeste's heart plummeted as her aunt continued to talk. Grace said almost the exact opposite of what Celeste had been hoping to hear. She struggled to put on a brave face but her hopes were dashed to pieces. Everything Aunt Grace said to her had sounded so final.

"People change, baby." Her aunt had gone on to say, after a short silence. "You can never really count on a person to stay the same as they were when you first met them. And the one thing I want you to *always* remember is that the only thing that's constant in life *is* change."

Celeste kept thinking about what Aunt Grace had told her as they waited for their dessert to arrive. She had no idea what her parents' relationship had been when they first met, but the way they communicated had always seemed strange to her. She had been made into an unwilling go-between, with her mother forcing her to keep her informed of her father's comings and goings. But her father had been even worse, by having Celeste deliver his cryptic messages to her mother when he got ready to leave their house.

He would walk right past Angela on his way out of the door, never saying a word. Instead, he would look for Celeste and have *her* tell her mother where he was going, and sometimes when he planned to come home. "Tell your mother," he would say over his shoulder before getting into his car to leave.

Celeste had felt proud of herself as she told her aunt that she had refused to do it one day. She had decided not to put herself in the line of fire, knowing her mother had already been having a bad day. Celeste had been so happy to have someone to spill her guts to that she never noticed how livid her aunt became as she confided in her.

"What on earth could my brother be thinking to put this baby in such a position?" She wondered.

Grace had grown angry with Winston *and* Angela; she struggled to keep her true feelings from surfacing as they finished their dessert. Finally, she managed to calm herself long enough to tell Celeste that she would understand all of it better after she was older.

"But true love heals all wounds," she had assured her niece, after a moment of silence. "True love never dies and there is no conflict on earth that's too big to work out if love is really there. Never forget that, sweetie."

By the time they were in their taxi and headed home, reality had begun to sink in for Celeste. It had never crossed her mind that her aunt might mention any of their conversation to her father. She was never certain that she had, but Celeste realized later that there had never come another time after her lunch with Aunt Grace that her father had asked her to deliver another message to her mother. And eventually, something must have sunk in with her mother too because she had finally stopped asking Celeste where her father went after he left home.

Everyone had seemed surprised at how well Celeste took the news that her parents were separating. Occasionally, she wondered whether anything would have been different if Aunt Kristin had still been there. She and Angela had always been close friends, and they had spent a lot of time together before Kristin left for Ghana. They had all been a bit distressed when Kristin left to teach for two years, but having her move to Africa permanently had been especially devastating to Celeste. She had always assumed her aunt would be there whenever she needed her, even after she was old enough to realize Kristin wasn't really a blood relative.

Lately, she also wondered whether Aunt Kristin might have been able to help her control the new person she found herself becoming. Things had been spinning out of control quickly and it was getting kind of scary. Celeste had no idea what came over her to make her do some of the things she did lately—like slipping out again that morning to meet Malaya.

But as soon as the thought left her mind, Celeste remembered exactly what had made her to go behind her father's back again so soon. It was something she had heard in Malaya's voice when her friend called her. Celeste had already resigned herself to spending the day in her room and had actually been having fun. She had made a game of cleaning out her closet for clothes that Charlotte would donate to the Junior League. Celeste had been squeezing her now-oversized body into outfits that she knew she had outgrown, and amusing herself by prancing around her room in front of the mirror. She had been having a great time laughing at the way her unmistakable new curves pressed against the seams of dresses and pants she tried on. And she had been just about to tell Malaya that she couldn't come out too, but there had been something in her friend's voice that made her change her mind. It was so noticeable that Celeste *couldn't* ignore it. She forgot about the promises she had made to her father and followed her instincts instead. They told her that Malaya was in some sort of trouble, so she had left the loft to go meet her as soon as they hung up.

Her friend had been acting so strange lately—even for Malaya. She had even started talking in codes when they were on the phone sometimes; then, she would act as though it had never happened when Celeste asked her about it later. But by the time she caught up with her at the mall that morning, Malaya's mood had changed completely. She was laughing and clowning around as she usually did when there weren't other people around them. Malaya had even bought Celeste a blouse while she waited for her to get there, just like the one she had bought for herself.

Celeste's luck held out again and she made it home before her father. She could hear Charlotte rummaging around on the other side of their living room space, so she crept up the stairs quietly. Her new blouse was in a bag that she held behind her until after she was safely in her room. She hid it in the back of her closet where it would have to stay for at least two weeks, and then quickly cleaned up the mess she had left all over the room. She was getting into so much trouble lately but she certainly couldn't blame her friend for it. Malaya had always been able to get away with bending rules at her house; she didn't even have a curfew, at least not one that seemed to matter. And sometimes, Celeste thought Malaya deliberately tried to get into trouble. The only thing that had changed lately was that Celeste had found herself caught up in doing the same crazy stuff as her friend. She had been doing things she would never have dreamed of doing—at least the old Celeste wouldn't have dreamed it.

Her father had really scared her a few weeks earlier, after he said he didn't feel comfortable with her being at Malaya's house. For one horrible moment, Celeste had thought he was trying to tell her that he wanted their friendship to end. She had braced herself as soon as he started the conversation, glancing quickly at Charlotte and wondering whether she had finally managed to have her way. Her stepmother had never seemed to like

179

her friend. She had been icy cold towards Malaya since the day they met, and had tried all sorts of things to keep them apart.

But thankfully, her father had only meant she wouldn't be able to spend the night at Malaya's house. He had always liked Malaya and had refused to join in on her stepmother's crusade against her. Her father told Celeste that he preferred her not to go there at all, and he had made her promise that she would keep her visits short whenever she did. Celeste had breathed a sigh of relief when her father said her friend was still welcome at their house. The two girls had been best friends since their first day of school, when they had naturally gravitated toward each other. They had become like sisters over the years, though they had been separated for a brief time after Celeste's parents divorced. She and Trazi had moved with their father to a different area of town after that; Celeste could still remember how sad she had been when she and her friend separated and had to say goodbye.

But Aunt Kristin had told her once that there was something good that always came out of any situation. And sure enough, Celeste and Malaya had found each other again just as Trazi was leaving Washington to join the navy. She had been clinging to her brother as his time to leave grew closer and one day, she had gone with him to visit an old friend from elementary school. As it turned out, Trazi's friend lived right next to the house where Malaya and her family had lived for years. The girls had been elated to see each other again, so unexpectedly. They were even more excited when they realized the house where Malaya's family planned to move next was very close to the loft. It meant that they would go to the same school again and be able to see each other every day.

Her father had seemed almost protective of Malaya sometimes when she was at their house. Celeste had overheard him tell Charlotte once that Malaya reminded him of a baby bird that had fallen from its nest; shivering alone on the ground, as it waited for something or someone to come along and decide its fate.

Chapter 23

Winston

*W*inston made a point of checking his email as soon as he was out of his one o'clock meeting. There had still been no response from his daughter, even though he had emailed her as soon as he booted up his computer that morning. He had finally come up with the perfect way to verify whether Celeste stayed home whenever he asked her to.

He leaned back in his chair, giving more deliberate thought to his crafty little princess with a slight smile. He pictured the look of innocence she would no doubt have on her face that afternoon when he got home. He had been able to count on her being practically glued to that computer he had bought her for Christmas whenever she *was* at home. And there was an alert featured on her email account that played a tone whenever a new message came in. Just to be certain, whenever he was testing her he added a subject that would get her to open the message and respond to it right away. The subject of the one he had sent that morning was, 'Do you want to meet me to get pizza for lunch in the mall?' If she had been at home, as she should have been, he knew for a fact that Celeste would have answered that email right away. His daughter had never let an opportunity pass to have him and his wallet join her at the mall.

And if, on the off-chance, there had been some kind of problem with her computer, Winston knew for sure that she would have called him several times by now, pleading with him to get the problem fixed. So all of that made him ninety-nine percent certain that his daughter had left home right after he had that morning.

He had always loved his son, of course, even after they started fighting all the time as Trazi got older. But his "Baby Blue," as he called Celeste sometimes, had always been his heart. He had been calling her by that name since he first caught sight of her astonishing dark blue eyes in the hospital, just after she was born. He had been bewildered too that they were so strikingly similar to Kristin's eyes. Both of them had eyes of almost the exact color and intensity, although he and Angela both had dark brown eyes. Winston often caught people doing double-takes after getting a glimpse of both his daughter's and his former wife's eyes. Their deep pigmentation had a hypnotic effect that seemed capable of sending someone into a trance if they weren't careful, or if they paused for more than a quick glance.

It had become painfully obvious to him that he had looked into his daughter's baby blues longer than he should have, but thanks to the new technology he was finally on to her. He was also finally beginning to accept that his little girl was growing up. He had to brace himself for the inevitable because he realized it would happen whether he was ready for it to happen or not. And he could see that she was going to be a knockout too, just like her mother. What a nightmare!

Winston was already painfully aware of the stares his daughter got from men on the street. He couldn't help noticing it whenever they were out in public together. It was bad enough to see teenage boys doing it, but when he caught men *his* age drooling over his thirteen-year-old daughter it was hard for him to restrain himself. The only reason he even tried was that he knew how mortified Celeste would be if he just lost it and made a scene.

In the meantime, she seemed oblivious to all the attention she attracted, and that was even scarier for Winston. Kristin had tried to assure him that wasn't the case at all, but he couldn't forget that his Celeste had always been a spirited child. She was used to catching the eye of strangers from the time she was a baby too. Now it seemed that those experiences made her quite comfortable with talking to people she didn't even know. When he was with her, the glaring looks he kept on his face were usually an effective enough deterrent for any would-be suitor they happened across. He would cringe whenever he thought about what might be going on when he wasn't around; if he thought too much about it, Winston would literally have nightmares.

He could remember praying that his daughter would be a late bloomer when she was just a few months old. He knew that he had to count himself lucky though, because thirteen *was* late these days for young girls to start blossoming. He had tried not to notice how her jeans started to fit her all of a sudden. Charlotte had blown him off when he mentioned it to her, but after a while he just couldn't take it anymore. He had browbeat his poor wife until she finally agreed to take Celeste shopping for larger sized clothing. But even *he* had to admit that it hadn't made much of a difference.

That had also been the moment that Winston realized he would have to adjust, if he were to have any chance of remaining sane. He was still trying to recover from a phone call from his daughter a few months earlier. She had been so excited to tell him that she had just started her menstrual cycle. Was she trying to make him have a stroke?

That had been his only thought as she rattled on and on, giving him all the details. Apparently, she had assumed he would want to know about it right away because she had just blurted the whole thing out without any warning. It had become very clear to him as she babbled on and on that he would never be able to help her with such things, no matter how much he might want to. And he had never been able to rely on her *own* mother to take care of her. Angela's imbalance during her pregnancy had never righted itself, as they had all hoped it would. Instead, she had developed a drinking problem to add to it after Celeste was born. She had already been to rehab three times and his daughter barely even knew her mother.

But he had done his best to be a good substitute. He thought that he deserved some credit because of her calm reaction to everything when her cycle *did* start. But when his daughter tried to have the kind of conversation she wanted to have with him that day, he had been forced to acknowledge that she needed someone else to guide her into womanhood. For a split second, he had considered calling Charlotte. After all, she was his wife. When they were first married, he had been optimistic that his third wife would not only find a way to coexist with his daughter, but he had hoped, and even expected, that she would develop more than a passing interest in her. After all, Celeste had been the main reason he had even considered remarrying. His daughter had only been nine when he and Charlotte married, so he had dared to hope at one time that they might eventually become friends.

But it would soon be five years since he had introduced Charlotte to his children. Trazi had already decided to move out, and there was nothing close to a friendship that had formed between his wife and Celeste. Now, with his daughter's volatile hormones being added to the mix, Winston had little hope that the situation would ever change. He had actually been relieved later that day when he got home and found a note from Charlotte. She had taken a train into New York to do some shopping, the note read, and wouldn't be back until the following afternoon.

He had hesitated only briefly before dialing Kristin's number, still in a daze from his conversation with Celeste. He knew that Kristin would be busy packing up her house for her move to Ghana, but he had been prepared to beg for her help if need be. He would have done anything to get her to come over to talk to his daughter and take care of her.

※※※

After Trazi left home, Winston's concern about those guys who always hung around across the street from their loft had grown considerably. He had already made a point of letting them know that Celeste was his daughter the year before, and that he had his eyes on them. He had gone out of his way to find something out about any guy he had seen lounging on the church steps on a regular basis. He would comment on whatever it was that he had dug up on them as he walked past the church on his way to and from the train station.

"They don't have steps for you to sit on over on Davis Boulevard, brother?" He would never stop long enough for the young buck he had questioned to ask how he knew so much about him. Winston *did* wait until he had seen the startled look on their faces, though. That was all he really wanted. He wanted his knowledge of them to be a mystery, and he only had to make similar comments two or three more times before they got his point. After that, they would wait until after they thought he had already left for work before they started gathering on the steps. Winston knew that they would start leaving the block just before it was time for him to come home too, if he took the train – like clockwork.

For the life of him, he could never understand how they could be content to be so idle. All they ever did during the summer months was to sit on the steps, day after day, making one failed attempt after another to validate their manhood with their lame catcalls. He had watched them for hours once from his bedroom window, as they tried to get something started with any young female who walked by. He could tell by their relaxed body language as they sprawled on the steps that day that they probably assumed he had already left for work. As he looked down on the young men, Winston thought about his grandfather and wondered what they would have been like had they grown up under his influence, as he had. Winston's own father had died in an automobile accident when he was still a young man of thirty-seven years. Winston's mother had begun taking him and his sister, Grace, to Jamaica every year after their father's death. They would visit their mother's parents for a week and then they would all spend one or two nights with their paternal grandfather, before his mother and sister returned to the States. His mother would leave Winston with his grandfather for the whole summer. She told him she wanted to make sure he didn't miss out on having a father too much.

For the first couple of years, Grace had been envious as it got closer to the end of their school term, while Winston bubbled over from his excitement. He had been anxious to go back to Jamaica every year for a while, because he lived a completely different lifestyle there on his grandfather's farm; especially compared to all the rules he lived with in Washington with his mother. But once he finished the seventh grade, Winston's feelings about going to Jamaica every summer had begun to change. He discovered all the fun his friends were having during his absence back in D.C. After that, it wasn't long before his excitement about spending time with his grandfather turned into dread.

He began to resent the brutal chores that would be piled on him from the moment he arrived on the island, although they were the same chores that he had once thought of as being fun. Winston had refused to listen to anyone's explanation as to why it was so important for him to learn how to care for a goat. He had to laugh to himself when he thought back to the summer he had finally yelled at his grandfather, saying that he had never seen any goats in Washington. It was the day that he had finally taken a stand, and unintentionally blurted out all his feelings about everything. Afterwards, his grandfather had still insisted that he take care of the goat, of course, and anything else that he came up with. Winston had been a man himself before he fully appreciated what his grandfather had taught him about being a man.

Looking down from his bedroom window at the young guys on the church steps, he knew right away that most of them were growing up without a decent father to show them how to act, or what to do. Otherwise, they would be doing something other than just resting on the steps all day. He was terrified that his daughter might end up marrying someone like that. The thought had made him shudder involuntarily and move away from the window.

185

His mother had a much easier time of steering him and Grace away from the friendships she didn't want them to have. For one thing, they had lived on Washington's "Gold Coast" for the first seven years of his life. Before his father died, everyone who lived near them had been acceptable to his mother's high standards. But she had been forced to ramp up her efforts to monitor their friends after they moved to northeast D.C. and they had been left without the income that their father earned as a physician. Their new house was modest, but it was in a very quiet and stable neighborhood. It didn't compare at all to their old house on the Gold Coast though, and Winston never caught on that his mother had managed all his friendships once they moved there until he was well into junior high.

He had never bothered to let the young bucks across the street know that he was on to their schedule. He knew that he had their attention now, and that was all that mattered. All of them knew that Celeste had someone who loved her and who cared about what happened to her. Winston had no doubt that they would respect his daughter, because now they knew that he was the kind of man to do whatever was necessary to make sure they did. And that would have to do for now since Trazi was away.

His son had been the only person other than Kristin, oddly, that Winston had ever trusted to look after Celeste. He thought briefly about calling Trazi to get some ideas from him on handling his sister. In the end, he changed his mind because he wasn't sure that Trazi wouldn't just hang up the phone on him before he had a chance to say why he was calling. It was one more reason for him to regret the way that his son had left his home, and that they had not found a way to resolve their differences.

His sister had turned into little Miss Pinocchio almost overnight, and Winston was certain that she could no longer be trusted. But since he and his daughter had always been close, he knew he would figure something out eventually. In the meantime, he had to find a better way to keep track of her and keep her safe from herself.

He allowed himself a rare moment to think about Kristin. He remembered something she had said to him about Charlotte on the night that Trazi had left their loft in the middle of the night. Their son had been missing for several hours; he and Kristin had both been worried sick at the idea that their seventeen-year-old son was traveling around D.C. in the middle of the night all alone. Both of them had been extremely jumpy until he finally made it safely to Kristin's house, still very upset about their fight.

Her maternal instincts had always been strong and had gotten the best of Kristin that night. Winston had immediately conceded that she was within her rights to be upset before he arrived at her house, and he had been prepared to deal with her anger when he knocked on her door. He had been driving around for hours looking for Trazi himself, and finally decided that what he was doing was fruitless. He drove to Kristin's house instead to wait with her for news about their son, and he had been pleasantly surprised to find that she was glad he had come. They kept all their energy focused on Trazi that night, praying that he would make it to his mother's house unharmed.

Kristin had kept her temper in check, but she made it clear to him that she believed Trazi's version of what happened at the loft. Instead of being angry though, she had calmly told Winston that she believed everything was in Divine Order and they would all have to wait to see what would happened next.

Winston had been even more surprised when she asked him abruptly whether he thought Charlotte might be battling some sort of internal demons. Coming from anyone else, Winston would have thought the question to be malicious. But he knew from her expression that Kristin's concern was genuine, especially when her next comment was in the context of his wife's influence over Celeste.

Kristin had been extremely generous with him that night, despite her apprehension about Trazi's safety. They had finally fallen asleep together on her living room couch and only woke up at the sound of their son putting his key in her front door shortly before 6 a.m.

It hadn't taken very much effort for Kristin to convince Winston to let Celeste stay with her for a few weeks after that night. Trazi shocked everyone a few days later by announcing that he had enlisted in the Navy; he already had his travel orders before either of his parents knew anything about it. Kristin thought it would be important for Celeste to spend as much time with her brother as possible before he left for boot camp, and Winston agreed with her, despite Charlotte's unexpected objections.

He dropped Celeste off at Kristin's house the night of Trazi's high school graduation. Winston had been surprised that he felt oddly left out when he thought about the three of them being together without him.

Chapter 24

Back to Africa

Kristin leaned back in her chair as far as she could go and stretched her arms in a long lazy yawn. From outside her office, she looked like a cat waking up from its afternoon nap. She rubbed both her eyes with closed fists and then stood up to swing her arms in a circular motion to stimulate her chi, or energy force, after having sat for so long. Part of the reason she had bought the wooden chair in the first place was that it was stiff and uncomfortable. Her intent had been to use it to help her maintain her focus as she worked. The hard mahogany wood kept her from becoming too relaxed, since she already worked with her shoes off most of the time. The other reason she wanted the chair was that its carvings and cow-skinned seat reminded her of a chair that her grandmother once had.

She had spotted her chair sitting among other wood carvings in a small shop in Sokoban Wood Village, not far from Kumasi. Kristin had gone to a great deal of trouble to have the chair moved to where it now sat in her office. It had taken a few days before she got used to the animal skin stretched across its cushioned seat, but she was glad that she had decided to buy it. When she and her siblings were small children, they had visited their grandmother for two weeks every summer. Her grandmother's cow-skinned chair had been a constant source of torment for her back then. The prospect of seeing it had always dampened Kristin's enthusiasm about going to visit her grandmother. Kristin, her brothers, and her sisters would all race each other at meal time to avoid having to sit it. Both the back and seat of her grandmother's chair had been made from the skin of a black and white cow. Kristin smiled as she remembered how terrified she would always be; invariably, she was the one who lost the race more often than not, resulting in her having to sit in the dreaded cow chair during most meals. One of her biggest fears, courtesy of her older brother, had been that the chair would somehow come alive, if she let her guard down, to swallow her whole.

Her other cause for concern had been the new set of kittens that her grandmother always seemed to have. Kristin had developed a phobia of cats some time after her fourth birthday and would be terrified the whole time she was at her grandmother's, because the scrawny animals would often pop up abruptly through missing floorboards in the small house.

But it wasn't as though staying there had been her only option whenever they "vacationed" in the country town her mother had grown up in. Her father grew up in the same place and his relatives didn't keep pets inside their house. They had indoor plumbing too and a few other modern conveniences, many years before other African Americans in the area. Kristin had always been tempted to stay with her father at his family home. There, she could have not only avoided the cats but she could have spent time with her other cousins too. But she loved being around her grandmother so much that she had always braved her fears.

She and her sibling had enjoyed sleeping on the pallets her grandmother would make for them and their cousins, who had often visited at the same time. Their grandmother would fashion several beds together from old quilts, arranging them around the living room floor like sleeping bags. Kristin loved finding bits and pieces of her own favorite clothing in the quilts. Before the lights were turned out, she would lie on the floor remembering dresses she had once worn that were now part of their bedding. Her mother would always bring a bag filled with more of their old dresses for her grandmother to use to make new quilts for them. And since there were never any floorboards missing from the living room floor, she felt safe from the cats as soon as the door was closed. She knew they couldn't get into the room although she could still hear them, and she would sleep peacefully throughout the night.

Since her grandmother didn't have indoor plumbing they had to use an outdoor toilet whenever they stayed with her, which Kristin also dreaded, and she would avoid eliminations for as long as she could. But she had loved walking deep into the woods to a natural spring that ran behind the house to get water. Everyone would bring buckets and containers of all sizes to fill and carry back to the house to be used for cooking, drinking, and bathing. Her grandmother could carry a bucket of water on her head, just like the women that Kristin saw carrying water in Ghana.

She had watched in fascination as her grandmother chopped wood and stacked them in her front yard in small more uniformed pieces. The younger children had never been allowed to touch the sharp ax, of course, but they had all helped bring wood chips into the house to use as fuel for the pot-bellied stove that also provided heat during winter months. There was an abundance of love in that small tin-roofed house and that had made up for anything else that might have been missing. It had been worth all the trouble Kristin went through to avoid the cats and the cow-skinned chair.

Her grandmother had also been the local midwife and herb lady in the small Alabama town, until she was well into her seventies. There were many who had depended on her for healing advice and treatment during a time that Blacks were not allowed to go to formerly all-white medical facilities. The whole community had relied on her grandmother; she prescribed herbs that she grew in her garden to treat fevers and other illnesses, and people had frequently called on her to perform minor surgeries and to administer first aid. Black *and* white women had come to her for advice on prenatal care; they sought her skills as a midwife, since even the closest white hospital had been miles away. Her grandmother delivered nearly all the babies that had been born in Clarke County from the time that she started her practice, until the mid '60s. She had made the cow-skinned chair herself too; one of the many connections to the Motherland that often survived due to isolation of small rural towns.

Kristin had been sitting on her mahogany chair for nearly eight straight hours. She had only been out of it long enough to pour herself a fresh cup of Moringa tea, or to make a quick visit to the small bathroom at the opposite end of her office. She would get so wrapped up in her work sometimes that she would actually forget to eat. The Moringa plant had grown to be a vital element for their Foundation's future; the powerfully packed nutrients in the tea kept her body supplied with what it needed to keep her going.

She had been so focused that she never noticed her assistant coming into the room, but the flavorful aroma coming from a large platter was indisputable evidence that Amina had been there. The smell of spices cooked into the grilled fish drifted over to Kristin from a side table until her fixation was finally broken. And once her concentration had been disrupted, her mind refused to focus on anything other than anticipation of the meal she had been brought. Sitting next to the steaming fish were large bowls of Moroccan couscous and fish stew – two of Kristin's favorites, along with fruit and other side dishes.

She smiled to herself as she realized Amina often used the same method to get her to stop working long enough to eat that Kristin's mother used to get her attention when she was a child. She and her sister had stayed after school for scout meetings on Tuesdays during elementary school, and their mother would make the most scrumptious graham cracker-crusted dessert on those days. She had never once had to remind Kristin or her sister to come straight home after their meeting was over, because the prospect of eating their mother's special dessert was all the motivation they needed.

It wasn't until after her stomach started growling when she smelled the fish that Kristin was conscious of how long she had been working. She spooned some of the fish stew into a bowl and shoveled several pieces of tilapia onto a large plate, adding a generous helping of couscous and salad greens. She also spooned chunks of mouth-watering mango onto a smaller plate to round out the meal. Then, she picked up silverware and quickly put it and her filled dishes onto a tray that she carried to her more comfortable loveseat.

She and Amina had intuitively been in sync since their days together at KNUST, seven years earlier. Her assistant was quite used to her habit of closing herself off in her office to concentrate, and the closed door was their unspoken signal that Kristin didn't want to be disturbed. This time, Amina had been so quiet when she brought the food in that Kristin had no idea she had been there at all.

Their first board of directors meeting had been scheduled for the following Monday, and board members were due to begin their staggered arrivals over the coming weekend. Kristin had been working like a possessed woman for the past two weeks, trying to make sure everything was in place. Time seemed to move faster as they got closer to the date, and she had spent the entire day carefully going over their agenda. She had also double-checked all the arrangements that had been made for the small group of people who would help her direct the charter for the Diasporan Exodus Foundation, the nonprofit organization she had founded. She went over each itinerary hour-by-hour with a fine-toothed comb, beginning with their arrivals and reception at the airport. For most board members from the States, it would be their first time in Africa; she wanted to make certain their experiences were as close to perfection as possible.

Kristin had also reviewed all the documents she planned to reference as the board moved through their three-day agenda. The material had been copied and assembled into notebooks that were already placed around a long table in the hotel conference room that would serve as their board-room. All writing tablets, pens, and other takeaways for the meeting had been inscribed with the Adinkra symbol she had chosen as the official motif for the Foundation. The emblem had seemed to jump out from the pages of Adinkra symbols Kristin had been studying. Initially, she had been attracted to it because she truly felt the success of their mission would take the equivalent effort of that required to fit a square peg into a round hole. But once she learned that "Boa Me Na Me Mmoa Wo," the symbol's meaning, translated to "Help Me and Let Me Help You" in English, she knew it was exactly what she had been searching for.

That had been the first of many signs Kristin began receiving once she took her first formal steps to create her Foundation in the U.S., with its objectives carried out in Ghana. She had taken it as a clear sign that the Universe was still directing her path. The motif she had chosen symbol-ized *cooperation* and *interdependence*; the very core of her Foundation's mission and a perfect reflection of her intent. There were two arrows in the symbol that moved toward each other from opposite ends; each containing a square or circle, with one arrow forming the base of the other. Kristin interpreted their positioning as the arrows seeking to merge together, with the two completing a larger circle that she viewed as the Diaspora that had been scattered all over the world. And to her, it was the perfect depiction of what the Diasporas journey back to the Motherland would entail.

She felt that the level of adjustment required for the square and circle to fit snugly together was an accurate barometer of what would also be required for her Foundation's success. The symbol was the first item on the agenda for their board meeting and would likely take center stage at future meetings as well. The strategies the board would devise to move their goals forward would be as challenging as fitting a square peg into a round hole, as the two cultures merged together. But she was positive her vision was attainable and she had already begun picturing the day that a new symbol would be created to celebrate their unification.

Kristin had personally arranged the name plates for each board member around the table, giving thought to each person's background and to the information she had learned about them. Most members representing the

American side would be meeting each other for the first time, although most were well known within their own areas of expertise.

She had sent each board member a photo and curriculum vitae of other members, hoping it would be a starting point for conversations after formal introductions had been made. Kristin looked for common interests they might have outside of the Exodus Foundation as she formalized seating arrangements. She mixed their Ghanaian board members in with board members from America, an arrangement she planned to continue whenever they met as a group. She hoped it might spark professional associations as well as friendships, all of which would be beneficial to the Foundation's overall objectives as they sought out the best for both cultures.

Their travel agency had purchased a beach resort that sat on the Gulf of Guinea in Accra, as a lodging option for their clients that would also lend itself to a culturally rich experience. Their board members would stay at that hotel and the meeting was also to take place there. Kristin had already achieved her agency's main objective of expanding opportunities for African American groups to travel to Ghana. The travel agency had grown quickly through referrals and now attracted clients from other nationalities and ethnicities, as well. But their marketing campaigns were still targeted toward African Americans making their first trip to the Motherland.

Kristin and Solomon reopened the agency's satellite office in Washington the year they took over as new owners. That office coordinated all itineraries that began in the States just as the original agency had done, and their agents arranged face-to-face meetings with clients whenever possible. If that wasn't an option, they would mail them questionnaires, using their responses to get a better sense of what clients were hoping to get out of their trip. The agency still personalized tours and tried to make as many of their clients' dreams come true as possible.

Heavenly Travel had already expanded their list of destinations to include the Northern Region. Their patrons would always rave about visits to Mole National Park, near Damongo, and the scenic drive to the well-known game and wildlife preserve. It was a destination that satisfied those who still presumed that they would find wild animals all over Ghana, before they traveled. Unfortunately, they also sometimes had clients who voiced open disappointment that cedis were dispensed from local bank machines instead of the U.S. dollars that they somehow expected. Everyone at the agency knew to keep a closer eye on those particular clients, and those who had similar notions. Their staff would make certain they were kept out of trouble while they toured the country; especially in the

Northern region, where the majority of people were Muslim and tended to be more conservative.

Along with pre-travel newsletters and materials that they routinely mailed, their agency now sent clients more detailed information about the history of villages and communities they would visit or travel through. Every time they sent out a mailing, they made a point of including some information about Ghana or West African culture in general. They would also discreetly include information about the community's needs, in an unobtrusive manner. The agency especially stressed the importance of their clients bringing school supplies with them for donations, since it was something that they could easily afford—even those who had to make smaller layaway payments to finance their trip.

Heavenly Travel suggested that they fill their suitcases with relatively inexpensive supplies, as Kristin and her friends had been urged to do on their first trip. They made sure their clients knew how much the items would be appreciated in Ghana. They also made their clients aware of how expensive it would be to ship supplies after they had traveled, due to their heavy weight. To encourage clients to stuff their bags with as many school supplies as possible before their trip, their agents always started tours with a visit to local markets in Accra, where they could find clothing that most already intended to buy, and wear it during their trip.

Not long after their grand opening, Solomon began making arrangements for their clients to witness festive ceremonies in the Ashanti region, with some rituals performed specifically for their tour groups. The ceremonies gave their wealthier patrons, in particular, an opportunity to present larger gifts in person that they had begun bringing in increasing numbers.

Within their first year, her business partner had also begun a program through Heavenly Travel that facilitated the adoption of any of their clients who were so inclined, by local families. A special rite would be performed to welcome the new American family member, culminating in a christening ceremony in which they were officially given their African spiritual name and new family name. Their agency suggested that a modest fee be given as an offering for the opportunity to participate in these stirring rituals, and all fees collected went directly to the adopted Ghanaian family. Most of their participating guests gave more than the modest donation they suggested, and those funds were given to the adoptive family as well. Heavenly Travel never kept one cedi of profit for arranging these "adoptions." They had only occasionally requested reimbursement for extraordinary expenses incurred as they staged more elaborate ceremonies for their VIP clients, but the Ghanaian families benefitted just as much in the long run. Any of their other patrons who happened to be in the country at the same time were invited to witness these ceremonies. The adoptees always made remarks at end of the rites, which often included a pledge of continued support after their return home.

The money or gifts they sent to their new families usually made a tremendous impact on their economic well-being. In some cases, it made up for financial support that may have been promised by a blood relative who had somehow managed to maneuver their way through the difficult process of obtaining an American visa, and for one reason or another, had failed to come through. But so far, to Kristin's delight, their 'adopted' clients had been consistent in living up to their pledges. The money that they sent "back home" often gave their adopted siblings new avenues for completing their primary and secondary educations. It also helped to sustain the family's household in many other immeasurable ways. As the number of people who benefitted from their programs grew, community support for their travel agency also increased. Their reputation for altruism quickly spread from the Ashanti Region to the Central and Greater Accra Regions, as the same opportunities were extended to families living there.

Earlier in the year, they had stepped things up a notch by adding luxury excursions to their offerings, specifically geared to the tastes of wealthier clients and Black American celebrities. The development of those plans had led them into building a second hotel at the midway point along the Accra-Kumasi Road. It was another first-rate hotel, with accommodations that were more suitable to the style of travel their VIP clients were accustomed to. They were treated to extraordinary once-in-a-lifetime experiences, with the high-maintenance care provided that they also usually wanted.

At least one personal concierge was assigned to each celebrity, and would be available to them during the entire time they were in Ghana. The concierge would greet their flight and help them through immigration and customs; they would also be on hand at the airport again when the traveller was ready to depart for home. The concierge would personally escort clients throughout their stay, if requested, and would even shop for their souvenirs; giving these clients an option of not having to travel with their own personal assistants. Or, Heavenly Travel's concierge could work directly with the celebrity's assistant to provide the same services, if requested.

Amina headed that division of their company and she had personally selected all the young men and women they had hired as concierges. She developed the protocol they were to follow, in addition to providing their orientation and general management. Kristin had requested that her own increasingly busy travel schedule be planned around some of their celebrity guests, as much as possible, so she could also be on hand at the airport for their arrival. If she happened to be out of the country or otherwise unavailable, Amina would fill in for her and greet these VIP guests, introducing them in turn to their personal concierge who would directly assist them during their travels. Either way, they made certain that their special clients got what they needed and what they expected while in Ghana.

Their agency had built up a solid reputation in only two years, of providing spectacular service and unique adventures for their guests. Their reward had been an exponential increase in business by the third month that their celebrity package rolled out. It had become so popular that those excursions now had to be booked over a year in advance. And, the growth in business had been almost exclusively generated by word of mouth.

Kristin had been particularly excited about the success of this phase. She had a long-standing desire to direct a significant portion of the millions of dollars that this sector of Black America seemed to spend so freely toward what she considered to be of "good use" in the Motherland. Heavenly Travel developed specialized information packets for these clientele, along with a list of significant goodwill opportunities available to them in Ghana. The materials the agency sent them included a suggested contribution for each opportunity, usually a minimum of ten thousand dollars.

She was certain that they could easily afford it, so Kristin had no problems in asking. And her instincts had proven correct because a majority of the Black American celebrities who had joined their growing list of clients, had been extremely gracious. They generously responded, when asked, to the needs of the Ghanaian people.

Since Kristin was sensitive to perceptions of favoritism, she had decided early on to turn over the responsibility for distributing gifts their clients brought, to Solomon. When she came to Kumasi to teach, Amina had steered her away from several unintentional breaches of protocol that she would have been completely unaware of, and Kristin had found the culture in Ghana to be very complicated at first. Since Amina was also Akan, Kristin heavily relied on her for guidance in showing the proper etiquette and respect whenever she interacted with local chiefs and elders.

Now, Kristin was finally beginning to learn her way through the maze of a culture that had seemed so different from what she was used to in the States. Amina had helped her understand that there were many divisions in existence among the people there, mainly as a result of illogical boundaries that had been created in Ghana and all throughout Africa, during colonialism. The Europeans had mixed non-homogenous groups together, many of whom had been traditional enemies, as a way of maintaining order and preventing dissension. Kristin now had a much better understanding of the different ethnic groups and sub-groups than she had started out with, but she still had no intention of unknowingly becoming entangled in a controversy over how gifts were being distributed.

In light of Solomon's political connections, it seemed best to leave him in charge of that. So far, the distribution seemed top-heavy on the Akan side, with most of the contributions going to families of that state. But they were, after all, the majority ethnic group and it was only logical that the Asante would benefit more because of Solomon's ties. Still, Kristin remained entirely hands off regarding those decisions. She relied on Amina's periodic reports to learn who had ultimately been selected as recipients, and only so she would be kept in the loop in case the subject of gifts came up during conversations she engaged in, as she visited local villages.

The soirees they arranged for celebrities were becoming more and more extravagant. Sometimes, a celebrity's entourage traveled with them and their group might end up being upwards of thirty people. For groups of that size, Amina would assign at least three people from her concierge staff to make certain everyone's needs were being met. They made every attempt to schedule their itineraries to coincide with important Ashanti traditional festivals, such as the Akwasidae, or Sunday Festival that was based on the forty-two day Akan calendar.

Their clients were taken to witness durbars, or processions of chiefs. Solomon's father, who was a paramount chief, would usually be the highest-ranking traditional ruler in these processions. Sometimes, Chief Asare would sit on a pillowed litter carried on the shoulders of young men, similar to the way Roman Emperors were carried. He would be shielded from the sun by colorful kente umbrellas held high over his head. Solomon's father would sometimes be clothed in all white, and sometimes draped in dazzling kente garments woven from threads of pure cotton or silk, depending on the occasion. In more elaborate ceremonies, the higher chiefs always adorned themselves in twenty-four carat gold accessories. Most of their clients automatically assumed it to be costume jewelry initially, because of the high price the jewelry would bring on the open market in America.

The durbars ended at a reviewing area where the paramount chief was seated, along with an entourage of lesser chiefs. His official linguist would sit nearby to intercede in any conversations that the people wanted to have and act as go-between. Young girls from local villages provided entertainment through dance and song, and each time Kristin witnessed a formal durbar, it seemed surreal. Her observations were shared by many of their travel patrons as well—both young and old alike. They often commented on how moved they would be by the ceremonies, and were especially affected by the young girls who danced the traditional Adowa (Monday) dance, passed down from generation to generation for centuries.

The common feedback they would get was that the pulsating beat of the drums, along with the singing and dancing, stirred a deep connection they had never been aware they had. Kristin understood what they meant because she felt the same pull of familiarity. Every time she heard the chanting and the drums, she would feel an unconscious yearning for some missing part of a collective past. It seemed as though her soul still remembered the dances that her ancestors danced in ancient Africa, as far back as the 4th century.

Many of the baby-boomers would confide rather sheepishly that the ceremonies reminded them of long forgotten episodes of Tarzan that they had watched faithfully on Saturday afternoons as children. The show had been popular once among their generation, and most had tuned in every week. The same songs and dances that were performed at the ceremonies they witnessed had also been portrayed on the show. Only on Tarzan, the chanting had usually been a backdrop for his weekly heroic rescue. There had always been some naive group of European visitors who inevitably wandered into hostile tribal territory. Unsuspecting, they would be captured and later rescued by Tarzan just in the nick of time. As the baby-boomers grew older, they realized how far fetched the storyline had been, of course. Most had dismissed memories of the show from their minds until they heard the chanting and the drums of the ceremonial dances in Ghana.

With few exceptions, their celebrity clients who were also entertainers were easily persuaded to provide a reciprocal performance at the conclusion of the traditional rites, or at the very least, they gave remarks of appreciation. Before long, the majority of their show biz clients had begun arriving in Ghana fully prepared to put on an unsolicited show, thanks to the candid photos and captions their agency often featured in travel brochures they sent to their clients.

Chapter 25

The Exodus Foundation

*K*ristin had arranged to have beautiful mud cloth bags made by the women of Ntonso and presented as gifts to her board members. Each bag had the Adinkra emblem and its Twi meaning: "Boa Me Na Me Mmoa Wo" embroidered on the front, just below the block lettering of the Foundation's name. They had already been delivered to the hotel to be distributed as board members checked in. Inside the bags were writing materials, along with a smaller bag filled with local gourmet treats wrapped in bright foil. Kristin decided to include the treats for her western guests in particular, who were used to a different time zone. She hoped the treats would provide enough sustenance to tide them over if their stomachs began begging for food while everyone else was still sleeping.

She had hand-picked an assortment of art on a recent trip to Kumasi Market, and the canvases were to be delivered to their rooms with luggage as board members arrived. Kristin had planned several days of sightseeing and shopping tours after their meetings adjourned, but it had dawned on her that some members might be on a tight schedule and need to head for the airport as soon as their business in Ghana was concluded. The canvases had already been rolled and packaged in cylinder cartons, ready to be checked-in with luggage on return flights. She had even thought of including a smaller color print of each piece. That way, her guests didn't have to wait until after they had reached home to discover what their gifts were.

Amina, who had continued to prove herself to be a woman of remarkable talents, had put together most of the briefing materials for the meeting. She had been invaluable to Kristin in getting the Foundation off the ground in many ways, and would soon transition from her post at the travel agency to one of the top positions with the Exodus Foundation full time. Kristin had already warned Amina lightheartedly that she would have to train her replacement first, before Kristin would consider her new move to be permanent.

She knew it would be tricky to wean herself from relying so much on Amina, especially with her travel arrangements. Kristin had still not quite recovered from a nightmarish experience she had the one time someone other than Amina took care of her travel plans. Her assistant had been away at the time attending to family matters, and Kristin had to rely on the person who sat in for Amina to arrange everything for an impromptu business meeting in the States. If only she had remembered in time that Mercury was in retrograde motion, she would have double-checked everything for herself. Kristin knew well that during Mercury's appearance of traveling backwards, snafus and miscommunications were common—especially relating to travel. But because of her habit of depending so heavily on Amina, it had never occurred to her to check the plane tickets she was given herself before leaving Ghana. Consequently, she had found herself at Gatwick Airport in London with no coupon to board her connecting flight to the United States. Her travel folder contained only her return tickets to Accra, from Baltimore–Washington International Airport back through Gatwick.

Kristin had her travel itinerary issued by British Airways and it confirmed that she had purchased a prepaid ticket for all four flights, but she had still been stuck in London for hours until Amina's harried substitute could get everything sorted out. It had been a costly mistake but one that could easily have happened to anyone. As a result, Kristin had not only missed her flight but she had also missed an important meeting that she had not been able to reschedule. That meeting had been central to all her other appointments, which meant the whole trip had been a disaster.

After that experience, she would become anxious every time she thought about leaving her travel arrangements to anyone other than Amina, since overlooking one detail could easily end in another catastrophe. The position required someone with great powers of concentration who was also quick on their feet. They would have to be able to fix issues that popped up because there was usually something that did. And the odds of something like the situation in London happening again only increased with the frequency of Kristin's travel.

But she would never dream of keeping Amina's talents so narrowly limited, just because she was good at her job. Not only would that not be the best thing for the Foundation, but she hoped Amina's new position would partially reward her for the enormous contributions she had already made. At the same time, Kristin had too much to contend with herself to be bogged down with the logistics of travel. They would find someone to take Amina's place, she was sure, but Kristin would be remain anxious until they found the right person for the job.

The reports that Amina had prepared for their board meeting would give their members from outside Ghana a detailed sketch of the country's evolving political culture. Amina had included a brief synopsis of the complexity added to it, from a Western perspective, by the power that traditional leaders still wielded. She prepared a profile of Ghana's ten administrative regions that included information on the major ethnic groups. She also added information on tourist attractions, natural resources, and various industries, including gold mining.

Another section of her prepared reports described responsibilities that fell under each ministry of the national government. It highlighted the Ministry of Tourism, which had been known for a brief while as the Ministry of Tourism and Diasporan Relations. That would be the ministry that their foundation would most often interact with, especially during the first phase of operations.

Kristin had selected the seven board members who represented the western side of the Atlantic only after giving them a great deal of scrutiny. She began the process by taking a closer look into the backgrounds of everyone on her short list that she only knew by professional reputation. After she had satisfied herself that everyone was of outstanding character with exceptional professional credentials, Kristin had set up her face-to-face meetings with each individual. She introduced the mission of the Diasporan Exodus Foundation personally, which also gave her the opportunity to gauge their immediate reactions to the specifics she outlined of what the Foundation intended to accomplish.

All the people she had in mind from the U.S. were relatively young, but their combined professional experience was well over one hundred years. Kristin had very high expectations for her board; to reciprocate, she would remain alert for opportunities through other board members that might reward them for their service.

Aside from their credentials, she only had one specific requirement for her board members: they had to share her vision for the Foundation's mission. She had selected members that she felt would appreciate its purpose, and who had a clear understanding of what was at stake. That was what she had been alert for during her face-to-face interviews with the people she met with from the U.S. She had stared into each person's eyes and searched for a sign; not only of their commitment but also their enthusiasm – something that she might have missed over the phone.

Since the board appointment process was of utmost importance, she had waited until she felt certain she had selected the right person. Only then did she extend an official invitation for them to join her in directing the Foundation's business. She expected that there would be many disagreements as they moved forward, especially in the beginning. She appreciated their diversity, but she couldn't afford to have anyone affiliated with the board whose passion did not at least match her own. That one trait was mandatory; it didn't matter what else the person might have otherwise brought to the table.

Kristin was confident that the men and women she had selected were more than capable of helping her to accomplish what her Foundation sought to do. They were people who believed in its core objectives and would help make what many would think to be impossible, possible.

She turned her full attention to the food that she had heaped on her plate. The West African seasonings gave everything a wonderful flavor that delighted her taste buds. It was the first time she had eaten since breakfast and before she knew it, she had wolfed down a second serving of couscous and several smaller pieces of fish; finally leaning back to digest it all.

It had taken her quite some time to confirm that all the documents to support her agenda items were in place. The systematic inventory she went through as part of her verification process, also helped to bring the Foundation's purpose more fully into focus. She found herself becoming anxious, as she considered the colossal responsibility involved in what they would be undertaking. The lives of hundreds of thousands would literally rest in their hands, and that thought had briefly made her feel overwhelmed by her own ambition.

A major objective for their first meeting would be to reach a consensus on their priorities for the first five years. There were vital elements that were required to be in place before they could successfully roll out their first phase of operation. Many other components would be mandatory in order to keep their programs running smoothly, as a full implementation of their mission would span generations. Literally, *everything* would need to be taken into account.

The Diasporan Exodus Foundation would finally bring Marcus Garvey's dreams into fruition. Their overall goal would be to assist scores of African Americans in migrating to the other side of the Atlantic Ocean. Their participants would make an unprecedented journey home to a country that most of them would likely know little about, in the beginning. Their journey would lead them to an entirely new world. Most would begin again in a physical, political, social, and economic reality that was completely unfamiliar to any they had known. And in that respect, their experience would be very similar to that of their enslaved ancestors in America.

But the important difference this time would be that they would travel the Atlantic in the opposite direction. This time, the Middle Passage would bring them home to Mother Africa instead of to a life of bondage. They would travel aboard a luxury cruise liner rather than being packed inside the hull of a ship, like sardines. More importantly, their passage this time would be entirely voluntary. And unlike the Liberian settlement, which had been founded using violence and by an exclusively white American Colonization Society (ACS), the African American expatriates in their program would be invited to Ghana. Their residents would be warmly received by both traditional and nontraditional leaders alike, and they would also have the support of the community.

Unlike with the ACS, arrangements that were being made for their passage back to Africa were motivated by a nurturing love, rather than fear or greed. Many of the abolitionists in America supported the ACS because they were afraid that the former slaves would never be fully protected there. But the Liberian settlement had been financed and controlled, in large part, by money that came from slave states. Unlike the abolitionists and other supporters, their motivation had been to get rid of freed slaves that they felt had become "agitators" and who had increasingly been inciting those who remained enslaved to fight for their freedom.

A deadly illness spread throughout the original ACS settlement in Sierra Leone and caused it to fail. Not long afterwards, the ACS forced the Dey and Bassa peoples, who had lived in the area around Cape Mesurado for centuries, away from their native land at gunpoint and established Liberia on a thirty-five mile tract of coastline north of Sierra Leone, in 1822.

Kristin knew better than to expect the majority of African Americans to be enthusiastic about the Exodus project, especially during its first few years. She had anticipated that a large number would recoil at the very notion of pulling up their transplanted American roots, and moving back to Africa. She was actually counting on a smaller number of participants initially. She planned to introduce her proposal for a six-month pilot program to the board of directors during their meeting, bringing fifty families to Ghana one year before the official start of the exodus.

Feedback from their pilot participants would help identify gaps that their careful plans may have overlooked. The timetable that she and Amina developed would give them ample opportunity to rectify critical issues before the news media got wind of their plans. Kristin fully expected to become the brunt of jokes on late night TV for a while too, after the Foundation was formally launched, but she could care less about such things. She had never concerned herself with naysayers either, because she had much more productive use for her thoughts. But that didn't mean that she was under any illusion about the massive amount of work that lay ahead.

She would be surprised to find more than a handful of their adult participants who had any knowledge of Marcus Garvey's vision. Even fewer would know that the Liberian "colony" had been financed and governed by the ACS for its first twenty-five years of existence. The colonists in Liberia declared their independence in 1847, but most Black Americans didn't know that the colony had continued its violence toward the indigenous people of that area for decades. Things had become so bad that an investigation had finally been conducted in 1929 by an international committee into reports of slavery and forced labor.

It wouldn't be much of a surprise to Kristin to find that their participants lacked substantive knowledge about their history either, since so little of it was being passed down. It was something she had always admired about Jewish people: they made certain their history was preserved and they taught it to their children. Kristin recalled how disturbed she had been on the other hand, after flipping through one of Celeste's 4th grade textbooks once. She had found two paragraphs on the entire Civil Rights Movement; a small space to devote to the years of non-violent protest that had put an end to Jim Crow discrimination and restored voting rights to Black Americans. Two paragraphs hardly did justice to the people of all races and religions who had lost their lives in solidarity with the movement. The same familiar photos were most often displayed as an official pictorial representation of that time in history. Kristin wondered whether the repetitious use of those photos somehow created a subliminal impression that the violent uncertainty of a decade had in reality been confined to only one or two disturbing incidents.

She had observed each generation of Black Americans become further removed from their accurate and uncensored history, although the majority had still managed to melt in the pot of American diversity. Some of those who had successfully assimilated showed considerable disrespect and disservice to those who had sacrificed their lives during the struggle for Civil Rights for all. As far as some Black Americans were concerned, the actions and personal risks of others now seemed of little consequence.

But to those who had yet to find their way, any distortion about their history and how they came to be in their current predicament only added to their troubles. Dr. Keenan had required his students to read a telling book written by Dr. Sidney M. Wilhelm called, *Who Needs the Negro?*[3] Reading it had been a real eye-opener for Kristin, because there was no denying the impersonal truth laid out in the controversial book. It had originally been written in 1970, when Kristin was still a sophomore at Tuskegee, and its contents had become a hot topic for discussion in the politically-charged town. The book questioned whether there would soon be any legitimate place for the masses of Blacks in America, as contributors to society. And as she read Wilhelm's unsettling theories, Kristin knew that what he had written was painfully true.

Over the years, she had watched the seeming inevitability of his predictions as they unfolded. Now, what had once been thought to be an indispensable demand for manual labor in the U.S. had all but completely dried up. During the industrial revolution, Black Americans migrated to northern cities in large numbers in search of jobs. Their mass movement triggered race riots, based on fears of poor white Americans that Blacks would take over the lower-paying jobs that whites had depended on to feed their own families. After their migration, the Black workers who found jobs had still been shut out of opportunities that others had to participate in labor unions and to bargain collectively for their rights as employees.

Kristin knew that as the Age of Aquarius settled in, advances in technology would only accelerate. The demand for unskilled labor was unlikely to emerge again at the scale it had once been, and unfortunately, as Wilhelm predicted, many Black Americans were still unskilled. Immigrants had

---

[3] Dr. Sidney M. Wilhelm, *Who Needs the Negro*, (Cambridge Massachusetts: Schenkman Publishing Company, 1970). [Reprinted in 1993 by Conquering Books]

come to the United States over the years and had bumped the unskilled Black labor force from the limited jobs that *were* still available. As a result, and true to Wilhelm's forecast, a subset of Black America had become entirely expendable. Large ghetto-like structures were the only housing options for many who lived in northern cities. Over time, they have been subjected to more government regulations and restrictions, as Wilhelm foretold, as the police take more liberties with them. And by virtue of their continued dependence on the government for their very survival, Kristin knew that Wilhelm's suppositions were not nearly as far fetched as they might have once seemed to some.

But during her own book research, Kristin had documented cases of other Black families who had a different fate. Some, like her paternal great-grandparents, had been given land by a former owner/relative who had decided to head west for a new start after the Civil War ended. There were former slaves who had bought land too that they paid for with money they had earned for the first time. And long before the war began, there had been Blacks who escaped or who had been freed in the North and who had owned property and businesses for decades before slavery ended. Regardless of whether it had been given or earned, the fact that they managed to own property gave them a definite advantage over those who didn't. Some were fortunate to have family members who had a strong enough drive to push everyone else forward, whether they wanted to go or not. Through sheer determination, they cultivated a better life for their children and improved the quality of their lives as they rose to the top. And in time, they even established social clubs whose charters pledged service to their communities, although many of these clubs eventually became opportunities to exclude other Blacks.

Their members insisted on being separate from those who had yet to rise from the conditions they had been left in after slavery. Perhaps they were driven by a sense of survival, but their self-appointed exclusivity set the standard for all Black Americans. This group became the litmus test and set the rules for determining whether or not a person was "a credit to their race." Their children received love, proper discipline, and good educations, and they were best prepared for the opportunities that emerged as a result of new civil rights assurances that became the law in the late '60s.

There would be new avenues through the Exodus Foundation for these Black Americans too, to reach even greater heights in Ghana. And Kristin's intention was to steer as much benefit from their successes in America back to the Motherland, as she could.

Chapter 26

Gimme That Old 'Skegee Spirit

*B*uilding support for the Diasporan Exodus Foundation within the Ghanaian government and the traditional tribal hierarchy had been a painstaking process, though nearly everyone Kristin spoke with had been generally receptive to the concept. They all viewed the Foundation's mission as being a win-win opportunity for both the African Diaspora and those living in Ghana. With Solomon's connections, the Foundation had made remarkable progress in establishing itself in the country within a very short period. Everything was finally coming together and there would soon be Black American immigrants arriving at their shores.

A major challenge had been in working through the many opinions held on how the Foundation's goals should be met. Kristin had been meeting regularly with key ministers of the government and their staff, and had made major inroads in developing important relationships the Foundation would rely on. They had been working closely with the Ministry of Tourism in particular, to iron out the specifics of their participants' immigration status prior to graduation from the Foundation's programs. The Ghanaian Parliament had already approved a five-year preferential class of citizenship for each new resident of the community their Foundation would soon establish. It would be an official tribute to each person from the Diaspora in America who had chosen to return to Africa. The special citizenship status would coincide with the Foundation's readjustment period, the time allowed to their participants as an opportunity to acclimate themselves to the new culture. Their special citizenship status would come with many privileges, but there were restrictions that came with it as well.

None of what parliament had done to establish the new citizenship status would have any effect on the existing immigration laws in Ghana. African Americans who weren't affiliated with the Exodus Foundation could continue to apply for Ghanaian citizenship directly, as individuals. But either way, African American expatriates would all have the same option of retaining their U.S. citizenship, as Kristin had done, along with their new Ghanaian citizenship. She had held on to hers primarily as an added convenience for traveling back and forth to the U.S. and to other countries.

It had taken months of lobbying, but she had gradually gotten through to the majority of the vocal political players in Ghana. She had shared story after story with them, trying to gain their acceptance of the same conclusions she had drawn about the psychological damage that had been done during American slavery. Most of the people she spoke with had progressively begun to develop a different viewpoint of Black America; one more favorable than their initial impressions. She had managed to persuade many influential leaders that a large segment of the population in America was still crippled by the aftereffects of their ancestors experiences. Above all, she had persuaded them to adopt a different understanding of the underbelly's lack of decorum, instead of taking them solely at face value. Now, many were not as quick to dismiss the underbelly or hold them in such critical light; they had begun to empathize with them instead.

As Kristin met with various groups, she would often play video clips of popular television shows in America from the '70s that she had Niyla send to her. She would bring groups together of all sizes to hold discussions after watching episodes of "Good Times" or "The Jefferson's." She would listen to their thoughts about what they saw and heard on the shows; in doing so, Kristin had learned much more about personal and business protocol that was observed in Ghana.

It had taken a host of meetings, a barrage of gifts, and frequent travel to some of the more remote areas of the country, but she had made remarkable headway. It had become even more clear to her that the underbelly would have to learn their true history—who they really were. She had always recognized that to be a requirement for the Foundation's plans to be effective, but now she understood more fully how necessary it would be for changing the perceptions that many Ghanaians had of Black Americans.

The Foundation had already begun developing cultural education seminars that would be required for anyone who worked for them. A different set of classes were being developed for the Ghanaians they would hire, and for program participants coming from the Americas. The classes, slated to begin one year before the first group of African American families arrived, would also be recommended to any associate of the Exodus Foundation. A presentation of both curriculum prototypes was on the agenda for their upcoming board meeting. Kristin had made certain they would be given adequate time for discussion, as one of her primary objectives for the meeting was to get board input on what they had developed so far, and ultimately conceptual approval of the classes.

Based on the board's recommendations, her staff would make any necessary changes before posting schedules for the free classes they would offer. The Ghanaian version would include a discussion of the concept of post traumatic stress syndrome too, with an emphasis on its application to American slavery. Those from Ghana taking the classes would learn that many of the Black Americans they would interact with in the program were not even aware that they exhibited certain symptoms of the disorder. The classes would help portray Black Americans as the spiritually troubled souls that they were, in need of nurturing love and support.

Their facilitators would share specific examples of opportunities that had been made available after Civil Rights laws were passed in America; opportunities that many had made no attempt to take advantage of. Kristin knew it would be a tough sell without any physical evidence to document the ongoing trauma being suffered. She believed in her heart that it was the true source of the underbelly's dysfunction, but there was no one left alive now who could verify the legitimacy of her claims.

It was only on rare occasions that some family member or friend might stumble across an old letter that had been tucked away some place, and revealed the graphic details of some heartbreaking event that had happened long ago. Sometimes, it would explain another family member's mysterious behavior or the source of their barely hidden pain. Aside from those infrequent occurrences, the damage that had been done to many had more often been passed down silently from one generation to the next. It took the form of subconscious behavior patterns—conduct that was automatically adopted by their offspring who naturally imitated their parents. Their way became their children's way, and later the same behavior was passed on to their children's children.

As she traveled around and spoke to different groups, Kristin would also talk about the posture that had been adopted for survival by a majority of slaves in America at one time. It was the stance of total submission or "shuffling," as many termed it. At one point, shuffling had been one of the only voluntary expressions that those who were enslaved had been allowed; aside from dancing, singing, and having sex. As they grew to understand their captors better, those enslaved discovered that shuffling often appeased their captors' violent appetites, so it was developed as an art form. It was a tool that could sometimes give them control over their own survival; an invaluable skill and one they taught to their offspring.

In Ghana, Kristin had observed the loving way that mothers connected with their children, even as they sharply disciplined them as was needed. It had caused her to look more closely at the contrast in the way that many African American mothers interacted with their children; this time in the context of the slave experience. She came to realize that the beatings that had been common, especially during and immediately after slavery, and all the other harsh treatment of African American children by their parents had likely been an offshoot of the art of shuffling for survival. Most likely, in the beginning the punishments and beatings had been used as another desperate means of managing their captors' violent behavior. Back then, a parent's ability to control their children had been essential; their obedience without question might well have been a matter of life or death. Initially, Black parents had likely been very sincere about the assurances they gave that their punishment would hurt them more than it hurt the child. They did what they felt necessary to protect their children from unrestrained retribution at the hands of someone who cared nothing about their welfare.

Those parents who had still allowed themselves to feel must have been terrified of the consequences that might have been brought to bear had their children's behavior been left unchecked. And those same parenting skills that had once been used to protect Black children, had also been passed down to each subsequent generation. Eventually, no connection was made to the original intent, although the punishment Black parents doled out was still often more severe than the infraction their child committed would reasonably warrant.

Seeing how Ghanaian women interacted with their children made Kristin certain that in the beginning, Black parents had about as much of a desire to actually hurt their children as Moses' mother had when she was forced to leave him in a basket on a riverbank. The beatings that Black parents used during and right after slavery had probably been the lesser of two evils, and at least back then their children stood a better chance of *understanding* why they were so severely punished.

When some parents taught their children about shuffling, they also taught them how to compartmentalize it. Those children grew up understanding that it was all an act; that shuffling was reserved for specific times and that it was never who they really were. Other parents gave their children no explanation at all, and Kristin thought it was likely due to the fact that they had never been given an explanation themselves. Many Black parents never knew the origin of the severe beatings they had often been given—they were harsh with their own children because it was what they had learned from their parents. They never knew that it had all started as a means of survival, so they failed to realize it was no longer necessary.

Kristin thought the same was true in general about shuffling. Children learned to shuffle from watching their parents; they passed the same behavior on to their children, until soon there was a whole generation of Black Americans who would bend to the will of any white person they encountered, particularly in the South. She knew that shuffling was still practiced in some parts of the U. S., where enforcement of the law was still in all-white hands, as it had once been all over the country. Many Backs in those communities would still fall back on their inherited shuffling skills. And Kristin was certain that Emmett Till's relatives in Money, Mississippi had tried to teach him the basics of shuffling too, after the fourteen-year-old came South from Chicago for his fateful visit in the summer of 1955.

But there were many Blacks who showed contempt for those who shuffled, although they had never spent one day in their shoes. That same mockery fueled the antagonistic debates between Booker T. Washington and W.E.B. DuBois, and it took on a different dimension once a closer look was given to their backgrounds. There had been a considerable difference in the early life and upbringing of the two men. DuBois was raised in the small town of Great Barrington Massachusetts, which had an overwhelmingly large white population compared to the large black-to-white population ratio in the South, where Washington had been born. DuBois was born after slavery had already been abolished, unlike Washington, who had been born a slave. DuBois's mother was of African descent, but she had been born free in the same small town of her son's birth. Her father had been freed from indentured servitude almost a hundred years before the Civil War began.

DuBois and his mother certainly had their share of hardships after his father deserted their family, but Black people living in Great Barrington would have never been perceived as a threat. His hometown environment was in stark contrast to Virginia, Washington's birthplace, and most of the South. The Black population far exceeded the number of whites in the South, due to the large number of Africans who had been brought in to work the plantations.

That ratio was the main reason the level of fear was so great for whites in the South, and for their use of extreme measures to keep the enslaved under control. Their fear always escalated after a successful or near-successful slave rebellion. Similarly, the large black population in Haiti had no doubt motivated Napoleon to send his secret step-by-step instructions to Major General Leclerc in 1801, to annihilate Haitian revolutionaries.

Kristin would always point out during her talks that DuBois, who had spent his final years in Ghana, had always known exactly who he was. He knew when and where he had been born and he could trace his father's lineage to the French Huguenots. Dubois had never been taught to shuffle by his relatives; there would have been no reason for it in Great Barrington. Shuffling had never been a skill that his life might literally have depended on, and it was doubtful that DuBois would have had personal knowledge that such a skill could indeed save lives. He could have easily led the life of a white person at any time, had he chosen to do it, with the physical features and level of education that he had. He never experienced any of the scars of injustice that other Blacks suffered until much later in life, after he had decided to embrace socialism and Pan-Africanism.

Kristin had planned for extensive discussions on shuffling to be part of the classes the Foundation intended for their American participants too. Many would already be familiar with the extreme brand of humility that had seemed so effortless for some Blacks to assume. Most had never stopped to consider that the behavior was unnatural, and for some it could only be sustained with the aid of corn liquor or sexual promiscuity as a distraction from it. The classes they would offer their American participants would take a deeper look into the root of those behaviors. They would talk about the shame that had often been a part of it, especially for the men who already felt helpless because they couldn't defend or support their families. Kristin believed it was partially that shame that kept Black parents from explaining what they had gone through to their children. They never made it clear that excessive sex and alcohol had sometimes been the poor man's prescription for treating depression and low self-esteem.

Over the last several decades, the underbelly's self-medication had morphed more into the abuse of illegal drugs that were always readily available in their communities. Those who were yet to be freed from their dysfunctions almost exclusively made up the two percent of the total welfare population that depended solely on government assistance, and well beyond the two-year average for all races who received assistance. Over time, the underbelly had come to consider welfare as a source of income, rather than provisional support. They were in the exact position of vulnerability that Dr. Wilhelm had predicted, yet most were completely oblivious to that fact. And if the government decided to discontinue welfare entitlements, as many had urged over the years, one sector of Black America would find itself without any means of survival, virtually overnight.

Kristin anticipated that a large number of Americans would likely grapple with their foundation's radical mission, at first. It would take time before some would be able to process the concept, and it would seem unimaginable to them until they could fully wrap their minds around it. Their unfounded prejudices and limited beliefs would cause many to dismiss the massive undertaking as being impossible, especially with the news media routinely playing a role in keeping the misconceptions about Africa alive. There was seldom a mention of anything associated with the continent that didn't involve war, poverty, issues of poor health, or corruption. And while it was true that those issues did in fact exist in Africa, they also exist in other parts of the world, as well—including America. There were many environmental issues and physical limitations that might make the average Black American somewhat wary of a move to Ghana, and those issues continued to depress the masses of people living in Africa. But Kristin also understood that they were issues that the African Diaspora in America was now equipped to help manage and resolve.

Those who had been captured and somehow managed to hold on to their core identity during slavery, produced descendants who were now more than capable of helping to lead Africa back to its former glory. They had attended some of the best colleges and universities in America, especially its historically Black colleges and universities, or HBCUs. There were many Black Americans who had well over fifty years of solid experience as educators, physicians, researchers, scientists, and entrepreneurs of all kinds. There were prominent Black alumni and former residents of Tuskegee alone who had left quite a mark in their professions. The small town could boast nationally acclaimed scientists, architects, engineers, military generals, pilots, radio and television personalities, civil rights leaders, rock stars, and everything else in between — even sex therapists. Kristin herself had been married to a rocket scientist. She had many friends who were professionally talented and who could render critical support to the Motherland to help it thrive again.

In return, Black Americans who no longer had a sense of who they were would have an opportunity to transform their lives. Her vision was to guide the Foundation's participants gently into relearning the ways of the ancestors. That which was lost during the mass kidnappings and enslavements could be gradually restored. Her intention was to nurture the underbelly; their Foundation would provide everything they needed, and they would be given the tools to become self-sufficient in their new environment and new lives.

Kristin envisioned the underbelly graduating from the Foundation's programs and settling all over Ghana, and eventually migrating to other countries in Africa as well. The Foundation's work would be the beginning of a far-reaching restoration that would eventually span the entire continent. As the Diaspora learned its way home, their transformation would also be a catalyst for the transformation of the Motherland.

As Amad drove her into the rural areas of the country during her breaks from teaching at KNUST, Kristin had often been brought face to face with the challenges affecting the people of Ghana. Each time, she had thought of someone she had known personally at Tuskegee who would have been more than capable of resolving whatever issue she had come across. She had friends, relatives, and former classmates who were talented enough to find solutions for agricultural issues, and others who were qualified to provide nutritional counseling and guidance. She knew people with the skills to build schools in Ghana, and teach classes that ranged from preschool through university level. She knew people who were school administrators and others who were skilled practitioners of nursing and of human and veterinary medicine, as well. There were many Black civil, electrical, mechanical, and nuclear engineers that she could count among her friends. Although they were no longer in frequent contact, they had always made a point of updating and exchanging contact information whenever they ran into each other during Homecoming weekend. They had all been influenced by the 'Skegee Spirit in one way or another.

As she planned her strategies for recruitment of the mentors they would need for their community in Ghana, Kristin had no doubt that she would have widespread support from the Tuskegee alumni. The 'Skegee Spirit had initially been conceived by Lewis Adams, who had been born into slavery and had been a talented blacksmith, shoemaker, and tinsmith. Although he had never had much formal education, Adams was a successful businessman who not only knew how to read and write but was also said to have spoken several languages.

It had been Adams who artfully brokered the deal to get financial backing for the establishment of the "Negro Normal School in Tuskegee." The school was founded three years after Reconstruction ended in the South—the price paid for Black voter support in an Alabama state senate election. Booker T. Washington's philosophy on the approach that Blacks should take in recovering from slavery had been very similar to Adams' vision for starting the school to teach self-sufficiency. Washington accepted Adams' invitation and left his teaching position at Hampton Institute to take charge of the new school in Tuskegee. As principal, Washington lured George Washington Carver from Iowa State Agricultural College, now Iowa State University, to bring his talents to Tuskegee as well.

When Washington contacted him, Carver had already secured his future in Iowa as the first African American faculty member. He had been born a slave as well, and had witnessed a Black man being lynched when he was a child after he had left his home in Diamond Grove Missouri, at the age of nine, to further his education. Carver had encountered discrimination at Iowa State, but was well respected by the time he left his position there. He was a skilled botanist and horticulturist and had also been held in high regard for his talent as a musician and artist.

Carver had been approached by other Black schools before he was recruited to join the Tuskegee faculty, and he had also considered moving to West Africa to use his talents to help uplift his people there. His 'Skegee Spirit had been even more aligned with Lewis Adams' vision, while Washington's skills as an orator and his ingenuity at "shuffling" had helped to secure long-term funding to operate the school. In the midst of all the rioting and racial violence of the early 1900s, Washington's reputation among Tuskegee's endowment patrons and corporate sponsors had been one of being "an apostle of accommodation" and he was pushed front and center as the official "Negro leader." His approval, and sometimes urgings resulted in solid financial backing, not just for Tuskegee but for many other Black colleges and universities.

Washington was a pragmatist, ego notwithstanding, and he kept his focus on producing tangible results that would advance his people in the 'Skegee Spirit. He discovered a simple means of "lifting the veil of ignorance" from their heads as he promoted business development through the Negro Business League and other private ventures.

When R.R. Moton took over as president in 1915 on Washington's death, Tuskegee had an endowment of well over 1.5 million dollars —a considerable amount of money at the time. Despite his many critics, Washington left Tuskegee's future financially secure.

Kristin had often speculated on the different direction Black history might have taken, had Washington not died a few months before a scheduled visit by Marcus Garvey to the small college town.

Chapter 27

A Square Peg in a Round Hole

*K*ristin stood firmly in the 'Skegee Spirit when she took the helm of the Exodus Foundation. The energy it carried had guided her through finalizing the governing principles that she would present to her new board for acceptance.

The 'Skegee Spirit had still been very much alive and well on Brickyard Hill, where she had grown up. She had participated in countless programs and activities sponsored by the college in partnership with the town. Kristin had tutors throughout elementary school who were college students and she had frequently gone on field trips to the George Washington Carver Museum. She had also gone on campus to see all the latest operas, ballets, and off-off Broadway musicals that had come to town, right along with the college students. And when she started school there herself, she and her friends had sung about "that old 'Skegee Spirit" all the time. They would put their hearts and souls into the song at football games, as they urged the Golden Tigers on to victory. She and thousands of other Tuskegee alumni still met up as often as they could to affirm that the old 'Skegee Spirit lived on. They all proclaimed loudly that it was "still good enough for them" as they sang off-key in the "Dust Bowl" during Homecoming football games.

She knew that it would take that old 'Skegee Spirit and much more to undo the centuries of damage that had been done in Africa. Land borders had been drawn up purposely during colonial rule to mix rival tribes together and separate homogenous nations, creating disharmony that had been encouraged and left unchecked over the years. And as colonialism usurped the hierarchy of traditional leadership, many unwelcomed changes had been forced on the lives of the people.

The Europeans had eventually realized they wouldn't be able to eradicate the "strange" culture entirely by forcing an end to it. Their goal had been to replace it with British cultural influences but it had soon become apparent that the culture's core had merely been driven underground. So, the British had taken a different tactic that began with cultivating "friendships" with many of the traditional leaders. Unfortunately, there were some leaders who had been persuaded to trade their power and influence over the people they ruled for their own personal gain. They were led into putting their desires above their duties and obligations to protect their people and ensure their welfare. It was an evolution of history that was to be included among the topics raised during the Foundation's orientation classes.

Once their mission was fully underway, Kristin expected to affect change in many of the issues the people of Ghana faced daily and that she had been so affected by on her first trip, helping them to improve dramatically. Prosperity had a way of causing even seemingly insurmountable obstacles to melt away. She also strongly believed that their Foundation's presence would help to ease the tensions that still remained between various ethnic groups too, and other long-standing internal disagreements.

The critical obstacle for the Foundation would be the cultural divide between the returning Diaspora and native Ghanaians. That was the reason their classes were to be mandatory, so that any disharmony could be detected and closely monitored within their community. Kristin could clearly see the endless possibilities that would exist with a successful synthesis of the two groups. The unlimited potential and benefit to both sides would outweigh any growing pains encountered and would make it more than worth the effort taken in getting there.

She was staking her reputation on the number of Black Americans who would be willing to leave the U.S. for a new start in Ghana, being much higher than most people imagined from the onset. She was also confident there would be an enthusiastic response for volunteers from among her HBCU peers. No doubt, there would be many talented Black Americans who would be eager to come to Africa to live, especially with what she had in mind for their new village. She would remind them of the vows they had made back in the '70s to make the pilgrimage to Africa one day. For the most part, her former classmates would have already seen their children through college and given them their needed boost for starting their lives. A large percentage would have already traveled out of the country at least once. Her friends would expect cultural differences as an inherent part of life outside the United States. Kristin expected that more than a few would see her Foundation as offering them an amazing opportunity for the second half of their lives.

She planned to select at least twenty of the fifty families who would participate in their pilot from this group of Black Americans. She would also target them to make up thirty percent of the first official group of immigrants, who would begin arriving after the pilot ended. The Foundation would need a substantial number of solid families to live in each village community at all times; to serve as mentors and be available to act as buffers between the underbelly, as they made adjustments to their new reality, and native Ghanaians, who would live in the village as well.

Kristin kept all of these yet-unknown brave pioneers in mind as she made her day-to-day decisions about the village they would create and operate. She thought about them as she carefully went over her scheduled presentations and as she put the agenda together for their first board meeting. She would personally select the fifty families that would comprise the trailblazing pilot group, and she would rely heavily on her intuition during that process. Amina was to provide her with a prescreened list of seventy-five families, and Kristin would then read the brief summary that Amina and her staff were to write about each family member. Kristin planned to listen to her Spirit and let it guide her in identifying twenty-five families from that list who would likely be more suitable to be among the second group of arrivals, rather than the pilot.

She planned to maintain close communications with the pilot families once they arrived in Ghana, and to hear their impressions of the village first-hand. She would arrange to meet with each family member individually within their first few weeks of arrival, providing her with an opportunity to get to know them better so she could become better equipped to select mentors from among their ranks. The mentors would help support the next group of immigrants adjust to their environment, a role that would become even more important as their numbers grew. It was Kristin's plan to eventually select one person from the mentor group to serve on the board of directors, in recognition of the vital role they would play.

Everything would hinge on the brave souls who would volunteer to be at the forefront of their ambitious undertaking, so this group was never far from Kristin's mind. She would have fleeting thoughts about them as she contemplated the Foundation's goals and timelines; she also considered them as she determined how the Foundation's projects should be prioritized. And she especially thought of the pilot participants as she made decisions on which projects would be better served by their Ghanaian executive board versus those that would be best handled under the auspices of American board members.

She felt a special obligation to this first group for the faith they would be demonstrating in her vision. It would take extraordinary courage to be first on their mission designed to benefit the masses. As pioneers, they would be the ones who would be most affected by any decisions the board made when they began their meeting on Monday. They would be first to suffer the consequences too, of any grave omissions in planning. The pilot families motivated Kristin to do her very best to get it right the first time, so their exodus village would live up to everyone's hopes and expectations.

As people began to take their programs more seriously, she suspected that there would be attempts made to manipulate the public's perception of their intent. She was fully aware of the need to be vigilant in that regard and to do all she could to make certain their mission was clearly communicated. The news media would be in the mix after their official launch and she expected to have their mission questioned, with possible insinuations made that it would pose a threat to someone or something. Kristin had always felt that Dr. Wilhelm overlooked one key factor in the book he wrote about the declining value of the American Negro. That factor was the untapped power that the underbelly had as consumers, a means of legitimate power that few Black Americans seemed to realize they have.

Kristin had witnessed its effective use in Tuskegee politics as a child, when the garnered strength of a boycott in 1957, led by Dr. Charles Gomillion, then-Dean of Students at Tuskegee Institute, proved an effective counter to the State Legislature's redistricting plan that would have effectively excluded Blacks from voting rolls in the city. Dr. Gomillion had also been lead plaintiff in a landmark 1960 Civil Rights case, Gomillion v. Lightfoot, which led to the U.S. Supreme Court's ruling that gerrymandering was unconstitutional. That decision was a great setback for local politicians in Tuskegee and other parts of the country who sought to skew election results, although the town itself had never fully recovered.

She knew well that the underbelly could always be counted on to spend the money they got from their welfare checks. They bought goods that were of the poorest quality too, and therefore produced at the lowest cost. Over the years, their spending had evolved and some in the underbelly had more recently become the largest consumers of "bling."

Kristin was aware that the corporations that produced these products would be reluctant to see their profits disappear without a fight. So the Exodus Foundation had prepared itself to send out quick rebuttals to counteract any misinformation that might threaten the Foundation or its milestones. Just like Booker T. Washington, Kristin was well aware that the proof of their mission would be in the pudding. She was determined to keep her eyes on the prize, as Civil Rights workers had done during the '50s and '60s. And fortunately, the universe continued to send her the help she needed, sometimes before she realized she needed it.

The last time she had been in the States, she ran into an old classmate at Washington's Ronald Reagan Airport. They had both been on long layovers, and Kristin had an opportunity to tell him about the Exodus Foundation in great detail. She had casually mentioned the attacks she expected against their organization as it grew in notoriety, and she had been taken completely by surprise when her friend offered to come to her aid. He had been a math major at Tuskegee and was now a professor at a prestigious east coast university, where he had completed his advanced degrees.

Her friend had taken notes as they talked and shortly thereafter, much to her amazement, he sent her a report containing some fascinating calculations he had made after reaching home. Based on the parameters she had given him in answering his questions, the report documented the probability of various misinformation campaigns being launched against the Foundation. He had even included statistical data that showed the order in which the campaigns would most likely be set in motion, along with their current chances of success.

Kristin and Amina had used the report as a basis for their new public relations charge. According to the report's contents and based on the success of past misinformation campaigns of a similar purpose, the first scenario would likely be to play the "race card." That was something Kristin took very seriously because she was more aware than most that race was still one of the most explosive topics in America. She and Amina had considered how some tactics might conjure up strong emotions and images that were contrary to what the Foundation was all about. Kristin had no intention of allowing that to happen, and she was prepared to discuss with the board their proposed counter-campaigns that could be implemented and timed to coincide with major milestones of the Foundation. She had instructed their new PR Department to communicate their objectives in as unambiguous a manner as possible, to avoid any distortions. Thanks to the 'Skegee Spirit of her classmate that she had just "happened" to bump into at the airport, they would make sure that the threat of these undesirable campaigns would be mitigated to the fullest extent, particularly during their first years. They would make clear that the Exodus Foundation's objectives had little to do with white America, other than to reveal the truth about the Diaspora that had been hidden for nearly two centuries. They would make it known that their sole ambition was to uplift the underbelly of Black America, and help restore Africa to its ancient greatness.

What had been done to those enslaved in America was already done and had been over for a very long time. It all really was in a past that no one could change. But everyone still deserved to know the truth about what happened, and why. The innocent white people who had never owned slaves or used tobacco products, but were killed during the slave rebellions in the U.S. deserved to know the truth too. They deserved to know that the people living like caged animals during slavery were in fact human beings. They had only been made to act like animals after their inalienable rights as humans had been withheld for generations, and they could no longer restrain themselves from lashing out at any and all who stood in their way.

Kristin would keep laying the truth on the table at every turn for as long as it took. Their foundation would have to get to the core before they could effectively clear up racial distortions that had existed for so long, and been passed down from one generation of White and Black America to the next. Kristin believed it would be the only way the underbelly would ever be released from the internal pain that many did not even realize they had. It would free them of the dysfunctions that prevented them from building futures for themselves and their families.

The Foundation would make a point of recognizing progress that had been made by Blacks in America at their official launch ceremony. Kristin would underscore success stories in her speech, both before and after Black Americans were finally extended equal social, professional, and educational rights of entry. Not unlike some ancestors who had decided to remain with the rival tribes who had held them captive, Kristin also knew that many Blacks would decide to remain in America. Many had fully assimilated into the culture and were making regular and outstanding contributions to it. For them, the thought of any other culture, including those of African countries, was foreign.

But she expected that a large percentage of the Black Americans who chose not to return to the Motherland would at least begin to visit. As tourist facilities and roads continued to improve, she expected that many more African American tourists would be attracted to Ghana. They would come to visit friends or relatives who had decided to make their exodus. Perhaps their children would decide to move to Ghana after they became adults, because of memories they would have made during their vacations in Africa when they were younger.

Heavenly Travel would begin offering new affordable family packages soon after their pilot participants settled into a routine in Exodus Village— their new home for their first five years in Ghana. Kristin suspected that over time, many of their new travel clients might also decide to settle in Ghana on their own. Their agency would schedule regular tours of Exodus Village to give them a chance to see for themselves how well their residents had assimilated, so they could decide whether a move to Africa might also work for them.

There were major details that still needed to be worked out on how expatriate residents would be eased into mainstream society, but Kristin couldn't afford to dwell on thinking that far into the future—not yet. She often reminded herself of the famous quote by Broadway philosopher, Annie Hall: "Tomorrow is always a day away." They would have five years after their first residents arrived at Exodus Village before the second phase of their plans was to be set in motion, and when the details of mainstreaming had to be worked out.

There was no doubt that the projects their foundation planned to sponsor would bring a significant financial boost to Ghana. There were many African Americans who were already living there and who had been making significant contributions to the collective for decades, but the Foundation would have a targeted mission. It planned to bring home to Africa as much of the knowledge and expertise that the Diaspora in America had learned there. And perhaps more importantly, they would leave the worst of what they had learned in America behind.

Kristin had become more and more certain that the Exodus Foundation was the vehicle of change that she had dreamed about while she had still been a professor at Hunter University. Her foundation would pave a road out for the underbelly; it would lead the Diaspora in America back to Africa—to save her and be saved by her.

❋❋❋

She had started a daily ritual of driving the short distance from where she lived to a nearby mountain crest every morning. From there, she had the perfect view for bearing witness to the miracle of the sun as it cleared the eastern horizon. She would close her eyes and meditate on the birth of each new day and these daily exercises strengthened her awareness of Source Energy. Kristin would find herself visualizing different aspects of her Foundation's goals and milestones as they were being reached. She would daydream about how it felt as all their plans came to fruition. It always stirred up very pleasant thoughts as she pictured her vision for Exodus Village being fulfilled in many positive and delightful ways. She saw smiles of joy on everyone's faces as she rode through the village, taking in all that had been accomplished. During these sessions, Kristin would allow her creative mind to wander and fill in the details of how their objectives might be accomplished. After she had finished her fantasy session, she would usually be left with a feeling of pleasant anticipation about whatever she had daydreamed about, and it would stay with her as she drove back down the mountain.

But sometimes as she meditated, her fears called out to her instead; hoping to convince her that she was in way over her head. On those days, as had happened that morning as she reviewed plans for her board meeting, there would be moments of doubt that would creep into her mind. She would feel a knot of apprehension form in her stomach as she second-guessed herself. It made her wonder whether she was trying to do too much too soon, and occasionally she would begin to think of the Foundation's mission as being too great an undertaking for just one woman.

She would shake these doubts from her head whenever she felt them enter her mind. Most often, she would turn her thoughts to her "shero" Rosa Parks instead, and to all that had been changed throughout the world thanks to her 'Skegee Spirit of fearless courage. The wood-framed house where Mrs. Parks's family had lived when she had been born was very close to Kristin's family home in Tuskegee. The Parks' home had long since rotted away and no one Kristin knew could pinpoint exactly where it had once stood, because the area was now overrun with vines and other vegetation. Kristin had always felt a special connection to the gentle warrior of the Civil Rights movement, long before she was told that they had, at different times, shared the same neighborhood. On the mornings when she felt her courage begin to wane as she focused on centering herself for meditation, Kristin would think of the large framed photograph of Mrs. Parks that hung prominently on the wall of her office, facing her desk.

The picture was an enlargement of a mugshot that had been taken as Rosa Parks was being booked into an Alabama jail during the Movement. Kristin had been fascinated by the photo from the time she first saw it, and she had hung it close by for inspiration. The older woman's normally serene face had been transformed into one of defiance as the picture was taken. She had stared straight into the eyes of the white sheriff's employee who had taken the photo, with steadiness and control. It made Kristin think of the Queen Mother of Asante and her defiance of the British military. There were other fearless Black women who had also refused to move from their seats on the Montgomery Alabama buses, but Mrs. Parks' refusal had sparked a movement that ultimately changed the rest of the world.

It had been quite by chance that Kristin happened to be back in the States on business shortly after the woman she had so long admired made her transition. She had been unexpectedly blessed with an opportunity to pay her last respects to Rosa Parks at her Detroit memorial service. Initially, Mrs. Parks had been honored with a service in Montgomery and then taken to lie in state in the Capitol rotunda in Washington, D.C. It was the first time that a female had been so honored and after thousands of visitors filed past her casket to say their goodbyes, her body had been finally flown to Detroit for burial.

Chills would still run over her body whenever Kristin thought back to that service and the loving tribute that had been paid. One flamboyant minister in particular had raised the energy in the sanctuary another octave as he offered a prayer of gratitude for Mrs. Parks, toward the end of the service. It was a beautifully orchestrated tribute done in the traditional excited mannerisms of a Black southern minister. Between the thunderous applause by the people who had been fortunate enough to attend the joyful service, the minister had eloquently said "thank you" to the ninety-one-year-old Civil Rights icon. On behalf of everyone, he thanked Rosa Parks in Mandarin Chinese, Danish, Hebrew, Greek, Yoraba (West Africa), Japanese, Portuguese, Spanish, German, French, Italian, Russian, Kiswahili (Kenya), Zulu, and several other languages.

He thanked her for having the courage of her convictions, something that had captured the attention of the nation and the world. "Her actions that day," the minister told the packed Detroit audience, "became an iron rod thrust into the segregation machinery of the Dixicratic South. Her bravery precipitated the end to that era. One heroic woman helped move an entire universe closer to peace, justice, and love."

And it was true what he said. Rosa Parks's defiance had been the catalyst for a paradigm shift that many had perceived as being immobile. She had taken a personal risk that day on that Montgomery bus and started a chain reaction that ultimately led to freedom, justice, and equality for the Diaspora in America. Mrs. Parks' courage inspired a young Dr. King to push forward with the Civil Rights Movement against all odds. Her 'Skegee Spirit resulted in many African Americans having meaningful opportunities to share in the American Dream.

The civil rights won for Black Americans had been naturally extended to women of all races and cultures. Those new laws were applied to the physically and psychologically challenged too, and to people whose sexual orientations were considered different from "the norm."

One woman's single act of bravery had literally changed the world!

Kristin would offer a prayer every morning as she started back down from the mountain crest. She would ask God to guide her path so that she would fulfill the purpose she felt in her heart she had been created for—her contribution to the world. She prayed to be used as an instrument to help transform the heavy energy that was still held by the Earth—the residual effects still lingering from all of suffering during the African slave trade.

She prayed that God would use her Foundation as a catalyst for significant and positive change for the Diaspora, for Africa, and ultimately for the world. Her Foundation's objectives were not based on separation but on the divine restoration of the African continent. The Exodus Foundation would take the lead in returning that which had been unlawfully taken away for hundreds of years.

Their major challenge, she knew, would be in finding the best way to fit a square peg into a round hole, as the Adinkra symbol she had chosen suggested. On the surface, she knew that it might seem an impossible feat to many, but Kristin's shero and many others had proven that anything was possible.

And she had no doubt that the Diasporan Exodus Foundation would be successful in its mission.

Chapter 28

Winston and Celeste — 1999

*W*inston struggled with the tall lean CD tower, tussling with it back and forth until he finally got it to slide across the rug. He positioned it on the left side of bookshelves that now spanned the longest wall in his new music room. He had already moved an identical tower to the opposite side of the floor-to-ceiling shelves, straining his now seldom-used muscles in the process. The shelves were filled with various titles he had collected over the years, ranging from home gardening to books on nuclear propulsion. He made one last adjustment and then shifted his head to one side to be sure that the front of the tower lined up perfectly with the front edges of the bookshelves. Satisfied that everything was in just the right spot, he plopped down on the overstuffed leather chair behind him that he had moved to the center of the room so he could sit facing his handiwork. He could finally breathe a sigh of relief because all the physical work needed to complete the project was over.

Moving the two mahogany tracking stations around had been no joke. Just getting them out of their crates had nearly worn him out. The muscles in his arms still ached as a stinging reminder of the exertion they had been subjected to all day. Fortunately, he had remembered the Ezy-Move Disks that were designed for moving such heavy objects around. Before he had taken on getting the second tower out of the box, he pulled the round orange pads from the kitchen cabinet where they had been tucked away for years. Moving the second piece of furniture had been much easier, but he had still wrestled with it for ten or fifteen minutes. Winston had seen an infomercial advertising the disks and had ordered them immediately. It hadn't been the first time he had been captivated by one of the compelling commercials that usually came on late at night. He would watch them sometimes when he turned on the television for a few minutes to wind down before getting into bed, after he had been working late. Many a time, Winston would find himself mesmerized by their slick marketing techniques, if he paused long enough to be pulled in by the ads as he channel surfed. The next thing he knew, he would find himself with a phone to his ear ordering some specialty product or another he had just watched being demonstrated. More than once, he considered the effects the commercials had on him and wondered about advances in the subliminal technology that had been talked about so much years earlier.

Usually, he convinced himself that he could find the perfect use for whatever it was at some point later in time. He had ordered all kinds of stuff over the years and had yet to find a purpose for most of it. The kids would tease him mercilessly on the days that they got home from school and found one of the all-too-familiar UPS trucks in front of their house. They would wait for him to come home to open the box that had been delivered, so they could have a big laugh at his expense. Winston had to laugh himself sometimes, especially if enough time had gone by for him to have second thoughts about his purchase.

But that hadn't been the case at all with the Ezy-Move Disks. Even Celeste had conceded that they were a wise purchase that afternoon when they were delivered to the loft. The greatest effort involved with moving the second tower had been for him to lift each corner of it just high enough for his daughter to slide one of the disks underneath. After that, it had only been a matter of pushing the heavy wooden furniture across the rug. Even with the orange disks doing their magic and most of the work, lifting the solid mahogany had still given his undisciplined muscles cause for complaint.

Winston reached behind to knead the tight knots that were forming along his shoulders. Satisfied that they had started to loosen a bit, he stretched his long, chocolate brown arms out in front of him and grabbed the remote. He winced as a bolt of unexpected pain shot through his biceps, before turning his music on in one fluid motion. He had programmed all the components of his state-of-the-art sound system to be controlled by just one remote, which now included his two new jukebox towers.

From the vantage point of his worn leather chair, he now had easy access to everything he needed. Several bags of his favorite snacks were piled in a colorful wicker basket that sat on the mahogany table next to his chair. He didn't have to leave the room to satisfy his thirst either; he had bought a new compact refrigerator that fit snugly beneath the table, filled with bottles of Dasani and unsweetened fruit juices. There was also a small wine rack nearby that held several bottles of his favorite wines.

Winston took a sip of water and selected Freddie Hubbard's "First Light" from the jukebox menu. He sank back into the chair with his eyelids closed and allowed himself to be enveloped by the mellow trumpet sounds. The CD was one of his all-time favorites, although deciding which music he liked most had always been difficult for him. But that disc had been among the first he had catalogued after the music tower was installed.

"Ah, yes," he murmured to himself, satisfied that the surround speakers had been placed at just the right angles. He felt the tension leave his shoulders as his muscles began to relax, and decided he would take a quick break while his daughter looked around the loft for more of his CDs. She had already brought in the bulk of them from his study, which was simultaneously being transformed into a dedicated office. After they had finished their cataloguing project, he would not only have the music room of his dreams up and running, but he would be able to work from home a lot more often too. And that would make it a lot easier for him to keep track of his daughter.

Winston had several major projects starting in the next few months, so the timing of everything had been perfect. His daily commute had always broken his concentration and used up too much of his creative energy, so all he needed was to have teenage nonsense distracting him on top of everything else. He knew that his change in routine would throw Celeste off balance for a minute, and give him the jump he needed to get a handle on her situation. That would be just one of the many benefits of owning his own shop.

He was glad that he made the move from NASA, although for some reason he was always reminded that he and Kristin had planned for it when they first moved to Washington. Leaving had been a real risk for him because he seemed to have a knack for nuclear propulsion and had been doing quite well. He had even been able to relocate from NASA's Greenbelt office during his last year to their headquarters down on "E"

Street in the District. The change had also meant moving into more of an administrative role, and it had been a welcome change for him in winding down his career.

Charlotte had never given him the support in starting his own business that Kristin had promised he would have. But he had gone ahead and fallen back on his undergraduate degree in spite of that, after a long ten-year stint with the space program. His engineering firm had been doing quite well in the few years of starting it. Months earlier, after he first realized he would need to keep a closer eye on Celeste, he had decided to convert their guest bedroom into his new music room and library. It was now the second largest space on the first floor and nearest to the living and dining room areas. Like the other bedrooms in the loft, it was completely soundproof and perfect for him to really crank up the volume when he was in that mood.

All morning long, he had been trying to think why he hadn't converted the room sooner. It had rarely been used, except for whenever his sister Grace decided to visit, but he was fully prepared to give up his bedroom for guests, if he had to. He and Charlotte could always sleep on the pullout sofa that converted to a queen-size bed that he had bought for the music room, whenever his sister came. He would gladly make the occasional sacrifice as long as he got to keep his music room.

He and Celeste had been going through piles of music all morning, listening to different cuts that had brought back all sorts of memories. He had given his daughter a formal introduction to what he called "real" music. He kept teasing her that her generation wouldn't even want to listen to the music of their youth once they were older, because it was far too loud and much too obnoxious.

"But that's assuming, of course, that you're still able to hear it," he had added, smiling. He couldn't understand how his kids' generation tolerated such high decibel levels, especially when it was directed into ear canals through the earphones they always used. He shuddered to think of the subconscious impact some of the lyrics had on such impressionable youth.

He and his daughter had started their ambitious project of cataloguing his music as soon as they had finished breakfast that morning. As the day went by, both of them had been pleasantly surprised to find that they still enjoyed spending time together. Winston had started a special ritual of spending time alone with both his children when they were small, because his own father's absence had made him sensitive to how much a child needed time with their father. Before she became a teenager, he had arranged outings with Celeste regularly. It would be just the two of them—

even when he had been on the strictest deadlines at NASA. It had been a way for him to keep up with what was going on in both his children's lives. He had put a lot of thought into finding things that he and Celeste could do together and that his daughter might really have an interest in. But lately, she had rejected anything he suggested. His daughter had made it pretty clear that she had no further interest in participating in their outings too. Just like that, she had cut him off.

That was one of the reasons he had decided to use the time they would be working together on his CD collection, as a chance to talk candidly with her about a few things. He had frankly been surprised that she agreed to help him so readily. Then again, he knew that she had been a bit nervous in the last few days that he was close to finding out about some of her little "extra" activities. But who knew how long it would be before he had another chance to bond with his daughter? He had finally come to grips with the notion that his baby girl was growing up. It was all happening much faster than he would have liked, but he realized nothing he could do was going to stop it. Celeste would be fifteen soon; before long, it would be time for her to head off to college. He would use the opportunity he was given that day wisely. And who knew? He might be able to exert one last bit of influence over her before she took full control of her own life.

Winston had only one major goal in mind for her that day: to convince her to start thinking about college as a real part of her future. He would help her see the experience as an opportunity to have fun and meet new people, because he certainly didn't want to make the same mistake he had made with her brother. Winston had just assumed they were all on the same page about college, but as hard as he tried he had not been able to convince his son about the merits of getting an education—no matter what career he decided on later, including the military.

It had been all push and pull with Trazi for a long time, though. If he had only been thinking quickly enough, he would have pretended to be thrilled about his son's plan to join the Navy right out of high school. After the fact, Winston had realized that would have almost guaranteed that his son would have changed his mind about going into the military, before he signed his enlistment papers.

He still hadn't given up on his son, but he was determined that he wouldn't go down the same path with Celeste. His ace in the hole was the differences between his two children, which were like night and day. Winston couldn't imagine the set of circumstances that would have persuaded Trazi to spend a whole day with him, for instance, doing anything.

By the time they were finished that day, Winston planned to have all doubt removed from his daughter's mind about continuing her education after high school. He had initially hoped to get her thinking about where she might want to go to college, which, of course, he hoped would be Tuskegee. So far, they had gotten off to such a great start that now he was optimistic that she might start thinking about what she wanted to study, too.

It hadn't been long after they started working that morning that it became apparent that he had grossly underestimated the time required for them to complete the project. His music collection had turned out to be much larger than even Winston thought it would be. The process of cataloguing each CD was painstaking too: he had to type in the title, the artist's name, and release date before putting the disc into the mahogany towers he had moved to either side of the bookshelves. Celeste had already brought in enough CDs to fill up the first tower and the second one would be half-filled before they were finished.

They had both been getting such a big kick from hanging out together that neither of them had qualms about canceling their previous afternoon plans. Once they got the ball rolling, not finishing it was something that neither of them considered. The whole project had been typical of Winston: he would put off doing something for the longest time and then—wham! He would throw himself into it, springing into action like a whirlwind. It tickled him to see that his daughter appeared cut from the same cloth. She seemed to enjoy being with him that day just as she had when she was little. It had only been after she started growing up that Celeste had begun to treat him like he had a plague or something around her friends. Except, that is, when she needed money for shopping.

Winston smiled in satisfaction as he considered the progress they had already made. He had always loved music and when he first started work-ing for NASA, he had rewarded himself for all his hard work during grad-uate school. His starting salary had been more than adequate to take care of his family, so he had given himself permission to buy all the music he had ever wanted. As soon as the new technology became available, he replaced his vinyl record collection that he still had from college with digitally mastered remakes. Before long, he had collected just about all the music he had liked when he was in high school and he also bought all the sounds that he and his friends had partied to when they were at Tuskegee.

He bought new music too, especially during his first few years at NASA. He bought reggae, blues, and jazz, of course, and his taste even expanded gradually to include a little rock and some hip-hop. Even if the lyrics were positive though, he still didn't care for most of it. It was too challenging for him to try to understand the words and have to put it all together with the music at the same time. Winston enjoyed the classics too; he had several operatic CDs and recordings of world-renowned symphony orchestras playing Bach, Beethoven, and the like. Celeste had always referred to it as "Bugs Bunny" music when she was smaller, but he realized she enjoyed classical music too. Winston even had a few country-western CDs, although the lyrics had been all written by Lionel Ritchie.

Overall, he was quite pleased with his music collection—and extremely protective of it. Other than his music, his clothes, and the chair he was sitting in, he had taken little else when he left the home he had shared with Angela for almost ten years with his children.

Angela. What a mystery she was! He thought back to how the two of them had calmly discussed the breakup of their marriage over breakfast. It had hardly seemed to matter much to her at all. Initially, they agreed on a legal separation as a way of giving the children time to adjust. After they had hashed out everything, the two of them had sat down with Celeste and Trazi to explain what was happening as best they could.

Surprisingly, neither of the kids had seemed the least bit affected by their decision to break up, so they had agreed to forego a trial separation. Everything had been amicable between he and Angela, and since the kids seemed okay he had not felt the urgency to find a new place right away. After all, he had been sleeping in his office for over a year, and their divorce would only be a formality as far as the marriage was concerned.

Since he had no idea what the housing market was like or how long the whole process would likely take, he had hired an agent right away to start looking around for him. Winston figured it might take some time before he found something that would be a good fit for him and the kids. As it turned out, the agent he hired had been very enterprising. The man had started sending him listings almost immediately, although Winston had not even been remotely interested in any of what he had shown him in the beginning. He had frankly begun to consider the man a bit of a nuisance until he got the phone call about the loft. Once again, the agent had been excited by what he described as the "perfect property." So what else was new? It wasn't as though he hadn't heard the same description used before. But Winston had finally agreed to take a look at the loft, primarily because of the agent's persistent phone calls. As soon as he pulled into the drive in back of the building, he understood why the man had been so relentless. It was exactly what Winston had in mind.

The loft was well over 5,000 square feet of intricately designed space on three separate levels. The blueprint maximized the effect of the structure's open flow, and at the same time there was a distinct feeling of privacy in areas where seclusion was needed. Winston had never pictured himself living in a loft, but as soon as he went inside he knew it would be the perfect place for him and the kids. The design would allow them all to entertain their friends separately and with plenty of breathing space. With the kids getting older, Winston thought it would be great for the times when the weather would force them all inside.

The loft had a huge gourmet kitchen but he had really been drawn to the unique designs for each of the bedroom entrances. Their doorways were tucked inside hidden niches just off the long hallway on each level. The walls, doors, and ceilings were all insulated for sound, so they all had loads of privacy. The master suite was on the top level, with the kids' bedrooms on the second floor, and a guest room built on the ground floor. Each bedroom was spacious and each also had its own bath. Skylights were scattered across the open space on the top level and in the master bedroom; the lighting throughout the whole space was excellent.

The property it was built on was very attractive too with a large well-tended garden bordering the front courtyard. It was enclosed by a black eight-foot wrought-iron fence that provided additional security. The structure had been designed so that it didn't give off a sense of imprisonment with iron bars on all the windows and doors. But the surrounding neighborhood was another story. It was different from any that the kids had ever been exposed to, but Winston had never intended for them to grow up in a sterile environment. He didn't see the point when they would only have to adjust to the real world later on. He had decided that both of them would benefit from having exposure to some of the unpleasant realities of life. That was how he had grown up, after his father died. They had to move away from the house and neighborhood he had lived in until he was nine-years-old, to a much smaller house in a different area of the city.

Ironically though, after he was older he felt he had become a better man because of the many experiences he had after his father's death. His life had changed almost overnight when his mother decided to use their father's insurance money as a safety net after all the bills were paid. Winston had been required to find a job early in life to earn money for the things that he wanted too, because his mother had already been working practically day and night to pay for all the things that he and his sister needed.

He knew that the area a few blocks over from the loft was a little seedy, but that was the way many of the neighborhoods were in Washington. And he had every intention of keeping his children physically safe and out of harm's way. He began to think of the coarse area near the loft as an opportunity, rather than a drawback, though he imagined that his mother wouldn't feel the same way.

Winston had made up his mind to make an offer on the loft by the time he had driven back across town. As he maneuvered his black Mercedes through the thick Washington traffic, his only concern had been the distance that their new place would be from Kristin's house. Aside from that, his only other anxiety had been in finding the proper protection for his music during their move. That was how he ended up finding the towers in a small shop just off "M" Street in Georgetown. It was just around the corner from the place where he had found the brown and orange Persian rug that lay underneath his bare feet.

Winston had gone into the store looking for temporary carrying cases to supplement the CD holders that he already had for his music. He had been looking for something that was secure enough to trust to the professional movers, who, aside from moving his music would mostly be moving the kids' stuff and his clothes. The elegant carvings around the top of the towers had attracted his attention as soon as he walked inside the store. He had been even more intrigued after he discovered the jukebox that was hidden inside the beautiful mahogany cabinetry. Winston thought about the towers long after he had left the store with the temporary cases he had come in for. Later, as he and the kids settled into the loft he realized he would still need to do something else soon to protect his music.

His tailored sound system was linked by speakers he had installed himself on all three levels. He could attach a device to the receiver and connect the system to all the speakers at the same time, with the flick of a switch. He usually reserved that for the holidays, when they had people over and he wanted to have the same music flowing in all parts of the loft. The sound quality was clear, crisp and exactly what he had always envisioned. The music flowed endlessly from one room to another, reminding him of the schools of fish that he and Kristin had watched swim all over the Atlantis Hotel in fascination, during a second honeymoon trip to the Bahamas.

The only down side to the whole setup was that his CDs had begun to drift away. Both his children had learned to appreciate old school music, and pretty soon there were parts of his collection scattered all over the loft. He became frustrated when he wasn't able to put his hands on the music he had an urge to listen to, so eventually he went back to Georgetown and bought two of the towers. He had been very relieved that the store still carried them, and had them delivered to the loft the very next day. But they had sat unopened in the same spot the delivery men had put them in for several years.

The towers had been a bit pricey even for Winston, who never had an aversion to the finer things in life. He had decided he had to have them from the moment the salesperson showed him their library feature. Once he and his daughter finished cataloguing all his music and he had activated the system, the discs would not be physically removable until they had been properly checked out by an authorized user. Winston had already programmed a list of valid checkout locations as part of the system's set-up. A location and an estimated date of return would be required before the music could be removed from the cabinets. And if the disc was not checked in by the due date, an email alarm would be sent to Winston's computer. There was even a snooze feature on it that would generate a second email if the CD had not been returned after an additional forty-eight hours. As system administrator, he could always override anything at any time or grant an extension beyond the return due date.

The disarray of his CDs had been unsettling for quite some time, but the morning that he couldn't put his hands on Chaka Khan's "Rags to Riches" CD had been the last straw. His aggravation prompted his memory about the towers that had been left sitting in their guest bedroom. He realized it was time to put them to use so he could bid farewell to frustrations about his missing music. When he and Celeste were finished, he would be able to push a button to locate anything he wanted to hear, when he wanted to hear it. And he had already warned her there would be zero tolerance if she couldn't produce the music he was looking for right away.

Winston was still a bit curious why his daughter hadn't put up a bigger fight about staying with him to finish the project. He wondered absently whether she and Malaya were fighting over something, and knew that Charlotte would be overjoyed if that were the case. She had never owned up to it, but he could tell that his third wife never liked his daughter's friend, although he never understood why.

Malaya had a gentle spirit about her that made you naturally want to protect her. He was glad that his daughter had chosen her as her friend, and that they were close again after having been separated for so long.

But he still had a nagging feeling that something else was going on with Malaya's family—something that he couldn't quite put his hands on.

Chapter 29

The Big T. I.

*C*eleste had taken on the task her father had given her much more seriously than she would have expected. She had been assigned the legwork for their cataloging project, and her dad had sent her all over the loft looking for his CDs. She would bring them back to the staging area they had set up in his new music room as she found them; she had even been sent out to the garage looking for disks in Charlotte's SUV and her father's Mercedes. A huge pile of them was sitting in the middle of the floor so they would have ample room to work. She had already helped her father catalogue the first set of music, then he made her start her search all over again to make sure she hadn't missed anything.

Everyone had always known that her father was into his music, but she had been surprised to find out just how deep his love of music really was. He seemed to like classical just as much as he liked "old school" and she had been surprised to discover that he also had a passion for the violin. She had surprisingly found herself falling in love with Noel Pointer after her dad played cuts from his "Phantazia" CD. The musician could make the strings of his violin seem like they had a voice; Celeste could listen to his music over and over, just like her dad. He had kept her running all over the place, but she wouldn't have traded the day they were having together for anything in the world.

She only wished that her brother had been there because she was pretty sure Trazi had never seen the side of their father that he had been showing her all morning, either. If Trazi could have only heard the things their dad had been saying, especially all the stuff about what he had gotten into while he was in college, Celeste just knew that it would have brought the two men closer together. And she already knew that she would never be able to describe it all to her brother later. It was definitely something that he would have had to be there himself to believe, because she had hardly been able to believe some of it herself!

Her father's sudden openness with her had been even more surprising, and some of the things he had told her about his past behavior had been disturbing, to say the least. She had been shocked by the glimpses he had given her into the person he had been before he was their father. She found out more about him that day than she had ever imagined she would know. Celeste had always thought of her dad as the reserved professional type—except for those times when he and her mom had their friends over for card parties, when she was younger.

But that day, she found out that her father had once been someone else altogether. And the younger version of him had really thrown her for a loop, because he had told her stuff about himself that she would never have imagined or believed, if he hadn't told her himself.

※※※

Celeste used her foot to push the door of the music room open and then emptied her arms of a small stack of CDs, certain this time that she had found the last of them. Her father still hadn't moved an inch from where he sat; when she looked closer, she started laughing as she realized he was rocked out in his chair, instead of working. Winston didn't even realize he had been sleeping until after his daughter started shaking his shoulder to wake him up.

"Hey, if I'm still working you should at least be awake!" She was still laughing as she watched him struggle to resume consciousness.

"Yeah, you're a laugh a minute." Winston rubbed the corners of his mouth in case there was drool that his daughter hadn't yet spotted.

"What time is it?" He had no idea whether he had dozed off for a few minutes, or whether he had been asleep for an hour.

"Well, I think it's definitely time for you to be awake." Celeste persisted, laughing at her father who was obviously still disoriented. "All right, I guess it must be time for both of us to take a break," she added.

She was still laughing as she headed for the kitchen to make something for them to eat. When she returned, they took an official break and feasted on the tuna sandwiches she had made, some chips, and juice that came from the small refrigerator under the table. Once they were done eating and had cleaned up after themselves, they both rolled up their sleeves again to tackle the remaining music left to be catalogued.

Since she was done with her roundup duties, Celeste helped by reading the name of each CD that she picked up from the floor out loud. Winston would rattle off the group or artist's name and the approximate date that the music had been recorded. The user interface for the jukebox software was displayed on the television screen nestled between books on the lower bookshelves. He would type in the information as he talked and with the push of a button everything about the music was added to the tower's search library. It could be easily located after that with a search based on the artist, the title, or the date that the music had been recorded.

Celeste had always been captivated by the way music would take her father back in time when he listened to it, especially back to the time he was a student at the Big T.I. "And that's Tuskegee Institute, *not* University." He was always quick to point out to anyone who listened. Winston would sometimes go on and on describing all the ruckus that the students at Tuskegee had made after the administration announced a change in the school's name to reflect its university status. He told her that quite a few alumni *still* stubbornly referred to the school as Tuskegee "Institute." They also identified themselves as alumni of the "real" Tuskegee, as they put it.

Whenever her father say that, Celeste was always tempted to mention what Kristin had told her a long time ago. Her aunt had told her that when they were students, the word "Institute" and the city's name were all that had remained intact after the *first* official name change back in 1937. Kristin told her the original name had been Tuskegee Agricultural and Normal Institute when her grandfather had been a student. And he went to school when both George Washington Carver *and* Booker T. Washington were still there.

Aside from all the interesting things that she had learned about Tuskegee that day, Celeste had learned a lot of other stuff. Her father had told her about some of the music groups that had been popular when he was in school, and some of them still were. He had told her some of the groups' former names, if they had them; stuff about performers who had left the group at some point along the way; their family connections to other entertainers; and all kinds of stuff like that. She had always known that Tom

239

Jenkins was her father's frat brother, but she had no idea that he had also been one of the original members of the Commodores, or that the group had a different name when they first started out. Her father had spent the rest of the afternoon trying to remember the group's first name but had never been able to think of it. But no matter how little or how much he remembered about any particular group, he could always tell her exactly what he had been into when his favorite music had been recorded.

"At one time, Tuskegee was one of the safest places in America for Black people to live in large numbers, he said of the town where he had gone to college. "It's smack dab in the middle of the Deep South, but you would never know it by the people who lived there. The college was founded three years after federal troops were pulled out of the South at the end of Reconstruction. Instead of the people living there being terrorized by the violence all around them during the Civil Rights movement, there were few racially motivated incidents that directly affected residents."

Then her father's mood had grown somber as he told her about the most devastating and violent exception. "Sammy Younge, Jr. was the first Black student to lose his life during the Civil Rights movement," he said sadly. "He was a very popular student activist from Tuskegee, and he was killed by a white man who escaped punishment, thanks to Jim Crow laws still in effect at the time." Winston explained that the reference he had made was to laws passed in many states to enforce segregation. It had been named after a black character in a once-popular minstrel show.

"But even with Sammy's death the majority of Black residents still weren't overly concerned about their safety during the Movement. All throughout the turbulence of the '50s and the '60s, children still grew up feeling safe there even as all the violence went on around them."

Much to her surprise, her father had answered any question that Celeste asked him that day, and he had given her as much detail as she wanted to know. He had her cracking up laughing when he described how much it had taken for the city kids, himself included, to adjust to being in Tuskegee at first— especially at night.

"There were even fewer street lights in the town when I was there than there are now," Winston told her with a smile. "Back then, it would be seriously dark at night, especially surrounded by all those pine trees. Many of the kids who came to school there had grown up in the city. They were used to all kinds of activity on the street and in their day-to-day lives— buses, fire engines—some kind of noise all the time. Grace and I had been taught from childhood to be on guard anytime we were away from home.

My mother even taught me to be wary of strangers I would see on a daily basis—like the people at the bus stop."

Winston told Celeste how Tuskegee had been a big contrast to all of that. He mentioned how much Kristin loved watching the city kids at the beginning of the fall semester. She had apparently gotten a big kick out of watching the horror register on their faces after it had sunk in with them that their parents actually intended to drive off and leave them there.

"She used to say she would imagine them as little kids sometimes, being dropped off in the woods for summer camp." Her father said laughing.

"Your Aunt Kristin told me that she would sit on the fountain in the middle of campus for hours on end, once the dorms opened and the new students arrived. She said that for her it was like watching the movies, since there was little else to do there. Many of the students would fly into Atlanta and then drive the one hundred and twenty miles to the school. The physical drive gave them an undeniable picture of just how far they were from the rest of civilization." Winston was laughing again.

"Is it that bad?" Celeste had started laughing too because watching her father laugh was contagious.

"Well, let's put it this way," he finally answered. "The main downtown portion of Tuskegee is roughly the equivalent of four city blocks. It's also the county seat and buildings around the county courthouse date back to the Civil War. They're all built around this square with a tiny park in the middle. And, the Daughters of the Confederacy apparently have an indefinite lease on the land, so there's this statue in the park of a confederate soldier on a horse that they had put up. It's right there in the middle of the park, in memory of Confederate soldiers from Macon County who had been killed during the Civil War. Looking at the statute makes it hard to forget that you're in the South, but other than that it's very easy to forget.

"Students generally avoided that area because other than the ABC store (alcoholic beverage control), there was little else around the square that had any appeal at the time." Her father told Celeste that getting a fake I.D. hadn't been nearly as easy back then either. He said it was rare for an underage student to try to buy liquor; they always found someone who was legal to do it for them.

"And very few students had a car at the time I was there either, and public transportation was literally non-existent."

"What? How did everyone get around?"

"Well, for the most part students were rendered completely immobile back then after their parents left in their rented cars." Winston was watching his daughter's face closely for her reaction.

"That's what Kristin found so funny? Wow, that's cold!" Celeste was laughing again at the mischievous side of her aunt Kristin that she hadn't known about either.

"Yeah, exactly." Her father agreed with his daughter with an odd look added to his smile.

"Most of us felt like we were completely stranded, especially the ones from larger urban areas. All we had access to at first was what the school provided on campus, or whatever we could find in the one or two small shops at the edge of campus. If you couldn't get excited by greasy chicken there wasn't much for you on "the Block," as we used to refer to the short row of stores close to the main gate."

Winston told his daughter that most students usually gave up and resigned themselves to being in Tuskegee eventually—it was just a matter of time. Sooner or later as reality sunk in, they realized their pleas to their parents were falling on deaf ears, so they would finally settle in. "Why?" Winston could tell by his daughter's question that she was becoming quite anxious at the prospect of being in Tuskegee—not his intention.

"Well, unfortunately, a good number of the parents had gone through their own shocking adjustment in Tuskegee, when they had been brought there by their own parents as freshmen. They knew their kids would like it there once they settled in.

"And did they?" Celeste was curious.

"Yeah. That was the beauty of it. There had been nothing much that had changed in the little town in over a hundred years, when we were there. We city kids gradually turned to our fellow captives and commiserated with each other over everything we were giving up—like Sabrett hot dogs, Chicago pizza, and Philly cheese steaks." Winston was laughing again at the old memories.

"You should get Kristin to do her imitation of the city kids when they first get to Tuskegee some time. It's a riot—especially when she does her, "I really miss my concrete" routine. She is *hilarious* with that one, and I'll bet she hasn't forgotten it.

"That's pretty funny, Daddy."

"Yeah, it is. He was still laughing. "As I said, eventually most of us gave up and learned to just accept our fate. We learned our way around the small community and with a little luck we met someone who was born in the town and had access to a car. Then, we could make an occasional trip to Auburn or to Montgomery to shop or to get fast food. If we got real lucky, we got to spend the night in Columbus after the Tuskegee-Morehouse football game, or in Atlanta for a couple of days to go to the jazz festivals they used to have every year."

Her father told Celeste that many of the same students who had such a time adjusting to Tuskegee had fallen in love with the town after they had lived there for a few months. A lot of the city kids eventually learned to relax too, and value dirt over concrete. Every year after graduation there were at least a few graduates who would stay on for a while, though too few stayed long enough to make much of a real difference. There were too few reasons that the town gave them to stay.

While the latest administration had made some recent improvements in the infrastructure, Celeste learned that Winston was dissatisfied with the overall progress of Tuskegee in general, especially over the past couple of decades. He ranted on for several minutes about the way he said the school's history had been literally allowed to burn to the ground and heaped into a ditch somewhere, referring to the loss of Huntington Hall. The spirit of interdependence and cooperation between the school and the town that Kristin had always talked about, had apparently become virtually non-existent. There were many historic buildings and houses that had been allowed to crumble and fade away, despite having such a reputable architecture department at the school. Her father said he could never understand why the old buildings hadn't been used to teach students the art of historic restorations, which could have helped the town's ever worsening appearance at the same time. Winston seemed to be definitely of the opinion that a change was greatly needed.

Celeste had been stunned when her father told her how involved he had been with the student government association while in school. He had casually mentioned how he had come very close to being expelled during his senior year.

"Okay, this is what happened," he told his daughter, amused by the shocked look on her face. "All I did was organize a very peaceful protest. It just happened to coincide with a meeting of the school's board of trustees, that's all." Winston made light of the incident to try to ease his daughter's obvious concerns. But he actually *had* come very close to having his college career end due to the incident. It had been the second time he dodged a major bullet after making a dumb decision. He explained to his daughter that the board membership at Tuskegee had always been made up of top executives, or the owners of some of the country's wealthiest corporations. Winston told her he had timed their student protest with the start of the board meeting because he figured the people who pulled the money strings should at least know how the students felt.

"We had protests all the time back then," he explained, still trying to calm her concerns. "Protest was just in the air that spring. I had been hearing from a lot of students how upset they were by rumors of plans to allow significant portions of Dr. Carver's research and specimens to be moved to a museum in D. C.

"Booker T. might have been the one who brought the money into Tuskegee, but the primary reason for the school's international reputation was Dr. Carver's scientific genius." Winston proceeded to tell Celeste all about Dr. Carver's generous help to black and white farmers alike. "His expertise in crop rotation and soil restoration had helped save a southern economy that had once been based exclusively on cotton production. Dr. Carver had earned a reputation for removing all kinds of agricultural roadblocks in the south and his work had brought him and Tuskegee national and international recognition.

"As the rumors continued to circulate about the school's plans to remove his research specimens, some students became outraged that the administration would so callously decimate the museum that had been built as a tribute to his legacy. The Carver Museum brought people to visit the campus from all over the country and the world. The students had grown very upset over time that the president would just allow his legacy to be taken away. Dr. Carver purposely preserved everything so schoolchildren from the surrounding towns could come to Tuskegee at any time to see the results of his work."

Winston, at least, had always been aware that the students were low on the decision-making totem pole. He explained to Celeste that his plan had only been to remind the board members through a show of their numbers that without the students there would be no school.

"The problem," he told his daughter, "started when a small group of students got unruly. After that, everything eventually erupted into loud protests and general disorder.

"But even though the students were being rowdy," he added, "I can truthfully say that none of them came to the rally with the intent of committing any acts of violence against the board of trustees. We were students, for goodness sake, protesting what we felt to be a grave injustice to the spirit of Tuskegee and to its legacy of supporting the community."

He informed his daughter that shortly after the crowd grew more spirited, the same smaller group of students pulled another surprise move on everyone, including him. Before he could realize what was happening, they had somehow managed to lock several of the board members inside the administration building where their meeting was being held.

"Most of the board had already been nervous ever since they arrived on campus after their two-hour drive from Atlanta, when they first realized a student protest was going on. Once they had a glimpse of the angry crowd of Black faces through the glass doors of their meeting room, it was more than some of them could take. But just seeing the terror on their faces had only worked some of the students up more. They had been insulted by the stark fear they saw on the mostly-white faces of the board members. After that, things went rapidly downhill and for several minutes, completely out of control."

"So what happened?" Celeste couldn't believe what she was hearing.

"Well, some of the students somehow blocked campus security from entering the building too. They were able to keep them out during the entire twenty-minute siege."

He told his shocked daughter that it had taken all he could muster to finally convince the students to unblock the doors. And after they had, Winston apparently pushed his way through the crowd and into the building.

"Several board members left campus as soon as the doors were opened and the way had been cleared," he added. He went on, telling Celeste how he had miraculously been given a chance to talk to some of the members who had chosen to remain on campus after the students were finally disbursed. "They weren't as shaken up by their unexpected capture as the others had been," he explained. "And they also seemed to appreciate that we were all students, albeit rambunctious ones, and not some group of murderous felons.

"I can't remember exactly what I said but it must have been pretty persuasive. Somehow, I managed to avoid any disciplinary action for having organized the protest in the first place." He told his daughter that he had even managed to convince the administration to agree to hear some of the students' grievances in the process. Surprisingly, they agreed to reduce the number of specimens that they had originally planned to remove from the museum, as a compromise."

Chapter 30

The Ignorant Bench

*I*t had never even registered with Celeste before that day that her parents had been in college during the free-love pot-smoking days of the '70s. Her father stopped short of admitting to smoking pot himself, but he sure seemed to know an awful lot about it for someone who never did. And, she had the strange sensation that he was just waiting for her to ask him about it, although she never worked up the nerve. He *did* say that there was pot at most of the parties he and his friends had gone to, usually in a back room somewhere. It was very easy for someone to get a "contact high" back in those days, he told her, from just being in the same room where other people were smoking. Her father said that was how the cancer researchers probably knew to look at second-hand smoke as a contributor to lung disease and cancer.

Her dad had even mentioned a little about his relationship with Kristin that day, although Celeste noticed that he had also kept an eye out for Charlotte, who had been making an occasional appearance, at the same time. Celeste had always known that her father met her mother at Tuskegee, but she had just recently put together that he had met her Aunt Kristin there too. *And* that Trazi had been born in Tuskegee. She had never thought about that at all until shortly before her aunt left for Ghana to stay.

Her dad had agreed to let her spend a whole week at Kristin's house and she had followed her aunt around from room to room like she always did. Celeste had kept Kristin company while she finished packing her house during the day, and then they would usually do something together in the evenings. They had gone shopping for last minute things that Kristin wanted to take with her; they visited a few museums one day; and they made one last trip to the Kennedy Center together to see the national symphony, with Isaac Stern playing the violin.

It had been quite by accident that Celeste stumbled across several photos of her father and aunt on the day before her dad was due to pick her up. The pictures had fallen from an album that Celeste didn't remember seeing before; surprising, especially considering how much rambling she had done in her aunt's house over the years. She had noticed the album as soon as she walked into the room, partly because it was lying on a table that was draped in a beautiful piece of chartreuse silk kente. She had been drawn to the fabric and only picked the album up out of curiosity once she reached the table.

Celeste remembered being completely caught off guard by the photos that fell out of it. The one thing that she noticed right away was how happy Kristin and her father looked together—happier than she had ever seen either of them look. There was a small newspaper clipping in the album about her dad too, from the Tuskegee News. It was a story about a summer internship he had been awarded at NASA in Houston. After she had picked it up, Kristin walked into her bedroom and discovered Celeste reading the article. Celeste had been surprised to see a look of alarm on her aunt's face for a quick second, and then Aunt Kristin immediately began looking around for the photos that had been in the album.

Then she started telling Celeste assorted background information about the article she had been reading, all the while looking around for the photos until she finally spotted them laying on a side table where Celeste had put them. Kristin explained that the article was about Winston's first official association with the space agency, and she had seemed relieved that Celeste had turned her attention away from the photos. Celeste thought that Kristin seemed to be talking a lot faster than normal too, telling her all about her dad's internship and that he had started working for NASA a few months after they met at Tuskegee.

"He was dating someone else at the time," Kristin added, "but it was the beginning of our friendship and us getting to know each other."

Celeste remembered thinking that her aunt must have still thought a lot about her father to keep all that stuff, especially after so much time had passed. Then, just as quickly, she decided that Kristin had probably kept it to show their grandkids one day—maybe.

Celeste had been drawn back to the photos again a few minutes later, and she could sense Kristin's anxiety as soon as she picked them up. She realized that both her aunt and her father still looked just as young as the couple in the pictures. Their hairstyles and the clothes they wore were the only things that made you realize the photos had been taken years earlier. And it was hard to miss the love that radiated between the two of them.

After a few awkward seconds of silence, Kristin had finally volunteered that the pictures had been taken during the spring after they were married, at an "All Day Music" festival on campus. Her friend Niyla had taken them, she said, while they were just sitting on the grass listening to the music in the warm sunshine.

"We had a music festival every year, usually on the same weekend as the Tuskegee Relays. It was a really big deal back then and we were always excited when that weekend came around." Celeste noticed that Kristin had shifted the conversation completely away from the photos.

"Students would come to Tuskegee from all over the South for the music," Kristin went on, "and to watch the track and field events across the street in the stadium. Your father was president of the student government association at the time, and every year the SGA would come up with at least one big name group to play in the festival. And we would always have other local and college bands completing the line-up.

"It was great fun and we were having a ball that day," she finished.

Kristin looked wistfully at a photo of her and Winston sitting on a blanket eating grapes for a few seconds, and all Celeste could do was to stare at her in surprise. It wasn't until then that she realized there had been an element concerning her father and aunt Kristin that had somehow completely escaped her attention up until that point.

"We would walk over to the Dust Bowl, as we called it back then, and watch the championship track meet for a while," Kristin told her. "Those races were always exciting too. There is a long list of future Olympic athletes who had attended rival HBCUs and would come to Tuskegee to compete with our track team. For several of them, those earlier races had been the beginning of promising careers and later helped prepare them for their run for the gold.

"But at some point, we would tear ourselves away and go back across to the yard to find a spot as close to the Fountain as we could get. If we spotted friends, we would lay our blanket next to theirs and eat sandwiches and fruit and just listen to the music."

Before she had run across the photos, Celeste had never even thought about the relationship her aunt had once had with her father. Kristin had always been a part of her life and they had always been very close—in many ways, much closer than Celeste had ever been to her own mother. Even with her living in Africa now, Celeste still thought about going to see Kristin more than she thought about going to see her mother who only lived a few miles away.

Celeste had known instinctively that day that it would have been fruitless for her to try to get anything more out of her aunt. There had been just a few more seconds of silence and then Kristin steered the conversation away from the one that clearly made her so uncomfortable. She only talked more about Tuskegee after that, and she had the same nostalgic look on her face that her father had as they worked on his music collection.

Celeste didn't get any more information from Kristin that day, but her father had seemed more than willing to talk about their relationship. Her interest in knowing more had certainly been stirred after seeing the photos and she had been dying to know more them every since that day. She kept bracing herself to ask her father for more details every time he mentioned Kristin's name, but she was surprised to find that she was also a little afraid of what he might tell her.

Besides that, she had been reluctant to change the carefree mood of their day together with something serious. And instinctively, she knew that would be exactly what would happen if she asked her father probing questions about his relationship with Kristin. He had seemed much more relaxed that day than she had seen him in a long time, and he was obviously having the time of his life telling her stories about his life in Tuskegee— "back in the day," as he had referred to it.

Winston would laugh so hard as his memories surfaced that Celeste could barely understand what he was saying at times. One thing he seemed to enjoy talking about most was his adventures on the "Ignorant Bench."

"The what?" She had stared at her father thinking that he had to be kidding when he said it. "What's an Ignorant Bench?"

"It was an institution at Tuskegee at one time, Sweetheart." Winston was already laughing at the punch line that he hadn't bothered to share with his daughter yet.

"Okay, I can't swear to this," he went right into the lie, "because this story has only been passed down by word of mouth. But legend has it that when Booker T. had all the former slaves line up to lift the veil of ignorance from their heads, there were some that he just couldn't help."

After saying it, her father broke into hysterical laughter and Celeste laughed with him, although she still didn't fully get the joke. She remembered him taking her to see a statue of Booker T. Washington once, when they went to pick Trazi up from his grandmother's house. The statue showed him pulling a blanket or something off another's man's head, but that had been when Celeste was only five years old.

"Over the years, there have been a number of students who somehow were able to get into Tuskegee," he continued with his bogus explanation, "although the veil of ignorance had clearly not been lifted from their heads either. At any rate, those students claimed this concrete bench that sat in the middle of all the other student activity, as their own."

After he finally stopped laughing again, Winston told his bewildered daughter one tall tale after the next about something that had happened as he sat with his ignorant brothers on the semi-circled bench that sat right in front of the Student Union building. A shady cedar tree grew in a small patch of landscape right behind the bench, and it provided just enough shade for them to be able to sit there comfortably all day during the spring, fall, and summer semesters.

"Our main objective," he confided to his daughter, "was to irritate as many female students as possible; kind of like pulling their hair in the first grade." He was laughing again. "Since the Ignorant Bench was on the beaten path to just about everywhere on campus, the majority of students would walk past it every day—either going to class, to the gym, the library, or to get something to eat in the cafeteria. The only alternative was to take a really long detour that went around the far side of the Student Union building. And a few women actually did that too, just to avoid the harassment."

"Okay, Daddy. This really isn't funny, but please tell me it was at least a joke."

And once again, she could hardly believe what she was hearing from her own father when he answered her. Winston gave her as many details as she could take about their relentless harassment of female students, who were only walking past the bench minding their own business. Celeste couldn't believe that he still thought it was funny either!

Then he told her that for the most part, he and his sidekicks had only goaded the women they were attracted to and might be interested in dating—like that made a difference. He actually told her that they would yell things out to poor female students like—"Hey slim, you want some fries to go with that shake?"

"It was unbelievable!"

Between his laughter, her father told Celeste that depending on the response they got or the lack of one, they might just decide to continue their barrage of corny remarks until the unfortunate woman was completely out of earshot.

"The safest thing," he explained, "was for the girl to just look at us, give us a sweet smile, and then continue on to where she had been going. I can tell you that it wasn't usually a good idea for her to be a smart-aleck either, unless she was really cute; especially if she was the sensitive type and couldn't handle the inevitable retaliation."

Celeste was still looking at her father with her mouth wide open as though he was an alien.

"Or worse still," he went on, pretending not to notice, "would be for her to try to ignore us, because that just changed the game and made us all heckle the heckler instead. Everyone else on the bench would turn on the unfortunate guy who had been outdone by the female student and start 'Jonesing' him; giving him some of his own medicine.

"And you know we weren't going to tolerate that." Winston said it as though it actually made sense to him. "Whoever the heckler was, he had no choice at that point but to redirect the laughter away from him."

He admitted that it had been pretty much a losing proposition for most young women at Tuskegee back then. He explained that he had the internship in Houston during the summers, so he had missed out on all the fun that went on during summer school when no one had that many classes.

"But it was a real blast for us because nearly every woman who walked past the bench was subjected to us."

"Daddy, are you serious?" Celeste had still been waiting for the punch line; for her father to tell her that he had been joking. Eventually she realized that he wasn't going to say that, and that she really had no idea of who her father was. He had always seemed so reserved to her except when it came to his music.

"Don't worry, sweetheart." Winston provided her with reassurances once he saw that she was taking what he said too seriously.

"Everybody knew it was all in fun. Some group of male students at some point had been bored one day with nothing but time on their hands, so they decided to start this clever new institution to pass the time.

"We really didn't have a whole lot to do back then," he explained. "There was absolutely no entertainment in the little town." He had at least offered some kind of excuse for their behavior, but it was still crazy. Winston told Celeste the Ignorant Bench tradition had been passed down from year to year and it gave the guys, at least, something to look forward to.

"But don't think there weren't any sisters who were willing to go toe to toe with us—it was really just a matter of confidence. He spoke as though his assurances made a difference of some kind.

"We really never meant any harm," He assured his still-skeptical daughter. "The object of the game was strictly entertainment." He ended with a broad smile on his face.

Celeste kept staring at him in disbelief. Her mouth was still open and she wished she had thought to tape him, because she knew Trazi would never believe her. Once again, if she hadn't been there to see the words come out of his mouth herself, she wouldn't have believed it either.

Her father had seemed completely oblivious to her reaction as he continued down memory lane, and just kept right on telling her about one shameless escapade after another at Tuskegee. Most of it was before he and Kristin got married, because he told her he had straightened up his act after that, especially when Trazi was born.

She would never have guessed any of what he told her about his college life. He still got a lot of pleasure just from talking about it now, so she knew he must have really enjoyed himself while he was there. She had no idea he was capable of most of the things he had been telling her. Aside from the times that he and her mother had friends over to play cards, he had always seemed pretty straight-laced to her from her earliest memories. She kept looking at him and really trying, but she still couldn't get a picture of her father sitting on anything called an "Ignorant Bench."

She had to admit that some of his stories were funny though, like the one he told about this football player, who had started in on some sassy young sister one day. Winston said the woman had just fired right back at the guy, tit for tat, as soon as he said the first thing to her.

"And the stuff she was saying was way funnier than anything this guy came up with," he told his daughter. "All the guys on the Bench just cracked up. We were holding our stomachs and laughing so hard they hurt. The football player was embarrassed, obviously, so he wouldn't give up.

He kept trying to get the best of the young woman, saying anything he could think of to get us to stop laughing at him and start back laughing at her.

"But nothing this guy came up with seemed to faze the female student one bit. She just kept right on walking past the bench; she kept the same deliberate pace that she had when they first spotted her coming as she continued toward Huntington Hall and her next class. She didn't speed up the slightest bit as some of the other women would do, or give any kind of indication that she was rattled by anything the guy said to her.

"So, finally," Winston said, "the football player glanced back at the bros on the bench, and then turned around toward the woman's quickly disappearing frame. He had an almost desperate look on his face.

"Man," he called out in a loud enough voice for everyone to hear, "that sister's behind is so big, if a fire broke out in her dorm and the firemen told everybody they needed to haul ass, 'ole girl here would have to make two trips!

"As soon as he said it, everybody started hooping and hollering and laughing all over the place. We gave each other five and slapped each other on the back, and the ripple of laughter was so spontaneous that even the girl had to look back over her shoulder with a smile. Then she exaggerated the sway of her very large hips and kept on her way without ever skipping a beat."

Celeste and Winston both were laughing out loud the whole time he relived that episode. Both of them were almost in tears from laughing so hard, and after they had started to calm down Charlotte came to the door to ask them what was so funny. That made them start laughing all over again, and it had taken several minutes before Winston could stop himself long enough to answer her.

After Charlotte had left again, he told Celeste that a lot of the regulars on the Bench had been members of the football team. "They could get away with a lot more than most of the other students because of the money that the football program brings the school.

"Unfortunately, he told Celeste, "a lot of them seemed to think registration was the culmination of their academic activity for the semester, instead of being the prelude.

"But somehow, most of the football players had managed not to "punch out" of school, at least not before their eligibility to play ran out. Don't get me wrong," he clarified. "There were a lot of football players who were on the ball academically too."

Winston had always tried to talk to both his children about the world as it really was. He could never understand why people would let their guilt, or shame, or whatever, keep them from passing on valuable experience they had learned in life to their children.

"A lot of those guys very seldom went to class though, unless they were in one of Dr. Keenan's classes. Their coaches always urged them to register for his classes to bring up their GPAs, but Dr. Keenan didn't care what the coach or the athletic director said; if the players didn't show up for class regularly they didn't pass.

"And then, there were the guys like me," he told his daughter. "We were really serious students although you wouldn't necessarily know it. It was seldom that I ever skipped a class, because it would've thrown my whole schedule off. Some of us were involved in the more productive extracurricular activities on campus too, aside from playing ball.

"Don't ask me why, but for some reason back then it had seemed pretty cool to pretend to be ignorant."

✳✳✳

The pair had nearly worked their way through the entire pile of CDs on the floor so they decided to take one last break before making a final push to finish the cataloguing project. They sat quietly for a few minutes, sipping water and listening to Thelonius Monk. Celeste watched her father and saw a smile slowly come across his face that she couldn't describe.

Then he started talking about how the women at Tuskegee had become a lot bolder before he graduated, which had taken all the fun out of the Ignorant Bench.

"It was Kristin really," he finally said. "She was the one who set the stage for ending our twisted little avenue for amusement. Without any warning, she just took a seat on the Bench one day. She just sat there waiting for over an hour, just chatting with the fellas until I got out of class."

"Wow," Celeste's response came right away. "That was pretty bold." She herself couldn't imagine trying to infiltrate such a male dominated den.

"She really was bold." Winston was still smiling. "She picked one of the prettiest spring days to do it too. Everyone was out on the yard and they all saw her sitting there. She even talked to some of her friends as they walked by."

"Go, Aunt Kristin." Celeste felt proud to know that her aunt had taken a stand against all those barbaric male students.

"We were married at the time, but we had been going at it for almost a week. We used to have these back and forth arguments that couples sometimes have—about nothing mostly. As I got closer, I could see all the bros in the background from the corner of my eye. I could tell they were watching to see what would happen next. They had been waiting for me to get there to see what I would do once I saw Kristin sitting on the Ignorant Bench."

"So, what did you do?" He had Celeste's full attention now.

"More like what I didn't do." Her father still had the strangest smile on his face. "I already knew Kristin was mad at me and I could see that she was being just a little *too* nonchalant as I walked toward her. We had left things pretty badly between us before we had to head toward the yard that morning. There was no way I was about to play the fool and say anything about her sitting on the Bench on top of that—especially with all the bros watching. I wasn't about to take a chance on what your Aunt Kristin might do." His mysterious smile only broadened as he said it.

"Kristin has never been known to mince words when she gets angry, and I could see trouble in her eyes from a long way off."

Celeste's interest had piqued again at the mention of her aunt's name. She was dying to know more about the relationship she and her father had.

"So, what did you do?" She asked again. She didn't want to seem too eager and have him end the conversation.

"I did what I had to do," he answered, laughing again.

"I said whatever I had to say to get her off that bench and away from my boys, 'cause I knew she might start to blow at any minute.

"But after that," Winston continued, trying to stop himself from laughing, "things on the Ignorant Bench were never quite the same. Kristin started waiting for me there in the afternoons regularly, on the days I had the Big Injun's math class," he said of his tall broadly-built East Indian professor. "She did it whenever she felt like it, so it was only a matter of time before other females on campus followed suit. Kristin finally broke through all the taboos and overcame the ignorant." He started laughing all over again.

Celeste had been trying to make out the expression on his face as he talked about Kristin. He pretended like he had been disappointed that all of their sick little fun had been brought to an end. But beneath his words, she was pretty sure he had been proud that it was Kristin who had been the one to end it. Celeste knew for sure that he never looked that way when he spoke about her mother—even during their best of times.

Then, he leaned back in his chair with his arms folded and his hands clasped behind his head. They had finished their break and were almost done with the entire project. Just like that, her father took on a more sober tone, as though the spell he had been under all day had been broken. He seemed to remember all that he had been saying to his daughter, and he made a quick turn back into father mode.

"Looking back, I guess we took some pretty big risks back in the day," he told her finally. We were very lucky back then," he said, still in a much stiffer voice. "The main reason we got away with so much was because Tuskegee was a small majority Black college town.

"Booker T. made a brilliant move when he convinced Dr. Carver to come to Tuskegee," Winston said to his daughter. "Did you know that Carver had been drawn toward Africa too, and he had considered going there to develop his talents?"

"No, Aunt Kristin never told me that." Kristin had always talked to Celeste a lot about Black history, just as she had with her son.

"Yup, it's true. He had been set for life at Iowa State already, but he wanted to do something to help Black people who were struggling to get their footing after slavery. I guess Kristin told you that he left home by himself when he was little, only because he had literally learned all there was to learn in Diamond Grove Missouri."

"She did tell me that," Celeste interrupted. "When he was nine—I can't even imagine doing something like that."

"Well, that's good to know." Winston smiled at her.

"Dr. Carver had all kinds of adventures on his way to Iowa too," he said after a pause. "He actually saw a Black man being lynched."

"Aunt Kristin told me that." Celeste's energy felt heavier as soon as her father mentioned the hanging. It made her feel sick to her stomach.

"That lynching never left Dr. Carver's mind." Winston's tone was serious. "He wanted to use his talents to help his people and he decided on Tuskegee as the best place to do it. He spent a lot of time and effort helping Blacks in rural areas all around the town. That's why he was so careful about documenting his research and the specimens in his lab. He wanted it to be a place for Black children in Alabama to be able to come and see it, and maybe be inspired to become scientists themselves. Which is why the students were so angry that the school's president would just let all of it get shipped off somewhere." Winston had become instantly upset again as he thought about the Carver Museum being stripped of many of the things that had been there when he first came to Tuskegee as a freshman.

"Dr. Carver actually taught the students how to make the bricks that they used to build the first academic buildings and dormitories, you know. It was his talent that put the tiny little town on the map, and helped shape it into a one-of-a-kind place for Black people in the South.

"It became a prosperous little place—and a very sheltered environment. There were kids in Tuskegee who went on cruises with their families as far back as the '50s. All of it was pretty odd since Montgomery, once proclaimed the "Cradle of the Confederacy," was only thirty miles away. The majority of people living in Tuskegee had either been students themselves at one time, or they had sent their children to school there. They either worked at the school, or its hospital that served the surrounding community faithfully for decades, until it became tainted by the scandal of that unconscionable U.S. Public Health Service study. People who didn't work at the school mostly worked at the veteran's hospital, whose expansive grounds was leased to the federal government by the college.

Winston told his daughter that the students felt like they belonged in Tuskegee. He said he had often overheard some of the townspeople saying something about what "one of those students" had done. He said he always heard an undertone of affection in their complaints, as though they were talking about a misbehaving child.

"Any disruptive behavior by students was usually looked at by the community as more of a harmless prank made by grown children. We could definitely tell that we were welcome there back then."

He hastened to tell her that although Tuskegee was still somewhat sheltered, compared to other places in the country, it was no longer safe to take the kind of chances they had taken as students. "There's no getting away with what we could get away with anymore, not even in Tuskegee.

"But back in the day, it was the safest and most nurturing place in the country for young Black college students. And we definitely took advantage of it."

※※※

By the time they had finished for the day, Celeste's head was reeling from all the things she had learned about her father.

'Is he finally starting to accept that I'm not just his little girl anymore?'

She wondered whether that could be true, as she helped clear away the discarded plastic cases from CDs that were thrown all over the Persian rug. Something told her that her dad had still held back on telling her some things, but she had a feeling that it might have been because it was some-one else's story to tell.

It had been such a perfect day and it left Celeste trying to remember why they had stopped hanging out as much as they once had. It made her feel good too, about how easily he had canceled his plans with Charlotte for dinner. She could tell by her stepmother's body language that she had been more than a little upset about not being consulted beforehand about the change in plans. Celeste had been a little surprised that her father just blew off Charlotte's complaints about having to make alternate dinner plans at the last minute. He casually mentioned having seen a sign in the window of the pizza place around the corner that they sometimes ordered from. He told Charlotte they were running a weekend special— and they delivered.

He had hardly seemed moved at all by her sulking for a change. Instead, he calmly explained that the project and the time spent with his daughter were more important to him than what they ate for dinner that night. Celeste could tell that Charlotte had been shocked at first, but she gave up eventually and left them in peace.

She and her father kept right on hanging out and having fun. Every now and then, they would get up and start dancing spontaneously to the music. Her dad taught her a few steps that they did at Tuskegee when he was in school. Celeste always knew that he secretly wanted her to go to col-lege there, although he said he would support any choice she made. She had been hoping that he was serious about that too after she found out Tuskegee didn't even have a commercial airport. She hadn't been so sure that would fit in with what *she* had in mind for college, and very little of that had to do with studying. But after hearing her father reminisce about his adventures all day—sitting on the Ignorant Bench, under the "Wine Tree," or on the Fountain; she thought it was pretty cool the way the stu-dents had created their own fun "in the middle of nowhere," as her father often described Tuskegee.

She had begun to be intrigued by the place again after the first few hours of talking with her dad. By the end of the day, she had started thinking that Tuskegee might not be such a bad place for her to spend a few years of her life. Her mom, her dad, and Kristin had all suggested that she go down for Homecoming one year so she could see the campus for herself. All three of them had told her that Homecoming was one of the few times out of the year that there was something going on there. The little town would usually be packed with thousands of alumni who came from all over the place every year. The old joined the new, and everyone joined in on the festivities as the town came alive for three days.

They all said everyone looked forward to Homecoming weekend, that is all except for Kristin's older sister, Rena, who managed the hotel bar that was usually at the center of everything. Rena was an alum too, and while it was nice for her to see her old classmates on the one hand; on the other hand, she always had to work all weekend long. Homecoming meant much longer hours for her and having to listen to many of the alumni complain about the archaic methods that were put into place just to buy a drink. She got tired of hearing their criticism about the tokens they had to buy first, which meant having to wade through the crowded hotel to stand in yet another line outside the lounge.

By the time Celeste and her father were finally done that afternoon, she found herself wanting to go down for Homecoming herself to check it out. But she decided she would wait and mention it to her father on another day. She didn't want to seem too enthusiastic, just in case she changed her mind later.

Winston smiled to himself as he watched his daughter pack away the trash she had picked up from the floor. He was glad that he had reluctantly taken Kristin's advice to show his daughter a different side of himself, because it certainly looked as though his ex-wife had been right. She had warned him that if he wanted to keep the lines of communication open with Celeste, he would have to accept that she was growing up. Even after they had been together all day, his daughter was still lingering in the room long after they had finished. Normally, she would have been long gone, but she had even helped him straighten the room up without having to be asked.

'Maybe I haven't lost my little girl after all,' he thought hopefully, as she kissed him on the cheek before heading upstairs to her room.

Chapter 31

Trazi

*T*razi had looked at his watch three times in less than fifteen minutes; impatient for the long hand to reach the five o'clock mark so he could call his sister. He figured she would be home from school by then and most likely be the one to answer the phone. He had still been avoiding their father whenever he had that option. He hesitated because he wasn't sure he would have the nerve to hang up if Winston did happen to be home and answered the phone instead of his sister. And he definitely didn't want to talk to Charlotte. Trazi hoped that he would never have to see or speak to *that* witch again in his life. He still couldn't believe his father would ever think he would be attracted to her. What a joke!

'I guess I must really be homesick,' he thought to himself after looking at his watch again for a fourth time. It had definitely been a good thing for him to be out of Washington for a while, but he had been in the Navy now for two years. After the distractions of boot camp and A School were behind him, and he had adjusted to being attached to his ship, Trazi had really begun to miss his family. As he continued to wait impatiently for his sister to get home he thought about calling his mom for a brief second. It would be nearly ten o'clock in the evening in Ghana and he knew that she often worked late hours. But he decided that he wouldn't risk breaking her concentration when he didn't really want anything except to hear her

260

voice. Besides, he and Celeste would be flying over to see her in the next few months. They would have plenty of time to catch up then because his mom was planning to take a few days off to show them around the country.

Trazi had even considered giving Angela a quick call. They had all been holding their breath now for months hoping that she would actually make it this time. Everyone that is, except for Charlotte. All she ever thought about was herself. So far, things had seemed promising for Angela; from all indication she had finally turned her life around this time. But Trazi still decided he would wait until he had talked to his sister first, in case there had been some setback that he didn't know about yet. The last thing he wanted was to be blindsided and left unable to think of anything to say to her. Angela's gentle spirit had always reminded him of his mother's in some ways, although she was nothing like her in many other ways. When Angela and his father first got married, it had seemed to him like having *two* mothers for a while.

Once he was older, he had come to appreciate the way that his parents had handled their divorce. They had remained friendly with each other and had worked out agreements for support and custody of him without getting any lawyers involved. They had ended their marriage peacefully, without any of the usual arguing and fighting that some of his friends' parents had done. For the longest time, he had happily shuttled back and forth between his mom's house and the house that his father lived in with Angela. They all had made it seem perfectly normal to him: He had a different set of toys for each place, and he stayed with each parent on alternating weeks until he started grade school. And he had always spent all the holidays with both his parents.

Trazi had been thinking back to those times a lot lately. Those had been some of his happiest memories, since he was too small to remember much about when his parents were married to each other. He had only been three years old when they split up. As far as he knew, his mom and Angela had always gotten along well together. They had really been more like sisters at first but a lot changed once Celeste was born. Trazi had started first grade only a few months after his sister arrived. After that, he had only spent weekends with his mother and Celeste started going with him when he did, before she was even old enough to walk. For his sister, it had always been as if she had two mothers too.

He had always been fond of Angela but he wasn't at all surprised when she and his dad got divorced. The older he got, the more convinced he became that his parents were still very much in love with each other. He wasn't sure if his father had figured it out yet, but his mom had come close to admitting it to him once. He had caught her off guard and asked her while they were in the car; deliberately waiting until that time so she wouldn't be able to make her usual escape. His dad had still been married to Angela at the time, but the look on his mother's face had told him that his suspicions were true.

The sad thing was that even *he* could see that Angela didn't care what his father did, or with whom. Trazi had seen that clearly after they had only been married a few years. Eventually, his first stepmom had pulled away from all of them, but now Angela had finally begun her journey back. He had always known that the same sweet person he had known before was tucked inside of her somewhere. But for the past fifteen years, the old Angela had only made brief appearances from time to time. She had never really been the same again after she was pregnant with Celeste.

For a little while, before his sister started grade school, it had seemed as though things had gotten better for his father's second wife. They would see the old Angela much more often and everyone had hoped that her emotional state had finally balanced itself out. That progress didn't last very long though, and before any of them knew it she had slipped right back into her old habits. She started retreating into herself again and away from everyone else. Trazi remembered that he had first seen the change in her a few months before his sister was born.

At first, no one else had seemed alarmed. Then, he would hear his dad's whispered conversations to his grandmother or his mother, when Angela was out of earshot. They had all seemed to believe the reason for her acting so strangely was the baby. They all said his sister had caused Angela's hormones to be out of balance. Trazi had been about to turn six at the time and had no real concept of what any of it meant. But since the explanation seemed to satisfy everyone else, he had accepted it too. He remembered how excited he had been when his dad called him at his grandmother's house in Tuskegee to tell him that he and Angela were on their way to the hospital to "get" the baby, as he had put it.

Trazi had also felt more than a little apprehensive, because he had never forgotten that it had been the baby who was the cause of Angela's peculiar behavior. But after his grandmother brought him back to Washington and he saw Celeste for himself, all of that had changed. His little sister was the cutest little squirming baby he had ever seen in his life. As with nearly everyone else, Trazi had been instantly hooked as soon as he saw Celeste.

All the reservations he had about the mysterious creature that had been growing in his stepmother's stomach had vanished instantly.

He had been immediately protective of Celeste too as soon as he got home. He would follow Angela from room to room when she was holding her. That was how he happened to be first to notice that something was still very wrong with his stepmother. He saw how she avoided touching Celeste, or even looking at her unless she absolutely had no choice.

Trazi had been terrified when he realized how seriously his sister's care was lacking after their father would leave for work everyday. He had been far too young to know anything about taking care of a baby, but he could see the difference in the way his mom handled his little sister. She would talk softly to Celeste and stroke her tiny face. His mom was always very careful as she fed her too and as she changed her diaper. Trazi had felt relieved watching his mother gently rock his little sister until she stopped crying.

Then, all of a sudden, his mom stopped coming over as much as she had, and when she did come she didn't stay very long. His dad told him it was because she wanted to give Angela time to bond with Celeste. Trazi could remember being alarmed after his father said that; he had never seen Angela doing any of the things his father described as bonding. He knew it would be a long time before his mother started coming over again, if she had to wait for Angela and Celeste to bond. So, even though he had only been six years old, Trazi began to think of himself as Celeste's guardian and his sense of responsibility for his sister had never lessened. His father had been working some pretty long hours at NASA back then, so someone had to look out for her.

It wasn't long before he had learned how to change her diaper if she was already lying down in her crib. It was something that Angela avoided for as long as she could, usually until Celeste had pooped and the smell left her with little choice. He had been afraid again when it was time for him to go to school in the fall. He would race the few blocks home every day as soon as school was dismissed. His father finally decided that Angela wasn't getting any better and he hired a full-time nanny a few weeks later. The woman only took care of Celeste during the daytime at first. Then, Winston extended her hours and she stayed with them until he got home from work.

Trazi had been a little uneasy about leaving his sister with the strange woman, since none of them really knew her. He would follow the woman around relentlessly too, as soon as he got home from school. He kept it up until he had satisfied himself that she took care of his sister the way that his mom did. The only difference was that she didn't kiss Celeste all over her face as much as his mom. But he still hadn't been completely relieved of his anxiety until his mother started coming to their house more frequently again. By then, it had become all too obvious to everyone that Angela needed more help than other new mothers usually needed.

Trazi remembered how he had been scared to death the first time his mother let him hold Celeste without having anyone else to help him. Both of his parents had stood close by and watched him, both smiling nervously. Somehow, he had managed to keep his little sister from squirming out of his hands and onto the floor. He had never been more proud of himself as he was that day, and he had never been as grateful for his mother as when she finally took his giggling baby sister from his arms.

After Celeste grew older and learned to walk steadily on her own, he had been allowed to take her to the small playground behind their house by himself. He had proven that he was trustworthy by then, although his mom made him promise that he would never take Celeste outside unless she or his dad were home with him. After she started school, he had taken it upon himself to walk from his school every day after it was out, to his sister's school so he could wait with her until Angela came to pick them both up. Usually, by the time she got there Celeste was the only child left. Trazi didn't like the thought of his sister sitting on the steps all by herself so he always went there to wait with her.

One day, Angela was over an hour late in getting there. Trazi could tell that she had been drinking too as soon as he and Celeste were in the car. He had been scared to death for himself and his sister during the short drive to their house. He had decided that he would take Celeste by the hand another day that Angela was late, and the two of them walked the nine or ten blocks home instead of waiting for her. He had been so afraid that Angela might be drinking again and they were almost home before they saw her car pull out of the drive and start in the direction of Celeste's school.

And she hadn't been at all apologetic. She had only stopped long enough to tell them that she was going to run a few errands and would pick up pizza for dinner on her way home. His sister had innocently told their father all about their adventure when he got home later that night. And without another word, Winston arranged to have a taxi service pick Trazi up from his school every day from that point on. He was to wait in the taxi at Celeste's school until she was dismissed, and then the driver would bring them both home.

Trazi didn't think anyone blamed his father for finally ending the marriage. It had become increasingly difficult to ignore their family's dysfunction and everyone could see that the marriage union wasn't of benefit to anyone. He had even overheard his grandmother say to his father once that he had gone far beyond the limit that any other man would have gone before walking away.

There had been no discussion about custody arrangements because it had been understood without saying that both Trazi and Celeste would move with their father to the loft he finally bought. It was farther away from his mom's house, but she had been away in Ghana teaching when his father and Angela divorced. He knew his mom wanted him to stay with his father because as she put it, he was well on his way to manhood. She told him that his father could teach him all the manly things that she had no clue about.

Trazi never told her at the time but he had secretly fantasized that she might move into the loft with them after she got back from Ghana, and then the four of them would have been a *real* family. He had been more upset than his father that his mom hadn't come home that Christmas. If she had, Trazi was sure that he could have helped make the dream he had come true. But by the time she finally came back, his father had already married Charlotte. She tried to hide it, but he was sure he could hear disappointment in his mother's voice, even across the thousands of miles that separated them when he called to tell her the news.

Trazi had to sigh deeply in exasperation whenever he thought about his father's hasty marriage to Charlotte. Both he and his sister had been caught completely off guard by his sudden decision. His second stepmother had seemed so artificial somehow. Charlotte had never really looked at him or Celeste when she talked to them; it was always more like she was looking in their general direction. They didn't know how to tell their father how they felt about her because he seemed to like her so much. They waited for him to ask them what they thought about her, but he never did.

Trazi guessed that it had been a reasonable expectation on his father's part to think Charlotte would be motherly toward them, but everyone except their father and grandmother could see that Charlotte barely had more than a passing interest in him or Celeste. With his mother living in Africa, and his dad working such long hours with his own business now, Trazi still felt that it was up to him to take care of his sister even though he was away in the Navy.

His ship was attached to the Naval Station in Norfolk, which made things a lot more complicated. That had been his one regret about leaving home; it had left him unable to keep a watchful eye on Celeste, especially now that she was a teenager and mobile. The young thug wannabees, who hung around across from their house in the summer, gave him nightmares. Trazi had watched his little sister with them for almost an hour once from the window in his bedroom. She had been giggling and talking to this skinny young kid—Bennie, they called him.

Celeste had been only twelve at the time and although she was openly flirting, it was still innocent enough on her part. As a man, Trazi knew those guys wouldn't see it that way at all. His sister had naively been inviting trouble with her body language and he was pretty sure she wasn't even aware of it. He could tell that she had no clue those guys were just sizing her up, and all the back and forth banter between them was just exposing how naïve she really was.

He could see straight through those guys and he didn't want Celeste mixed up with any of them. It had been all he could do not to run downstairs and drag her little behind back into the house. The only thing that had stopped him was the realization at the last minute about how mortified his sister would have been if he had. She probably wouldn't have spoken to him for months afterwards, if not longer.

So he had just stood watching them from his window and waiting impatiently for his sister to come inside the house. And as soon as she did and he had given her time to settle down in her room, he walked to the store down the block as an excuse for stopping off on his way back. He wanted to have a little chat with the guys who were hanging around on the steps. Trazi knew that he had a reputation around the neighborhood as a nice guy. It was also well known that he had a short fuse if he was pushed the wrong way, at the wrong time. He sat down on the steps with the guys to talk, just in case Celeste came to her window and saw him.

He quietly talked to all of them about his sister, but he directed his attention to the one called "Bennie" in particular. Trazi told them how he had watched them from his window sometimes, as they tried to talk to every girl who walked down the sidewalk. He even joked with them about it a little, but he also made sure they understood the consequences of taking things too far with his sister.

A few days later, he made a point of coming to Celeste's school to walk her home. He did his best to sound casual as he struck up a conversation with her about how she should handle men that she ran into when she was out alone, or with her friends. He tried to make it seem like a game and hid how serious he really was from her, because he also knew she was stubborn. Trazi coached his little sister on how she should respond to older men especially, in a way that politely said "hello" in answer to their greeting. But at the same time, her tone would say, "don't say *another* thing to me because I am not interested in hearing anything else you have to say."

To his relief, Celeste bought the whole thing and she caught on pretty quickly, too. Everyday after that, she would wait for him to get home so she could relay the conversations she had with different men who tried to talk to her. Trazi had been more horrified than their father had been at how quickly her body was developing. His little sister had changed drastically almost overnight. He could only imagine how much attention she was attracting now that she was fifteen, and knowing that she and Malaya were travelling around together only made it worse. His sister's friend had always been a knockout, even when she was little. She had come to the airport with Celeste and his parents to see him off to boot camp, and when he saw the two blossoming thirteen-year-olds together like that it made him franticly wish he had reconsidered plans to move so far away from his sister; especially at a time when she would need his protection the most. But it was too late by then; he had been issued his travel orders and had been expected to report for duty at Great Lakes.

※ ※ ※

Trazi looked at his watch again and quickly walked to the small bank of phones outside his bunk to dial their number at the loft. As he listened to the sound of the phone ring on the other end, he was sure that his sister would be home because it was already twenty minutes past five.

He hung up abruptly as soon as he recognized Charlotte's voice, not caring whether she would suspect it had been him on the phone or not. He still couldn't believe that witch had actually tried to get his father to believe he was trying to *hit* on her, of all things. Or that his dad had *believed* her!

"Where is that girl?" Trazi was getting more anxious now and considered what his next move should be in tracking his sister down. Their father had always been adamant about both of them coming straight home from school. They had to check in first before they went anywhere else. The only exception he made was if they had a school activity that started right after school. Trazi was positive that their father hadn't loosened his rules for Celeste. Since he had started working from home more than he worked at his office, it was just possible that his sister was using that excuse to get in some unaccounted for time. But he knew that it was far too close to the end of the school term and unlikely that anything would be going on after school—at least not for sophomores. There would be too many senior activities going on instead before their graduation.

He had given Celeste more than ample time to get home, even if she had lingered around for a few minutes before starting off. His mind immediately went to the alley that led behind the post office and for the millionth time, he regretted that he had ever shown it to his sister. He knew her well enough to know that she had probably ignored all of his warnings. He could almost hear her quick mind moving the first time they had walked home through the alley. Celeste had been in third grade at the time but it hadn't taken her long to figure out where they would end up, or that it would have taken much longer for them to get home if they had taken the sidewalk.

Trazi slowly began to panic as he wondered whether something bad might have happened to her. For the first time in a long time, he wished that he and his father were on speaking terms again. It had been almost three years since their fight and it had been pretty bad too; but Trazi had refused to back down. And he certainly did not intend to apologize to Charlotte for something he never did.

In a way, he was glad it had happened the way that it had because he had been able to spend some time with his mom before there was an ocean separating them. He knew his mother had been dying to ask him a thousand questions about the night that he had left his father's house. But she had respected his wishes and accepted only what he had told her; she never tried to force him to say any more. Part of the reason he had been so reluctant to talk to her about it was that he knew how hurt his mother would have been to know his father had taken Charlotte's side over his.

After the two weeks Celeste had stayed with them, he and his mom had hung out together for the whole weekend before it was time for him to leave. They had created their own set of memories that Trazi would always look back on happily. His mother had come up with the idea of going on a treasure hunt for all the buildings and monuments in and around Washington that appeared as images on U.S. currency—both paper and coin money. They had a great time driving all over the city together. They would grab a nearby tourist when they were close to one of the monuments or buildings, asking them to take their picture in front of it. It had taken the longest time for them to find the image engraved on the back of the dime. They had looked all over the city with no luck, but both refused to give up. Finally, they stumbled upon the image quite by accident after missing a turn off the GW Parkway. They found themselves headed in the wrong direction toward Rosslyn, and Kristin had quickly swerved her Saab onto the ramp leading to Roosevelt Island at the last minute. It was there that they had found the missing monument in the center of the island – the last piece of the puzzle.

His mother put all the pictures they had taken while Celeste was with them and the ones from their monument hunt into a photo album. She brought it with her to the airport to show it to him before he had to board his plane. He had only seen them that one time since photo albums weren't on the list of authorized personal items he could bring with him to the Recruitment Training Command for boot camp. As he looked at the pictures, his mother's smile told him she had been as happy to have his sister with them as he had been. Until that moment, Trazi had never really realized how much his mother genuinely cared for his little sister.

"Where is that girl?" He was suddenly aware of the time again. He started toward the phone banks for enlisted personnel again, this time with the intention of calling his father. He had punched in the first three numbers and then stopped with the phone still in his hands.

"Maybe I'm being too hasty," he decided, putting the phone back onto its cradle.

"What if she's not in some kind of trouble? Celeste would never forgive me if I got her busted long distance for no reason."

He was still so used to taking care of her that not knowing what she was doing with her time every day had become very distracting. He had been working on a plan that he hoped would help undo the damage that his rash decision to join the navy had done, but he couldn't count on it just yet.

Trazi checked his watch again and he knew that if his father had gone into his office that day, he would be back home by six at the earliest. He would call again at fifteen minutes of six, and give Celeste a little more time to get there. He reasoned that she might be taking her time in getting home to avoid having to spend time alone with Charlotte.

And he definitely couldn't blame her for that.

"I'm going to have a long talk with that girl," he concluded, unable to concentrate on a book he had decided to read to keep his mind occupied.

He also realized he was going to have to break the ice and start talking to his dad again. His sister was leaving him with little choice.

Chapter 32

A Thin Line Between Love and Hate

Malaya hopped out of the shower and quickly flipped through the clothes hanging in her closet, trying to find something decent she could put on. She was so excited that her cousin Nathan had called; they made plans to go see the new exhibit at the Hirshhorn Museum and he was due to arrive at any minute. She couldn't believe how just a few minutes earlier she had been moping about the house alone, and bored out of her mind. Then, just like that, she was running around her room trying to get dressed before Nathan got there to pick her up. She had also been praying that she would be ready when he got there, so they would be long gone before her mom and stepfather got home. The two had left the house together over three hours earlier for one of Lil' Sam's soccer games. If the game wasn't already over it probably would be soon. She knew they might all come walking in the house at any minute, unless they decided to stop somewhere on their way back.

Things had only gotten worse for Malaya as the years went by; if it weren't for Celeste, she didn't know what she would do. After almost a year and a half, she still wasn't used to her grandmother not being there anymore. Sometimes, when she first woke up in the morning Malaya would forget her grandmother was gone. For a few minutes, it would feel like she was in the room with her sitting on her bed. Malaya would finally decide she would tell her grandmother about Sam, and then cry for hours once she realized it was too late. She had missed her chance to tell her grandmother what her stepfather had been doing.

At least Sam had finally stopped coming into her room, right after she started having her period. But he still gave her the creeps the way he was always looking at her – especially lately. And he had insisted to her mother that she couldn't have any male friends although she was already fifteen years old. She couldn't even go out on group dates like everyone else her age. And Malaya could tell that Sam didn't like how Nathan had started showing an interest in her either, not one bit. He would start acting crazy on the drive home from Uncle Paul's house whenever Malaya spent any time talking to her own cousin. She always looked to her mother whenever Sam started in on her. She could never understand why her mother never set Sam straight. Why couldn't she have a boyfriend? And Nathan was her cousin!

Malaya had refused to listen to either one of them about Nathan though. And she had even been bold enough to talk about the museums that she and her cousin visited when they were at the dinner table at Uncle Paul's house once. As she had expected, first one of her aunts and then another responded by commenting on their trip. Pretty soon, nearly everyone at the table had added something about the museums they had visited, the train schedule, or their favorite Smithsonian exhibit. Finally, Uncle Paul had even made a comment about the Air and Space Museum, resuming control of the dinner conversation. After that day, the trips that she and Nathan took had the official approval of the family. And she knew that Sam would never go against Uncle Paul by trying to keep her from going.

Malaya was so glad that she and Nathan had discovered they had common interests. She had even started looking forward to their family dinners now. The pair would try to sit next to each other whenever possible, and now Malaya finally had someone she could talk to after dinner was over. She had something she could be happy about for a change. Nathan was only a few years older than her but he seemed much older. He had become the big brother that she had never had. Her cousin was a lot like Uncle Paul too in many ways, and Malaya could see that he was going to be just as big of a man as his father was. But her cousin also reminded her of their grandmother. Malaya felt safe when she was around him and they had become very close over the past few months.

They had already explored several of the Smithsonian museums together, and sometimes they would take the train and the bus, if necessary, to festivals that were held in different parts of the city. They would usually meet at the train station and she had wanted to meet Nathan there that day too, but he had just put an old car on the road that he had been working on. He finally had it running so he insisted on picking her up at home. And she had been flying around her room trying to get ready so they could leave as soon as he got there.

She had just finished the top button on the black and gold embellished shirt she had finally decided on, to go with the black matching skirt she had already slipped into. She thought she heard Nathan's car pull into their driveway and Malaya grabbed her purse and hurried toward the stairs so she could save him the trouble of getting out of the car. But she stopped dead in her tracks when she looked toward the front doorway and saw Sam instead, glaring up at her. He could tell by her hurried movements that she was on her way out and had hoped to leave the house before he got home.

"Where are Mom and Lil' Sam?" Malaya hoped she didn't sound too unnerved as she asked the question. She said a silent prayer that her mother and younger brother would be coming up the drive and through the doorway at any minute.

"Lil' Sam is at his cousins' house," Sam answered her finally. "And your mother had some shopping she wanted to do." His voice held a conspiratorial tone and he started moving toward her, as though he thought she would be pleased to learn that they would be alone.

Malaya fought the urge to run back up the stairs and lock herself in her room, and she moved forward quickly instead. She was quick enough that she made it down the rest of the stairs and past Sam before he could block her way. Nervously, she moved around him to go and stand by the living room sofa. She could look out the picture window and be able to see Nathan's car when he pulled up. She was calculating in her mind how close he might be to their house by that time.

"So where do you think you're going, all dressed up?"

Sam's voice was almost a growl; he had started moving in her direction again, slowly.

"And smelling all good too." He was sniffing the air just like the wild animal Malaya had always known him to be.

"Nathan and I are going to an exhibit at the Hirshhorn." She answered him lightly and hoped that by mentioning her cousin's name, Sam might be dissuaded from whatever sinister thoughts she could see forming in his mind.

"He should be here any minute." She tried to sound confident as she gave him that extra bit of information.

"I should have known," Sam said accusingly. "You and Nathan seem to be spending quite a bit of time together lately." He snarled at Malaya in a low voice, his displeasure evident. With every step that he took toward her, she moved a step in the opposite direction. She could see in his eyes that he was becoming annoyed with the prospect of having to chase her.

"I'm almost sixteen years old and there's nothing wrong with us going to the museum." Malaya snapped at him. "We're cousins!" She yelled the last part in a desperate tone, in response to the slimy look he was giving her that implied more to her relationship with her cousin.

"Why can't you understand that?" She was shouting at him in frustration, praying that Nathan would hurry up and get there.

"What does that matter?" Sam shouted back at the teenager. "I'm your father." He lunged forward suddenly as he said it and grabbed her arm, managing to catch her off guard.

"You're not my father!" She screamed at him, as she tried to free herself from his grip. "Stop saying that!"

Before she could get away from him, Sam gave her a hard shove backwards. Malaya lost her footing and fell back into the sofa cushions. Sam was on her in an instant.

"Yeah, I've just been waiting for you to get a little older," he confided hoarsely. He was leering at her in a way that had always made her feel sick to her stomach.

"But I guess you're old enough now." He was looking her up and down as though he could see her naked body through her clothes.

A deep-set panic came over Malaya after hearing what he said. He had pinned her down before she had a chance to regain her equilibrium. Now, he shoved his hands under her skirt roughly as she wrestled with all she had to get away from him. She closed her eyes so that she wouldn't have to see his leering expression. Malaya kept turning her head from side to side to keep him from kissing her lips, frantic to get away. Then abruptly, she felt Sam's limp body fall across hers.

When he did, Malaya screamed at the top of her lungs, still unable to understand what had happened. Then she realized Nathan was standing over both of them. He still had the broken table lamp that he had hit Sam with in his hands.

After she saw her cousin, Malaya started scrambling again to try to get from underneath Sam. When she couldn't move him off of her, she covered her face in her hands to hide her shame. Nathan let the broken lamp fall to the floor and reached down to pull his young cousin up and into his open arms. They heard Sam fall to the floor from the couch next to the lamp.

"Nathan! Oh, thank God." She was crying into her cousin's chest. "I'm so glad you got here before..." She pulled back from him and covered her face with her hands again to hide her embarrassment. "Oh God. I'm so ashamed!"

"You don't have anything to feel bad about, Malaya." Nathan held her as tight as he could. He released one of his arms from time to time to pat her on the back. He was trying to get her to stop shaking so much.

"This pig is the one who should be ashamed!" He looked down angrily at Sam's limp body.

Then Malaya looked toward the front door and saw that her mother was standing in the doorway. She had obviously heard the noise from the street and was staring at the scene in the living room with a shocked look on her face.

"What in the world is going on?" Vivian shouted at her nephew and ran quickly past him toward her husband, without giving Nathan a chance to respond. Sam had begun to stir when he heard Vivian's voice, and was struggling to regain consciousness.

"Aunt Vivian, what's going on is that your husband has been molesting your daughter!" Nathan was very angry at his aunt's response; he had said it in disgust as he took a few steps in her direction. Malaya cringed at hearing his words.

"How could you possibly not know what was going on?" He wanted to know. His father had taken Nathan aside months earlier, and asked whether he had noticed how strange Malaya acted whenever Sam was in her company. Once he thought about it, Nathan realized there had been a big difference in the way his cousin acted when they came over for family dinner, versus the way she was when she, Lil' Sam, and their mother dropped by their house occasionally. After the conversation with his father, Nathan had made a point of observing Malaya more closely the next time they came for dinner. He agreed with his father that something was not right, and the two men had been determined to get to the bottom of whatever it was.

"What?" Vivian turned around quickly to face her nephew. She had an incredulous look on her face. "That's impossible," she concluded. "What are you talking about?"

Then she turned to look at her daughter as though she had just remembered she was in the room. It was a look that Malaya had never seen before. The woman in front of her no longer seemed like the mother who had always wanted to dress her up in pretty dresses.

"How dare you make an accusation like that?" Vivian shrieked at her daughter, moving a few steps toward where Nathan and Malaya were standing. "After everything Sam has done for you! You ungrateful little..."

"She didn't have to make an accusation, Aunt Vivian." Nathan interrupted his aunt's tirade and stepped in front of Malaya to protect her.

His father had recently told him how their own parents had worked from sun up to sundown to take care of their large family. Their mother had to work at the home of a rich family most of that time, because it paid the steady income that their growing family needed. She had spent most of her waking hours taking care of someone else's kids so that she could feed her own. Nathan's father had told him that he and his sisters and brothers had gone without their mother most of the time that they were growing up. Paul and Vivian's mother had to sleep at that family's house too during the weekdays, and she had to take care of her husband when she was home on Saturday and Sunday nights.

Their father had done whatever work he could find—mostly manual labor. He worked long hours and was usually too tired to spend much time with his children during the week after he got home. Paul told his son that their parents depended heavily on him and their next oldest sister instead. The two of them had to take care of all the others and themselves too. He told Nathan that his youngest sister had always needed much more attention than she got while growing up. He told his son that it wouldn't surprise him to find that Vivian had chosen to ignore what was right in front of her—especially if it meant an end to her getting things that she wanted.

Nathan was still baffled that his Aunt Vivian had been so quick to take her husband's side against her own daughter.

"I saw Sam with my own eyes," he finally told her forcefully, after he saw that he still wasn't getting through to her. "When I came into your house, Sam was trying to rape your daughter!"

Vivian became outraged by what her nephew was saying. She looked first at Nathan and then at Malaya, unsure of what she should do next.

As they were talking, Sam had managed to pull himself up from the floor. He had stumbled into the kitchen quietly and now was suddenly back with a long knife in his hand. He lunged dramatically toward Nathan, poised to strike. Vivian was the only one of them who still had her back to Sam, and the only one who didn't see him trying to attack Nathan. She had no idea what was happening or even that Sam was no longer lying on the floor. All she knew was that her nephew had suddenly started moving in her husband's direction again, so she quickly moved in front of him to try to shield Sam from what she imagined to be another attack against him.

Malaya could see the inevitability of what would happen as soon as it was all set in motion. She started screaming again at precisely the same second that her stepfather plunged the knife into her mother's back. But even seeing that his wife's blood was spilling all over the floor wasn't enough to stop Sam from coming after Nathan. He thrust the knife at him wildly again and again, as the younger man dodged his attempts. Eventually Nathan, who was far stronger that Sam, took the knife away from him. But Sam still refused to give up on his attack, until finally Nathan stuck the knife blade into his chest as he tried to deflect it from piercing his own. Nathan had been left with no other choice but to do what he had done to save himself.

Malaya was still screaming uncontrollably as Nathan hurried to the phone to call an EMT and the police. But by the time the paramedics arrived, Sam had already bled to death. And Vivian was barely alive from all her loss of blood. They quickly and carefully loaded her into the ambulance and took off toward the hospital with sirens blasting. One of the EMTs gave Malaya a mild sedative and that calmed her down long enough to talk to the police. She confirmed Nathan's account of what had happened and told them that her cousin's actions had been entirely justified.

She was still in partial shock as Nathan helped her pack some of her and her brother's things, once the police had finished with their questioning. And the two were completely silent as Nathan finally drove his cousin back across the Anacostia Bridge, to his father's house.

❊❊❊

Malaya tried to decide whether she would ask Lil' Sam one last time whether he wanted to go with her to visit their mother, but she thought she already knew the answer. He wouldn't want to go to the hospital and Malaya could hardly blame him because she didn't want to go herself. She watched her little brother playing outside with the cousins he now shared a bedroom with, from her old bedroom window. She had cried for joy when Uncle Paul told her that his twin daughters had volunteered to move into the guest bedroom downstairs. That meant Malaya could move back into the room that had been her bedroom until her mother met Sam, and they both moved away. Everyone in the house had pitched in to help her paint the room a new color that was more to her liking.

As she looked down at her little brother, Malaya could truthfully say that he was the only reason that she would never regret that her mother had met Sam, in spite of everything that happened. They had shared the same bedroom for years before her brother was old enough to know his father. Now, even though he had known him, her brother was still not yet old enough to know what he was really like. Sam had spent very little time with his son, so the biggest concern that her brother had after his father's death was that he would no longer be bought most anything he wanted.

Everything had been quite a bit different at Uncle Paul's house than her brother had been used to. Living with their uncle and his family had been a challenge for both of them at first, but having his cousins to play with all the time made Lil' Sam's adjustment much easier.

It had now been six months since the day of his father's death and their mom's accident, as their family members chose to call it. The blow that had been meant for Nathan had paralyzed Vivian from her waist down. She had already undergone five surgeries but her chances for a full recovery remained slim. Everything had changed so quickly for all of them that day. Malaya still had nightmares, especially about seeing her mother get hurt. She still loved her mother in spite of all the accusations she had made against her, and in spite of the way she had been acting toward Malaya since Sam's death. Malaya even felt bad for her mother, but on the other hand she had finally been released from the hell she had lived with for most of her life.

Uncle Paul already treated her and Lil' Sam as though they were his own children, and he had arranged for them to see a therapist every week. It had been the therapist's idea for Malaya to visit her mother. Her doctor didn't exactly push her, but every month or so she would urge Malaya to visit her mother whenever she felt strong enough. That morning had been the morning that Malaya woke up feeling that it was the day to face her mother. She had lost far too much of her life already and she felt ready to do everything she needed to do, to be made whole.

Malaya had a thousand questions that she wanted to ask her mother, questions she had always been too afraid to ask before. She involuntarily slowed her footsteps as she neared her mother's room. She peeked around the doorway before she felt ready to move into full view. She was very nervous about seeing her mother again and she wasn't at all certain about the kind of reception she would get.

Vivian sat in a wheelchair with her back facing the doorway. She stared out the window onto the well-maintained grounds of the spinal rehabilitation center. She had been moved to the facility after recovering from her most recent surgery. Uncle Paul told Malaya that the physical therapists at the center were working hard to find out if there was a chance that her mother's ability to walk might be restored.

"Hi Mom." She spoke the words softly. Malaya waited, not sure whether her mother had actually heard her.

Vivian turned around slowly at the sound of her daughter's voice, suddenly realizing Malaya had grown into a beautiful woman. She looked almost identical to the way Vivian had looked when she was her age. She avoided looking into her daughter's eyes and then turned back toward the window to resume staring blankly out of it.

Malaya waited a few minutes after her mother did not utter a sound. She was unsure of whether she should try again and she tried to think what her therapist would have advised her to do. She had no yearning to see her mother at all. And despite what her therapist thought, she didn't feel the least bit better for having come to visit her. Both Nathan and Uncle Paul had encouraged her to visit Vivian too. Everyone kept saying that it might help her during her process of recovery. They said that it might be good for her to talk to her mother, to tell her everything that she needed to say—about what happened with Sam and what he did to her.

Her therapist had told her she would find it difficult to have a normal life if she kept her feelings bottled up. That was what had convinced Malaya to take the bus out to Virginia to visit her mother. She went to see her because a normal life was the one thing that she had always wanted.

"Lil' Sam asked me to tell you that he said hello."

Malaya started again after a few more minutes had passed. Her mother winced sharply when she heard her say Sam's name.

"He's starting to get used to his new school," she went on, not knowing whether her mother would be interested in hearing about her brother's progress or not. But Malaya couldn't think of anything else to say.

"He seems to be doing okay there," she continued, after still getting no response from her mother.

Vivian sat very still. She kept right on ignoring her daughter with a very rigid demeanor.

"Mom," Malaya started one last time, after it was clear that her mother did not intend to talk to her.

"Did you know what Sam was doing to me?" She asked the question of her mother finally. "Are you blaming me for what happened to him?" She felt her eyes begin to tear up in frustration. She had hoped to get Vivian to say something to her. Her questions hung in the air expectantly for several minutes.

Finally, Vivian wheeled her chair around to look directly at her daughter. "I don't know what you're trying to pull Malaya, but I happen to know that Sam loved me," she said forcefully. "And you're going straight to hell for all of the lies that you've been telling about him."

She didn't say anything more. She stared at her daughter with such a look of hatred in her eyes that it was chilling. For the first time in her life, Malaya consciously disobeyed something her grandmother had always taught her, that she should always respect her mother. She looked straight into her mother's eyes for what might very well have been the last time. She had lost any respect she had left for the woman who had given her life. She couldn't imagine how their relationship could ever be restored.

"Mom," she said slowly. "I've been in hell for a very long time—since the day you brought Sam into our lives, actually. But for the first time in a very long time it's starting to feel more like Heaven, or at least that I'm on the road to Heaven."

With that, she turned around and walked back out of her mother's room leaving the door wide open. Vivian sat in the chair and stared helplessly after her daughter.

Chapter 33

A Mother for Celeste

*N*o one had ever said anything to Celeste about why her mother hadn't been awarded custody of her after Angela and her father divorced. As she grew older, Celeste suspected that her mother's drinking may have been a major factor. They had never had a close relationship and now she wondered whether that played a role in the sadness that she would sometimes see in her mother's eyes. She had been wondering about a lot of things since her dad sat her down and told her what had happened to Malaya.

Celeste couldn't recall anything said about Malaya's mother having had a drinking problem, but the more she thought about it, Vivian had never seemed all that connected to her daughter either—not really. It had dawned on Celeste that her friend's mother and her mother had quite a lot in common. She only wished that she could be there for Malaya now, but Aunt Kristin said it was probably too hard for her to be around other people just yet. Malaya had steadfastly refused to talk to Celeste, even after her dad called several people to find a telephone number to reach her at her uncle's house. Celeste understood, of course, under the circumstances, but it made her feel even more hopeless since she was about to fly out of the country and Malaya wouldn't even know she was gone.

She thought back to her conversations with her friend over the years, about her relationship with her mother before she met Sam. Malaya had told her that she and her mom had been close when she was a little girl. She told Celeste they had done a lot of things together back then and Vivian would even let her stay in her room while she got dressed to go out on dates. Her mother would put makeup on Malaya's face sometimes too, she said, and even perfume. Malaya had told Celeste once that her mother's dates always said she looked like a carbon copy of her mother, if they happened to see her daughter when they came by to pick Vivian up. She could also recall that her friend had gotten very quiet after she said it—just for a little while. Now Celeste knew that she must have been thinking about her stepfather that day. It was all so awful to even think about.

Her friend had never said one word to her about any of what her stepfather had been doing to her, but now everything about Malaya made perfect sense. Celeste wondered what she would have done if her friend *had* told her about it. She might have told her dad, but then she remembered the time when he had stopped her from spending time at her friend's house. Was that the reason? Did her father know that Malaya's stepfather was hurting her? Did Malaya's mom know?

Celeste and her own mother had finally started the process of getting to know each other. She had started realizing how strange it was that although she was fifteen-years-old, she and her mother had never had a real relationship. Her mother had always been in her life and Celeste only had vague memories of the times that Angela had been away in rehab hospitals. But since she hadn't played much of a role in her daughter's daily life, the times she was away hadn't had much effect on Celeste at all; although now she was old enough to be curious about it.

Her mom had told her that her efforts to change their relationship was part of her twelve-step program. For the past two years, Angela had been trying to make restitution to everyone she had hurt by her alcoholism. She had approached Celeste gently about it at first, and still never put any pressure on her. Angela had explained to her daughter that her behavior during Celeste's entire life had been greatly affected by her alcoholism. She had asked for her forgiveness, for not being the mother that she knew her daughter needed. Angela had even told her that she was grateful to Kristin for being the mother that she should have been.

The conversation had taken Celeste entirely by surprise, although Angela had arranged for their talk in advance. After fifteen years, her mother told her that she wanted to work on building a bond between them. And of course she had forgiven her mother; Celeste had the same relationship with her all her life, and had no idea what it would mean to have a different one. Her father and Trazi had always taken care of what she needed, and in many ways, she had always thought of Aunt Kristin as her mother. She was glad that Angela was doing so much better now, but on the other hand, Celeste didn't feel that she had missed out on anything. And since she would be grown soon, she wasn't particularly interested in having some-one else telling her what to do either.

But she was willing to try for her mother's sake. All of them wanted Angela to be healthy, so Celeste had been making an effort to include her mother in things that were going on in her life. It was one of the things she wanted to talk to Aunt Kristin about when she saw her. She had thought about talking to her dad, but Celeste knew that he wasn't fully convinced of her mother's recovery.

"I'm just not getting too excited about it yet, that's all." She overheard him tell her grandmother, after her mother had been released from rehab the most recent time.

"Let's not forget that this is the third time around."

It made Celeste glad that she hadn't told him about what had happened at her mother's house, a few months after she came home. Celeste had just turned twelve and had gone to spend the weekend at her mother's to celebrate her birthday. Angela had been waiting in the doorway of their old house as her father pulled up to drop her off. Her dad had only waved to her mother and he never got out of the car. He hadn't been close enough to her notice anything out of the ordinary.

But Celeste had noticed, as soon as she came within a few feet of her mother. She could smell the strong scent of rum that was coming from a large glass of what looked like cola in her hand. She had hurried past Angela without looking directly into her eyes, as if that would somehow make the contents of her mother's glass disappear.

Once she was inside the house, there had been no doubt that her mom had been drinking again for some time. There were dirty dishes piled in the kitchen sink, competing for space with large Styrofoam boxes that held remnants of days-old food from the sandwich shop down the street. Celeste had been overpowered by the smell of decaying food, combined with liquor, stale cigarettes and ashes.

Still without saying a word to her mother, she had begun to clean up the mess. Celeste had found half-empty liquor bottles all over the house and she poured their contents down the sink as her mother stood by watching her. She swept the floors and changed her mother's bed sheets. She even tried her best to scrub grease stains from the wool rug on the living room floor. She knew that it had been one of her mother's favorite things in the house, and her mother had started crying when she saw how determined Celeste was to clean it. Angela had once told her about the trip that she and her dad had taken to Costa Rica before she had been born. Her mom had bought the rug there and Celeste remembered her saying what a hard time they had getting it back to Washington. But it had almost been ruined by the grease that had run out of an overturned and partially eaten box of chicken that had been laying across the rug.

After she had finished cleaning the house, Celeste sat on the couch in the living room the entire time she wasn't sleeping. She could still remember being terrified as she watched her mother for the rest of the weekend. She had been afraid to visit her old friends in the neighborhood, as she usually did. She thought that if she stopped watching her mother for even one minute, Angela might find a liquor bottle that Celeste had missed while she was cleaning.

Her strategy had apparently worked because Angela didn't drink any thing else before Winston came back to pick their daughter up on Sunday evening. Although Celeste never knew it, that had been the last time her mother would ever drink again.

※※※

The shrill sound of her doorbell startled Celeste after she had pushed the buzzer, as it usually did. She rubbed the ear that had been closest to the sound and used her key to let herself into the apartment. First, she scanned the small living room quickly as she always did when she arrived. Celeste smiled to herself and released the deep breath she had taken as she crossed the threshold.

Satisfied there was no evidence of liquor smells or bottles, she called out to her mother as she ventured down the short hallway toward her sewing room. Angela had moved into the smaller living space a few months after that weekend Celeste had stood guard over her. The sewing room started out as a second bedroom, but her mother had finally converted the space to a workroom for her craft. Celeste found her there sitting at her sewing machine, busy working on one of her creations.

It had only been a few months since Angela had gotten started in her new business. She designed handmade sleepover bags for adults, usually made from beautiful tapestry and canvas fabrics. Her business had just begun to take off and Angela had given the very first bag she designed to Kristin. The two women had spent a lot of time together before Kristin left for

Ghana. Angela told her daughter that the bag had been a gift of apprecia-tion to her aunt for introducing the concept of metaphysics to her, and for all of their soul-searching and healing conversations.

Celeste couldn't remember seeing her mother so enthusiastic about any-thing before, and she felt bad again that she would have to cancel their plans for the afternoon. They had planned to have lunch together at a veg-an restaurant that Angela had been telling her about for weeks. It was close to her apartment and had opened only a few months earlier. It was to be Celeste's first taste of raw food and her mother had described all the food she had tried at the restaurant as being flavorful and delicious. Celeste had actually been looking forward to going, to her surprise. She hated that she would have to disappoint her mother but she really had no choice.

It had completely slipped her mind that she still needed to get one last immunization before she was to board her flight for Ghana the follow-ing day. It was something that Celeste should have done a week earlier actually, but the travel clinic had agreed to work her in that afternoon between other appointments. Celeste had no idea how long she would be at the clinic or how she might feel after getting her last shot. So she had reluctantly called her mother the night before to tell her she would have to cancel their date.

"Hi Mom," Her greeting still held an apologetic tone. She crossed the room to kiss her mother on the cheek. "I'm so sorry about today, but I promise I'll make it up to you. And, I'm going to bring you back some-thing really special too."

"Oh, that's okay, baby. You're really special to me."

She tried hard not to show it, but Celeste could tell that Angela was very disappointed. They had decided to start doing at least one thing together every month and it was to have been their first official mother-daughter outing.

"We can just do it when you get back from Ghana."

Angela had really been looking forward to starting a real relationship with her daughter. The pair had spent more time with each other over the past two or three years than they ever had before, but there was still something that had always kept them from developing the close relation-ship that Angela now wanted to have with her daughter. That was why she had convinced Celeste to agree to do something each month with her that would also give them more time to talk; force them to talk, really. Angela had thought of going to the raw food restaurant because it would be some-thing different for Celeste. It would've also been a good icebreaker if their conversations became awkward, or if things became too emotional. But of course, she understood how important it was for her daughter to get her hepatitis vaccination before she traveled.

"I'm just glad that you had time to stop by; I have something that I wanted to give you." She had a glint in her eyes that seemed as foreign to Celeste, as it was pleasant.

Angela walked over to a closet on the other side of the room and pulled a red and brown tapestry bag from it that she had just finished making the night before. It was an overnight bag she had made for her daughter to take with her on her trip to Africa.

"It's mainly for you to use on the plane," she explained, "and for the time you and Trazi have to spend in Zurich at the airport before you catch your flight to Accra."

"Mom, this is gorgeous!" Celeste had taken the bag from her mother's hand and was turning it from side to side, admiringly. She was very impressed by all the details of her mother's workmanship. It was clear why her business had started growing.

"Aunt Kristin is going to be so jealous when she sees this!" Celeste told her mother happily.

Angela blushed from her pleasure. She had made the bag in a compact size that was perfect for Celeste's small frame. There were two deep zippered pockets on either side so she could easily get to her passport and plane tickets as they were being processed in and out of airports. There were also two larger pockets inside the bag for other things that she needed to keep in a more secure place. Her mother had the bag packed with everything that her daughter would need for her trip: There was some underwear and a pair of cotton socks; a soft face cloth and some moisturizer; and a travel sized toothbrush and toothpaste. Angela had packed other toiletries that she thought her daughter might need too, when the flight attendants woke everyone up on the plane after it met up with the eastern sunrise over the Atlantic.

Celeste could tell that Angela had spent hours making the bag; she had even monogrammed her initials on the front flap. The teen was touched that her mother had done something so special for her, and they hugged each other lovingly for the first time she could remember, before Celeste finally had to leave to get to the travel clinic. She still felt guilty as she stood on the platform waiting for the next METRO train. On instinct, she had dreaded the idea of having lunch with her mother when she suggested it at first. But surprisingly, Angela had persisted and she told her daughter that she understood why she would hesitate. But Angela also said she was determined to find a way for them to develop a closer bond.

Now, Celeste was beginning to think that it might actually be a good idea. Maybe it really would be possible for them to have a real relationship, instead of the surface one that they had always had.

The question of whether she would ever bond with Angela had gradually slipped from her mind by the time her father drove her to Dulles airport the next day. By then, Celeste was only filled with excitement that she would see her brother soon, and that they would both see Kristin the next evening in Accra. She and Trazi had planned to meet up at their departure gate as soon as Celeste and her bags had been checked in. The flight that her brother had taken into Dulles was to land only an hour or so before they were both scheduled to board the Swiss aircraft for Zurich.

It was the first transatlantic flight for both of them, and it had taken a very long time to fly over the ocean. They hadn't seen each other for over a year so they talked away much of the time. They explored Kloten International Airport together during their three-hour layover in Switzerland and by the time they boarded their connecting flight, they had finally run out of conversation. But before they knew it, the plane was preparing to make its smooth landing in Accra that evening on schedule at 6:40 p.m. The travel bag her mother had given Celeste had come in very handy during her trip, and she was even more determined that she would find something special as a gift for Angela while she was in Ghana.

She and Trazi were both stiff from their long flights, but they were far too excited about being in Africa and seeing Kristin again to give anything else much notice.

Chapter 34

Reunited

Kristin waved eagerly as soon as she caught sight of Trazi and Celeste coming into the air terminal. She had already dispatched Amad to help them navigate their way through immigration. Now that they were finally in Ghana, she was impatient to have them both by her side. But first, they had to be processed into the country. She watched carefully as Amad introduced himself and then turned to wave in her direction. It was only then that the children spotted her and eagerly waved.

They were quick to collect their bags and Amad stood close by as they worked their way through the foreigner line to the customs and immigration table. Once they had reached the table, Amad stepped forward quickly and spoke with officials on their behalf. In very little time, their travel visas had been verified and their passports stamped, clearing them for entry into the country.

They practically ran the remaining distance that still separated them from Kristin. All three stood embracing in the middle of the busy airport until Amad finally pulled their bags from them, and led the way outside and away from the thick crowds. It had been nearly three years since they had all been together and they were reluctant to let go of each other at first, even long enough to get inside Kristin's waiting vehicle. Trazi and Celeste were animated in their excitement and had difficulty deciding whether to focus their attention on the streets of Ghana they were seeing for the first time, or on Kristin.

Luckily, they were able to do both because Kristin interrupted their eager conversations from time to time, to direct their attention to points of interest they passed on the way to their hotel. The daily Swiss flight touched down in Accra in the early evening so she had arranged for them to spend the night at the La Palm Royal Beach Hotel. By the time they had driven the short distance from the airport, Trazi and Celeste both realized they were completely famished. Since Kristin had already checked them into the hotel, they went straight to the restaurant for a late dinner, while Amad made certain their luggage was delivered to their room. He then bid them all an early good night so he could retire and prepare himself for their drive the following morning.

After he had left, Kristin spoke with the kids about what an asset Amad had been to her. She told them he had been assigned as her driver when she taught at the University of Kumasi, and miraculously, he had been available again when she came back to Ghana to live. She had hired him on the spot to work at Heavenly Travel. Amad was such a skilled driver, she said, that he had been invaluable to her in getting around the country for her meetings.

"I've grown to rely on him in many ways," she told the children, as they waited to be seated in the dining room, "almost as heavily as I've come to rely on Amina." She said that her relationship with Amad had gradually developed into more of a familial bond, as well. "I literally trust him with my life.

"And you're going to love Amina and Solomon too. But you won't get to meet them until after we've made our way slowly to Exodus Village, I'm afraid."

Kristin told the kids she had planned a roundabout route to the village. "I want you to see as much of Ghana as possible while you're here," she said. "I must apologize though, because there were a few meetings that would have been impossible to reschedule, so I have fit them in our travels too.

"Amad will be with you for the few hours here and there that I'll be distracted by business, though," she added hastily. "And he's told me that he is happy to take you wherever you want to go whenever I'm tied up."

The buffet-styled restaurant Kristin chose for their first taste of Ghanaian food offered a variety of delectable dishes to select from, and everything they tried lived up to Trazi's and Celeste's expectations. They savored each delicious morsel as they all caught up on the major developments they had missed in each other's lives. The energy between them felt much the same as it had back when Celeste and her brother had visited Kristin on weekends when they were younger.

As had always been the case, Kristin insisted on hearing what had been going on in their lives first. Celeste volunteered to start and as she talked, Trazi and Kristin both worried about how Malaya's situation might have affected her. Celeste seemed so sad as she told them what she knew and that she had been unable to reach her friend before leaving for Ghana.

Hearing what Malaya had been going through all those years, and right under their noses, had been very disturbing to all of them. Kristin tried to console her niece by telling her that her friend probably just needed time; Malaya would most likely reach out to her when she was ready.

After a short silence, Celeste abruptly changed the subject. She talked carefully about selected things that were going on at her school, and she missed the knowing glance Trazi gave his mother when she wasn't looking. At one point, she stopped talking in the middle of a sentence as she described an incident that had taken place at her school. It was so obvious to both Trazi and Kristin that Celeste was leaving out quite a few significant details about her life.

"My mom's business has started to do really well," she interjected, after the conversation began to wane. "Can you believe she actually made this bag?" Celeste held up the tapestry bag that she still had by her side. It was small enough to double as a purse, in some situations like that evening.

She could see that Kristin was genuinely impressed with the bag. Her aunt pretended to be jealous, commenting that it was even nicer than the bag Angela had made for her.

"Please, tell your mother that I'm glad to hear that she's doing so well. And tell her that I'm jealous, too," she added playfully, "because your bag is absolutely *gorgeous!*"

Kristin had never said anything to either of the children about Angela's alcohol addiction, or the emotional challenges they had all gone through over the years with her. At first, she had decided they were too young to understand. Later, after she had begun to delve more into the power of thoughts in creating both the circumstances you want *and* don't want, Kristin had made a conscious decision not to focus any attention on the behavior that *none* of them wanted.

She had always been amazed by the synchronicity of the Universe in orchestrating her life. Angela had stopped by her house unexpectedly just as Kristin was starting to recover from her health challenge, when she had nearly overdosed from cayenne pepper during her Master Cleanse fiasco. Angela had never stopped by before, and until she did, Niyla had still been the only person close enough to be family who knew what Kristin had been going through. Angela's only explanation for coming was that Kristin had been on her mind for several days. And after that first visit, she had stopped by regularly, bringing Kristin samplings of nourishing vegan soups from a restaurant not far from where they both lived. Kristin had been exceedingly grateful to Angela, because she was being very careful of the foods she was putting back into her body during her recovery. The time that the two women spent together created a new bonding experience; it provided new depth in their long-standing unconventional friendship. They had spent hours talking about the books that Kristin had sent to Angela while she was in rehab the last time.

Kristin had been happy to introduce Angela to metaphysical meanings of symbols and religious texts that they had read and memorized as children. She managed to convince Angela that everything one needed to help manifest their dreams could be found simply outlined in easy-to-read books that were written by spiritual leaders such as Deepak Chopra, Wayne Dyer, Catherine Ponder, and others—for all who had ears to hear.

As she sat listening to all of the positive comments that Celeste could finally make about her mother, quiet tears began to form in Kristin's eyes. She had been confident before she left the States that Angela understood the New Thought concepts of spirituality, but she also knew that much more than an intellectual understanding was required. Kristin knew the Universe would always provide for the needs of Angela's heart and soul so that she would never "want" for anything again. But in order for her to make it work in her life, Kristin also knew that Angela would have to believe it as she did, with the same faith and certainty that she expected to see the sun rise every morning. She had to know it in her heart without question, and it appeared now that Angela finally did.

The conversation dwindled as all three became lost in their own memories about Angela's struggles over the years. They were soon sitting in silence over the remnants of food left on their table. Hearing the confidence in Kristin's voice as she spoke about Angela's recovery had also reassured Celeste and Trazi that it was for real this time. They were all glad that Celeste would finally have the chance to know the same Angela that every one else knew.

Trazi broke through the silence a while later, tapping the side of his crystal water glass with a fork.

"Ladies, may I have your attention for a moment, please?" He asked mysteriously. "I have a very important announcement to make."

Celeste and Kristin turned to look at each other at the same time, as if to ask whether the other one had any idea of what his big announcement might be. Their blank expressions changed to curiosity and they looked back at Trazi expectantly. They had both picked up on him being somewhat evasive when they had asked him general questions about life in the military earlier. Both of them had begun to wonder whether he might be involved in some sort of top security operation at first, but then they dismissed the notion, laughing. They realized they were just out of practice with having to drag information out of Trazi.

"I waited to get you together so that I could tell you with great *pleasure* that I will be officially discharged from the U.S. Navy on the twenty-fifth of next month."

Both Kristin and Celeste were completely speechless for a few seconds. Then they got up at almost the same time to hug Trazi, in a delayed reaction to his good news.

"How on Earth did you manage to get discharged?" His mother asked, although she already knew the answer. Still, she was almost afraid to believe what her ears had heard. "I thought you had at least another year left before your tour would be over."

"You just gotta have connections, that's all." Trazi teased her.

He knew that his mom and sister had been very nervous about his decision to join the Navy. They both tried to be supportive and not let it show, but he knew them far too well. Trazi could tell how they really felt no matter how well they tried to hide it. He had spent hours trying to assure them that his chances of being assigned outside of the U. S. were marginal. But by the end of his first year, he had been rudely awakened to just how subject to change his military assignments would always be.

Truthfully, he had begun having second thoughts about the military long before that. Once he finally moved beyond his original insistence on enlisting, he was able to admit to himself that his primary reason for doing it had been to get back at his father. That was when he realized he had been trying to cut off his own nose to spite his face.

But being the pragmatist that he was, Trazi had immediately gone to work using all his spare time to find a way out. He had come up with a seldom-used method of exchanging the remaining time he had left for military service into some type of civilian service, instead. Once he found something that he wanted to do, everything else had just fallen into place. He had used some of his father's connections, without consulting him of course, and he had maneuvered his way into the Naval Environmental Leadership Program.

"I'll be assigned to a joint project that's being sponsored by the Departments of Energy and Commerce, in conjunction with the Navy," he announced to a still stunned Celeste and his mother.

"It's a partially classified project but I *can* tell you that our research will focus on alternative fuel sources, specifically plant based options. Our overall task will be to develop strategies to replace segments of the petroleum market demand, as a first step toward decreasing our country's dependence on foreign oil.

"It's gonna open up a whole new commercial market too," he ended. "But that's about all I can say to anyone who hasn't gone through a security clearance. Otherwise," he kidded, "I would have to kill you right after I told you."

He laughed out loud at the stale joke, a trait that Celeste and Kristin knew well he had picked up from his father.

"But the best part of all of this is that I'll be working in northern Virginia." He looked directly at Celeste as he said it.

"From now on, I'll be right outside of Washington so I can keep a better eye on my little sister."

"That's wonderful, Trazi," Celeste realized she actually meant it too. She knew that his transfer would mean an end to some of the stuff she had been getting away with, but maybe having her brother close by was exactly what she needed. It would make her clean up her act before she got herself into real trouble.

"I wanted to tell you on the plane," he teased Celeste. "But we all know how hard it is for you to keep *anything* to yourself, and I wanted to be the one to tell mom." He reached over and pulled one of the braids that Celeste had gotten her hair styled in for their trip, as only a brother would do.

Kristin was still fighting back tears of joy. She had imagined the conversation they had just had about her son countless times. There were variations to parts of it, but her daydream had always ended with her son announcing his early discharge from the Navy. It had been a struggle for her to keep the vision clear at times; but whenever it was clear, she had used it to keep other more fearful thoughts out of her head. It helped her conjure up a host of positive images as she shooed away any other thoughts from

292

her mind. She would stop thinking about Trazi altogether on the days that she found herself surrounded by negative thoughts about him. And, when she had imagined him telling her about his discharge, Kristin had always seen him as being as strong and as healthy as he currently was.

There had not been one valid reason why she should have believed that her son would be honorably discharged before his time was up, but she hadn't let that stop her. Kristin had let the Universe take care of those details. She had taken her mind off *how* his discharge would happen. Instead, she had written down several affirmations about it on note cards, beginning on the day that her son had left Washington for boot camp. After she had written them down, she had taped the affirmations all over her kitchen and bedroom so that she could see them first thing in the morning, and as soon as she came home. And she had brought the cards with her when she moved to Ghana, creating the same ritual at her new home.

Kristin would recite them daily until she had reached a point where she could hold the same positive vision herself that the affirmations would induce. She had rehearsed the feelings of joy she would have when her son finally told her he was being discharged. She had played it over again in her head, whenever she felt nervous about his safety or that he might be deployed overseas. Now that he had actually said the words that she had been longing to hear, Kristin could feel the very same feeling of joy that she had always imagined!

As with everything else in Africa, she had noticed that her thoughts had also grown increasingly fertile in Ghana. She had come to feel quite at home with co-creating her life there—or at least *most* areas of it.

Since she knew the error of interfering with someone *else's* will, Kristin had only prayed that *God's Will* be done in her son's life. At the same time, she felt certain that it was not God's Will for Trazi to travel thousands of miles across an ocean to kill people he had never met before, or had any previous dealings with.

As Trazi continued to talk about the research he would be involved in, Kristin felt another boost of confidence in her vision for Exodus Village. She had continued her early morning ritual of meditating and then sitting quietly on the mountain top once she had finished. She still envisioned key milestones for the Exodus project being completed; she saw their first major goals reached, and she saw herself checking them off their master project plan. Each time that she had the visualization there would be more of the details brought into focus. The more she practiced, the more conscious Kristin became of precisely how she wanted everything to be set up and implemented. She had been routinely and miraculously manifesting her visions from the immaterial into form, for quite some time now.

Her favorite daydream of late had been one in which she clearly saw herself on the set of a major U.S. television show. She would always be impeccably dressed as she made casual small talk with the show's producers, who waited with her in the Green Room for her cue. A few minutes later, she would be called on stage for an extensive interview with a very popular talk show host. Kristin always saw herself as being extremely focused and at ease during the taping of the show, as though television interviews were something she routinely did. She imagined herself speaking candidly about her personal life, discussing relevant sections of her books, current events, and then talking extensively about the mission of the Diasporan Exodus Foundation.

She had come to think of her now-routine visions as an expression of faith. They had helped her grow more self-assured in their repetitious familiarity and they had helped her remain undaunted by any roadblocks she encountered in her plans. She had learned to view those detours as signals that she needed to reconsider her strategy, or sometimes consider a new plan altogether. Kristin's daydreams about her television appearance would always be essentially the same; only her outfits would change to suit her current mood. At the end of the most recent version of her dream, she had watched herself thank the host for her generous donation that was being made to their Foundation. Kristin had accepted the check with great excitement, knowing that it would easily cover a major portion of their operating expenses for nearly a year.

"We have so much to be thankful for." Kristin looked at Trazi and Celeste with a wide smile on her face. "For Trazi's discharge and for the three of us being together again, after such a long time."

They all raised their tea glasses in a toast.

"So, come on Mom. Tell us the latest," Trazi urged his mother after taking a sip of the iced tea. "We're dying to know everything that's going on with the Foundation." He and Celeste had already exchanged the bits of news they each knew on the plane, but it hadn't been very much.

"Well, let me think where to start...." His mother began. There were so many different facets to the Exodus program alone that Kristin now found herself in a continuous stream of decisions, phone calls, and meetings with notes from all of them constantly swirling through her head.

"I guess I can sum it up by saying that things are going great, and they're getting better all the time." She had picked up that affirmation from one of Catherine Ponder's books and she used it often. As she kept telling herself only positive things, the Universe miraculously made good on her promises.

"Right now, everyone is busy getting things ready for the arrival of our pilot residents."

"When will that be?" Celeste's tone was excited.

"Well, we're about a year out before our first ship leaves the U.S. for Jamaica, the last stop before it begins its journey across the Atlantic.

"Our Foundation is just starting to hold preliminary discussions to gear up for our commercial operations, which will officially start shortly after the pilot begins. Unofficially, we have quite a lot going on at the same time.

She outlined a few of their high-level plans, promising to fill in all the details as they travelled around Ghana.

"You're going to be able to see at least the beginnings of most of it for yourself," she assured them. "And what I can tell you now is that the only thing that's going to stop us at this point is God. Otherwise, it's all going to happen, and very soon!"

She could feel chills running up and down her spine at the level of confidence in her voice, in talking about the Foundation's plans. It was such a long time in coming. Her dream had started out as a gentle, nagging persistence that over time had firmly attached itself to her mind. It had taken shape and now it was getting closer every day to its full physical manifestation. Her vision for the Black American underbelly would soon become a reality.

"Well, we want to hear everything," Celeste chimed in. "We've really missed you a lot but what you're doing here sounds so exciting! I had no idea there was so much involved. I really hope I get a chance to help you with it one day."

"That would be wonderful, Sweetheart!" Kristin was not surprised by Celeste's offer in the least. It was a part of a new vision that she had already begun to form in her head.

"Mom, what else can you tell us about the Foundation? How does it all work?" Trazi had been mulling over what his mother had told them so far and wanted to hear more.

"Okay, but it's always hard for me to know where to begin. There are so many different components," she started again.

"I've met with all the Ministers of the national government here, at least once, and our Foundation has been working closely with two in particular. For the most part, everyone here appears to be very committed to the Exodus Foundation's success."

"We do have one hold out," she admitted. "He's a major political player but I'm sure he'll come around soon enough."

"And I'm very happy to say that I have managed to steer clear of any direct involvement with the major political parties here; at least to the extent that I can.

"And you have no idea how much effort went into being able to truthfully say that." She added after a pause, with another big smile on her face. Kristin moved her glass to one side to make room for a slice of banana peanut cake that a server had just brought to their table. They all concentrated on the cake for a few seconds, luxuriating in the rich taste of the dessert.

"Ummmm." The sentiment was echoed in succession as they each took a bite.

"We had a little bit of a challenge at the very beginning," Kristin admitted, "as we started trying to drum up support." She ate another generous spoonful of cake before continuing.

"Some people thought that what we wanted to do was impossible, because there are so many different ethnic groups in the country already. They gave me all sorts of reasons why we could never do what we're currently doing.

"But you know me," she reminded them. "I refuse to listen to anyone who doesn't have at least *something* positive to say. So I made a list of all the reasons they had given us for our supposed failure and just knocked them off the list one by one. Our Foundation has had an amazing response here despite all the predictions made by naysayers.

"Many of the ethnic and political divisions here have already slowly started to fade somewhat, as people from the five major groups have moved from rural areas into the city. Now different groups all live together in many urban areas, although they have naturally conjugated together to a large degree within them. Whatever differences initially formed the basis for having ten subdivisions of the largest *major* ethnic group, the Akans, must seem far less important to at least some degree to people now living together in larger cities.

As African Americans start to blend into the population, those ethnic subdivisions will likely seem even more tolerable, eventually."

"What do you mean?" Celeste wanted to know.

"Well, a contrast between any of the ethnic groups or subdivisions here will become more obvious when the comparison is being made to us—or at least for the first few years or so. It's definitely going to take some time before we all become a naturally homogenous group here, but we'll be moving in that direction all the time. The American culture is generally thought of as renegade too, in relation to British culture. There will be conflicts in expressing proper etiquette because of the lingering British influence here: *tomăto–tomăto.* That sort of thing.

"I think the surprise to Black Americans will be that many British traits are still infused within the Ghanaian culture, especially among the "haves." The British forced its mores onto Ghana's culture after they over-powered traditional rulers and took control of the government. As strange as it may sound to Americans, some West Africans may actually feel more connected to *anyone* from the U.K. than to the average Black American. That's one of the major reasons that our cultural sensitivity classes I mentioned earlier, are going to be so important."

"Yeah, now I can see what you mean," Trazi agreed.

"I saw the same kind of scenario play out in Tuskegee. Kids who had grown up in the city and were used to having an infinite variety of stimulation, suddenly found themselves in the middle of nowhere. It was an absolute culture shock for them because overnight they had nothing to do and no way of getting around to do it—other than walking. Except, most were terrified because there were no street lights." Kristin was laughing at her flashback of freshmen from northern cities being dumped at Tuskegee by their parents. "They knew they were in the Deep South and all that many had heard about it was its connection to the Klan.

"I'll tell you what we have in mind for that, later," she said, still smiling at the images of the city kids from her seat on the fountain.

"One of our biggest decisions was where our village would be located. Once we secured the land we needed, we had planned to just start putting one foot in front of the other and keep going until we got everything done.

"The big surprise is that our land is located in the Ashanti Region. And the King himself has pledged the considerable resources of the Asante nation to help us achieve our goals."

"Wow. That *is* major," Trazi commented. "How did you manage that?"

Kristin had made certain that her son learned the true history of the slave trade as he grew up. He was aware of subtle tensions that had always existed between Ghana's largest ethnic group and Black Americans. He knew that the Akan were said to have had a major role in the operation of the slave trade and the Asante formed the largest of the Akan states. Trazi also knew that many of them had been captured and enslaved themselves, especially towards the end of their nation's association with the British.

"I actually stumbled onto our land quite by accident," Kristin continued, "if you believe in accidents, that is. Last year, after I had finished some meetings in Kumasi, I asked Amad to drive me to see Lake Bosumtwi because I had heard so much about it. Solomon had mentioned the lake to me several times; but somehow, I had never made the twenty-mile trip from Kumasi to see it. Going to see the lake meant taking a different route back here to Accra, where our travel business is headquartered. I didn't even understand how strange it was that I had never been to the lake before until after I finally went. Amad and I had literally driven all over Ghana during the two years I was here teaching, so I still can't believe how close I lived to Lake Bosumtwi, yet had never seen it.

"Amina is from the Fante subgroup, also one of the ten Akan states. She had mentioned Lake Bosumtwi to me too, and she suggested it whenever we started talking about new properties for the travel business. At any rate, I guess something made me finally hear them both after Solomon mentioned the lake again. He thought it might be a good location for a smaller, more intimate resort property for some of our celebrity clients. And once I saw it for myself, I absolutely agreed with him and Amina, as I'm sure you will too once you see it. The lake has a beautiful backdrop of the rain forest. The unspoiled environment surrounding our property makes it the *perfect* location for the type of spa offering we all had in mind.

"It's a fascinating place, really. According to archeological reports, a huge crater fell over a million years ago and formed the lake's eight and a half kilometer diameter, roughly the equivalent of five and a half miles. I've since learned that it is close to a mass grave that was dug to bury a large battalion of warriors, who had been killed during an ancient battle.

"The lake, and much of the area surrounding it, is still held sacred by the Ashanti people. There are important rituals and ceremonies that take place there that the king participates in, as occupant of the golden stool."

She gave them a brief account of the attempt that had been made by the British to capture the stool, which symbolizes the essence of the entire ethnic group.

"The area is still treated with respect because of the warriors who sacrificed their lives for the survival of the Asante nation-state. It's an area that completely escaped Western influence when the British occupied Ghana.

Many of the people living near the lake don't speak any English at all and they also don't appreciate having their photos taken randomly by tourists, by the way. Special permission has to be granted to visit some areas near the lake like the Abrodwum Stone, considered the lake's spiritual center, or the Ekoho Forest, where even farming is prohibited.

"It's been that way for as long as anyone remembers, which is why it's one of the only areas in Ghana where the rain forest is still in its pristine condition. The people don't even allow metal to touch any part of the lake. Special wooden planks called *padua* are used to fish there or to relax on the water.

"But, at any rate, after we left the lake, Amad drove us south toward the coast along the Kumasi-Yomoransa Road. As we got close to the road that led into Obuasi, on an impulse I thought we might as well take a brief detour to see the gold mining town too. I had still been thinking about our new celebrity tours at the time, and perhaps extending them to Obuasi after we opened the spa on Lake Bosumtwi.

Well, interestingly, Amad ended up taking a wrong turn, something I've never seen him do before or since. He was quick to realize we were travelling east instead of west, but there was something vaguely familiar about the landscape after we took the turn so I asked him to keep driving in the same direction for a bit. And that's how we stumbled on the land that Exodus Village is being built on as we speak.

"The closest thing I could think of to explain the feeling I had is that it was like coming home; even as we drove through the undeveloped land. As soon as we were back in Accra, I asked Amina to make some inquiries and described the approximate location. She found out who owned the land and we quickly purchased a small tract of it, figuring it to a good starting point. I was hoping that we would be able to buy more of the land around our tract, as we started to grow. It really is beautiful country and I think you'll see why I fell in love with it as soon as we get there.

"That's a very interesting story," Trazi agreed. "What are the chances of you just finding it like that?"

"Yes, I know. But, the amazing thing is that I had a call from Solomon two months later, saying that we had been asked to come to Manhyia Palace in Kumasi. As it turned out, the land we purchased was in the Ashanti Administrative Region, which means the Asantehene is the traditional ruler where our village is being built. The King himself asked me during our meeting whether I thought a bridge could really be built to reconnect

Africa with her lost children in the West. He said that he had often asked himself the same question.

"Through our intermediary, I quickly assured him that I *did* think that. When he asked us about the Foundation's latest developments and I described the parcel of land we had just purchased, it still never occurred to me that the king would have been well aware of our purchase. He had been advised, of course, by the local chief of the area through the paramount chief.

"So I was caught completely off guard when he presented us with an extraordinarily generous gift: the title to large parcels of land that were on either side of the land we had just purchased. I could barely believe what I was hearing—he had given us all the land we needed for Exodus Village.

"That is amazing!" Celeste and Trazi agreed together.

"Yes it is," Kristin echoed. "You really have no idea. It was something that I had never dreamed of, which is another reason that it's best to let the Universe take care of the details of what you desire," she added with a smile.

"The Queen Mother and her attendants were also with us in the room for the meeting, although they were seated a short distance from the King and his entourage. I immediately turned toward her after thanking the king and made a silent gesture of gratitude and respect. By now, I know a lot more about the behind the scenes influence that the Queen Mother usually has. Instinctively, I knew she had played a major role in our being presented with the land.

"Almost overnight, we had all the land that we need—enough for our residential communities, our farms, and for the different industries that will support us locally. We even have all the land we need to build an industrial park for our commercial ventures in the Ashanti Region.

"We were told that the land was being presented as a gift to the African Diaspora in America, from all of Asanteman. They have given us our official home in Ghana."

"That was some gift," Trazi observed.

"My God—yes!" Kristin responded triumphantly. "It blows my mind every time I think about how everything has just been falling into place. We have been spared a tremendous expense, not to mention all the time and effort that would have been required to buy the land.

"The Asantehene has decided to become personally involved with Exodus Village, as I said. As traditional ruler of the largest tribe in Ghana, he heads a hierarchy of powerful paramount chiefs. And as occupant of the golden stool, which symbolizes the unity of Asante, he is head of the Asanteman Council as well. We are thrilled to have his support because it carries a great deal of influence.

"What makes all of this even more significant," Kristin explained, seeing the puzzled look on Celeste's face, "is the history of the Asante involvement in the slave trade. Once again, it's where learning our true history becomes paramount. The classes we offer will make sure that all our residents and mentors understand more fully what African tribesmen had to draw on at the time. Once they see that the cruel and dehumanizing practice of slavery in America could never have been expected, we will begin to turn the tide. The talking drums couldn't be heard from the other side of the ocean. The Asante aligned themselves with the Europeans only to secure and extend their territory and it gave them a tremendous edge over their opponents. They were fierce warriors and defeated the British in several wars when their alliance ended, until the early 1900s with the final heroic battle led by the Queen Mother of Ejisu."

Kristin gave them the highlights of the last major battle before the British established full control over the country.

"I could start to see how complicated it would be to try to place blame for the slave trade on any particular group," she told the kids, "as I was researching the last book I wrote. Even if everyone conceded that it was fair to blame the descendants of the people who had actually perpetrated the crime, how would responsibility ever be assigned? The slave trade generated massive profits for many nations, corporations, banks, religious organizations, and family trusts. Many are still financially sound or profitable because of money they got as a result of slavery.

"There have been all sorts of organizations coming forward in the last few decades with their apologies, admitting their role in the slave trade. They've expressed remorse on behalf of those who actually participated in it. And I know that many might say that an acknowledgement or apology isn't enough, but I happen to think it's a good start. In reality, it's one of the few things that can be done at this point, since no one is prepared to make financial reparations. And even if that was the general consensus, what amount of money would it be worth and to whom would it be paid? We can't forget that some of the indentured Africans owned slaves in America themselves, after they had gained their own freedom.

"No one can go back and change what happened, no matter how much we may want to do it. But it is important to know our true history and what actually happened and why. I don't believe we will ever have a fully sustained recovery without that. As painful as it is, the truth has to be brought to light—no matter what comes with it. It's the only way to go forward.

※※※

Kristin happened to glance down at her watch and then she quickly looked over at the wait staff. "Oh my goodness! Look at the time!"

There were several young men and women standing nearby, politely waiting for them to leave. She had no idea that it was so late; it was long past time for the restaurant to close. As she looked around the room, she realized they were the last patrons there.

"Come on, you two." She got up from the table hastily and pulled out money to leave a sizeable tip.

"We can finish talking in our suite. It's past time for us to get out of here so these poor people can finish their work and go home."

Kristin apologized sheepishly to the cashier as she paid for their meal, nodding to the other staff. She led Celeste and Trazi outside the main building and onto a sidewalk that ran near the entrance. It led them down the side of the building toward their suite.

"So, how's your father?" She had deliberately waited until they had walked a distance before she asked the question. She wanted to be outside so that her expression would be shielded by the night sky. Kristin never would have made it as a poker player because her face usually revealed exactly what she was feeling. She had been waiting all evening for one of the children to mention Winston but neither of them had. She found it strange that neither of them had brought up their father even once. They were getting close to the thatched bungalow that their suite was in and she hoped her voice sounded casual.

"How are he and Charlotte doing?" She blurted it out without thinking. When neither of them answered right away, Kristin wished that there was some way she could have taken the question back, or at least rephrase it.

"He's okay." Celeste's response was soft and abbreviated. Kristin was relieved that Celeste had answered before she had time to do more damage.

"He's working hard as usual. I guess Charlotte is about the same."

After a brief pause Celeste added, "He asked me to tell both of you hello."

"Well, at least that answered why *Trazi* had never mentioned Winston," she thought to herself. Apparently, her son and his father were *still* not communicating after three years. But Celeste was a different story. Kristin was curious why she had waited until she was asked before she delivered Winston's greeting. Was it possible that she had made the whole thing up? Maybe, it's the jet lag," Kristin reasoned a few seconds later. She remembered the five-hour time difference between Accra and Washington and considered whether Celeste was just having a hard time adjusting on their first night in Ghana. Maybe she was feeling fuzzy-brained since it would have been much later had in the evening had she been home.

'Maybe I'm just paranoid,' Kristin concluded shortly afterwards. She began to think that maybe it was the Universe's way of telling her that it was time to move on. Maybe she should start showing an interest in that gentlemen Solomon kept trying to get her to date. Celeste obviously didn't really need her anymore; or more accurately, she was at the age where she would probably not listen to her anymore.

At any rate, Kristin's mind told her that it was high time for her to leave it all alone and go on with her life.

"You two must be exhausted by now," she said quickly. She changed the subject so neither of them would feel obligated to say anything more about Winston. They had reached their suite and she was still fishing for the room key. They would spend one night in one of four suites built into the circular building that looked like a large cabana. It was very similar to the one that Kristin and her friends had stayed in on *their* first night in Accra. She pointed out Trazi's bedroom, which was off the small sitting area in the center of the suite. She and Celeste were to share a larger bedroom on the opposite end. The room had a casual style that matched the hotel's quiet sophistication. There were beautiful pieces of art scattered over the walls, providing bold splashes of color.

A large bathroom connected the two bedrooms and was decorated in a lovely mixed travertine tile. A third door led from the bathroom back into the sitting room, which was equipped with two small sofas, a television, and a few more pieces of furniture. It would have been very comfortable accommodations for the three of them for several days, but they would be leaving Accra early the next morning.

"The people of Ghana stand to gain tremendously from all the projects we have planned," Kristin told the kids, after they had settled into the suite. "Our goal is to give as much of a boost to Ghana as we will be giving to the thousands of lost African American souls who will soon start arriving for refuge. The gift of land has put us in an extremely favorable position, one that we will definitely use to our advantage. His graciousness has immediately removed any lingering doubt that our plans will become a reality."

"But what about the government?" Celeste wanted to know. "Does the king have power in Parliament too?"

"He has quite a bit of power," Kristin answered her, "but it's all unofficial. When the British forced their system of colonialism on Ghana, they attempted to eliminate traditional leadership. After independence was won, Parliament remained the country's official governing body and enforcement of the law was split between traditional and non-traditional legal remedies.

"The Ashanti king's influence is similar to that of the royal family in Great Britain, with many differences of course. Having the king's support and influence has been very helpful to us in getting laws passed through Parliament that we need for our operations. His influence most certainly helped in the negotiations for special citizenship status for our village residents.

"The Ghanaian culture is deeply rooted in protocol," she continued. "It's the same in most other African countries too, so it's vital that we show the same respect for their codes of conduct. Besides, inadvertently stepping on the wrong toes could easily lead to massive delays in meeting our timetables.

"But how do you possibly keep track of all this?" Trazi asked.

"In a word—Amina," she responded quickly. "I don't know where I would be without her, honestly, and I'm sure you'll be just as impressed after you've met her. She has remarkable talent and is just as committed to the Exodus Foundation as I am. We just had our first board of directors meeting a few months ago, and everything went quite well.

"I plan to formally nominate the Asantehene as our Executive Chairman when we meet again in about six months. We currently have three ministers who serve as board members and three paramount chiefs, as well. Each chief is from one of the regions where we plan to set up our first commercial operations. Eventually, we'll have an additional board seat reserved for a prominent entrepreneur in the country, with a two-year seat rotation. We'll have a similar seat reserved for each of the five major ethnic groups, and we'll rotate these positions among each subgroup. Every major group in Ghana will be able to provide input into what we'll be doing here.

"I've been relying heavily on recommendations from Amina on everything," she added, "and on Solomon too. They both gave me advice on which ministers and chiefs to invite as board members. I've learned so much about the culture from them, but not nearly enough to be on my own yet."

"What about board members from the U.S.?" Trazi asked her. "I'm curious how you decided who you would ask."

"That was a tough call all right. I was especially happy to have two of our American board members join us—they were both in school with me at Tuskegee. One of them is an extremely talented architect and city planner. The other is an agricultural scientist who has been heavily involved in research. He also teaches soil science and enrichment at Tuskegee, but more importantly to us, he's recently become involved in research dealing with organic hydroponic farming. We're relying heavily on his direction for our soybean and Moringa farms, since we'll be using them in our commercial food production—our first product offerings.

"I know how versatile and nutritious the soybean is, but what is Moringa?" Trazi wanted to know.

"Oh my goodness, it's this amazing plant that can grow very well in this climate," Kristin answered. "It's an all-around wonder and I'm convinced it was Moringa seeds that inspired the story about Jack and the Beanstalk. The plants can grow up to six meters high, if not trimmed back, and up to thirty centimeters wide." Kristin had joined the rest of the world in thinking in terms of metric measurements since moving to Africa. She forgot for a second that Trazi and Celeste would have no concept of what she had described.

"That's close to twenty feet tall and just under a foot in diameter," she explained.

"Good grief, that does look like a giant beanstalk!" Celeste agreed.

"Right. It can grow in all types of soil conditions too, and it loves the sun. But we won't be letting our trees get that tall. We'll trim them to make sure we can reach the leaves and seedpods that are produced as the plants mature.

"For what use?" Trazi wanted to know.

"We're already using the leaves in dishes our nutritionists have been experimenting with. They provide a very high source of calcium, vitamin C, vitamin A, potassium, iron, and many other essential vitamins and minerals. It's truly a miracle plant and we plan to cultivate it for many of our needs. Eventually, we'll have classes to teach everyone how to grow their own Moringa, and how best to take advantage of its many benefits.

"And one of the most important parts of the plant is its seeds. When dried and ground into a powder, the seeds can be used to clean the dirtiest of water. Everyone is already comparing Dr. Grant, our new board member, with Dr. Carver, partially because he has been so tenacious in his agricultural research. I can't wait to see what he does with Moringa.

"We have two other board members from America who are my former students at Hunter, Kristin added. "One of them is a prominent civil engineer, who has been involved in substantial renewable energy projects all across the globe. She's very well known internationally in the areas of geothermal, solar, and wind energy technologies. She has patents on a number of devices that can increase the harvest of direct energy currents, and we plan to make full use of her here in our solar plants.

"Now that sounds pretty interesting," Trazi commented.

"Yes. And the other young man has solid government relations and public policy experience. He's held several top-level administrative positions with the federal government over the last three decades. And he has a reputation for achieving remarkable results in managing large groups of people. The final two American board members both have medical backgrounds. One is a physician, who's on faculty at Morehouse School of Medicine in Atlanta; the other is a retired public health administrator from the State of California.

"Right now, we primarily have a working board because that's what we need. We're planning to put everyone's talents to good use for as long as we can. Dr. Grant is actually on a sabbatical from Tuskegee until he can get us up and running. I still wanted to keep the size of the board relatively small for now, and I've deliberately selected a clear majority of voting members from this side of the ocean. Politically, it was impossible to whittle the board size any smaller; but on the other hand, it is a working board so it's a win-win for us either way.

"We believe the immediate benefits that the people of Ghana will see will come from the substantial increase in tourism we're projecting, and that will gradually create more jobs to help fuel the economy. I have the feeling that in a few years we're going to have people traveling to Ghana just to see our village."

Trazi felt himself swell with pride as his mother kept talking. He had been an adolescent when she took her first trip to Ghana. He remembered being resentful when she told him she would be gone the first time for two weeks. He had been having some crisis at the time that he could no longer remember. Now, for the first time he understood the far-reaching scope of his mother's vision. It made him a little guilty as a grown-up that he had once prayed for her to abandon her plans and stay home with him.

"I've become a celebrity of sorts here recently," Kristin was saying. "I'm getting invitations now to speak at schools, and more recently I've been invited to some of the more exclusive events that are given by some of the country's wealthier residents. But no matter where I am, I use nearly every chance I get to further dialogues about our two cultures. We talk frankly about misconceptions that have, more often than not, been accepted as fact. I've told them all about my experiences growing up in Tuskegee, how my family once hosted tribal chiefs and other African officials who visited the college and how they would come for dinner at our house on Sundays after church. The experience was made possible by our minister's wife, who was then Dean of Women at Tuskegee.

"I've been telling everyone I meet here how fortunate I consider myself for having had that experience. It was a rare opportunity for an African American child, at a time when many of us based all our impressions of Africa on episodes of Tarzan, or on pictures of naked women plastered on the cover of National Geographic. And of course, more recently, many Black Americans have been basing their impressions on nonsense movies like *Coming to America*.

"What many don't know, and what I didn't realize until I lived in Kumasi is that many of our African cousins grew up with the same derogatory portrayals of us in mind. Amina was first among my friends here to tell me about it. After talking to her, a number of things about the relationship between the Diaspora and Africa clicked in my mind. Since then, I've had many people confide when asked directly that they grew up believing Black Americans were either too simple or too lazy to take advantage of the things America has to offer. In the meantime, literally millions of Africans dream of having the same opportunities that my generation has had available since the late '60s.

"In the past few decades, many West Africans have made judgments about us after watching *Good Times* and *Sanford and Sons* on cable television. You should hear what the elders here think about Lamont's character, and the way that he blatantly disrespects his father—even if he was someone like Fred Sanford. The elders here are not subjected to that type of disrespect. They also don't have to spend time worrying about providing money for their burial expenses either. They can expect to be properly buried by their children, as part of the ever-continuing cycle of life and death.

"When you look at it from both sides, it's easy to see why there are so many unflattering and persistent opinions that have kept us so far apart. Since I've learned about the prejudices that many Africans my age hold about us, it's helped me understand the sometimes-standoffish behavior that I've heard Black Americans complain about some Africans who visit the U.S. It also explains why they become so upset when the son they send to America for an education decides to marry a Black American woman. But before we are actually in a position to get to know and understand each other better, those kinds of reactions are going to continue. They will see us through the same lens of preconceived judgment as many Black Americans see Africans.

"For example, I don't think it's really clear to many of us until we've traveled to Africa, or spend time in substantive conversations with Africans, just how difficult a process it is for West Africans to get travel visas for America. It's something that has made me look differently at any African I see in the U.S. frankly, from that point on. I always wonder how they had managed to get there. We have such a tendency to give stock to appearances alone that a lack of interest in having expensive designer clothes, or at least the latest styles, somehow gives us the impression that the person doesn't have the funds to buy them.

"In the meantime, people like African cab drivers who have established a niche in the U.S. that allows them to support their families there, have to be constantly on the alert for the criminal element of the Black underbelly. That, as can be expected, gives them justification for everything they already believed about us before going to the U.S.

"They don't even have mortgages here in Ghana, so they have a very hard time understanding why so many Black Americans are willing to spend a lifetime paying high rent on property they will never own. Many immigrate to America for opportunities that aren't available in their country. As soon as they arrive, they see many African Americans who aren't trying to take advantage of any of the breaks available to them, only confirmation of what they had already been told about us. They witness the high rate of Black Americans who drop out of school—not to work and support their families, as might be the case in Ghana. In the U.S., they drop out so they can have more time to hang around on the street and do nothing—unless, of course, they decide to sell illegal drugs or find some similar way to get fast money.

"When you add that to all the thinly veiled insults they frequently get from Black Americans in the States, it gets a lot easier to understand their attitudes. Many of us are so convinced about our own superiority that we aren't even aware that the feeling is mutual. It's just like the way things were when we finally found pride in our blackness. After everyone had been forced to struggle with the adjustments of integration, it took a long time for many whites in the U.S. to realize there were many Blacks who didn't want integration either. And many Black mothers certainly didn't welcome their sons' new white girlfriends with open arms.

"I think it's fair to say that the majority of Black America would have been very happy back in the '50s with separate, but equal—if it had really been equal. The problem was, in reality it was more like separate and inferior. Blacks were protesting because they were tired of raggedy every-thing—raggedy schools, raggedy schoolbooks, streets and houses. Black parents didn't just start out wanting to be forced to send their children into dangerous environments everyday to learn, especially since their kids had to get up much earlier and spend hours being bused to a better school. Most Black parents just wanted better schools—with better books, better teachers, and a safe environment for their children to learn in, just like any other parent would want.

"I would have to say that a great number of Black Americans won't be capable of understanding their African cousins fully, not until they make the journey here. To be honest with you, I'm not sure that I did myself.

"One major drawback might have threatened to keep the two groups from reaching any kind of realistic détente. From the Black American per-spective, there is still silent resentment about the obvious role played by other Africans in helping the Europeans enslave our ancestors.

"The king's gift might be perceived as being suspicious at first, but I'm convinced that after time for reflection the majority of Black Americans will see it as we do—as an amazing offer of reconciliation.

"Somehow," Kristin told them earnestly, "we're going to have to learn to overcome all the heavy, negative energy that's still left around from all of this, before our plans can be executed smoothly. That's why we're counting so much on our re-education campaigns. I predict it will happen in much the same way as things transpired with integration in the U. S.

"As impossible as some of it might seem right now, a good portion of the conflicts will resolve themselves automatically once our children start growing up together. They'll be exposed to each other without our biases, and they will learn to live peacefully together as blacks and whites have done in most places in America. We're definitely not under the illusion that this will be an easy task to check off though."

Kristin could see how sleepy Trazi and Celeste were, and realized it was time to call it a night. She stood up to signal to them that it was time for bed. They had both been staring at her in awe. It was a brilliant plan that she had put together and one they were dying to learn more about.

"That's why that same topic is going to be on the agenda at every board meeting until we get it right. So far, we've had some frank discussions and everyone seems to be on the same page as far as its importance is concerned. After we cross this major hurdle, everything else will be relatively smooth sailing.

"But can you even imagine what it will be like once the barriers that have separated us all these years are permanently removed?"

"This is so exciting, Aunt Kristin." Celeste stood up too. It would have been way past her bedtime in Washington and she was so sleepy that she could barely stand. "I can't wait to see Exodus Village."

"Me too." Her son agreed.

"So, should I start calling you Ms. Garvey now?" Trazi teased his mother, as he got up from the couch and started moving toward his bedroom. He referred to Marcus Garvey and his *Back to Africa* movement during the early 1900s.

"Hey, if the shoe fits!" Kristin smiled at her son. She could see that he was proud of her and it warmed her heart.

"Okay guys. Seriously, let's get some sleep," she suggested.

"We're going to need an early start in the morning," she told them, "right after breakfast. I have quite a bit planned to show you in the short time you're going to be here." She was smiling again, so happy to have them both with her in Ghana.

"You guys had better get some sleep, because after tonight you'll have to wait until you're back on the plane to catch up on it."

Chapter 35

Butter and Honey Shall They Eat

*B*ecause their bodies were still on eastern standard time, Trazi and Celeste were both awake bright and early the next morning. Eager to get their first clear look at Ghana in the light of day, they had been out exploring the hotel grounds for almost an hour before Kristin woke up. They wandered over to one of the restaurants overlooking the Gulf of Guinea, and stood against the fence that protected visitors from a steep drop off the cliff to watch a beautiful sunrise over the waters of the gulf.

Kristin was finally awake by the time they got back to their suite. After they had all made a quick stop at the breakfast buffet, Amad loaded their luggage into the Land Rover and everyone piled in. Soon they were off towards the Volta Region for a meeting Kristin had scheduled with three local businessmen in Akosombo for later that morning. They were to discuss possible options for financing the smart grid technology they planned to install in Exodus Village to manage energy usage.

"We'll be using hydroelectric power from the Volta dam at first, until we're ready to move into solar and wind energy production that will allow us to supply our own electricity." Kristin explained.

"What are smart grids?" Celeste asked.

"They help manage the storage and usage of electricity," Trazi answered before his mother had a chance to speak.

"That's exactly right. The smart grids will primarily manage the solar and wind power we harvest. It will provide data on peak usage times and other valuable information that will allow us to make scheduling adjustments, as needed. The technology will also help us make sure we have a sufficient amount of stored energy as a supplement during the rainy season every year. We're going to keep our connection to the Volta dam and still be able to use that source if need be, but our plan is to eventually become self-sustaining. Since the technology is bound to catch up with the inevitable demand for natural energy sooner or later, I would imagine that better longer-term storage mechanisms will be available to us fairly soon," she added. "And who knows, we just might develop what we need ourselves."

She explained that the Foundation had hired a meteorologist from a firm in the U.K. several months earlier. "He has pinpointed the exact locations on our property that would be optimal for building wind farms," she told them. "For the kind of commercial-scale farms we plan to operate, we were advised to build farms in an area with at least an average of class-three wind speed. Our meteorologist has identified two different areas near the place where I normally meditate every morning. The sustained wind speeds there are much higher than what we require."

Kristin told the kids that her second meeting that day was scheduled right after the first one, and that its purpose was to start purchase negotiations for a stretch of land bordering Volta Lake. Their plan, she said, was to construct a new four-star hotel and resort that would overlook the water. Kristin had convinced officials in Akosombo that the city would soon be in need of many more hotels to accommodate the increased tourism they anticipated after Exodus Village welcomed its first residents.

"After that meeting, I have one final appointment tomorrow in the Volta Region. I'm scheduled for a breakfast meeting with an architect that we've been working with. Coincidentally, he was already scheduled to be in Akosombo while we're there, so since both our schedules are so busy we decided to take advantage of the unexpected opportunity. He actually contacted me as I was on the way to the airport last evening to pick you guys up.

"I *really* would have rescheduled these meetings if I could have," she assured Trazi and Celeste. "The architect has some preliminary sketches to show me for the spa we're looking to build on Lake Bosumtwi. But we'll still have plenty of time together in Akosombo," she promised. "For some reason, there always seems to be enough time for everything here in

Ghana, just like it was in Tuskegee. It always seems easy here, like Sunday morning." Whenever Kristin heard Lionel Richie singing that song, she felt certain he must have been thinking about the hometown they shared.

The kids were as surprised by the road conditions as Kristin had been during her first trip to Ghana, after they had finally left the city behind and were out in the countryside. Kristin had finally gotten used to it from all her traveling over the past few years. It was one more thing that was taken for granted in the United States, although more and more cities there were also becoming notorious for having huge potholes in their streets.

"We've been hoping to get some of the businesses interested in forming joint ventures in the areas where the roads are the worst," Kristin confided, "especially where there's a lot of tourist traffic. We're going to have to do something, but so far our efforts have been slow-going. We're not going to give up though; we're determined to make our tours a little less hazardous for our clients if we can." She was smiling in a good-natured way. "In the meantime, we just try to hire the best drivers we can find," she said laughing, as she looked over at Amad.

After they had driven a few more miles, Kristin turned around toward the back seat to get a better look at Celeste and Trazi in the daylight. It was hard to believe Winston's daughter had grown up so fast; she would be sixteen in only a few months and Kristin could tell by her body language that she was still a good girl. She was very proud of the young woman that Celeste was becoming.

After Kristin realized she had been staring at the teenager like she was watching her on television, she quickly turned her head toward her son. She didn't want the poor girl to think she was insane, after all. Kristin was so happy that Celeste and Angela had been given another chance and might be able to develop a real connection with each other this time. In her heart, she had always thought of Celeste as her own child though, as much as the son that she had actually given birth to. And she knew that feeling would never change, no matter what happened between Celeste and Angela.

She looked at her son more closely too and was jolted by her sudden realization of how much he looked like his father at that age. Trazi could have *been* Winston, he looked so much like him now. She would have been the last person to suggest the military to anyone, but she had to admit that her son had gone into the Navy as a boy and would come out of it a man. She smiled at him before she turned back toward the front of the car.

313

"We haven't been able to get much going with any of the townships or businesses so far." She continued talking after she realized her voice had just had trailed off and she had never finished her thought.

"There are some very complicated reasons for their inactions sometimes too, but we also have road restoration and construction projects at the top of the Foundation's list of things to do. We're going to resurface some of the roads that lead into our village before our pilot program gets underway.

We're also putting together a proposal for Ghana Railway Corporation, hoping to collaborate with them on developing a high-speed commuter rail system. But that won't happen until the second phase of our operations at the earliest. Our plans for the new rail system wouldn't affect the current railway operations at all, except for possible scheduling changes that might need to be worked out.

"What we have in mind is a high speed system that will make it easier for people to travel around the country. Not only would that pave the way for increased tourism, but the people living in rural communities would be able to take advantage of employment at our commercial enterprises when we get started. It would mean they wouldn't have to crowd into larger cities anymore just to find a job. But either way, you should find it much easier to get from city to city the next time you're here."

The hour and a half drive from Accra to Akosombo went by fairly quickly. Amad pulled into the drive of the Volta Hotel where Kristin's meetings were scheduled to take place. It was also where she had arranged for them to spend the night. Trazi moved into the front seat of the Land Rover after she got out and waved them off. Then Amad pulled the vehicle back out onto the street and they were off for a tour of the city.

He pointed out different markets as they passed them and gave them some of the highlights of the city's history. Celeste had her first opportunity for shopping when he took them on an accelerated visit through Agomanya bead market. The young girl had been completely overwhelmed by the sheer volume of colorful glass beads in the market. As they walked from one stall to the next, she saw even more beautiful pieces of artful beads and jewelry than in the previous one. She finally picked out several pieces and several varieties of singular beads too, in smaller quantities, thinking that her mother might be able to use them somehow in her tapestry creations.

After they left the market, Amad drove them to see Volta dam and they went on an abbreviated tour of Akosombo Hydroelectric Power Plant. They were surprised to find out that the massive facility not only provided power to almost all of Ghana, but also to countries as far away as Togo and Benin. By the time they had taken their brief walk around the power plant and had an up-close look at the dam, Kristin's meetings were scheduled to be over. They swung by the Volta Hotel to pick her up and were soon on their way once again.

This time, Amad drove them through a different part of the city. After a short while, they turned off the road they were on and he pulled the Land Rover up next to a pier. Kristin, Trazi, and Celeste got out of the car and walked up a plank that led to a small ship docked at the harbor. The three of them boarded the Dodi Princess, a double decked luxury vessel, as Amad left to visit nearby relatives. They took a relaxing cruise around Lake Volta, which Kristin said had been the largest man-made lake in the world at one time. "It was formed in 1965," she said, "as a by-product of constructing the Akosombo dam, which also resulted in major tourism in this area."

As the three sailed around the lake, they had lunch under the canopy of the ship's upper deck. It cruised over the waters at a leisurely speed for hours, giving them more time to catch up with each other and to enjoy being together. There was a gentle breeze that stirred the air from time to time, as the vessel made brief stops along Dodi Island and several smaller islands. They were all fully relaxed by the time they returned to the pier and found Amad waiting.

Later, as they settled into their suite for the night, everyone felt the effects of their long day. By the time they had taken turns having a long, hot shower, they were unanimous in deciding to have their dinner sent up to their suite. None of them felt much like dressing again so they could sit in the hotel restaurant to eat. The kitchen staff was very accommodating and set up a stem table on their private balcony. They served themselves from a delicious variety of food that had been placed on warmers on the table. Everyone filled themselves with plantains fried in red palm oil, grilled tilapia, and red-red chicken in a sauce of black eye peas, with gari, a condiment made from marinated ginger.

As they ate, they took in the beauty of the Volta River that ran nearest the hotel's border, appreciating the magnificent orange sunset that painted the sky as the sun sank slowly over the water. Kristin mentioned that she always made a point of checking out her competitor's best offerings whenever she traveled. That way, she would have an idea of what their travel agency was up against. She considered the owners of the Volta Hotel to be one of her major competitors in Akosombo, and it had certainly lived up to its reputation for luxury and hospitality. But with what they had in mind after Exodus Village opened, there would be more than enough tourists coming there regularly to benefit all the hotels in the city.

The next morning, the kids decided on a walk around the grounds of the hotel as Kristin left for her breakfast meeting. They gambled that they would have enough time for a canoe ride along the Volta River that came nearest to the hotel. Trazi hired a young man who looked to be around sixteen to row them out onto the river for a quick smooth ride. Exotic birds calling out to them from the nearby bushes, breaking through the cool stillness of the early morning with their urgent sounds. The scenery was breathtaking, and they knew the mixed melody of the birds would be permanently etched in their minds. They continued their cruise for as long as they thought they could, and ran into Kristin as soon as they had walked back through the front doors of the hotel lobby.

She had just finished her meeting and had stopped by a small stand for newspapers and to buy snacks for their drive, so the three walked back to their suite together to collect their things. By ten o'clock they had eaten their breakfast and had all piled back into the Land Rover, ready to head out. Amad pointed the car toward the Accra–Kumasi trunk road that lay to the west and connected the two cities.

Trazi and Celeste held their breath and were nearly frozen by fear as he drove across the Adomi Bridge, linking the Volta Region to the Eastern Region and the rest of the country. The bridge formed an eight hundred and five foot arched suspension across the Volta River at Atimpoku and Kristin had been so busy chatting about the bridge's construction that she never noticed the expressions on the children's faces.

"It's still a major tourist attraction," she rattled on, unaware, "in spite of some structural damage that was found last year. At the peak, the bridge is suspended two hundred and nineteen feet above the river." Kristin had yet to notice how quiet they had become or seen their shocked faces. She kept right on talking about structural problems that had been found after the inspection was done. Finally, Amad cleared his throat to get her attention. He had glanced into the rear mirror earlier and seen the look of fright in Celeste's eyes and even in Trazi's.

Kristin turned and looked back at the kids and saw that their faces were nearly drained, especially poor Celeste. Then she quickly tried to assure them that the Ghana Highway Authority had already finished all the critical repairs from what had been found lacking. She felt really bad as she tried to convince them that the bridge *had* been re-inspected and certified as being safe. "The inspection report confirmed that all of the past issues had been resolved and no new ones were found," she assured them.

Kristin went on to explain that she had only been speaking of minor repairs that were still needed. There were many people who had urged that the bridge be completely restored to its original condition. She stressed again that there were no immediate threats posed, either to them or to the structure itself. But she could remember how apprehensive she had been the first time she was with Amad and they approached the suspension bridge. She could only imagine how much her thoughtless comments contributed to the kids' terror and she wasn't surprised that they looked scared out of their minds.

After they were safely across the bridge and all the "suspense" was over, everyone settled down again and the car was quiet for quite some time. Amad continued to guide the Land Rover smoothly away from the city of Akosombo, and eventually they turned north toward Kumasi.

"Our agency has a hotel just south of here," Kristin told them after Amad had steered them onto the Accra-Kumasi road. It's only about thirty minutes away but we would be sure to be delayed there, and probably would have lost at least an hour's drive if we stopped. And I really don't want to risk driving through the mountains at night, if we don't have to."

Amad drove in a northwesterly direction for over an hour before Kristin looked out of her window and saw that they were nearing Nkawkaw. She had planned for them to stop there for a late lunch in the small city whose name literally meant "red, red." It was located in the mountainous Eastern Region and was a major town of the Nwahu Mountains, roughly at a midpoint on the Accra–Kumasi Road. The once thriving transportation hub connected the Eastern and Ashanti Regions. Kristin asked Amad to drive them past Nkawkaw Park first, so Trazi and Celeste could have a look at the 5000 seat stadium there. She told them it was the home turf of the Okwahu Stores United Nkawkaw, a Ghanaian football team—or soccer, as the sport is known in the States.

A short time later, Amad pulled the Land Rover into the Ecowas Point Motel, where they sat down for a leisurely mid-afternoon meal in the motel's restaurant. They were all glad to be out of the car after hours of driving, and it was only at Amad's urgings that they pulled themselves away from the serenity of the quaint inn to get started again. He reminded Kristin of the potential risks involved in driving over the mountainous road into Kumasi after nightfall. And with that reminder, she didn't need any further prompting.

Soon, they were on their way again, ascending the Nwahu Mountains at a steady pace. Trazi and Celeste were captivated by the breathtaking views from the mountain peaks; they stretched their necks from side to side to take in as much of the scenery as possible. Kristin revealed that it had been the plentiful mountain ranges in Ghana that persuaded her to buy the Land Rover they rode in, since she travelled around the country so frequently.

"Mom, I'm still not getting a clear picture of how everything is going to work in Exodus Village." Trazi had been quiet for a while, still trying to put everything together that his mother had told him since they arrived.

"I guess I really should have started by giving you an overview of what our Foundation's mission is about," his mother answered after a time. You'll have to bear with me though, because I'm sure to start skipping around again without having my usual notes in front of me."

"Well, I can see that it is a massive project," her son empathized, "and definitely not the kind of thing that you could sum up in a few paragraphs."

"That's certainly the truth," Kristin agreed before starting again. "At its highest level, the Diasporan Exodus Foundation's plans are to relocate African American individuals and families to Ghana. The Foundation will pay their transportation expenses and we will fully support all their living expenses in Exodus Village for a period of five years. That's the amount of time we agreed on to give our residents an opportunity to readjust.

"We're going to provide them with family and career counseling and all the other services they are accustomed to having, from housing to entertainment. We're providing them with education and skills training too, including on-the-job training in a field that has the potential to support them and their families here. We're basically giving them everything they will need to make a new start—butter and honey to replace the option that many of their children would otherwise have—like petty crimes, or life in the fast lane of some small-time drug trade.

"Okay, I get it now. And I think five years should probably be just enough time," Trazi interjected.

"Well, we certainly hope so," Kristin responded. "We're also planning to help our residents use what they learn with us after they leave. They won't just be pushed out of the gate after graduation. We're going to help them assimilate into the culture; by the time our pilot residents are ready to graduate, we intend to have several of our planned commercial operations up and running as a possible option for their support. Our former residents and a specific percentage of residents living in the areas surrounding our facilities will be given preferential treatment for hiring through set-asides," she finished. "And we have tons of commercial projects in our pipeline, so we'll only be adding to their employment potential as we proceed.

"Wow. That's wonderful Aunt Kristin. But how are you going to decide who gets to come here?" Celeste wanted to know. She had always been practical in her thinking—all the earth signs in her birth chart pretty much guaranteed it.

"Well, that's going to be a tough decision, Sweetie, because we'll have limited resources and we expect to have long waiting lists once we're up and running. We're putting a number of mechanisms in place to make sure that we only bring the right folks here to start with.

"All of our individual applicants will have to be at least twenty-one years of age; right now, they'll also have to be native to either the United States or the Caribbean. And, they must have lived in one of those places during the twelve-month period prior to filing their applications. Our main criteria is that each of the individual applicants, and at least one parent listed on our family application must be a direct descendant of at least one African who was enslaved in the United States or the Caribbean.

"We had quite a debate over that one, but we finally decided to accept descendants of indentured Africans in the U.S. as well. We hesitated because of evidence that shows that some of the indentured Africans owned slaves themselves after they were freed, and because of their later treatment of natives of what is now called Liberia, where the ACS set them up. We considered it, but in the end we decided we wouldn't make any distinction. First off, it's doubtful that many will actually know that much about their family's history, but we realized whether their ancestor was taken from Africa as an indentured servant or as a chattel slave for life, the bottom line was that they were brought to America in chains."

"But that's still a big list. How are you possibly going to narrow it down?" It was Trazi's turn to ask.

"Well, you know me and my essays," she answered. They both remembered that having Trazi write essays had been Kristin's preferred method of punishment as he grew up. She would have him write a brief essay, sometimes after she had yelled at him first for whatever he had done. As part of his punishment, he would have to write down exactly what he understood to be wrong about his past behavior, as well as how he planned to correct it. Trazi absolutely *hated* having to write the essays, but his mother had soon discovered it was a far more effective punishment than any thing else she thought of. And, she rationalized, there had always been the possibility that writing about his behavior might have a positive subliminal effect.

"We're having our applicants write essays," she went on, "and just tell us why they want to come here." She still smiled at memories of her past tussles with her son. "It's a major part of our selection process," she continued, "and we'll use their essays to flag people we don't feel are a good fit, for any number of reasons. "Anyone who is at least sixteen will have to write one, although we'll accept a much shorter version from the older children. But what we want to know is what's on their minds. We need to know we're not bringing a bunch of teens here who really don't want to be here. But we won't care anything about anybody's grammar or anything like that. We'll also have volunteers ready to assist anyone who doesn't read and who can help them with their essays. They can also be taped, if need be. But we have to get an essay from everyone beyond the age of sixteen. It's not something we're planning to advertise though; all they'll be told is that the essay is required. I'm convinced that's going to tell us a lot about our applicants and that's what we're trying to get at. We'll have people pouring over them and we'll use what they wrote to help us make cuts during our first round of elimination.

"Before they're read, they'll be classified first and then sub-classified. They'll be arranged according to a number of factors such as city versus country dweller; with or without children; steady employment or chronic unemployment; and similar categories. We'll select people from each group, but we're organizing them this way to keep groups with some of the same built-in cultural biases together. We also won't be equipped to deal with any chronic health issues either, unfortunately, especially those that might be aggravated by the climate in Ghana. Those will be automatically disqualified at this point.

"But how are you possibly going to keep track of all that?" Trazi asked.

"We have an amazing network of volunteers in place already—thanks to the Hunter, Lincoln University, and Tuskegee alumni associations. Some of these volunteers are interested in moving to Africa themselves, at least for a while. Others have no interest in even coming here for a visit, for whatever reason. But they have all been donating a tremendous amount of their time and technical expertise already, in every area we're involved in. We have a talented group of computer experts at our disposal, who have been designing interfaces that we'll use to keep track of all the data.

"Everyone will be given what the software industry refers to as a "primary key." That's a series of numbers and/or letters that uniquely identifies each person individually. It's like a social security number; that's how the IRS knows exactly how much money a person earns by the end of the tax year. They track it by the social security number and they have another kind of number for businesses.

"By doing a search using one of our resident's primary keys, we'll be able to pull up all the information available on that person. As long as a unique number is used to index the information we put in the computer, it will be automatically linked to that particular person. From there, we'll be able to run reports that will give us all kinds of information on our applicants and our residents—like their city of origin and specific social circumstances, and the like. It's going to help us keep track of exactly who we have living with us, and where they go after they leave.

"Yeah, computers are really opening up a whole new world," her son observed.

"You are exactly right, Baby." Kristin ventured off into telling them about the astrological age that the planet Earth had recently transitioned into, a measure based on the Earth's precise wobble on its axis. "We've moved from the Age of Pisces, which started around the time of Jesus' birth, into the Age of Aquarius. Computers, advanced technology, science, independence, and caring about the rest of mankind are all parts of the energy that the Age of Aquarius brings—and we're just starting it. We're all living in a very miraculous cycle of the Earth; a major change that only occurs every 2,160 years or so. There's no one alive who can tell us what the experience will be like and its beginning effects are very pronounced. This current new-age shift is even more miraculous. Since Aquarius itself represents the energy of change, like that of the sign's ruling planet, Uranus; the change associated with the dawning of the Age of Aquarius has been quite sudden and unexpected.

"But at any rate," Kristin returned to her point, "we anticipate having the majority of our initial applicants come from the lower and lower-to-middle income brackets—especially in the first few years. We will also be accepting mentor applications at the same time, but those will go through a different route for processing although their essays will still be required. And while we certainly don't intend to discriminate against anyone based on their net worth, we'll be asking applicants who have financial resources beyond a certain level to make a one-time contribution to our administrative budget."

"Well that certainly seems fair," Celeste agreed, "especially since they won't have to pay for anything once they get here."

"We think so too, Sweetie, and we hope they'll see it that way. We won't even ask them unless we're fairly certain they have the means of contributing. I think that most will agree that the benefits we're offering them at Exodus Village will far outweigh the cost of a one-time donation.

"I can't wait to see what you've done so far." Celeste was anxious again.

"I can't wait for you to see it either, Honey. Exodus Village will be a completely sustainable green community and all our commercial enterprises will follow suit. I really am sorry we have to take such a scenic route to get there, but it's because of where my meetings were already scheduled. No trip to Ghana would be complete without visiting Kumasi and the Volta Region, though. They would have been on my list of places to take you while you were here anyway, so you guys are just getting to see them on the front end of your trip."

"Well, don't worry about it, Mom," Trazi asserted. "We understand all about your schedule now. It's not a problem for us at all because we're having a blast just being here, and we can't wait to see what's next."

"Good. After my meeting in Kumasi tomorrow morning, I'll be all yours—I promise."

"I really want to know all about what you're doing here," Trazi said. "It's so much more involved than I had ever imagined."

"Well, it has certainly been exciting to watch everything come together," Kristin agreed. "There have been so many people who have worked very hard to get us here, and the results are finally beginning to show. We're going to run Exodus Village like a well-oiled machine, efficiently providing needed services to our residents. We'll have all kinds of non-essential services available as well, and everyone will contribute based on their aptitude and interests.

"We also have to keep everyone as healthy as possible, because we don't have a budget for long-term care or anything other than emergency and routine health services. That's the main reason why the "SAD" diet that most of our new residents probably have been on, will be out."

"What's a SAD diet?" Celeste was curious.

"It's an acronym for standard American diet. The reason it's so sad is because it's so unhealthy; almost exclusively made up of white sugar and white flour, processed foods, red meat, and the usual assortment of additives. None of that will be available to our residents here and it will give us a huge advantage in minimizing medical costs. We already have full time dietitians who are working on recipes, and they'll be offering classes on how to make dishes with vegetables, herbs, and spices that help control blood pressure and other easily managed health issues that the American health care 'industry' currently exploits for profits.

"Everyone will have a required health assessment done before they leave for Ghana. And those who are physically able will be required to maintain a certain level of physical and mental activity once they get here. Our wellness coordinators will tailor specific schedules of activity individually, and we will actually monitor these for compliance. We'll be taking all kinds of proactive measures to help everyone develop and maintain their good health.

"So you'll have gyms too?" Celeste wondered.

"Yes, we're working on a variety of physical activities, but each community in our village will have its own recreation building. In it, there will be a very large gym, a pool, and some other state-of-the-art sports equipment. We've done quite well with fundraising for our first rec building, so a good portion of it is already completed.

"And I just realized that all this time I've been misleading you a bit, implying that the amenities in Exodus Village are free," Kristin corrected. "It would be more accurate to say that money won't be required in Exodus Village because everyone, including older children, will be required to make a regular contribution to the collective—whatever work that's best suited to them. We're still working out all the details for aptitude tests and skills training, followed by on-the-job training in most cases. Our village will be the size of a small American city when we're at capacity, and we'll provide most of the same services. We'll have our own farms, factories, and commercial enterprises; we'll had a need for dressmakers and tailors, childcare operators, housekeepers, teachers, and everything else you can think of. It's going to be all village-sponsored so the people living with us will have many opportunities to learn new skills to support themselves when they leave us, either through employment or maybe their own businesses."

Kristin fished through her bag for some wrapped candy that she passed to Amad, Trazi, and Celeste.

"But how can someone possibly know what they want to do when everything is so different here?" Her son asked the question after some thought.

"It won't be easy, Sweetheart, but we'll help them with that process too. It's all going to start when they board our ship in the States—and yes, Trazi, it will be christened the *Black Star*, after Marcus Garvey's ship." She was smiling again.

"After our residents arrive in Ghana and have taken a few days to get settled, their mentors will begin meeting with them to talk about their goals and aspirations. During this process, they'll have an opportunity to look more closely at all the different possibilities that exist for them here. And as I mentioned, that might include creating their own businesses as well. It's going to be a continuous process, with their counselors formally reviewing their goals with them every year.

"We'll be having our residents move to a different community in Exodus Village each year too, as a way of helping them keep their focus. Their move date will coincide with the anniversary of their arrival. Their family counselor in their new community will review their goals with them again once they get settled into their new homes."

"Why do they have to move so much?" Celeste was curious.

"Well, mostly because we want to make sure that the notion of the village as being a temporary arrangement stays fixed in their minds," Kristin answered. "We don't want our residents to become complacent or get too cozy. We're going to have a total of five communities. After our pilot program of fifty families is completed, we're planning to bring in one hundred new families each year. Half of that number will be arriving approximately six months after the first group of pilot families gets here, if all goes well with the pilot. And we're making all of our population projections on the high side; we're estimating an average of ten members for each family, which means having twenty-five hundred residents in Exodus Village at full capacity.

After residents move into the fifth and final community, their relocation counselor will take over and assess where the family is as soon as they are settled, in terms of either their original or their modified goals. Their final counselor in the fifth community will work with them more closely on completing any required steps needed to meet their goals. That will also be the official start of their relocation support, which we will provide for three additional years after our graduates leave the village.

"So Mom, how are you planning to control all these people once they get here?"

"That's an excellent question, Trazi. We'll have regulations in place to maintain order, of course, which will benefit and protect our residents as much as anything else. We have considered anything related to restrictions on them very carefully, but at the same time we fully intend to enforce those policies that we adopt.

"It was something that I personally tussled with for a long time before we finally came to a resolution," Kristin said quietly. "None of us want to see the bad behaviors that were picked up in America brought back to Africa. Still, we also didn't want our village to have a feel of confinement either, or be unwelcoming. Too many of the people who will be coming to us have been in those kinds of environments all their lives. The whole idea is to give them something different that will make them feel nurtured and secure, and give them a fresh start.

"We had a spirited discussion about the issue of maintaining order at our first board meeting, and then we left it as an open item for our next meeting. But, once again, through the synchronicity of Divine Providence, I ran into another old friend at an airport in the U.S.

"I had met Brother John at Tuskegee on the first day of freshman orientation. That was our first official campus activity and we bonded instantly. We spent a great deal of time together that first year, and in the Spring, Brother John and I met this other young brother that we both found fascinating. He was a member of the Nation of Islam and had come to Tuskegee on a pre-engineering scholarship, by way of Temple No. 2 in Chicago.

"I'll tell you, this brother spoke Arabic like he had been born in Saudi Arabia. We were very impressed with his knowledge of Islam too; it was like experiencing a brand new world. Brother John converted before the end of that semester, and I have not knowingly put another piece of pork in my mouth since hearing that brother talk to us about swine," she smiled.

"Anyhow, Brother John was very intrigued by the plans that I shared with him about the Exodus Foundation, when we ran into each other at the airport. We continued to correspond by email after that meeting and our conversations just kept naturally evolving over time. I kept him up-to-date on what was going on here and by the time the issue of providing order for our village came up again, I had learned about my friend's connection to the Fruit of Islam – the FOI."

"Are those the guys in that movie about Malcolm X who waited in a line outside the jail, when Denzel, I mean Malcolm, was inside talking to the police?"

"Yes, Sweetie—that's them," Kristin answered Celeste with a smile. "The FOI is organized into highly disciplined units and they are known as the "brave fighters for Allah." They've always provided protection and security for people within Nation of Islam communities, but they've also been known to provide security for national leaders too, on occasion. They even provided the security detail for the Asantehene's trip to America a few years back. They have a dignity and presence about them that commands respect and requires little physical force. John told me they have to take an oath to tell the truth to members of their community, and it's taken at the expense of their own lives if they go back on their word."

"Wow, that is serious! That was really cool the way they all turned and marched off at the same time in that movie," Celeste countered, still somewhat distracted.

"Yes, well they're just that disciplined in real life too, Sweetheart."

Kristin told them that as it turned out, Brother John had been playing an important leadership role in the FOI for the past twenty years.

"He was one of the key players in creating the security agency they've been operating outside of the Muslim community for years."

"I never knew they did that," Trazi commented.

"Many people don't, but the FOI has contracted to provide security at public facilities in the U.S. for years," she told him. "According to Brother John, they have long-term contracts in several large urban cities and their actions have reinforced their reputation for maintaining order without the use of physical force.

"And I am absolutely thrilled that Brother John has resolved our issue of security in the best possible way. He has agreed to take full control of security at Exodus Village. We've worked out arrangements for him to recruit and train special FOI units that will travel with our new residents on board the *Black Star*, starting with our pilot group. They're going to board our ship in Annapolis and will remain with our residents until they arrive in Elmina, nearly four months later.

"Wait, why is it going to take them so long to get here?" Trazi asked.

"Oh right. That's something else that I failed to mention earlier—and it plays a large role in our plans. Our new residents will stop over in Jamaica for three months on their way to Ghana. Our re-education programs officially begin on their second day out from Annapolis, but the real preparation for their arrival in Ghana will take place in the Caribbean. It's actually going to be quite an operation, but I'll tell you more about it later.

"In terms of our security, we were initially given an option by the Ghanaian government to either assume responsibility for order inside Exodus Village, or leave that task to them. Even before we knew how we would be able to do it, I felt strongly that *we* should retain authority over the underbelly at all levels until they make the adjustment to being here. They're going to be quarantined in Exodus Village in a sense, until they are ready to mix in with the rest of the country.

"As I said before, I have all the confidence that once our new residents learn about their true history, have been provided with years of nurturing care, and have been taught how to stand on their feet; the vast majority will willingly accept what is being offered to them and change their lives for the better. We're going to give them butter and honey so they'll refuse evil and choose the good.

"And now, we have Brother John and the FOI to maintain order and security until they make their transition–truly a gift from God. John is arranging for the FOI to use the travel time and limited space on board our ship to become well acquainted with each new group. The FOI will have full responsibility for the group they travel with during their five years in Exodus Village, and after they've graduated and left us, that particular FOI unit will rotate back to the U.S. Brother John will ask them to do it discreetly, but by the time the ship arrives in Jamaica they'll be able to pass along vital information to the people running our re-education camps about potential issues.

"Your re-education camp?" Trazi's voice sounded concerned.

"Well, you know me son—I've always been one to take short-cuts with words. I guess I'll have to think of a new name for it, but that's essentially what the purpose will be. Jamaica will be the place where we administer the first aptitude tests to our new adult residents too—anyone within the age range for mandatory skills preparation and certification. We're going to do our best to match an applicant's interest with their actual potential for succeeding in whatever they choose to learn to support themselves. They'll be matched to a training program that comes closest to their interest, but there will also be a human element in the process. We won't just go by their test results alone.

"Our residents will begin overview classes in Jamaica so they can get a better feel for the training they've signed up for, especially if it's something new to them. It gives them a chance to change their minds and switch to something else before they get here, where their training will become more intensified.

"But the main focus in Jamaica will be to teach our new residents about the culture of Ghana, as well as their own history as slave descendants. Aside from that, we'll also identify people we don't feel are suitable for our program at all. It'll be easier to do it there rather than after they've come all the way to Ghana. The climate and culture in Jamaica are also very similar, so those who have only lived in northern cities will be able to start adapting to West Africa.

"We will teach them about the triangular trade routes that operated during the slave trade as well, so once they board the ship again they'll know that they are traveling the "Middle Passage" across the Atlantic in the reverse direction. Jamaica will be a symbolic stopover but our residents will be reliving history in a sense. We hope that what they learn in Jamaica will be on their minds during the two weeks it will take for them to cross the ocean.

"They'll be issued their new Diasporan passports as they board the ship again, bound for Ghana. Those will be the passports they will use for their official entry into the country; we'll be collecting their other passports during the same process that their new ones are issued.

"Why?" Celeste wanted to know. "Won't they need them?"

"Well, the only reason they would need them in Ghana would be to leave the country, or actually to legally enter another country. We're going to have a very secure system of safekeeping their passports, and they will be given back as a part of their graduation exercises.

"But our residents will always have the option of withdrawing from our program at any time. In that case, their original passports will be given back to them immediately.

"As head of FOI security, John will represent the highest level of authority in Exodus Village," Kristin went on after a pause. "He's going to set up checkpoints at our entrances for residents and visitors alike to show their authorization to enter and exit. That's going to take some getting used to, I know, but we feel it'll be for everyone's benefit in the long run. Brother John is going to set things up similar to the procedures followed on military bases at the entrances, making sure that order is maintained at all times.

"Running into him was a blessing in another very important way, as well, and resolved another major obstacle we would have eventually faced. Our hopes are that our graduates will be able to assimilate into all regions of Ghana, but our prospects for gaining support for our operation in the North, where the majority population is Muslim, hadn't been at all promising before John joined with us. Now, he's become our unofficial ambassador to that region and will undoubtedly be a great asset to us when the time comes for resident relocations. Also, because with the FOI presence, we expect to have a larger population of American Muslims move to our village.

"Some of our policies might sound a bit restrictive at first, but it's for the good of all concerned. And that's what matters most. A major mission of our Foundation is to give African Americans in need of a lifeline, a brand new start here. We lost a great deal of ourselves during the ordeal of slavery in America," she concluded. "Many people still don't realize there was anything lost; they may never realize it until they've spent time in Africa.

"Each of our families and individual residents will be assigned to a Ghanaian adjustment counselor; they will have specific periods of time they will be required to spend with them. Sadly, we'll have no choice but to send residents who consistently fail to comply with our rules, and who are making no attempts to assimilate into the culture, back to the U.S. or the Caribbean. Their entry into the country will be on our Exodus Village passport, so unless they can work something else out with immigration authorities here to obtain a U.S. visa, they'll have to return home.

"And once someone has been expelled from our program, there will be severe restrictions put on any future travel visas issued for them in Ghana. But trust me, we already expect that there will be difficulties for some in making the adjustment to living here, especially those who have spent the majority of their lives in larger cities and know of nothing else."

'The city kids,' Kristin thought to herself, with a suppressed smile.

"Our board of directors has an appreciation for the amount of time it will likely take for the majority of our residents to make their adjustment. Hopefully, we'll never have to expel anyone but we've had to take into account that for some, the idea of living in Africa might sound better on paper than their actual reality. We certainly won't try to force anyone to stay, but we're prepared to do all we can to help everyone trying to adjust.

We'll also do everything we can to keep things from deteriorating to the point of having to deport someone. But as with everything else, we're preparing for that possibility. The Fruit of Islam has a well-earned reputation for their firm approach in maintaining order; they don't leave much room for compromise or discussion.

"If we do this just right, most of the people we accept will be serious about taking hold of their futures. We're going to be upfront with them from day one so we properly set their expectations. Everyone is going to know well in advance of leaving Annapolis what the consequences will be for intentional noncompliance with our regulations. I'm sure you can probably imagine how involved a process it will be to keep everything organized," Kristin told them. "That's exactly why all our procedures have to be well thought out and will be enforced.

"We have some critical milestones just ahead of us that will have to be completed and checked off by certain dates. But we're going to keep working steadily toward each of our goals, completing them in the sequence that the board prioritized.

"The land we were given is highly treasured in Ghana, because of the gold deposits that have been discovered beneath the ancient forests nearby. We plan on showing our appreciation by taking the very best care of it. Our commercial enterprises will always be in harmony with the environment and we're working on future projects that will help preserve, and even restore, sections of the rainforest nearest us.

"I can't imagine how things looked here before, because the land is still beautiful," Celeste commented.

"It is," Kristin agreed. "And as we continue to make our plans for our organization, minimizing our carbon footprint will remain a high priority. Our intention is to coexist rather than to destroy or control.

"Mom, how hard do you think it's going to be to get past all of the other stuff?" They had been riding in silence for a long time again and were nearing Kumasi. "I mean, this thing between our different cultures has gone on for a long time," her son continued. "Do you think it's really possible for all that to change?"

"Yes, Baby, we definitely believe it will," she answered. "Believe it or not, there were people who asked the same questions about integration in America at one time. There were so many who were dead set against it, both black and white. It was a violent and dangerous struggle; nobody really knew what would happen from one minute to the next. There was a much greater chance of failure in the U.S. with integration than we have for failure here now.

"There are many Black Americans who have already moved to Ghana on their own, and they've been here for decades. We just can't afford to leave anything to chance because of our numbers," she finished. "That's why we're putting so much emphasis on cultural diversity classes.

"The majority of our Ghanaian employees will work with us on five year renewable contracts, and most will live in Exodus Village the entire time. We're planning to place at least one family in each of our residential triplex groupings that will make up each community. And like my Aunt Mamie always says, "Living with someone is the best way to get to know them."

"We're really counting on our Ghanaian residents to help our transplanted residents make their transition. Everyone on our board understands that our biggest challenge will be in bridging two cultures together that are each broken into many factions. But if we don't do it, we're going to fail," she concluded. "That's really the bottom line. We have to figure out how to smoothly fit a square peg into a round hole."

✳✳✳

Kristin wiped back a tear from her eye and smiled as best she could. The children had only been gone a few hours and she already missed them so much that it hurt. She leaned back in the stiff cow-skinned chair in her office and let out a big sigh. She could still see the surprised looks on their faces when they finally saw Exodus Village for themselves.

She could see how proud of her they had been to see the form she had brought to her vision. It warmed her heart and Kristin realized the only thing that would have made it perfect would have been to have Winston there with them to see it too. Seeing the children had made her realize her feelings for him had only deepened after she left the U.S., but she was still determined not to let that distract her from her purpose.

She thought back to how strange Nana Adwoa's reaction had been to meeting Celeste, when Kristin had brought her and Trazi to Nana's house to introduce them. It had been even more peculiar than the woman's behavior with Kristin when the two of them first met. But Kristin had finally dismissed it all as just another of the older woman's eccentricities.

A stack of single pages on her desk caught Kristin's eye. When she picked up the sheets, she felt a boost of excitement when she realized they were the one-page summaries that had been created by Amina and her staff for each applicant. Kristin held in her hands the names of the people who would be selected as their pilot residents. As she scanned the pages in the stack, her attention was randomly pulled by some of the names she read and she placed those summaries to one side. She continued working through the stack, using her intuition to select applications that just felt right and had caught her attention for no concrete reason.

By the time the plane that had carried Trazi and Celeste away from Accra landed in Zurich, Kristin was once again fully focused on the Exodus Village pilot project.

Epilogue

*E*ven through the fog of her jetlag, Celeste immediately sensed something was wrong as soon as she spotted her father in the airport. He was standing alone near the baggage conveyor with his arms folded. Her first reaction was that he might have been thrown off by seeing Trazi walking with her. Her brother had changed his flight at Zürich's Kloten Airport impulsively, opting to fly back to D.C. with her instead of going directly back to Michigan as he originally planned. He had requested more days of leave than he needed before he left the base to go on their trip, so he wasn't due to report back for a few more days. Trazi had made an impromptu decision to use that time to start looking around for a place to stay, since he would be living in the area again in just over a month.

Celeste had been glad to have her brother with her for a while longer. She also hoped that things between him and their father could start being right again. There were a few awkward seconds as Winston reacted to the surprise of suddenly being face-to-face with his son, after three years of animosity between them. But Celeste could tell that after his initial shock, he was genuinely glad to see Trazi, too. To everyone's surprise, their father closed the space that separated them quickly and embraced his daughter *and* his son. Winston had even seemed relieved when Celeste told him Trazi's news about moving back to the area.

Then she began to think that her father might be worried that Trazi would want to move back into the loft with them, but his troubled look remained on his face even after her brother asked him for a lift to the hotel where he would be staying. They systematically gathered up all their bags and packages and loaded them onto the handcart that Winston had with him. From the corner of her eye, it seemed to Celeste that Winston became even more agitated as they started toward the parking lot to look for his car. By the time they spotted it, she had begun to worry about what ever it was that was troubling him, until she finally found out after they had everything loaded into his SUV, with Trazi's bags stuffed in last.

Winston placed his hand on his daughter's arm to stop her, as she started around toward the front passenger seat. He clasped her small hands tightly inside his and with the strangest expression on his face, he told her there was something that he needed to tell her.

"There's really no easy way for me to say this, Sweetheart."

A sense of foreboding immediately engulfed Celeste. She tried to steady herself for whatever her father would say next because she knew the news wouldn't be good. Her mind raced and she wondered whether something had happened to Kristin after they had left her at the airport. But her father had said it was something he needed to tell *her*, not her and Trazi. Before she had time to go through a mounting list of other horrible possibilities, she saw the tear that was streaming down his face. Celeste had never seen her father cry before.

Then she remembered something she hadn't thought about in years. She remembered the look that had been on his face when he came to tell her that her mother was going to the rehab hospital, that first time.

"Has something happened to Mom?" She searched his face for an answer. Winston took in a deep breath and then told her that a neighbor had called him a few hours earlier. "They found your mother in her apartment this morning," he said quietly. "They tried to get her to the hospital, Sweetie. They tried to help her, but it was too late." Winston looked at his stunned daughter closely with much compassion.

"Your mother passed away in the ambulance, Baby, before they ever got her to the hospital."

Celeste stood completely still and stared into her father's face. Her brows were furrowed because she couldn't understand how what he was saying to her could be possible. At the same time, she knew that her father would never say something like that to her unless he was absolutely certain that it *was* true. She was having difficulties with her thoughts. Everything seemed so strange outside of the airport and away from the travel hustle and bustle they had been in for hours on end. Somehow, all the chaos of the airport had apparently buffered the effects of her not having readjusted to the eastern time zone. Celeste stood in the parking lot in quiet confusion, trying to make sense of what her father had told her.

She thought about the beautiful kente fabric she had packed away in one of her suitcases. She had bought the cloth for her mother when Kristin took them to Bonwire Village. It had taken her a long time to pick out the beads for her mother too that she had bought from the market near Volta Dam. She had bought her mother the prettiest beige bedspread with a beautiful pattern of Adinkra symbols stamped across it. Celeste had planned on gift wrapping the bedspread and giving it to Angela at their first mother-daughter lunch they were supposed to have in a few days.

She was still silent as her father pulled her into his warm chest and hugged her. Trazi came around the truck and hugged them both, and the three stood crying together in the parking lot, oblivious to the stares of passers-by.

Celeste still hadn't said one word, even after they all got into the car and were finally on their way out of the airport parking lot. All she knew was that she felt sadder at that moment than she had ever felt in her life. She kept thinking about the mix-up in getting her hepatitis shot before she left for Ghana. Having to leave to get the shot had been the reason she and her mother had to postpone their lunch date.

'Would anything have been different if we had gone to lunch together that day?'

When she slowly began to accept what her father told her, she realized why she was in such disbelief. Although she loved her mother and they had finally started to get to know each other, her death would have absolutely no affect on Celeste's life at all—not really.

She wouldn't need to make any changes in her daily routine, although she and her mother had lived very close to each other now for several years. They had both been trying hard to have a closer relationship recently, but the new relationship had never gotten off the ground. It felt as though she had just learned about the death of a complete stranger, like the man who lived in the apartment over the cleaners who always had his music blaring.

Celeste was still crying softly when she and her father finally reached the loft. By then, she had stopped crying in grief over her mother's passing. She was crying now because she would never know who her mother was. She barely managed an audible response to Charlotte's greeting and then hurried upstairs to her room to be alone. She spent the evening thinking about the weeks that had led up to her trip to Ghana, when she and her mother had seen each other often. They had just begun to put everything from the past behind them, so they could have a fresh start.

She kept crying until she finally fell asleep, still engulfed in her sadness. Celeste began to find consolation in her dreams because there she could feel her mother with her. She showed her the presents that she had brought from Africa and she could feel that they made her mother very happy. Celeste wondered if that would have been the way things might have felt, if they had finally bonded the way they had planned.

In the early morning hours as the sun began to rise, she felt an onslaught of sadness again as the memory of her mother's passing flooded her mind. Angela's essence had already begun to fade a little and Celeste was anxious because she knew her mother would leave her soon. But before she faded away completely, Angela reminded her daughter of Kristin's love for her.

A chorus of birds chirping outside her window finally woke Celeste up from a peaceful sleep she didn't realize she was having. And miraculously, she smiled as she opened her eyes to greet the new day.

Can a Square Peg Really Fit Into a Round Hole?

Please share your thoughts with the author:
LSamuel@Ngratitude.net

www.ingramcontent.com/pod-product-compliance
Lightning Source LLC
Chambersburg PA
CBHW022207010726
47493CB00002B/447